FIRST DAYS AFTER

BOOK 1 IN THE CATACLYSM SERIES

JAY VIELLE

IN MEMORIAM

*—To my dear friend Kurt, who, years ago when I was
searching for some direction in life, told me:
"You need to write."*

*--And to my parents--whose love of the written word was
passed down to me forever. May I be lucky enough one day to
gain a tenth of their dexterity with it.*

I wish you all were here to read this.

MAP OF SETTINGS

Maryland, West Virginia, Virginia

The bus ride south

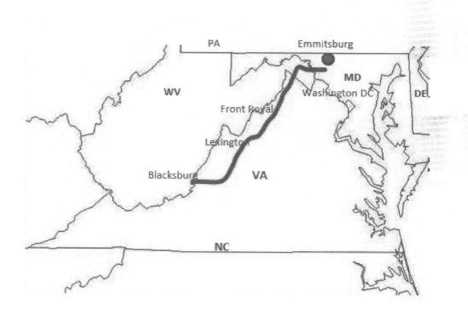

PROLOGUE

World War III Has Begun

It's almost hard to remember before The Cataclysm. That's what the media called it for the few, brief days they were still on the air as the bombing was going on. Catchy name. I can't even remember which network coined it first. Funny, it really wasn't that long ago. I mean, I remember stuff from my childhood, my college days, my first two years teaching, all of that stuff as clear as day. But the time leading up to it—The Cataclysm, I mean—that's all a blur now. Some of us talk about it when Jake isn't around. We ask each other questions, like "do you remember what went first," or "who teamed up with whom."

Seems nobody really has a good handle on it all. Those of us in our group, our band, our clan—whatever you want to call us—we're a pretty educated bunch—so I trust us to have a pretty solid grip on the facts for the most part. Which is good, because this may be the only collected history for all I know. Who knows—maybe there are pockets of people out there that we're gonna find and they're doing the same thing. But for now, I'm it. I'm the historian. The record keeper. The rememberer. The Camayoc, as my Incan ancestors might have called me. At least that's what my parents would have said.

My name is Eduardo Reyes Rosado. I am a lifetime resident of Frederick County, Maryland. I attended Hunter's Run High School, then went away to college, only to come back and return to my alma mater to teach. My parents are originally from Peru. They are naturalized citizens who moved to the U.S. in the 1960's to become college professors. I am—I *was* -- a history teacher at Hunter's Run High School in the northern hills of Maryland, just south of the Pennsylvania line. I say 'was' because all of that is over now. Everything is over. Life as we knew it is simply not there.

All of that started—I guess--about two months ago when the international pissing contest began. Our president taunted the North Korean guy. He taunted us back. At some point China threatened us if we used force that they would intervene. Then the Russians joined them, not wanting China to control another warm water port all by themselves, and suddenly they became our enemy too. Japan was with us, as was South Korea. That much of it was pretty clear in the days leading up to...It. The Cataclysm. The release of so many fucking nuclear bombs that the entire world as we know it will never, ever be the same.

As far as we can tell, the fighting began conservatively and traditionally. Fighter planes, warships, and soldiers. Standard stuff. The talking heads all threatened with nukes, but nobody wanted to be the first to use nuclear weapons. So, the mobilization of troops went on for about a month or so, and countries began lining up and forming teams. I have a saying hanging up in my classroom. Or rather, I *had* a saying hanging up in my classroom: "Those who do not learn from history are doomed to repeat it." So true. Just like World War I, countries began making those entangling alliances we all used to read about in our history classes. England, Japan, South Korea and the United States all squared up against Russia, North Korea and China. The big superpowers would have been enough, but then the "fringe countries" started getting involved. Venezuela declared war on the U.S., still defensive from the rhetoric coming against them from the White House.

Cuba jumped on board with them, and China and North Korea were very happy to have allies in the Americas. Europe joined in soon after, and Great Britain and Spain were our next allies. Libya and Syria joined in against Spain, and then when Pakistan and the Eastern portion of Afghanistan joined our enemies, India reacted quickly thereafter and joined our side.

You see where this is going, don't you? Malaysia sided with its Muslim allies. Australia sided with its English-speaking cousins. Followed by New Zealand. The Phillipines flip-flopped. South America took sides. The only place where you didn't hear any involvement was sub-Saharan Africa. I imagine if there's a place that goes on today like nothing ever happened, it's there.

But I would imagine that I'm not the only intelligent guy out there to figure that out. I'd bet my daily rations that those places are starting to get inundated with refugees about now, and that will only get worse when people start to take inventory on their resources and realize they can get there somehow. Taking notes is what I've been doing for almost two months now. Jake has me keeping track of things. He's a good big picture guy. Actually, he's a great big picture guy—which means he's a little shaky on details, which is why he has me.

Jake Fisher has become the go-to guy here at the school. He was a Social Studies teacher and the school's wrestling coach before the Cataclysm. Very successful coach. Hall of Fame successful. Jake is 49 years old and bears the scars of a man who spent his life in the pugilistic arts. His hands are gnarled, calloused, and he's obviously broken a few fingers somewhere down the line. His ears are slightly misshapen, showing a touch of cauliflowering like you see on wrestlers, boxers and MMA fighters. He walks with a slight but distinguishable limp, and according to him his left hip is artificial. He has a kind of rugged good looks you might have seen in the old Westerns, with perpetual five o'clock shadow, with temples graying just a tad. Not my type at all.

My type. I wonder if there even is a type anymore. It

probably should be noted that I'm gay. Not that it matters, really. I didn't really advertise it that much before the Cataclysm. New teachers have enough trouble being accepted. That said, I didn't hide it either. Hunter's Run is in a very red part of a state that votes blue all of the time. They don't particularly care for my views in our neighborhood. Never did. I didn't come out in high school because I knew it would be weird for me and really hard on my friends. Once I returned as a teacher, I had lived a little and had more confidence. I felt more comfortable explaining to conservatives why they didn't have to like my point of view, but they had to tolerate it in America. Not sure that matters one bit anymore. Everything has changed. Everything. Now there are only two kinds of people left in the world. Dead, and survivors. Well, turns out there's something else. But I'll get to that later.

I'm a survivor. Always have been. I have also always been a sci-fi geek. I've seen every post-Apocalyptic, Dystopian movie ever created. And as far as I can tell, in most of those movies the viewers had a pretty good idea of what they were dealing with. No power. No law. No order. Zombies. Whatever. But we had the misfortune of NOT knowing. Sometimes the power worked, sometimes it didn't. Some places got demolished in the bombings and had nothing. Others operated as if nothing had ever happened. But it was the not knowing—from town to town, from day to day—what was going on...that's what was so hard. Hindsight is 20-20. But we acted almost as if we had blinders on.

Every day the blinders would peel back just a tad to reveal new things to us, but in those blind moments, we had nothing but instinct to operate with. That's why telling this story is important. People will look back at us and what we did and wonder how stupid we must have been. But we weren't stupid. We were doing the best we could with the information we had in a landscape that was changing daily. So, let me tell you about what it was like at school on the day the shitstorm started.

CHAPTER 1

First Day After

J ake kind of took control once "the event" happened. It was total terror here at first. I'm told it was a lot like 9/11/2001, but I was too young to experience any of that, and can only remember my parents' fear when they watched reruns of when the planes hit the Trade Centers. I remember how all of their colleagues acted at the college. The general feeling of everyone was a lot like that this time too. People were freaking out when the first big bomb hit Hawaii. When the second one hit Los Angeles, they were panicking wildly. That's when some of the news shows were still on, and we could get information. It was about then that we began to hear which countries were allying with others. The school went into a lockdown. Nobody in, nobody out. That didn't last too long.

Parents began rolling up to the school to get their kids. Nobody was going to deny them that in a crisis, of course, so the normal rules of lockdown loosened a bit. At first, they weren't letting parents in the building, checking them at the door. Then when they started demanding their kids, it started a bottleneck, so they let them in with I.D. and had them waiting in the school lobby, our rotunda, until their kids came out. Both Jake and I had our planning periods when the news started coming in, so we were out of class and running off copies of papers in the library. I remember seeing the parents in the lobby, many of them barely hanging onto their composure. Jake came out and talked to lots of them. He was a kind of fixture around the school, having been here since the place opened two decades ago. He had a gentle, calming effect on them. He'd speak in vague generalities, shake hands, pat folks on the shoulder, and return offers of hugs from the ones who were leaving. Mostly girls. Guys don't hug it up when they're scared. At least straight guys don't. Too much of the machismo thing, I guess. Can't show feelings or emotions in times of crisis. Jake was like that too. Nothing fazed him. He was always smiling back then.

Always smiling. He used to be the biggest prankster in the building. Always joking around, being a smart ass. It was occasionally annoying, but most of the time people really enjoyed his humor, and they congenially put up with him even when he'd go over the top. All that changed with the East Coast bombing. Jake was on the phone with his wife at the time. The school went into lockout mode first. That's the "nobody in" protocol. It pretty much assured us that it would likely be the last period of the day for everyone, and with Jake and me having planning that period, it freed us up in ways that other teachers would not yet be. Jake called his wife to see how she was doing and what she'd heard. Jake's wife was a salesperson of medical supplies. Her region included DC, Baltimore and areas to the north, so she was on the road several days a week. She'd taken that job when her kids graduated from Hunter's Run. Jake's marriage had gotten a little rocky back then, and she responded by getting herself out of the house for a while, hoping that the occasional distance might make them appreciate each other more.

When Jake called, I was right next to him. I wasn't trying to listen in, but it didn't take much to hear everything in the library. They were talking about what they'd heard regarding the West Coast bombings. Laura—Jake's wife—was always listening to the radio when she was driving, so she had

11

more notes to compare than Jake did. Then suddenly, Jake's face froze. He said "Laura?" into the phone about six times. His face turned into stone, and he put his phone in his pocket. He turned to me with a look I've only seen him use before wrestling matches, and said, "we got cut off." Then he turned around and walked out of the library toward his classroom. That was the last day I saw him smile on any consistent basis. Now those smiles come and go unpredictably like the wind.

Nobody really knew where the bombs came from, or why we were unable to defend against them. That's just when everything stopped for good—at least around here. Radio went out. TV went out. Internet. Everything. We'd get occasional calls from people in isolated areas who had heard things, but none of them verified. One of the first of those calls came to Jake himself. Jake had a brother-in-law in Wyoming-- Marty--who tried to give him information for a while, but we couldn't be sure what he said was accurate. The brother-in-law said that there were reports of bombs hitting New York, Boston, Washington DC, Norfolk, Virginia, and several spots in Florida. All of those spots were big ports with military vessels there, so that news at least made sense. Jake told us what he'd said, but despite getting called back several times, Jake had trouble talking to him. He never told Marty that his sister might be dead, just that he'd had to hang up when they were speaking and that he'd update him when he knew more.

But Jake never heard from Laura again, and given Marty's reports and the silence in the surrounding area, we simply assumed the worst. The first hour or so after the East Coast bombs hit, the school hit mass hysteria. Kids were running out of the building by the hundreds. Teachers left too. I admit I was packing and getting ready to take off myself. It was Jake who stopped me.

"Eddie," he said. "Where are you going?"

"Home," I answered. "I don't want to be here if the world is at war."

"Yes, you do," he said. "This is exactly where you want to

be."

"What the fuck are you talking about, Jake? I want to be with my family."

"Have you heard from them?" he asked.

"No. They were in Washington, guest lecturing."

"And they haven't called you?"

"No."

"Where do they teach again?" Jake asked. "They're not at Hollowel anymore, right?"

"Yes and No. They both are doing guest stints at Georgetown this semester."

Jake looked at me seriously. His bottom lip stuck out a little, and he nodded ever so slightly.

"What?" I asked.

"Eddie, Georgetown's right by DC," he said.

"So? We have no idea what has happened."

"Okay, okay. I know. I just want you prepared for every eventuality."

"They haven't called yet," I said again. "It's been over an hour." I checked my watch. It had been over three hours. "I'm thinking maybe I should drive home." But I knew. I knew what the truth was. Anyone remotely close to Washington DC was gone.

"Leaving here might not be your best bet," he said. "Just think for a minute. If DC has been bombed, the radiation area is going to track very close to here. We're an hour from Washington, less as the crow flies. If DC has been nuked, it's gone already. The areas around it—outside the blast perimeter—they're going to go within days. The crucial areas are going to be the ones right where we are. People way outside of bombing zones—they're going to be OK. They might be without power, or satellite feed, but they won't be in danger of radiation. We are. We've got to hunker down here for a while, let the danger-ous radiation pass."

"Hunker down for a while? Define 'a while'."

"Impossible to know for sure, but if I had to give an answer? A month or two."

"A month or two? Are you out of your fucking mind? Live here? For a month? Where are we gonna sleep? What are we gonna eat? There are over a thousand people here!"

"Not anymore. Did you see that mass exodus of people over the last hour? Most of the people in this school took off. There is a decent chance that they signed their own death warrants by leaving. If the radiation trail makes it up this far, they are going to die a slow, horrible death out there over the course of the next couple of weeks. We are in a secure building. People can't get in unless we let them in. The walls are solid. Even the glass is thick. There is no better place to ride this out—apart from an actual bomb shelter—than in a school. This is the safest, most secure place in the whole town. "

I thought about that for a minute. He was right. Schools were built to last, and the most recent codes made everything super solid and secure.

"What about food?" I asked.

"The school cafeteria has enormous freezers. They're stocked for nearly a month ahead of time, and that's for over a thousand people. We can ration what we have."

"How about water?" I said.

"We're on town water, but you may remember that when they put this place in, we got our own reservoir to draw from first. We have our own water treatment plant just down the road. It may not be ideal, and in coming weeks it may be radioactive, but if we act fast, we can get some saved."

"What do you mean?"

"If they used the standard kind of nuclear bombs, radioactivity takes a little while to get here. If we can get something to put the water in--buckets, tubs, anything we can find—we can get safe water stored up for a while. It's not perfect, but it's better than nothing, and better than out there."

"Shouldn't we talk to the principal or something? I mean, he's the boss," I said. I thought about the question for a moment. It was sensible. It implied there was an order to things. Go through a chain of command. Except now, several hours after hysteria had hit Hunters Run High School, there was no chain. There were barely any links left here.

"He was the boss. But he's not here now. Most of the people that were here in this school have gone. Things have changed. There is no school system anymore, at least not right now. Survival takes precedence. Leaders lead," said Jake.

That was the Marine Corps talking. Jake had been a Marine officer before joining the teaching force. He had wrestled in college, then wanted to try and compete for an Olympic spot. He wasn't that good--at least that's what he always said--but good enough to get a shot at training for it. The Armed Forces had a World Class Athlete Program where soldiers essentially were professional athletes. They wore their uniforms, they lived on military bases, but they trained for their respective sports. The Marines had a particularly good wrestling team, and Jake managed to be on it for a while until he got hurt. Still, the whole Semper Fi thing is real. Once a Marine, always a Marine. Jake was oozing military just then.

"Look Eddie, I'm not trying to be a dick here, but if I'm right, then this is now a survival situation. It's not really time to think about asking permission or seeing who's in charge. We have a short time to get our shit together. It's your decision to stay or go, but at the risk of sounding harsh, everyone out there" he pointed to the window, "may be as good as gone, assuming they're not gone already. You're a smart guy. I need smart guys right now."

"For what?" I asked.

"To survive. We have a bunch of people still here either not sure what to do or on the verge of panicking. We need to get our shit together, unite these people, and make a plan."

I thought about that for a moment. Jake was right. We didn't know who was here and who wasn't. The power was still on for the moment, but that might not last. We needed to get a plan together, and Jake was already on it. Suddenly I got the sinking feeling that Jake Fisher might be my best ticket for survival. I decided then and there to join him.

"Okay, you're the boss, then. What's first?"

"Go to the Main Office. Get on the PA system and announce that anyone remaining is to report immediately to the cafeteria. "

"Okay, on it. What are you gonna do?" I asked him.

"Try and figure out what to say to these people," he said, exhaling.

I went to the Main Office. No one was in there at all. The door to the nurse's office was cracked, but it was empty too. I heard noise coming from down the office hallway from one of the assistant principal's offices. I thought about asking permission, then remembered what Jake said, and walked into the PA room. The microphone was sitting on the table next to the machine. One big, red, "on / off" switch was right there in the front. I figured that was about all there was to it. I held in the big "speak" button and cleared my throat.

"Mmm...hmm. Uh, anyone who is left in the building please report to the cafeteria at this time. Please." Realizing I had said 'please' twice, I put down the mic and walked out of the office and into the cafeteria. When I got there, Jake was in the front, sitting at one of the tables reading a book. It was titled "Hiroshima." I lifted my eyebrows and gave him a quizzical look.

"Internet's down, and I don't know a whole lot about nuclear weapons. These live in our school library," said Jake. Beneath the book he was reading were more books and all on the same topic.

"From what I'm reading, I have no idea why we still have power," he said. "But when I look out into town, I don't see a whole lot of lights, so my guess is we're on an automatic emergency generator, which explains why whenever we get a power outage the lights come right back on at a lower level. If that's the case, it won't be long before that generator runs out of whatever juice it's running on."

"So, you're saying the power could go out completely at any time?" I asked.

"Yup. This one book says that if a bomb detonates high enough in the air, the electromagnetic pulse that results from it could literally cause a blackout across the entire continent."

"Holy shit," I said.

"Yeah, holy shit indeed," said Jake. "It's possible that some of our defense systems caught some of their bombs before they hit their targets. No telling where that might be or what the effects are, and with no news, no internet, and no radio, it's impossible to tell what areas are affected and how badly."

"So, are you telling me that my folks might be alive?"

"No way to tell, Eddie. But where would they go if they were?"

"Here. To find me. I'm their only child." Jake exhaled with a flat, scrunched lip look at me.

"Look buddy, I can't keep you here. You have choices. If you feel you need to go, then go," he said.

"What are you gonna do?" I asked.

"I'm going to find out who's here, take stock of what we have, get a survival plan together," he paused.

"And?"

"And then go find my boys."

Jake had two sons in college. Tommy, the oldest, was 21. Vinny, the younger brother, was 19. They were both in Virginia, and both were on wrestling scholarships at two different schools.

"You think they could have survived?"

"I'm hoping that they're both far enough in the mountains that they should be OK. Bigger targets would be Norfolk, Northern Virginia, even Richmond. They're four or more hours away in the Shenandoah mountains. They could be— they should be alive. And I'm gonna find them."

"By yourself?"

"If need be. I wouldn't ask anyone to go with me that didn't want to," he said.

"Uh, no offense, Jake, but why would anyone want to go with you halfway across the mountains to find people they're not related to?"

"Understandable. Of course, they may feel like they have to."

"Jake," I said. "You just got done telling me that the surrounding area could be radioactive, and you're talking about traveling past DC to get to the mountains of Virginia. That's a four- or five-hour drive, assuming your car works and the highways aren't blocked. You just talked me into staying here where it was safe. So why would anyone want to leave?"

"Eventually, there might be...scenarios," he said evasively.

"Scenarios?" I asked.

"Things may evolve over the next few weeks or so. You never know." As he was speaking, people started wandering into the cafeteria, and Jake lowered his voice as they entered.

"What are you trying not to say?" I asked, this time a little concerned at what he might be holding back. Jake put his forehead into his hands, closed his eyes, then exhaled again.

"Jake!"

"Okay, well, I'm not trying to be dramatic, and I'm not trying to scare anyone, but I'm thinking ahead now, trying to put myself in other people's shoes, and my gut tells me that it won't be long before this place comes under siege."

"Under siege," I exclaimed. "What the hell?"

Some people turned their heads my way, and Jake waved downward to indicate he wanted me to lower my voice. He gave them a reassuring nod, then grabbed me and walked just outside the doors where we could talk.

"In times of crisis, people can be pretty stupid. They're impulsive, greedy, self-centered, and they tend to panic. Pretty soon, people who have survived will start running out of food and water. If the rest of the town is like this school, places have been deserted and people are trying to assess what they do and don't have. If they're already mostly out of electricity, it's possible they've noticed that the school has some lights on. That will attract them like moths. When they realize they're locked out, they'll start banging on the doors. If nobody lets them in, someone will start going for the glass, and in case you haven't noticed, this place has a lot of glass. There aren't too many places where we could hole up and defend ourselves."

"Why do you think we're going to have to defend ourselves," I asked, horrified.

"Human nature," Jake said. "Extreme situations bring out the extremes in people. Extreme good, extreme bad. Extreme heroism. Extreme villainy."

"Jesus. You think people will come after us just because we're here? And did you just use the word 'villainy' in a sentence?"

"I did. And I do think it's possible. And when they do, one of two things is going to happen. The trusting folks in our group will want to let people in. If those people are known to us, no big deal. We have other people in our group."

"That's thing one. What's thing two?" I asked.

"Those same folks let people in, those people turn out to be dangerous strangers, and we are forced to defend ourselves. Violently. Maybe lethally."

"Shit, Jake. You think it will come to that?"

"I don't know. I mean I really don't. But do you want to face either scenario if you can help it?"

"No. No I don't." I thought about it for a minute. "So, you think staying mobile is the answer?"

"Maybe. Maybe not. Ironically, the first thing I feel like we have to do, though, is set up and fortify this place. Even if it means eventually we can't stay, for now I feel like we need this place to be a stable environment," he said. He shrugged and said, "I'm going with a lot of gut here."

"That's because at your age it's what you have most of," I joked. He shot me an eye roll.

"How would you know? Are you eyeballing me again?" he smiled. Almost a real one. I laughed a little. Laughing felt necessary. "I can understand that, you big flirt. I am pretty easy on the eyes."

Jake was a teacher here when I was a student. I had always thought he was pretty cool, but word has it sometimes he could be preachy in class, and as a standard teenager, preachy people can turn you off a little. Any teen being told what to do by an adult bristles a little, even if it's a no-nonsense thing. That's what teens do. Getting to know Jake as an equal was another matter. I returned to Hunter's Run to teach after finishing college. I even taught in the same Social Studies department as him. Seeing him from the other side of the teacher's desk was a very different view. Jake Fisher could be a bit of a ham.

I had eaten lunch with Jake almost every day since I first got hired. He'd had a big sense of humor. He was a big prankster, a big smart-ass. I think he enjoyed being the faculty clown. He always was picked to M.C. events, like the pep rally, talent shows, stuff like that. He was the classic host. Everybody seemed to know and like him, even the students who never had a class with him. He was kind of like the local celebrity, on everybody's good side. It sounds dumb to say out loud, but I felt like the cool new kid when hanging out with Jake. It gave me some "street cred" with my fellow faculty members. As one of the youngest on staff, I was desperate to be taken seriously, and befriending Jake made it a lot easier.

One time at lunch it was just the two of us. In the quiet moment I had asked him why he was such a goofball all the time. The answer I got surprised me.

"Lowers people's expectations. People don't take me seriously, so I rarely disappoint them. Opponents don't take you as a threat, let their guard down. Then you can swoop in. If I act like the 'aw, shucks' country boy who's always joking around, folks don't expect much. Makes them lose focus. It's a distinct advantage."

I must admit that took me by surprise. He'd fooled me, at least to an extent. There aren't many middle-aged, white wrestling coach types who strike me as open-minded intellectuals. But Jake was. Knowing his military background with the Marine Corps, I was even more surprised that he wasn't homophobic. He never had a problem with my being gay. He joked about it all the time. Called me "Princess," always did off-color stuff; but I knew he wasn't judging me. I'm not sure how I knew—I just did. I don't think for a second he was closeted, or even bi-curious. My Gay-Dar didn't go off at all around him. But he made me feel comfortable being me around him, and that was important.

"I don't care who you kiss, or where you piss, Princess," he used to say. "As long as you're not an asshole. But do try and keep those effeminate little hands off my world-class tushy. This thing deserves better."

That was before. Now, Jake was different. His demeanor changed. The smart-ass had disappeared into someone quieter, more calculating, more stone-faced. Not that world-wide thermonuclear war wasn't reason enough to put a damper on your sense of humor. It was. But I think that phone call flicked a switch. He was on the phone with his wife, Laura, when the phone went dead, and the big bombs hit DC. That killed something inside him. All he seemed to have left was a desire to find his sons. A primal drive. I'm too young to really understand that. I'm not a parent. Hell, I'm still a kid by comparison with most of this faculty. I'm half Jake's age—so how could I possibly understand his mindset? All I knew was that Jake Fisher was sharp, tough, and a friend--and most likely, the safest place in a world gone mad was as close to him as I could get.

CHAPTER 2

Taking The Lead

T he cafeteria started filling up. Most were teachers, but a few students trickled in as well. The kids were the ones that had no families to go to. The poor, wretched, huddled masses that Lady Liberty speaks of wanting to give shelter to. Many of those kids were ones you'd predict. They wore Goodwill clothes, stayed on the social outskirts, and didn't quite fit in. Others were a unexpected. Lots of really bright, really awesome kids are actually alone in life. A surprising number of kids come to school because school is all they have. Teachers are parents, counselors, and friends. Some teachers might provide the only positive exchanges those kids will have all day long. Those were the kids who were filing into the cafeteria now. They had no place else to go anyway.

Jake asked me to get a head count. All told, there were 36 people there. Some teachers, some kids, some staff members and assistants, and two custodians. The custodians were crucial, because they held the keys to literally every room in the building. It seemed like a lot of people to me. I mean, why would anybody stay here when the Holocaust was going on outside? Yet here I was myself, inexplicably. And considering that the school had over a thousand kids, about a hundred teachers, and a couple dozen support staff, it was obvious that the vast majority of the Hunters Run community actually had fled very quickly. People sat down at the cafeteria tables looking somewhat in shock, unsure of what to do. Jake went to the podium in the front of the room and spoke up.

"Thanks for coming here. This is all very difficult for each of us. I understand that. Many of you have questions that probably no one here is going to be able to answer. While we're here we can trade what we know, discuss what we don't, and formulate a plan for survival for the foreseeable future."

Jake walked over to one of the custodians, Randy, who was in his school uniform with a light blue collared shirt and navy pants. He whispered something to Randy, who nodded, then left the cafeteria.

One girl started crying, and another came over to hug her. Her soft sobs gradually evolved into heaving ones, and the girl hugging her began to cry as well.

"What do we know?" a young male teacher asked. The teacher was Mark Longaberger, a social studies teacher who had been at the school three years. Jake looked around as if to direct traffic. An older female Physical Education teacher, Robin Eaves, held up her phone.

"I got people in Missouri who said Chicago is gone. No survivors. They had no power but were able to tweet out some things from the Midwest. St. Louis is on fire. People are looting and killing each other. The National Guard was called, but only fifteen Guardsmen showed, and they were demolished by the mob in a matter of minutes. It sounds really bad out there."

"I got cousins in Texas," said Melanie Richmond, the school secretary. She was a single divorcee who had no one to go to when the bombs dropped, having moved far from her home in the Lone Star state to marry her now ex-husband. "They say that the border wall is coming down in places. Houston is nearly empty. Parts of the city that were devastated by Hurricane Harvey only a few years back and not yet rebuilt were in flames. Everybody on the coast is trying to get their hands-on fuel for their boats. Lotta shooting going on in Texas."

"That's because everybody in Texas is a gun-toter," said Al DeFillipo, a science teacher in his early forties. "I bet they'll all have shot each other by the end of the week." Melanie shot him a scowl.

"They'll need those guns," said Wes Kent. "Mexicans will be streaming in trying to take stuff by now." Wes looked at me when he said it. Kent was an ultra-conservative math teacher. He didn't approve of me on several levels—starting with my 'ungodly choice' of dating other men-- and he also tended to lump every Hispanic into the simple group known as Mexicans.

"Eddie's Peruvian, Wes. And everybody everywhere is trying to deal with this whole situation," said DeFillipo. "And that attitude—and guns—are what got us into this mess."
Al, a science teacher through and through, was a liberal athe-ist. He was constantly in a verbal battle with Wes. The number of times I got drawn into debates in the teachers' lounge were too many to count.

I was glad that Al stuck up for me. It's a lot easier being gay and Hispanic in America in the 21st century, but the country's recent extreme politics recently had dominated nearly every debate. People tended to be fervently to one extreme or the other, and vocal about it. The number of folks who landed in the middle were pretty quiet about their politics. Reason was not something we saw a lot of in those days, and while Al was definitely on my side, he was also pretty aggressive about it. I just wanted to exist. I didn't necessarily want to be a gay activ-ist, or an authority on Hispanic immigration. Most of the time I just wanted to be me and be treated normally. Neither Wes nor Al ever really let me do that. Jake, however, was another matter.

"OK," said Jake. "Let's keep this productive. It sounds

like there's chaos pretty much everywhere, and devastation in quite a few places. We're going to have to hold together for protection and make some plans."

"Sounds like you have something in mind, Coach?" The question came from Lou Orville. He was a Math teacher working his way through grad school. He was young and able-bodied and coached the football team.

"I do," Jake said. "To be ready to ride this thing out—whatever it is—we're going to need to do some planning. The way I see it, we should be out of power already. I'm really not sure how we kept it this long. The only thing I can figure is there is an automatic generator, and it can't have much fuel left. We need to go to the ice machines in the cafeteria and the training room and put as much as we can in coolers as soon as possible. We also need to inventory the food in the freezers here and see what will spoil first, what can travel, and what needs to be heated. We're gonna get start getting hungry soon, and we'll need to make rations, decide if we want to venture out and see what's out there. You got a head count yet, Eddie?"

"I got thirty-six, *Jefe*," I said, using the Spanish word for "chief" or "boss." Jake cracked half a smile at that. He had been a linguist in the Marine Corps after his injury and was pretty fluent in Spanish.

"OK, thirty-six. Is anybody here on a special diet or allergic to anything?" Jake asked.

"Me, Coach."

A big hand went up. It was Glen Billings, the heavyweight on the wrestling team. He was a Type 1 diabetic and had been on an automatic pump at one time in his life. He'd had some real struggles over the years, and given the scenario now, he had to be nervous.

"Hey Big Guy. Yeah, I know your situation. We can get into the nurse's office, see if she has any blood monitoring stuff in there. In the meantime, your blood sugar starts to feel too high or too low, you let somebody know. Keep mindful of how you're feeling and stay around people, alright?" Glen nodded.

"What we need to do is go across the street to the Wal-Mart. That place has got everything we need," said Orville.

"They sure would," I said enthusiastically. "We should maybe see what's there, bring back the important stuff."

"What if everybody else probably has the same idea. You might run into some trouble there," said Robin.

"Or bring some back with you," added Al .

"He can handle himself," Mark Longaberger said. "He's 6'3" and 250 pounds. Who's gonna mess with him?"

"Is he bulletproof?" asked Robin. "Cause everywhere else in the country seems to be shooting it up."

"At least in Texas," added Al DeFillipo.

"I'm pretty big. Like he said, I can handle myself," Orville said.

"Keep in mind, something, Lou," said Jake. "You're responsible for more than just yourself now. You're a teacher, and we have students and fellow colleagues here who need us. We're a group of survivors now, not just a school building. What if you run into some unsavory characters at the Wal-Mart? What if you get followed by somebody with a weapon, and they get the idea to break into the school? Then we're all in danger, and you will essentially have put us there. So far, we're lucky to be alive. Hard to say how long our luck's gonna last. I suggest we wait a little bit, exercise a little caution first."

"So how are we supposed to survive just sitting here?" Longaberger yelled. He leaned over towards Wes Kent and whispered, "this feels a little like bullshit." The second comment was made with less volume, almost fading into whisper.

Jake made a calming gesture with his hands and lowered his voice a tad. "Mark, we are in a building that stores tons of food for over a thousand people a day for weeks at a time. We're way better off than lots of people right now, and we're safe. That's probably not going to last."

"Why not?" The question came from one of the crying girls, who had composed herself enough to pay attention to the two alpha males interacting.

"The way I figure," Jake began, "The first thing that's gonna happen is survivors will look for each other. You'll see folks helping each other, sharing, kindness, folks sticking together. That's usual after big tragedies. You see great human kindness follow close behind catastrophe. But after a while, when everyday survival starts taking over, you'll start to see a change. People are going to start huddling together in groups. Clans, gangs, whatever you want to call them. There's safety in numbers. Those clans are going to have to feed themselves, and when law and order is out the window, the easiest way to feed yourself is to raid someone else. Someone will figure out that we have stuff here and sooner or later, they'll try to break in. That's when we'll have to defend ourselves."

"Let 'em come," shouted Orville. "I'll put all 250 lbs. behind my fist and see how they like that." Robin Eaves and Melanie Richmond rolled their eyes, and the handful of football players hooted in affirmation.

"I'm glad that you are a big guy on our side, Lou. But remember, animals that have to fight to the death for every meal don't tend to live very long," said Jake.

"Well I ain't no animal," said Orville.

"No need to fret about something we don't have any control over. Preparing for the worst is a safe bet. Worrying about it or talking tough doesn't really help," said Jake. "I figure our best bet is to gather some food first, then get some inventory on what we need to cook first so that it lasts longer. Once we've established ourselves, created a system for rationing, and gotten a bit of a routine, then it will probably be time to find something to haul our supplies in. Then we try to create or snag some weapons. By then, it'll be time to start scouting around," Jake said. "For now, though, let's just try to get settled, see what we have, maybe make some plans in case folks decide to show up with bad intentions."

"What if you're wrong," asked Lou Orville. "What if nobody comes here?"

"Yeah, and what if we don't want to stay here? What if

we want to go someplace? It's a free country," said Longaberger.

"Yeah," added Orville.

"It WAS a free country," added Wes Kent. "We don't know what it is now. We might have to protect our own. Take down potential invaders."

Eyes scanned around the room after that. A chill hit me at the thought of what desperate people might do to us, to each other, to anyone.

"No offense, Jake, but who put you in charge? I mean, we can do whatever the hell we want. It's World War III out there. I mean, it's the Apocalypse, right? Doesn't that make it every man for himself?" said Longaberger.

Melanie Richmond looked at Longaberger with a sneer and shook her head, mouth agape.

"What? You know every one of you has thought it at least once since we heard about the bombings. I'm just the one who said it out loud," said Longaberger. "A-Poc-O-Lypse. Mad Max stuff. And in Mad Max, the aggressors get the lion's share of everything. Sorry if that hurts your feelings, Mel."

Melanie Richmond frowned.

"The thought that this might be Armageddon did cross my mind," said Wes.

"I thought it," said Orville. "Aint' gonna lie."

"We're all thinking it," Jake said. "And we're all probably fighting down some panic right now. Your gut tells you to grab a handful of whatever you can and go sneaking off to loot stores and buy weapons and God knows what else. I get it. That's human nature. But you all are going to have to suppress those thoughts for the time being and start thinking like a community instead of like an individual."

"Well maybe I want to think like an individual," said Mark. "Only the strong survive."

"Perhaps you're mistaking me, Mark. I'm not really asking," said Jake. "This is not the time for that kind of bullshit. You want to survive, you stick together, and you start now."

The room went quiet. Longaberger stared daggers at

Jake. Lou Orville cut his eyes back and forth at them both and frowned. Jake walked over to the table where most of the female teachers were sitting.

"Robin, can you and Mel take a little inventory on food? I'm looking for stuff that's going to spoil soon and also what stuff we have that is non-perishable. We'll need to eat the perishable stuff first before the power goes and it starts to spoil. Or at least cook it, so that it lasts longer," said Jake. Both nodded.

Then, almost as if on cue, the power cut out.

"Shit. Now we have to do it in the dark," Robin said.

"We can use my phone, it has a light," said Melanie.

"You might want to hold off on that for now," said Jake. There's not going to be anywhere to plug phones in here now. You might want to save everything you have. Try opening all of the cafeteria doors and use what's left of the sunlight. Just do the best you can."

"What do you want us to do?" asked Al DeFillipo. "I'm with you."

"Al, how about you take a handful of guys with you and get the ice chests from the training room and fill them up. Every last piece. It's always open, so you shouldn't need keys for that. Lou—I'm presuming a football coach has keys to the Physical Education storage. If not, Robin probably can loan you hers. Why don't you and Mark go snag all of the targets, bows and arrows from the archery sets and bring them into the gym. We're going to need weapons, and those would be a good start."

"I'm not particularly crazy about the way you're bossing everybody around," Lou said. Jake wheeled around, surprised. He stared at Orville incredulously for a moment and seeing that his look didn't affect the big football coach, walked over to him. Orville straightened up and puffed out his chest, readying himself. Jake reached up, and Orville stepped back for a second, as if ready to block a punch. Jake rested his right hand on the big man's shoulder.

"Lou, this isn't about you and me, or who's giving orders. It's about all of us. If you have other ideas, we can discuss them together. I'm not trying to boss you around, just try-ing to take actions now that will save us in the long run. You get it? This is what all my Marine Corps training was about. We stand together or we die apart. These are the tough times you've been preparing for all your life. Every pep talk you ever gave to your team about using sports as preparation for life— well this is it. This is the crisis where we see who was listening. Now, are you with me on this?"

The big man exhaled, softening. He looked a little em-barrassed, and he nodded at Jake.

"Sorry dude," he said. Jake patted him on the back twice and smiled.

"No sweat big guy." Jake exited the cafeteria and walked down the hall towards his old classroom. Once around the corner, Mark Longaberger checked over his shoulder and whis-pered to Orville.

"Man, you were totally right back there. Where does this guy get off? Who put him in charge? He's not the principal. You're bigger and stronger than he is. In the jungle that makes YOU boss, right? Why didn't you get in his face?"

"I wanted to, but he had a point, Mark. We have to be in this together. He's just doing what he thinks is right," said Or-ville. "We don't want to turn into animals, you know. He could be right."

"So, what makes him right? Why can't you be right? Why can't I be right? I don't need to be told what to do. I'm a grown-ass man. That guy's a dick," said Longaberger.

"Maybe. But for now, let's do what he says. Here, help me get those archery targets."

The two men walked into the PE storage closet and looked at the collection of games, balls, and sports equipment. It was a massive amount of space and stuff dedicated to playing. Just playing. Longaberger and Orville stared at the space and sighed.

"Never really thought about how much time and money goes into playing games," said Lou. "Don't need any of this stuff now. Shit just got real." Orville and Longaberger started gathering eight targets and a cart full of bows and arrows and wheeled all of them into the auxiliary gym. There was a mesh curtain hanging on a cable. Orville grabbed it like he'd done a hundred times and drew it across as the archery back-stop.

"This is ridiculous. How are these serious weapons? This isn't the 1500's," said Mark.

"They're better than nothing, and it'll cause some serious problems for anybody who wants to fuck with us," said Orville. Some of the football players had followed the two teachers and were carrying the bows that didn't fit in the cart. Glen Billings nodded in agreement.

"I always sucked at archery," said Glen.

"Dude, you're huge," said Tanner Heffner, a small, wiry kid who was wearing a football jersey. "You don't need a bow and arrow," he said smiling.

"Time may come when we all need a bow and arrow," said Orville. "You may want to start practicing soon. Bow and arrow could be a nice weapon to have if people ever decide to come here and cause trouble."

"Not if they have a gun. Bringing a bow to a gunfight is how the Indians lost," said Mark.

Al DeFillipo was shoveling ice into giant Gatorade coolers in the athletic training office, where there was an ice-machine. The machine's motor was off, and the office had no window, and it was hard to see in the fading light of late afternoon. Al was spilling ice on the floor and cursing to himself.

"Mr. D, don't sweat it. Let me help you." The comment came from Jada Allen, a young African-American girl who was one of several students that had come to assist.

"Pass them along once they're full, Jada," a woman said. The woman was Maureen Kelly, who taught Spanish and

French at the school, and was the director of the International Club—which was one of the small bastions of minority students in the building. Maureen was white but had married a black man from the Dominican Republic when studying there in college. A friend of DeFillipo's, she shared his politics, and was always welcoming to people of color or pretty much any kind of minority in the school. Many said that she and De-Fillipo had had an affair, which was what led to her divorce, but anyone taking note of the make-up she used to mask the bruises her ex-husband gave her knew the truth. She was a kind, big-hearted woman in her early 40's, who had always gone out of her way to be welcoming to me. Maureen was stacking the Gatorade buckets onto a large flatbed cart to bring back to the cafeteria. I was keeping tallies of how many there were.

"Make sure you wheel these back to Coach Fisher, Jada," I said. She looked disappointed.

"But I was gonna help Mr. D fill the rest of these," she said. Maureen's eyes cast towards DeFillipo.

"I'll do that, Jada. Do what Señor Reyes says," said Maureen.
DeFillipo felt the eyes on his back and pursed his lips. He looked back at Maureen.

"Really? Anything you want to say to me?" he asked.

"Just be careful, Al. That girl idolizes you."

"She's helping me fill ice chests, Mo'. Not asking me to sleep with her."

"Yet," said Kelly.

"Jesus, Mo'. What are you saying?" said Al.

"Just be careful, that's all. No harm in being careful, right? Especially now," she said.

Jada wheeled the cart back to the cafeteria with me and we approached Jake.

"Thanks, Jada. All the machines off, Eddie?"

"Yeah, Jake. Lights out, ice machine off. We won't have too long before stuff starts to melt," I said.

"Tell Al and Maureen to empty out the machine. No sense letting anything go to waste. Jada, you and Mr. Randy dump all of these into the walk-in freezer in the kitchen. Mrs. Eaves and Mrs. Richmond are moving things around in there as we speak. The ice will last longer in there. Everything's insulated. We want to dump everything we have and make the most of it for now. Thanks."

I stared at Jake for a moment. He had taken charge coolly and confidently, had managed to become a leader in tough times with people challenging his leadership, and was making decisions that made complete sense in a survival situation. I shook my head in admiration ever so slightly, and he caught me.

"Jesus, Eddie. You're not gonna hit on me now, are you? I got stuff to do."

"Nope. Too old. Too fat. I might go hit on that hunky football coach, though. He seems pretty macho," I smiled. "What did he say to you?"

"Nothing. I did most of the talking. I understand why he might be a little touchy about taking orders. Hell, for all we know, society is out there with no rules at all right now. But I know what I'm doing, and I'm not gonna let him screw that up just to get in a pissing contest with me," he said.

"That's good, hombre. 'Cause with the size of him, I think he's got more piss."

"Size isn't everything," said Jake.

"Spoken like a straight man," I said, walking into the kitchen.

CHAPTER 3

Getting To Know You

The first night in the cafeteria was sleepless for most of us. While the day had been horribly taxing and the effort to get things ready very stressful, the night--for many of us—was worse. Lying in a dark cafeteria on piles of our clothes was more than uncomfortable. It was unsettling. The not knowing was awful. The wondering, Am I going to make it through this? Is my family OK? What are we going to do next? All of those questions circled around my brain. Some of the kids dropped off the minute the sun went down. All of the stress of the day exhausted many of them. The adults, on the other hand, were another matter. With a sense of responsibility that is drilled into you as a teacher, most of us didn't sleep well, concerned about our students and our colleagues.

While the night may have been unsettling, the next morning, however, was another matter. By the time most of us had awakened, Jake had already done some cooking. There were french toast sticks and sausage patties waiting for everyone, the scent wafting into the main part of the cafeteria from the kitchen. What's more, the lights were on. All of the electricity was on. I couldn't understand it. But as everyone around me started to rouse to their feet and gravitate towards the kitchen and its good smells, I saw a smiling Jake Fisher standing behind the serving counter offering food to thirty-six people under his charge. In addition, I could smell coffee brewing in the teachers' dining room. Melanie Richmond had put it together.

Each of us got two french toast sticks and a sausage patty, and about half of us had a small cup of coffee. As we all sat and ate, conversations slowly and quietly began to spring up. Once everyone was served, Jake came and sat down next to me with his small plate and a glass of water.

"No coffee?" I asked.

"Never could get used to it," he said. "They practically forced it on you in the corps, but I couldn't stand it."

"Suit yourself. More for me," I added. Jake grinned back and stuffed a stick in his mouth.

"How'd you get the electricity on?" I asked.

"Wish I could take credit for it, but it just came on all by itself," he said.

"What does that mean?"

"It most likely means that whatever bombs hit, the EMP took out some local grids for a time, but they weren't permanently damaged—at least around here."

"EMP?"

"Electro-magnetic pulse. With nuclear bombs, everyone pays attention to the horrific destruction, but there is also an EMP that takes out all power within a pretty big radius. If the power plants or grids aren't destroyed, however, then things should just re-set I guess."

"You guess?" I asked.

"History teacher. Don't teach physics or electricity. Not a demolitions expert. Like you, remember?"

"Fair enough, but you were a Marine, right? Didn't you see action?"

"Yeah. Long time ago. Didn't see tons of action, either," said Jake.

"How is that? You were a soldier. How can soldiers in Iraq not see action or know how bombs work?"

"All depends on when and where you go. I went in just as the Gulf War action was slowing down. I went OCS. That's Officer Candidate School. Figured it's better to be the boss than the grunt that has to sweep up pigeon shit off of runways, so I chose to go OCS. That training took a while. You ever see Officer and a Gentleman?"

"No," I answered.

"You young, unwashed bastard. You truly have no upbringing. It's all about OCS. Actually, it's more about Richard Gere chasing Deborah Winger and pissing off Lou Gossett. But OCS is the setting."

"Richard Gere. Mmmmm. If I was older--I mean a LOT older--he'd be my type."

"You are so gay. I mean, not in the homosexual way. But the lame way."

"So, in one sentence you just offended non-heterosexuals and the handicapped," I said. "That's like twenty percent of the population. Gotta be a new record for you."

"Jake Fisher. Successfully offending people since the last millennium. Anyway, I finished OCS and most of the work was done in Iraq. I got sent in for clean-up duty. I basically oversaw guys cleaning up the mess we made after bombing the shit out of Saddam Hussein. Not really a forward position as combat goes," Jake said.

"Then you've never killed anyone," I asked. Jake stiffened.

"Never said that," Jake said, casting a glance downward.

"Sorry, I didn't mean," I stammered.

"Naw, it's okay. I mean, hell, we are sitting in the aftermath of a nuclear war. Not like we can afford to be too squeamish about our conversations, right? Yes. I have killed," he said.

"You don't have to talk about it if you don't want to. I didn't mean to touch a nerve."

"No, you didn't," Jake said. Then he took a deep breath, closed his eyes a moment, exhaled loudly, then nodded.

"We were picking up broken pieces of a building. It had

been a bank, but it was mostly rubble at that point, and we were trying to determine if it needed to be completely demolished or if it could be fixed up. I had a couple of engineers with me waiting for us to move a few things so they could go in and assess. I felt like they were being impatient, and since shit flows downhill, I got after the guys to pick up the pace. Rushed them a little bit. Didn't really make a complete check of the perimeter for people in the vicinity. Not well enough at least. We hadn't had any trouble at all for weeks, so I figured that today would be no different.

"So, I gave a cursory look at the streets nearby, but didn't check into one of the nearby buildings. Big mistake. A group of men dressed in black charged us. Most had handguns, one had an automatic rifle. He came in and sprayed the front of the building and hit a bunch of my men. Everyone ducked for cover as they came running up. One of my friends died in front of me almost instantly. His head was half blown off. I kind of snapped at that point. Kinda went a little psycho. I ran out with my pistol and shot the rifle-toter immediately. Shot him in the face three times. Then I turned on the others. There were five of them. I shot two, then ran out of bullets. One had his gun pointed at me. The rest was kind of instinctual."

Jake stopped for a moment. I could see he was starting to have some trouble finishing his story, but I didn't know what to say. He clearly wanted to finish telling it. Almost like confessing to a priest, but he was struggling not to show emotion, and I didn't want to press him. Men like Jake have an almost primal need not to show real emotion. It means weakness to them. I've never understood that, but then again, I was never a Marine, never a wrestler or a fighter of any kind. The men I spend most of my time with aren't usually macho, aren't usually afraid to show feelings. Jake, on the other hand, needed some help here, and I wasn't sure how to give it.

"Instinctual?" I asked. He nodded.

"Basically, with the martial arts training they give us —mostly Aikido and ju-jitsu type stuff in terms of disarming someone—I took the gun away from the third guy. I broke his wrist and the gun went flying in the street. Then I snapped his neck and he fell limp. I turned to the other two and reached down my leg for the knife that we always carry. They were scared, even though one of them had a gun. Not everybody who runs in to attack you is a fearless warrior, and those last two were scared to death. The fourth one I knifed in the throat. I could hear gushing noises as I pulled the knife out. The fifth one had already dropped his gun and pissed himself, and dropped into a ball on the ground, covering his head with his arms, with his hands up in a kind of pleading gesture. He was trying to surrender. I reached down, picked up his gun. I realized that it had been one of ours. Somehow this guy had gotten a hold of an American pistol. That really ticked me off for some reason. Not sure why. I flicked off the safety and shot him in the head."

"Jesus, Jake."

"All of the shooting had been heard by our troops, and a bunch of our guys ran our way, guns raised ready to back us up any way they needed to. When they got there, they saw me standing over a half a dozen of the enemy, covered in blood, gritting my teeth, shaking like a leaf. Both engineers were dead. One of the guys in my unit was dead, and two more badly wounded. One of the wounded didn't make it and died the next day. They were just kids, even younger than I was at the time. The ones who survived told this story about me that made me into some kind of legend. Told everyone in the compound what I'd done. They tried to get the higher ups to award me a medal, but it was determined that had I done a better job scouting the area first, the whole thing might have been avoided. The guys stationed there all treated me like some kind of celebrity, but I was messed up after that. I blamed myself for the deaths of my colleagues, and seeing what my rage had accomplished scared me. I got kinda fucked up in the head after that. They sent me home with PTSD three weeks later."

"Holy shit, Jake. I'm sorry."

"Once I got home, I became asymptomatic pretty quickly. They determined I was fine, so back to work I went. One of the kids in my unit who survived—his dad was a pretty important officer in the Corps. He came to see me. His son had told him everything. He had been hiding inside the bank's walls and watched me singlehandedly dismantle our attackers. Made me sound like Chuck Norris or something. The colonel said that he knew that the Corps would not reward me as I should have been due to the nature of the incident, but he still felt that my actions were valorous, and he wanted to do me a favor. He asked me what I wanted to do with my life, why I had entered the Corps. I told him I wanted to wrestle, and that I was hoping to try out for the all-Marine team, in their World Class Athlete Program. He put me on the Marine Corps wrestling team for the last two years of my service. I was basically a professional athlete for two years, training and competing. I had spent less than three months abroad, saw no actual combat, but managed to come away from Iraq responsible for nine people's lives—some of them American."

"Wow. That's some heavy shit," I said.

"Heavy enough," Jake answered. "How the Hell did we get on this topic again?"

"You were making excuses for why you don't know anything about bombs," I answered, smiling. Jake laughed at that. He nodded at me and smiled. "Oh yeah, that," he said.

"Discussing traumatic events makes me hungry, Eddie. If you are not gonna eat that sausage," he hinted, raising his eyebrows.

"You can have it," I said, forking it over to him. He grabbed it off my fork, stuffed the whole thing in his mouth, and started chewing.

"I thought you people liked sausage," he said laughing.

"My people? You mean Hispanics?"

"No. Gays," he laughed.

"Links? You bet. Patties? Not nearly as much."

Al DeFillipo walked over to the table where Jake and I were sitting.

"The ice machine is working again, and the freezer's on. Looks like everything is back up and running. You got any thoughts on that," Al said.

"We were just talking about it," I said. "What are your thoughts, science guy?"

"Science guy thinks it probably has something to do with the grid being out, but maybe not the whole source. I don't know. I'd have to know what kind of bombs they were using. Nice to have electricity though."

"My thoughts are that we take nothing for granted. Why don't you set up a schedule for some of the kids to haul ice once the machines have made some more into bins and coolers that we have put in the freezer. You never know when it'll run out," Jake said. "Has anybody had any luck on the internet yet?"

"No. That's the first place everybody went yesterday, and all communications were knocked out all day after the last of the explosions hit. Could a nuclear bomb knock out the Internet?"

"Nope," I answered smugly. Jake and Al yanked their heads around to stare at me.

"What? I Googled it right after the first ones hit," I said.

"And," said Jake.

"Well, the fact that I Googled it **after** the bombs hit should be a hint, Einstein," I said. Jake crossed his eyes and stuck out his tongue. "I copied it on my phone," I said, "Here," and clicked my cell phone on, opened up my memo page, and read what I had copied:

The bigger issue from an EMP would be the shutdown of critical systems and infrastructure like the systems that keep nuclear power plants stable, keep power grids running, manage your water and gas, and even run your car. All of those would be down temporarily. Whether or not you have internet access is a minor consideration after an EMP attack.

"Well, they got that last part right. Lots of other problems besides the internet. Besides---it sounds like the internet itself isn't the problem, it's the access that could be sketchy for some. Essentially, all power now should be considered unreliable and able to go in and out at a minute's notice. No telling what's going on with local government, also. Or if there even is any. For all we know, the Maryland state government is running things fine, double checking power grids and trying to assess damage," said Jake.

"Or thousands of people could be dead, and people are still trying to figure out what's going on," said Al.

"Or that," I said. "I mean, we could hear the bombs going off over Frederick and Camp David."

"Eventually, we're going to have to do what Coach Orville has suggested," said Jake, "and go out and see what's happening. My concern is with radiation. We don't know what hit where, how hard, and what the aftereffects will be, and I'm just trying to be safe."

"So, you agree with me now," said Lou Orville, sauntering up to our table.

"In theory at least," said Jake. "I never said it was a bad idea, just maybe not the first thing we oughta do."

"How long does radiation last? Isn't it, like, forever?" said Lou.

"Not necessarily. Depends on the power of the blast, location of the blast, and how much water is exposed," I said.

"Water," asked Orville.

"Fallout lands in the water, essentially contaminating it. Water can then, in turn, contaminate things around it."

"How do you know all this shit?" Orville asked.

"History teacher, remember? Hiroshima, Nagasaki, even that nuclear plant in the Ukraine, Chernobyl. Lots of info on that. The town of Pripyat, where Chernobyl was, started

41

getting some plants to grow back between 10-20 years. Saw a *60 Minutes* on that."

"Twenty years? We don't have twenty years. How are we gonna live?" yelled Orville.

"Slow down, Lou," said Jake. "Chernobyl was a different thing. It was worse than a bomb in some ways. The explosiveness of a bomb—that's the part that's bad. It spreads the damage, but as the blast radius grows, the damage lessens. Question is, where did the nearest bombs hit, and how big were they? No way to tell until some type of news gets up and running somewhere."

"Speaking of which," said DeFillipo, lifting his phone. He had the internet up and running, and an MSN news feed was running on it. He clicked the first article he could find. The headline was ominous:

WORLD WAR III BEGINS.

The article spoke of a multinational alliance with the United States, Great Britain, France, Spain, Canada, Japan, and South Korea all launching missiles and receiving word of counterattacks coming from Russia, North Korea, China, Cuba, and Venezuela. The article mentioned larger target cities in the U.S., such as New York, Los Angeles, Chicago, and Washington D.C., and how the capital had the best anti-missile defense system of any location in the world. It was also three days old. Nothing newer had been posted at all.

Al read out the article. It was what most of us remembered, but to hear it out loud, to see it written—that was different. It was no longer like we were playing at survival. We were actually there.

"Why hasn't there been an update?" asked Al.

"Hard to say," said Jake. "Could be a multitude of things. Maybe it's technical, could be a satellite got destroyed, could be the building sending it out was destroyed, or even the people doing it were killed. How long have you had service, Al?"

DeFillipo squinted as he thought. "It went out for me about an hour after the first warnings came out. Came on again briefly. Then nothing while the power was out. Then it picked up again just a few minutes ago. It's like you can't really know yet what works and what doesn't."

"Funny," I said. "When this place only had cable television, when I was a student here, internet was harder to get. It was considered more cutting edge. Now all we have is internet, but it seems like it isn't nearly as hard to damage as cable."

"Now *you* sound like an old man, Eddie," said Jake, smiling a little. "Teach you to make fun of me when I'm reading a book, won't it?"

Just then Melanie Richmond came running up to the group of us. She was out of breath and looked a little scared.

"Guys," she said. "We've got company."

On the athletic entrance of the building was a wall of thick glass. About eight to ten feet of it were doors, then above those, just a decorative wall of glass, with an awning of steel and concrete jutting out about fifteen feet from the doors for shelter. Standing under that awning in front of the doors were four figures.

Knocking.

Two were adult sized, one seemed the size of a teenager. One looked female from the distance.

"What now?" I asked Jake. His face went cold, and he stared off into the distance.

"Jake," said Melanie. "What do we do?"

"Now," he said. "We figure out who we are."

Everyone could hear the knocking, and everyone went completely still, as if not moving would keep people from seeing them. But they saw us. They knocked harder as they saw us look their way. They started yelling.

"Gather round, quickly," Jake snapped, and everyone quickly assembled into an extended huddle. One of the kids whispered "what should we do" only to have Lou Orville look at them as if they were stupid.

"You don't have to whisper," he snapped back.

"Shouldn't we let them in?" asked Maureen Kelly. "I

mean, they need help, right?"

"Hell no," Mark Longaberger answered. "You want to share food with them?"

"Yeah, and what if they're contaminated. They could spread that shit," said Orville.

"Really?" asked Robin Eaves. "Could they contaminate us?"

Suddenly everyone was looking at Jake, which made sense. He had calmly assumed leadership, gotten us on track, and given us a plan for survival. It's natural to look to our leaders for answers to everything. But Jake didn't have all the answers.

"I'm not really sure," said Jake. "We have to decide what our goals are, and who we are going to be. I'm not an expert on radiation, but I know that people wear suits to block them from it, so I'd have to say yes—if they are contaminated, or maybe their clothes are, I'm guessing they could spread it to us." Everyone gasped almost collectively at the thought.

"Not pumped about that idea, then," I said.

"No fucking way," said Lou Orville. "This is our place. They can get their own."

"They're human beings, not lepers," said Maureen.

"Lepers are also human beings, dear," said Robin. Maureen drew her mouth up in embarrassment.

"I say we don't let them in," said DeFillipo. "It's a matter of survival now. I'm sorry if that seems dickish, but it's how I feel." Longaberger patted him on the back.

"What if they need medical care? Food and water? Are we just going to let them die?" asked Maureen. "That's savage."

"Tough break for them," said Longaberger. "It's just the way it is."

"Just the way it is because you're on the inside," she retorted. "Something tells me you'd feel differently if you were the one knocking." The banging and yelling started getting louder. Nerves were beginning to fray, and most of us were staring down Jake.

"Why don't we start with finding out what they want,"

said Jake. Heads nodded in agreement.

"They're knocking on the fucking door," said Orville. "We know what they want. They want in. The answer is no."

"They're looking right at us," said Maureen. Everyone snuck a quick glance at the door, then most of the people turned their heads away uncomfortably.

"Let's go talk to them first," said Jake. "We're under no obligation to do anything right now, and we can be patient for the time being. Let's talk and see." Everyone seemed to like that idea except for Longaberger and Orville, who grumbled the entire time. Wes Kent was silent during the entire exchange, his face unreadable, but caution slowed every step he took. Jake took bolder strides and led the pack towards the other entrance. As we got closer, we could see their faces. They brightened at our approach, believing that we were coming to let them in. Then their faces dropped when we all stopped about ten feet shy of the door.

"Let us in," they yelled. Jake walked forward.

"Hi," said Jake. "Listen, we don't know much about who you are, where you're coming from, or what your intentions are, so please be patient for a moment."
They looked perturbed at that, exchanging glances. Jake walked up closer to the doors.

"Can you hear me?" Jake asked.

"Yes, we can hear you. And we still want to come in."

"I understand. But it's a bit complicated. We," Jake faltered, unsure of what to tell them. I looked around the group. So did Jake. Everyone was nervous. Jake struggled for something to say. Melanie Richmond stared at Jake as if to will him to speak. Orville and Longaberger just looked at the floor. "We," he stammered again, unable to bring forth the right thing to say. The people outside began to look at Jake with gazes that seemed to turn from pleading to impatient to perturbed. I decided to jump in.

"We're not sure we should let you in," I said. "We don't know what's been happening outside, we have kids in here that we're trying to keep safe, and, well, frankly, we don't know who you are."

Just then, Tanner Heffner spoke up.

"I know who they are," he said. "They're my family."

CHAPTER 4

Company

Almost as if on cue, everyone in the massive group of about forty people turned and looked at Tanner Heffner with their jaws agape.

"Tanner!" the woman outside yelled. "Tanner, it's us!"

"I see you mom," he yelled.

Longaberger turned to Lou Orville and whispered, "What the fuck do we do now?" Orville shrugged, wide-eyed.

"That's your family?" I asked Tanner.

"Yup. My mom, my dad, and my little brother, Will. He's an eighth grader. They went to get him when the bombings started and told me to stay put here at Hunter's Run."

"Did you tell anybody that?" I asked.

"Yeah. Glen knew." I turned to look at the massive Glen Billings, football lineman and gentle giant who was Tanner's best friend.

"You knew?" He nodded quietly back.

"Why didn't you say something?"

"What was I gonna say? We have been busy here getting things ready and prepared, storing food, gathering weapons. It's been non-stop for a day and a half. We didn't know what happened to Tanner's family, and his phone hasn't worked since the bombing."

While I was incredulous that we were all discovering this now, in this awkward moment, I supposed that the entire country at some level was experiencing this kind of uncertainty. Some things worked, some things didn't. Some power was on, some was off. Some people left school the minute the bombs started. Others had nowhere to go. It only seemed reasonable that parents who would have been at work with kids in different schools would have gone to collect the youngest first. Who knew what they were facing out there? Why did it take them a day to collect Tanner? It seemed we were about to find out. Jake moved towards the door and started to push it.

"Stop! What are you doing?" yelled Lou Orville.

"I'm letting them in. It's Tanner's family," said Jake.

"They could be contaminated," said Longaberger.

"He's right, Jake. How do we know they aren't a danger to us all?" Wes Kent asked, suddenly coming out of his quiet funk. "We discussed this."

"We discussed hypothetical strangers, Wes. These aren't strangers. They're...us," said Jake. Wes Kent approached the doorway.

"Why are you waiting until just now to get your son? What happened to you since yesterday," asked Wes.

"We were surprised—like everybody was. We went to pick up Will first," Tanner's father said, gesturing at his youngest son. We were on our way here last night when our car just stopped. I couldn't get it to start again. We saw and heard people walking nearby, sneaking around. We decided to spend the night in the car and come here when it was light again. Then for some reason, the car started up again, and we drove here."

"How do we know you're not contaminated with radiation?" asked Kent.

"They might not be, actually," jumped in Al DeFillipo. If they were here in Emmitsburg all day, and the bombs dropped in DC yesterday, and an EMP went off last night, there isn't time for the fallout to make it here by then. Most likely."

"Most likely," said Wes, frowning.

"Look, until we know more about what hit where, there's no way to be sure."

"Exactly."

"But it's unlikely."

"Unlikely," Wes echoed again. "That's not good enough. If we bring them in here, in our survival stronghold, and they end up contaminating it, we will have killed dozens of people. Unless you are carrying around a Geiger counter, I say we can't let them in."

"Are you kidding me?" Tanner's father, Scott Heffner yelled. "My son's in there. I'm looking at him. We have been a part of the Hunter's Run family for years. How can you keep us out?"

"Hunter's Run is over," said Wes Kent. That was before--before the "Cataclysm" happened. Now it's something else. And until we know you're safe, you can't be part of it."

"Wes, are you out of your mind?" Jake asked.

"Yeah, gotta agree with Jake. We know these people. It's kind of a dick move, Wes," I added.

"Dick or not—Jake Fisher, you yourself talked Lou out of scouting the area yesterday saying that he shouldn't risk contamination because now he was part of something bigger. Well, now that a hard decision has to be made, you suddenly don't have the balls to make it. You want to risk all of us for what? To be some kind of Lady Liberty? The wretched, poor, huddled masses weren't radioactive then. The world has changed now."

Jake was stunned into silence again. I turned and looked at him, aghast at what I'd just heard.

Al DeFillipo chewed on his lip and turned to me with an uncomfortable look. Al had flip-flopped his position, and his body language clearly showed he wanted to let the Heffners in.

"Wes," Jake said.

"No, Jake. This isn't your show. It's our show. These

people are not coming in."

"Seriously, Fisher. Leave the doors closed," said Longaberger.

"Mr. Fisher, that's my family," Tanner said. Jake turned around to look at the group. They were a mix of looks. Some wore the same visage as Kent, Longaberger, and Orville. Adamant. Negative. Exclude rather than include. Others looked guilty. Eyes cast down. Shame in their faces. But only Jake, Al, Maureen and I seemed to think that the Heffners should be allowed in.

"Are we seriously not going to let these people in?" I asked. A prolonged silence hung in the air. The group looked back and forth. Some faces were certain with their decisions, and their faces showed it. Others were uncertain, and their faces showed that. Then, suddenly, Jake stepped towards the door and reached. Lou Orville grabbed Jake's bicep. Jake turned and looked back in Orville's eyes. The look on Jake's face was one of cold fury. Like a controlled mayhem held precariously on a leash was about to be let go. Jake looked down at his bicep being held by Orville. He closed his eyes and took a breath.

"Not your call, Jake," said Lou. "Don't erase all the good you did today with one bone-head move." Wes Kent and Mark Longaberger walked up alongside Orville. The three of them abreast made a statement, and I could see Jake calculating in his head what the consequences of violence would be over this. Kent was a little younger than Jake by maybe six or seven years, and Orville and Longaberger were in their late 20's at their peak. Jake clearly had a middle-aged man's 'dad bod,' but was far from over the hill for a man in his mid-forties, but many was the day I'd see him limp into work with athletic tape wrapped around a wrist, or an ankle, or sporting a knee brace. Jake had taken a pounding in the past twenty years, and his body wasn't what it used to be. He closed his eyes and his hand fell softly away from the door. As it did, Mrs. Heffner began to cry.

"I'm sorry Tanner," said Jake. "I'm so sorry."

Tanner Heffner's lip began to quiver, and his face contorted, looking like he would begin to cry.

"Fuck all of you cowards," he said, and he bolted past the group of teachers and stormed out the door into the arms of his mother, who embraced him through tears. Tanner's father, Scott, turned red-eyed towards the mob of people who barred his entrance and began to shake with anger.

"God damn all of you," he said. "This place was like extended family. You'll regret this."

"No, we won't," said Kent. Just then, Maureen Kelly went running up to the doors with a bag. When it became obvious that the group was not going to allow the Heffners in the school, she had walked back and grabbed several food items and several water bottles and put them in a sack. Now she brought that sack past the group and to the doorway. She opened the doors and handed the sack to Tanner.

"I'm so sorry," Maureen said. "I feel horrible. Take this. I wish we, I'm so sorry," she said, starting to cry. She touched hands with Tanner's mom as she went back in and the metal on metal sound of the door slamming shut had a finality to it that made several people start.

"What do you think you're doing?" said Longaberger. "That was our food. We didn't say you could do that. You can't just give away our food stores."

"Get out of my face, you heartless bastard," she said. "You may have just condemned that family to a slow death, and you're worried about a couple of meals and some water. How dare you!"

Maureen Kelly was in full blown sob mode and ran off towards the cafeteria. Al DeFillipo and Jada Allen went running after her. A few other women and a handful of students with disgusted looks on their faces walked after them.

"Women don't understand," said Orville. "Too soft. Wanna save everybody."

"Don't worry about it. You were right," Wes Kent said to Mark Longaberger. Longaberger nodded dismissively. "Those people don't understand anything about where their food and shelter comes from. They'd have let that family in, and they would have cut into the food stores and maybe made everyone sick with radiation poisoning. You were smart."

"No, you were assholes," I said. "Easy to condemn someone from this angle. I pity you when it's your turn."

"It's not gonna be my turn," said Mark.

"No? Didn't you want to do recon yesterday? Look around outside? Wouldn't that make you 'Radioactive Man' then? Should we not let you back in after that?" Longaberger swallowed hard and looked nervously at Lou Orville, who had initially suggested the recon walk.

"As unpopular as it is to say, Eddie," Wes started, "We don't need three more mouths to feed."

"That's because your mouth is already fed," I answered.

"Yes, it is. Because I worked for it all day yesterday. I'm not surprised someone like you wouldn't understand working for something and wanting to keep it," said Wes.

"Whoa--Someone like me?" I asked. Jake's eyes narrowed, and he turned intently to listen.

"You Mexicans just flood in here and expect things to be handed to you," he said.

"Jesus, Wes," said Jake. "Are you serious?"

"I'm American, you asshole," I said.

"Your parents, then."

"My parents are Peruvian," I answered.

"Same difference. Mexican. Peruvian. You people immigrate here and expect everything to be handed to you from the government without doing anything to get it. And to make matters worse, you're a bleeding-heart homo."

"To make matters worse?" I was incredulous at this point.

"You people have about a million names for yourselves. How many letters are there now? LGBTQ, and whatever the hell else you want to label yourselves. You want to give a handout to everyone, just cause nobody liked you in high school. It's no wonder this country got blown to smithereens, with people like you running it."

That's when Jake stepped in.

"Okay, Wes, that's enough stupidity for one day. The number of things you just said that were inaccurate, wrong, and just flat-out stupid are almost too many for me to correct. For starters, Eddie's parents are college professors, which makes them smarter and more educated than you. And they came here for jobs that were offered to them, not for a handout, you ass. Second, he went to high school here. *Here.* He's a goddamn alumnus—which makes him not one of 'you people' but one of 'us people.' Lastly, the fact that he's gay literally has nothing to do with the fact that you just shut the door on a family from this community whose kid goes to school here, and who worked for six hours yesterday to make sure you had that food you so desperately wanted to hang onto. You're doing the white privilege thing even in a survival situation. It's unbelievable."

I could not have been more proud of Jake just then, listening to him. He was getting himself a little worked up, and I hadn't seen him like this before.

"I am ashamed of myself for letting you turn those people away, and if they haven't left the area by nightfall, I'm going to find them and let them in," Jake said.

"You are like hell," Lou said.

Jake turned on him and poked him hard in the chest.

"No, I am. And you are going to shut the fuck up. None of you here seem to get it. We survive together or we die separately. We have no idea what's going on outside this building. It could be a few damaged cities, or it could be the fucking Fallout Apocalypse. But one thing's for sure--to survive, we need to come together and work as one. And I can tell you now--I will not let you treat anyone else like that."

"Oh yeah," said Lou. "What are *you* gonna do?" He emphasized the *you*, as if to remind Jake that he was shorter, smaller, and older than the hulking football coach.

"Try me and find out, Lou," said Jake. "If size were all that mattered, we'd be dodging dinosaurs right now. You may be bigger, stronger, and younger than I am, but I didn't get this limp and these scars from playing pattycake for the past twenty years. Whatever happens to me, I'll make goddam sure you face the rest of the fucking Apocalypse without a top row of teeth or two functioning hands before I'm done. The same goes for you two as well," he said, gesturing at Wes and Mark. "The three of you just made a decision for nearly forty people. That won't happen again. We're going to establish some actual legitimate leadership now—one that we all agree on like the goddamn democracy we're supposed to have here—and then we're going to find that family, and let them in."

Jake stormed off, and the crowd of now thirty or so people still at this end of the building all looked at each other with wide eyes and slack jaws. I smirked. A big, loud smirk, sprinkled with an approving nod of my head, and slowly walked after Jake. As I walked away, I smiled and raised my eyebrows at Kent, Orville, and Longaberger.

"Gentlemen," I said, offering a mock good-bye salute, and headed back toward the cafeteria.

There was a great deal of chatter going on in the cafeteria when I arrived. There was no sign of Jake. People were discussing what had happened in little groups scattered about the cafeteria and the main rotunda at the school's entrance. Most were appalled at our not letting the Heffners in. Some, however, agreed with Orville, Longaberger, and Kent. Clearly the opinions were not one-sided. I saw Jada Allen looking distraught at a table by herself near the window.

"Jada," I said. "Did you see where Mr. Fisher went?"

She pointed down the hall. I figured he went back to his classroom. He was pretty worked up. I followed down there. His room was down the main corridor, then to the left, then once more to the right. The two-story academic wing of the building was just two squares on top of each other with a hall-way and staircase in between, and Jake's room was on the first floor. Mine was right above his on the second. As I rounded the second corner, I heard something that sounded like growling, followed by a large bang. I peeked into Jake's room and saw him throwing a chair.

"Dude, you alright?" I asked. He turned at hearing my voice, and for about two seconds the look on his face was frightening. The only word I can come up with to describe it is 'feral.' It was dark, vengeful, and profoundly committed. Com-mitted to what—I didn't know—but there was a kind of deci-siveness there that unnerved me. Jake and I have been friends since I returned here several years ago. I had always found him kind, helpful, insightful, and in no way threatening. What I was looking at now was the opposite. I was honestly a little scared, though I tried not to show it. He took a deep, tight breath in, closed his eyes and exhaled for about ten seconds.

"Jake?"

"Yeah, Eddie. I'm okay." He leaned on a desk, head drooped, eyes closed, arms tensed.

"You're not really selling me on that," I said. He smiled slightly.

"I'm mad at myself," he said. "I should never have let that go down. I was caught off guard. I wasn't ready for that." His voice cracked. I felt very uncomfortable. He'd obviously left to be alone, and I had invaded that sanctum. He sniffed, fighting tears back with some effort.

"Still processing Laura," he said. "I let that affect me."

"Oh shit, Jake. I'm sorry."

"It's alright. It's not like everyone else hasn't lost every-thing too. It's just that she and I had unresolved things. Issues. Stuff we were trying to work out. Things had been strained since the boys went off to college. We were talking on the phone when, well, you know when." I stuck my tongue be-tween my teeth and nodded.

"Yeah. I know when."

"I wasn't ready for that. To process the fact that my wife was in Washington when it got bombed. I'm also worried about my sons. I checked my phone—it had been plugged in here, and now with the power on, thought it might be charged and have some messages. The boys have not called."

He took another deep breath and visibly tried to steady himself. I could see some tears forming.

"They're down in the Shenandoah Valley at college. They should have been far from any of the bombings, but I just haven't heard from them. I don't think they even know about their mother," he said, coughing.

Jake was fighting through the guilt of a struggling marriage and the lack of contact with his sons. That's enough to trouble a man without having to wonder if any of them are dead due to a nuclear holocaust. He'd held it together for a day a half and gotten us to gel as a group. At least for a while-- until we locked out Tanner Heffner's family. Then something in him snapped, and he was starting to lose it. Jake controlled his breathing and stood up straight.

"But that's not even what bothers me the most right now," he said. I raised my eyebrows incredulously. If that wasn't eating at him, what was?

"When you're a Marine. A soldier of any kind. Even a combative athlete, like a wrestler, you have to have a certain battle mindset. On the mat, you might be wrestling a friend or someone you've known for years, but once you step in that circle, it has to be all business. You have to do whatever it takes to win, things that might otherwise damage your friendship. Off the mat, you can buy them a beer. Inside the circle, they're the enemy, and anything within the rules is fair game, even if it hurts or permanently damages them."

"Okay," I said. "That's a little dark."

"That's my point. You have to go to a dark place. A really dark place. You have to shut down forethought, cancel out your morals for a time. It's even worse on the battlefield.

You might have to maim, kill, even go after innocent people without hesitation, all to complete the mission. You'll endanger your sanity if you don't go to that place. That dark place. It's like shutting off the power to your brain, your ethics. If you hesitate in those crucial times, you can get someone killed. So you turn yourself into something a little scary. You have to.

"Okay," I said. "I'm listening. What are you trying to say?"

"Well, you hope you can turn the power back on, but for that short time, you've got to shield yourself from feeling anything remotely sympathetic. I've been to that place. You can feel the darkness taking over you. It's a survival instinct. But there's a toll. It steals from your soul when you return to sanity. You almost can't remember what you said or did, like it was an alternate personality. Then the come down after. It's hard on you. Hard on me at least. Some guys, they don't regret it. I always did."

"So, are you telling me that you were there just now? In the dark place? When you were threatening Wes, Lou, and Mark?"

"Yes," he nodded. "If they had gotten into it with me, I'm not sure what I would have done," he said, breathing in. "I'm so sorry."

"Don't be. I would have liked to have seen you kick their asses," I said. "That was a douche move. A horrible decision. An inhumane decision they made," I rambled.

"Decisions can be changed and unmade. You can't unbreak a bone or revive the dead," he said.

And right then I realized that when Jake said he was in the dark place, it meant he might have--would have killed those three. If he could. I'm not even sure with his training and experience he could have handled three big, young, athletic men. But that is most certainly what he meant. He was suggesting that for a brief moment, he wanted to kill them. Kill them for real. Despite all the death we had seen and experienced over the past couple of days, that thought scared the hell out of me. Actually seeing murder take place with people I knew. I processed that a minute, then started to back out of the room.

"Look dude, I'll leave you to your thoughts. I didn't mean to intrude."

"You're not intruding, Eddie. In fact, you're saving me a little. Let's head back to the cafeteria. My head is coming back to me, feeling a little more like myself again. We really need to establish some ground rules with the group now. This kind of thing can't happen again."

I nodded, smiled, and took a reassuring breath as we walked down the hall together. I was just starting to feel comfortable around him again, when I heard footsteps running down the hallway towards us. It was Glen Billings. He was carrying a bow and a quiver of arrows.

"Mr. Fisher! You gotta come fast. Something's happening. It's Tanner's family."

Jake shifted into a run and headed toward the rotunda in the main hall. You could see his legs and their perceptible limp as he ran. As we reached the large, glassed in lobby at the rotunda, we looked out the windows. About thirty yards away in the lane in front of the school, four men were beating on a car with what looked like a mop handle. They'd managed to crack a window, and a woman inside the car was screaming. It was Mrs. Heffner. Tanner and his father were trying to keep the windows intact, but Tanner's hands up against the broken glass were already bloody.

There was a crowd of about thirty people inside the school with their faces pressed up against the school doors and windows trying to look outside. All of them were completely frozen. Immobile. Disbelieving what they were seeing, and physically incapable of movement—or so it looked. It took Jake about four or five seconds to process what he was looking at. Then he grabbed the bow and the quiver from Glen's hands and slammed his way through the crowd into the door handle and went outside. The noise the door handle made was a loud pop, and it resonated throughout the rotunda. That door represented much more than inside or outside. It was a wall between the known and the unknown-- between the-safe-for-now, and the who-knows-what-is-waiting outside. Everyone was looking at it as if it were some kind of impassable line. Now they watched Jake walk towards the car. The three men stopped for a moment and looked up.

"Gentlemen, I'm gonna need you to back away from that car, please," said Jake. The men were a mix of ethnicities. One white, loaded with tattoos and wearing a doo rag; one apparently Hispanic, wearing a Barcelona soccer jersey, and one extremely tall black man in a dark shirt and cut-off shorts. The Hispanic one turned towards Jake and smacked the mop handle into the palm of his hand. The black guy took his hands off the car and turned.

"Yeah? Well I'm gonna need you to shut the fuck up," he said. The smaller white guy reached in his pocket and pulled out a knife. All three started walking towards Jake, who had managed to nock an arrow on the string of the bow. He slowed to a stop and dropped the quiver on the ground, and stuck two more arrows into the dirt.

"That's close enough, gentlemen," he said, jockeying the bow into position.

"Fuck you, Robin Hood," said the Hispanic guy, whose pace had quickened a bit, apparently in an attempt to get slightly ahead of his partners.

"Last warning," said Jake, drawing back the bowstring.

"*Chíngate cabrón,*" said the Hispanic.

Jake pulled the end of the arrow back to his cheekbone, exhaled, and released. And shot the Hispanic directly in the face. His head snapped back and he dropped hard to the ground clutching his face. The arrow had penetrated a cheekbone and gone into his mouth. Everyone in the rotunda had a collective gasp.

"Holy shit," Wes Kent said, almost whispering. Melanie and Maureen winced and turned away.

"Oh my god, oh my god, oh my god," Maureen repeated.

The white guy in the doo-rag and the big black guy halted immediately, wide-eyed.

"I got two more right here with your names on them," said Jake, nocking a second arrow. Both men started backing away slowly, the doo rag shaking his head in disbelief.

"I don't think so," said doo rag.

"I'm sorry, you're right. I don't even know your names," said Jake.

The large black man frowned, reached in his pocket, and pulled out a handgun.

"Oh shit," I said. I had been thinking about maybe going out to help Jake at first. If, for no other reason, maybe just to be another person, a small added deterrent, something to make them back off a bit. Then I saw them come after him, and then he put that arrow into the first guy's face, and I realized I was too far out of my element. I even felt a little queasy. But now, the second guy had pulled out a gun, and I was completely frozen.

"Okay, motherfucker," the black guy said. "My turn now. Drop the fucking bow or I do you." Jake held his aim and didn't move.

"Standoff," Jake said.

"No, it ain't no fuckin standoff, motherfucker. I can shoot you six times before you get off one more shot."

"Yeah, but can you hit me?" Jake said. "I've already established what I can do. Your friend over there might not live through the night. He'll die slowly without medical attention, which he probably isn't gonna get. You can join him if you want. You drop the gun and I'll think about not puncturing your lung."

"Bitch, you know who won the West, right? It wasn't the fuckin Indians. You got three seconds to drop that fuckin bow. One."

As he counted, doo rag started circling behind Jake, who was immobile and focused on the gun. He had the arrow pulled back to his cheek and was holding it there. The bow wasn't that powerful. It was used in Physical Education classes and had about a 40 lbs. draw. The arrows were target arrows, which meant that although they didn't have blunted tips, they also weren't terribly sharp. At that range, the arrow could do some damage to human flesh, but compared to the gun, the arrows were much less deadly, and I'm guessing Jake knew it. It was a bluff, but the damage done to the bleeding Hispanic thug had made it a credible one.

"Two," said the black guy. The white doo rag wearer had gone all of the way behind Jake now and was about to pounce on him. In order to hold his bluff, Jake had to focus on the gun bearer, but you could see his eyes track the doo rag guy. Ironically, in trying to help, doo rag had actually given Jake a chance, since doo rag's partner wouldn't shoot with him right there, but Jake had no reason to hesitate. I wondered if Jake was aware how close he'd gotten, then I saw Jake's eyes flit to the periphery just for a second, and he smiled.

"Jake, watch out behind you," I yelled, pounding my hand on the door. The black guy instinctively pointed his gun towards us behind the glass. Everyone screamed and dropped, and Jake let the arrow go. The black guy tried to turn away, and the arrow caught him in the rear deltoid, in his back shoulder muscle. He cried out, dropped the gun, which skidded under the Heffners' car, and started falling to the pavement, clutching at his arm. As he did, doo rag made his move and dove at Jake. Jake spun and met the attack with the bow, slashing it into doo rag's head. The combined impact jerked doo rag's head back and he dropped to the ground. As he shook his head and tried to recover, Jake was on him. He grabbed the guy's head in his hands and tried to snap his neck, a move I always had seen in the movies, and always wondered if it was realistic. It didn't work. It must've hurt like hell, judging by doo rag's face, but he wasn't dead or even immobilized. It did slow him, however, as doo rag reached for Jake's hands on his head, and winced, trying feebly to get Jake to let go. Jake set up to do it again and that's when the freight train hit.

The black guy had gotten up with the arrow dangling from his arm and attacked Jake in a rage. He hit him like a linebacker trying to make a tackle, and the two went tumbling into the ground. Jake was on his back, and the black guy was trying to hit him. He'd forgotten the arrow, and as he lifted his right arm to punch Jake, only to find sharp pain lancing into the back of his shoulder. He winced in pain and cried out. Then he feebly took a swing at Jake with his left, but Jake had time to block it. They struggled for a moment, then Jake reached up with his left hand and jabbed the arrow in deeper. The black man hollered out in rage and put his left hand on Jake's throat and started to squeeze. Jake choked for a moment, then reached up again, and this time yanked the arrow out, which came out easily due to its construction design for targets. The black guy howled and loosened his grip. Jake tried to wriggle out from under him, but the attacker recovered himself, winced and then tightened his grip—now with two hands—on Jake's throat.

Jake took the arrow and jabbed it hard into the black man's right eye. He flew backwards in pain, thrashing on the ground. Jake sat up, and as he did, doo rag was coming at him with his knife. Jake went from sitting to kneeling so quickly that I had to ask myself when it happened, but even on his knees, Jake was able to dodge the lunge like a bullfighter. As doo rag guy went flying by him, Jake snagged the wrist of the hand holding the knife. He dragged in a circle, making him stumble, taking him down, then up, then twisting the knife hand back towards doo rag's face. Then a final back step and a bowing motion threw doo rag violently to the ground, and the wrist—twisted hopelessly back upon itself and possibly broken, released the knife. Doo rag clutched his wrist and cried out. Jake picked up the knife, walked over to doo rag guy, who was on his side clutching a broken wrist, and slit his throat with his own knife. Everyone near me in the rotunda let out a collective gasp. The first man with the arrow in his skull had gone still. The second clutched his throat and slunk to the ground in a pool of blood. Two men now lay dead on the ground, and a third was badly wounded--and suddenly very afraid as well.

Then Jake turned back towards the large black guy, who by now was sitting on the ground holding his bloody, mangled eye socket in both hands and screaming. Jake walked up to him slowly. The black attacker was in shock, and at this point could see his death coming. Jake dropped down to one knee in front of him. The big man instinctively cringed, but Jake held up a hand gently as if to say, 'wait a minute.'

Jake leaned in towards him and appeared to whisper something to him. The big man answered him back. They had a quiet exchange for a few moments, then the big man got up and started to walk away, still holding his eye. Jake walked over to the car where the Heffners were. They looked like everyone around me: mouths open, jaws slack, disbelief in their eyes, mixed with a bit of horror. Jake knocked on the window, asked them if they were alright, then got down on his stomach and retrieved the gun from underneath the car.

"You guys keep this. It's got some bullets left, and who knows what you may find when you start to look. Either way, it's a nice deterrent from any would-be attackers."

Scott Heffner took the gun, and quietly thanked Jake.

"And if you all want to come join us now, you'll be welcomed."

They all got out of the car and followed Jake towards the doors. Jake picked up the quiver with the remaining arrows, slung it over his shoulder, and grabbed the fallen bow with his other hand and approached the door. No one spoke. Mouths still hung open. As Jake reached the door, he finally looked up and stared silently at everyone near the row of doors. I opened the one up in front of me and let him in. He gave me no eye contact as he walked past me. The Heffners entered and Jada hugged Tanner hard, and Maureen took Mrs. Heffner by the hand and walked her towards the cafeteria. I stole one short

63

glance at the stunned faces of Orville, Kent, and Longaberger, then smiled to myself before turning down the hall towards Jake's classroom.

CHAPTER 5

Recon

Maureen Kelly and Melanie Richmond sat in the cafeteria with the Heffners. Marianne Heffner was softly crying, almost keening. Tanner and his brother were whispering to each other, and Scott was trying to comfort his wife to no avail. Maureen and Melanie were whispering soothing messages towards Marianne. Al DeFillipo walked up to Scott.

"You okay, man?" he asked. Scott nodded.

"Nobody hurt, just scared," he said.

"Ugh, nobody?" asked Tanner, holding up his bloody hand.

"Here's a wet towel for that, Tanner," Mrs. Eaves said, walking up from the kitchen. "Might want to wash out any glass you might have in there." Tanner nodded, rose, and walked back to the kitchen.

"Thanks," said Scott.

"No problem," said Robin.

An awkward silence continued for a bit while Marianne Heffner started to get her breathing under control. Scott looked outside at the two dead bodies lying in front of the school and shuddered slightly.

"So, I never knew that Coach Fisher...I mean, holy shit.

He saved our lives," said Scott. Eyes shot around the room, which seemed a little less crowded than before. People had separated since watching Jake Fisher dismantle the attackers. No one seemed to acknowledge that any of it had even happened. I had followed Jake down the hall, figuring he was going to his classroom, but he went into the bathroom and locked the door.

"Jake, you okay?" I asked. No answer came. I called again twice more, then decided to head back to the rest of the group. As I walked by Jake's classroom, I heard an odd noise. I poked my head in and looked around, then realized it was some kind of ringtone. His phone was on his large desk, tucked away in the corner and plugged into the wall outlet. I picked it up just as it finished ringing. It read,
MISSED CALL: TOMMY

I ran back to the bathroom.

"Jake, Jake," I yelled. "Your son called. Tommy just called you."
The door exploded open and Jake came out, about to make a break for his classroom. I held up the phone to him and he took it.

"He just called. You just missed him."
Jake immediately tried to call him back, but no one picked up. His face, which had come out from the bathroom with a look of desperate hope, suddenly fell. His lips trembled a bit.

"Did he leave a message?" I asked. The face filled with hope again, and Jake dialed into his voice mails and listened on speaker.

Dad, It's Tommy. I'm okay. I'm stuck here on campus. Lots of guys have left already, but they're saying we should stay anyway, since the town was totally missed by everything. I've spoken to Vinny, and he's okay too. Dad, are you okay? I haven't heard from mom. Call me when you can. We have power for now, but they're not sure how long it will last. We love you dad.

Jake's face brightened, but he was fighting back tears.

His entire body sagged and he leaned on a desk, like a wrung out dish rag.

"He's okay. They're both okay." I smiled at the news.

"That's great. Are they coming back here?" I asked.

"Probably not. Neither one of them have vehicles. One of Laura's family members is storing one of them. She sort of lives in between the two. I should probably get a hold of her. God, there are so many people I should have gotten a hold of by now," he said, dropping his head on the table.

"Jake, you have been literally saving people's lives for two days. I think you can let yourself off the hook on this one."

Just then, Al DeFillipo walked in. He was holding his phone.

"9-1-1 is out," he said.

"What do you mean?" I asked.

"I just tried to call them. Tell them about what happened. There was just a message saying that 9-1-1 services were temporarily suspended. I've never heard anything like that before. There's just--nothing."

"I was afraid of that," said Jake.

"Of what?"

"If essential services are down, it might mean that it's like the wild West out there. It might be the kind of scene that spawns people like we saw today. Hooligans. Criminals. Outlaws. An 'anything goes' mentality."

"Jake. I gotta ask you. What did you say to that guy?" asked Al. "That last guy. The one you let go."

"I asked him if he was part of a group, or gang, and he said yes. I told him that if any of them ever came back here that I would not be so merciful next time. I told him to tell his people that this place is off limits, and if none of them ever came back, then I wouldn't have to come hunt them down one by one."

Al and I looked at each other nervously. Images of every dystopian society sci-fi book I'd ever read or movie I'd ever seen started running through my head. *Mad Max. Book of Eli.* The idea that they might be real and that I might be living in them was horrifying.

"I'm going to head back to the others, tell them about 9-1-1. You guys coming?" asked Al. I shrugged, then looked at Jake.

"So, what do we do now?" I asked.

"I need to try and get my head together and then try to text my sons, catch them up a little," said Jake.

"Then I think maybe we need to go do some scouting," he said.

"You know that's the opposite of what you said yesterday, right?"

"Every day's a new day," said Jake, lifting his eyebrows expectantly.

My deadpan face in response made him ruffle his brow disappointedly.

"I love you more than yesterday."

Nothing.

"But not as much as tomorrow?"

Nothing.

"You should know that song. It's Sonny and Cher. I thought you people were all about Sonny and Cher," he said with a smirk.

"Us homos only listen to Cher as a solo artist. Only you old farts listen to Sonny."

"Shouldn't we, I don't know, bury them or something? They're just lying there," said Melanie. The group was sitting in the cafeteria, just across the rotunda. The bodies of the two dead attackers were laying there, both in small pools of blood that had started to dry a little. The others turned to look at them after Melanie spoke.

"They are pretty gruesome to look at," said Al. "I can't

believe Jake did all that. He killed those guys. Like, really killed them. Jesus Christ."

The students were fascinated and horrified at the same time.

"I've never seen a dead body before," remarked Glen Billings.

"It would actually be a little scarier if you had," said his friend, Casey Kirby. Glen scrunched his face up and nodded. "Just sayin'" said Casey.

"Shouldn't we call the police or something?" Jada asked.

"9-1-1 doesn't work," said Al. "Who would we call?"

"It's like there's no rules out there," said Robin. "Is this how it's gonna be now? Is every place like this?" Just then Mark Longaberger threw up. It was spontaneous, projectile, and all over the floor of the rotunda.

"Ugh. God, I'm sorry," he said. "I'll clean that up." Wes Kent and Lou Orville were still staring at the corpses. Their faces had both gone a little pallid, and like their colleague, looked as if they might vomit.

Jake texted his sons. He let them know that he had been staying in the high school and trying to gather himself and organize the group with him. I noticed that he did not mention their mother, Laura at all. Once completed, Jake and I walked up slowly to the cafeteria, which lay just alongside the large rotunda, the school's main lobby where students generally entered, and in front of which Jake Fisher just took two lives.

Everything became instantly quiet, and all heads turned towards us. The awkwardness was palpable. Jake moved slowly, and clearly favored his bad leg. He rolled his shoulder and winced a little.

"Hey Mel," Jake said, "Can I get a bag of ice please?"

Melanie Richmond's eyes bugged, and she looked terrified of Jake as she awkwardly smiled, nodded, and shuffled off to the kitchen. The silence continued in the room, except for Jake's request. All eyes were on him, then on me as I sat down beside him. I started getting irritated, and my face must have shown it, because Scott and Marianne Heffner walked quietly over to our table.

"Mr. Fisher. Jake," Scott began. "I want to thank you for saving my family." Marianne was unable to speak. She had tears in her eyes, a wrinkled smile on her face, and she nodded vehemently in agreement. "Yes, thank you," she managed to whisper.

"Think nothing of it," said Jake. "I know you'd do the same if roles were reversed."

Scott nodded, took Jake's hand in both of his and shook it. Marianne brushed her hand down Jake's arm. She noticed a large bloody abrasion on Jake's elbow, presumably where he hit the pavement after being tackled.

"That looks like it hurts," she said.

"Not that bad, but thanks," said Jake. "My joints, on the other hand, aren't being so kind," he said with a soft smile.

"Here's your ice, Jake" said Melanie. He nodded and mouthed a silent thank you. He placed the ice pack on his shoulder, then used some old athletic tape to make it stay. The wrap job was far from professional, but the bag would stay for now. Jake wandered over to the cafeteria's edge where a giant bottle of hand sanitizer sat by itself. He pumped a dollop onto his elbow abrasion and rubbed it slightly. I saw him stiffen slightly when he applied it. It had to sting like hell. Jake's nostrils flared a little, and he mashed his lips together, but I never heard him make a sound. He walked back to me.

"Shit stings," he said, laughing a little.

"Never were known for your intelligence, were you?" I asked. Lou Orville was slowly wandering this way. Normally, Orville swaggered when he walked, like most popular football players. He usually had a look on his face somewhere between self-satisfaction and a smirk. Just now, though, he looked cautious in a way I'd never seen him before. I imagine that the recent action outside affected him a little. Hell, it affected all of us. Most people have never seen anyone dead. Even fewer have seen someone in the process of being killed, and only a small percentage have seen that happen through violence. The world just added another thirty-six people to that small list, and the tension in the cafeteria was palpable because of it.

"Uh, Jake," Lou began. Jake looked up and got eye contact. "Some of us heard you were thinking of maybe, going outside, scouting a little? You, you think it's safe then?"

"I don't know for sure," said Jake. "Not my area of expertise. But I know that we were terrified of it before, and now I've been outside and the Heffners are in with us, so my thought is that the damage—if there is any—has already been done. Might as well assess the situation."

Lou nodded. "I'm happy to be part of that scouting party. If you want, I mean."

"Thanks," said Jake.

"Listen," continued Lou. "I'm sorry about before. We were all just in survival mode, you know?"

"I know. Not exactly something you can really practice for, is it?" Jake added. "Sure, Lou. It'd be good to have you along. I'm thinking maybe this evening, when it cools off a little. We can go out, tend to the bodies, and take a look around. Check out the nearby area of town."

As we all sat and chatted in the cafeteria, and Jake nursed his elbow and shoulder, the tension eased a bit out of the room. Robin Eaves and Maureen Kelly teamed up to cook a meal for dinner—meat loaf and mashed potatoes. I can't remember a meal I liked or needed as much as I needed that one then. I've had many memorable meals in my short life so far. I still remember the steak and lobster that my first boyfriend and I shared in college. I remember the *cuy chactado* and *chuño* stew that my grandmother made for me when we went to visit her in Cuzco. Most Americans can't handle the fact that I enjoy eating fried guinea pig and a stew made of freeze-dried potatoes, but everyone can appreciate their grandmother's specialty. As good as all of those were, this meal offered some kind of normalcy. It was the epitome of comfort food, since all of us really needed the comfort right about now. We all sat together, all savored things that in another context we would have disparaged, insulted, and even refused.

After dinner, everyone pitched in to clean up, using as little water as possible. Everyone was in constant conservation mode all of the time, and as silly as it sounds, spam and powdered mashed potatoes felt a lot like splurging. Once the area had been cleaned, Jake wandered over to the auxiliary gym where the archery equipment had been moved. After rooting around in the Physical Education closet for a few minutes, he grabbed about twenty arrows and a bow for me, and then went into the media center and found some thick tagboard and began to roll it into a cylinder. Then he wrapped the cylinder in wrestling mat tape. Mat tape is used to keep sections of wrestling mat together during practices and matches, and it's incredibly thick and tough. When he was finished, he tied an adjustable belt he'd taken from a pair of football pants, and looped it around the taped cylinder, and *voila*—he had fashioned a solid quiver for my arrows to match the one he already had used earlier.

"You ever use one of these?" he asked.

"Here, in P.E. class," I answered.

'Any good?" he asked.

"Adequate. I had the mentality for it. Patient. Quiet mind."

"So, just like the Scottish girl in the Disney flick," he said, smiling. I laughed out loud and shook my head.

"Minus the red hair and the corset, of course," I answered.

"Um, are we sure you don't have the corset," he asked.

"Are you kidding me? You ever worn one of those? And how is it you never got fired again for being a raging homophobic?" I asked him.

"Cause I'm not phobic. I'm not scared of you, I just like to make fun of you," he answered.

"Fair enough," I said with a grin, and we met up with Lou Orville and Wes Kent at the rotunda.

"You guys ready?" asked Lou. Jake nodded, I gave the thumbs up.

"Wes isn't coming?" I asked, cutting my eyes towards Jake slyly.

"He...felt someone had to stay here in case someone approached. He and Casey and Glen will guard the doors," said Mark. Jake nodded again, then turned and raised his eyebrows to me.

"H-o-m-o-p-h-o-b-i-c," I silently mouthed.

"Who could ever be afraid of Merida?" he whispered back.

"Huh?" wondered Lou.

"Nothing. Archery joke," said Jake, and we all walked out the doors. Mark Longaberger stopped hard as we approached the dead bodies. He had vomited earlier at the sight of them. Now he was affronted with the smell as well.

"Oh God," he said, wincing and shaking his head.

"Lou," said Jake. "Why don't you and I drag these bodies someplace out of view of the windows and doors here?"

"Ugh. Okay," said Lou, grimacing. "What did you have in mind?"

Jake took a breath and pursed his lips.

"You really wanna know?" he asked. All heads turned at this.

"What, Jake?" I asked.

"You're not gonna like it," he said.

"Spit it out," I said.

"We really should spit these guys on stakes at the perimeter of the school," he said.

"Jesus," said Mark. "What the hell would you possibly do that for?"

"Send a message to anyone who might wander up on this place with similar ideas," said Jake.

"Hell of a deterrent," I said. "A little extreme, though."

"It's fucking horrific," said Mark. "This isn't the goddamn middle ages."

"No?" asked Jake. "Sure felt like it this afternoon."

No one answered that. Jake's arm was covered in the blood of three men, including his own, and despite his attempt to wash it off, the residue was clear. He had fought for his own life and the Heffners—and ours, if you get right down to it— and no one else had helped. As horrific as the idea was, it was also practical. Jake was in survival mode. He had been since the cataclysm, and here in the aftertime, he still was.

"Okay, maybe it's a bit much. But we can drag them to the perimeter of the school. The buzzards will make for a pretty creepy warning themselves," said Jake.

"Vultures," I said.

"Huh?"

"Vultures. Technically lots of things are buzzards, and most true buzzards are hawks. Vultures are what you're talking about. Two kinds, around here at least: turkey and black," I answered.

"A gay ornithologist," Jake said. "Who'd have thought?"

"Birdwatcher. Good hobby. You should take it up," I said. "And yes, I have found an unusually high number of gay birdwatchers per capita in this area."

Mark Longaberger stared at us with a knitted brow and a squint. "You two really ought to get a room," he said.

"Not my type," I answered. Longaberger gave a 'whatever' kind of shrug and shook his head.

"Don't worry, Mark. Neither are you."

The four of us dragged the two bodies to the side of the school where there were fewer windows. It bordered alongside one of the main roads up to the school. While they didn't make quite the statement that Jake initially recommended—two spitted corpses—they would at least keep most folks away. And the kind of folks who would not be deterred by them were a much bigger worry anyway. Mark decided to stay at the school. He threw up at least once more after moving the bodies, and he looked pretty green as we got ready to leave.

We wandered about a half a mile to the Wal-Mart. The

streets were empty. No noise, no cars, no nothing. I noticed that the streetlights were coming on now that the sun was going down. I guessed that meant that the main grid of the town was still working. The air was warm and dry, and the slightest of breezes blew. I noticed the lack of any food smells. Hunter's Run was fairly surrounded by restaurants, and there were always great smells circulating in the air. Not tonight, though, and the lack of smells was noticeable, at least to me.

We walked into the empty Wal-Mart parking lot. The doors at the main entrance had been destroyed and I was betting that looters had picked the place fairly clean. We walked slowly and carefully towards the main doors. Jake nocked an arrow and held the bow down at his side. He fumbled around his belt and felt for his knife. Satisfied that it was still there, he held up a silent hand to signal us to stop.

"What is it?" asked Orville.

"Thought I saw a shadow inside," said Jake.

"Uh-uh, no way I'm going in there," said Lou. "You guys see *Zombieland*? There's always somebody in there waiting to ambush you."

"Noted," said Jake. "But they also found women and Twinkies. Can't get chicks and Twinkies without going in, Lou," he added with a smile. "Sorry Eddie. Might not be anything but confections and lady-parts in here. Nothing for you."

I shook my head with a smile and noticed that Jake's level of smart-ass was starting to come back since getting the message from his son. That was good. It was hard to see him down, or brooding, and he'd been down since the Cataclysm. It was clear that he felt some responsibility for the rest of us. We had students with us, after all, and most of us didn't have much survival training. Jake did. It was also obvious that he was a dangerous man when he needed to be. I was glad he was on my side.

"Okay, we came here to do recon on this store, and we'd be idiots to turn around now. I will go in first. You guys cover me. If I run into trouble, I will most likely drop down. Just keep your arrows high if anybody comes after me."

"We shoulda brought that gun you gave Heffner," said Lou.

"In hindsight, maybe that would have been better," said Jake, "But I wanted the others to have something to defend themselves with. They're missing three of us."

"Mark can always throw up on an intruder," I added.

Jake sidled up along the front entrance wall, and we all pressed in behind him, bows ready. I almost laughed out loud at how we must have looked. A gaggle of dollar store Robin Hoods entering a busted out Wal-Mart. I can see the memes now. Jake turned, put a finger to his lips, nodded, then grabbed the bow with both hands and tip-toed in. He immediately backed into the wall adjacent to the entrance in order to get a better view. Seeing nothing after a few seconds, he motioned us in with his head. We all followed in carefully.

"Holy shit," I said in a whisper. The place was virtually untouched. The doors had been smashed, but now I suddenly realized that all of the glass was outside. Had someone had gotten locked in and busted their way out? Didn't make sense. But most of the stuff in the store was still right where you might expect it to be.

"Grab a cart," said Jake.

"Are you serious?" I asked. "We're going shopping?"

"Yes. We've found an unexpectedly full store with a broken door. How long do you think this place will be intact? We have been lucky enough to stumble onto it now. Might as well take advantage of it."

I shrugged, grabbed a cart, and put my bow and quiver in it. It made a clanking noise, and everyone jumped a little when I did it. Lou scowled.

"Are you trying to be loud?" he asked.

"Sorry," I said.

"Don't let your guard down," said Lou in a loud whisper. "Just because it looks empty in here, doesn't mean it is. Just because we don't see anybody yet."

"You're right, Lou," said Jake. "But I already have."

"Already have, what?" asked Lou.

"Seen somebody," whispered Jake, maintaining his gaze forward. "Look beyond that rack of clothes where the ladies' dresses are. That's a person crouching down."

A shiver went down my spine. There was clearly someone trying to hide behind one of the clothes' display walls. He or she was crouched down, tucking their head into the sweaters hanging in front. But a shoulder had remained exposed, and now I could see the outline of a shoe.

Jake pulled the bowstring back to his cheek, took a breath, and loosed an arrow. It made a whooshing noise before slamming into the separation wall that our mystery guest was hiding behind. It hit with a surprisingly loud thud, and the person fell back onto their buttocks, into a sitting position.

"*Pendejo,*" said the voice. It was clearly a woman's, but she was dressed in a very masculine manner with a baseball cap pulled down and her long hair tucked into the back.

"*No se mueva, por favor,*" said Jake, nocking another arrow quickly. His accent was very gringo.

"Who the fuck are you? Robin Hood?" the woman asked. I smiled at that.

"More like Zorro. Who are you?" asked Jake.

"Estela Fuentes," said the woman. "I am an assistant manager here. Or at least I was. And you're trespassing."

When she stood up, I realized that despite being dressed like a man with multiple layers and a ball cap, she was beautiful. She appeared to be in her early twenties, clearly Hispanic, with a defiant look in her eyes. Jake smiled.

"Mucho gusto, Ms. Fuentes," Jake nodded in a mocking bow. "And these are normal shopping hours, so we're not really trespassing, right? Are we the first ones to come here?"

"No. Just the first ones to make it in."

"What's that supposed to mean?" I asked.

"There were some gangbangers who came by earlier. They were beating on the doors, trying to get in. I warned them to go away. They didn't. So I shot out the door. They scattered and haven't come back. That was a few hours ago." That explained the broken glass outside rather than in.

"Why didn't you shoot at us?" asked Jake.

"You were quieter. I didn't hear you come in at first. Once I realized I had company, I remembered I left the gun over there," she pointed towards the back of the store. "I was trying to sneak back over to get it when you shot at me with that fucking arrow."

"Wasn't trying to hit you. Just get your attention. Sorry to frighten you. Probably scary enough being here all alone," said Jake.

"What makes you think I'm alone," said Estela.

"Because we got in. If there were someone else, there would have been a lookout. But you wouldn't have gotten caught with your guard down, not this far from your weapon." Estela looked angry at that and cut her eyes across the room to the gun section, scowling.

"Don't worry," I said. "We aren't going to hurt you. We work at the school down the street. Hunter's Run. We just wanted to see what was happening out there," I said. Jake turned at me admonishingly.

"No need to tell everything about us, Eddie," Jake said.

"So, you *are* Robin Hood," said Estela. "You're here to rob the place."

"Well," Jake said. "Yeah, we are."

CHAPTER 6

El Tejón

W ait, we are?" I asked.

"Essentially, yes," said Jake. "If you want to be honest about it. When we first thought we had found this place empty, weren't we planning on taking anything handy?" I raised my eyebrows and looked towards Lou. He shrugged.

"Actually, that was your idea," I reminded him.

"And you were going to go along with it," he reminded me back. "Does it make a difference that someone's here?"

"Well, yeah. Kinda," I answered. Lou shrugged again. He couldn't take his eyes off Estela.

"I guess it does," said Jake. "But Señora—whom are you defending?"

"It's Señorita. And what do you mean?" said Estela.

"I'm guessing that nobody here works on commission, and that you don't have a personal stake in the stock here, yes?" said Jake.

"No. Nobody does."

"And all of your workers, they just...left?"

"*Sí*. They all left. So?"

"So, if there is nothing but mass hysteria out there, with gangbangers trying to take whatever they want, then you have a choice, right?" asked Jake. I wondered where he was going with this.

"What choice?" she asked.

"You can lose your stock to a bunch of gangbangers whom you shot at earlier, or you can donate your stock to some dedicated public servants and needy children for their survival." Jake grinned.

I grinned wide and nodded. "Good point."

"Thanks," said Jake, offering me a nod.

"That's *mierda*," said Estela. "It's theft, either way."

"Not if you donate it," said Jake.

"I don't care if you're Robin Hood or William Tell, you're not going to intimidate me into giving you free stuff," she yelled.

"Okay then," said Jake. "We'll buy it."

"What?" said Lou, gawking at Jake. Jake waved the hold on gesture at Lou.

"Do you have change?" he asked.

Estela stared at him perturbedly.

"Afraid I only have big bills," he said. "So, are your computers working? I presume ringing me up, and getting change from the drawer for big bills is no problem, then?" She looked angry again.

"Eddie, do you have your credit card with you," Jake asked.

"Alright, shut up. Just take it. Take whatever you want," said Estela. "It's not like I could ring you up, for God's sake. It's not like anybody is here to tell me what to do either."

"You're sure?" he asked again. Estela exhaled and slumped a bit in the shoulders.

"Yes, dammit. Just take it all," she yelled. "You made your point, *pendejo*."

"*No soy pendejo, señora, soy ladrón*," Jake said. I smiled. Lou looked confused. I whispered to him.

"He said he's not an asshole, he's a thief," I said. Lou smiled and nodded.

"*Ustedes hablan español,*" she said. "And, I told you already, it's *Señorita*. And *pendejo* isn't really 'asshole,' you know," she said to me.

"Loose translation," I answered. "My parents are Peruvian. And as for the need to translate," I jerked my thumb towards Lou, "Dumb Gringo." Estela smiled.

"Hey," Lou said. "I'm right here."

"Accurate on both accounts," said Jake.

"Señorita," said Jake. "We did come to see if there was anything we could use, but we also came to see how bad things are around here. We've been stuck in the school for a couple of days, with little or no internet, cell phone reception, or news of what's gone on since the first bombings. We've been attacked by a pack of hoodlums and had to fight them off. Things seem pretty rough. We can help you if those guys come back, maybe in exchange for some supplies?"

Estela looked us up and down a few times. She frowned a moment, then exhaled.

"I suppose I can't hold onto all of this by myself for very long," she said. "Now that I've blown the doors open."

"That's true. Thank you anyway. Eddie, you and Lou snag some canned food, maybe some protein or energy bars. Whatever you can grab. Get bread and rolls too. Throw them all into a couple of carts. *Señorita?*"

"Call me Estela, *Señor.*"

"Estela then. I'm Jake. Estela, can you take me back to where you sell your weapons?"

"Yes. But leave me something, would you?" she said.

"I had assumed that you might want to come with us," said Jake.

"Wait, you're inviting me?" she asked.

"It's tough out there. There are thirty-six of us. I guess a few more now. We're holed up in the school, at least for the time being. Supplies are decent there for now. We'd love to have you."

"Gracias," she said, walking Jake back to the hunting

section. "It's just, I don't know what I should do. I don't really know you."

Jake grabbed another cart and began filling it with everything the store had. Shotguns, rifles, pistols, ammunition, bows, crossbows, knives, whatever could be used as a weapon. He also grabbed rope, duct tape, lighters, and batteries. Estela had to grab another cart to fit it all. Then Jake directed her to the camping section. He put several folding tents, cots, sleeping bags, and memory foam bedrolls in the cart as well.

"You guys planning on going camping or something?" she asked.

"Bad night's sleep for everybody. Figured the more we could do to help folks sleep the better. Besides, I don't know how long we're going to be there. We may have to move out soon."

"Move out?" Estela said. "Why?"

"Same reason as you. People have found us. They may want to try and help themselves to things that we have. Like the school building itself, for starters. It's almost like a fortress. But if we can't defend it, keep it for ourselves, then we may be better off moving on."

"Moving on to where?" she asked. Jake shrugged at the question. "Don't you know what it's like out there?" Estela said.

"Point of fact, Señorita, I don't. This is as far as we've gotten in three days. The internet isn't reliable. No radio is reliable at the moment. No television. We're blind and deaf, and only know as much as we can see. And I've seen about all I care to today. Do you have the keys to the gun cabinets?"

"Yes," said Estela warily. Jake raised his eyebrows, then jerked his head towards the cabinets. Estela nodded and began opening them.

"Look, Señorita," Jake said.

"Estela. I'm Estela."

"Estela, if you're coming with us, we might as well take everything we can."

"Yeah, yeah, I know," she said, as her eyes began to tear up. "It's just that, I told myself, this world is still okay as long as I have this place. I know you're right, but it's like I'm admitting defeat if I do this."

Jake looked at her a moment, then gave a reassuring smile and put his hand on her shoulder. "This is not a defeat. You are not giving up. You are trying to hold an untenable position in a world that has changed dramatically in the past twenty-four hours. You've got to find someone to trust. You can trust me. You can trust us. We're not bad people."

Estela wiped her eyes, nodded and smiled, then opened the cabinets, and helped Jake start dumping as many guns and ammunition as would fit into the shopping cart. She noticed how heavy they were when she pushed the cart along the aisle. She also noticed Jake's limp as he moved down the aisle collecting weapons, then turned to see where Mark and I were putting canned and packaged food into our carts. I waved and smiled, unable to imagine what the new member of our group must be thinking.

Then the tires squealed outside, and we heard four doors slam.

All of us turned immediately and looked at each other. Jake waved us down and we all dropped below apparel racks and tried to get a view of the entrance. Two shots rang out and the already splintered glass in the door frame exploded. Then the first of four men walked through the broken door and waved the gun in several directions.

"Knock, knock, bitch! We comin' in," said the first man, who was wearing a flat-brimmed Phillies cap and a matching vintage Mike Schmidt jersey. Behind him were two identical twins, who appeared to be bi-racial. One was holding a butcher knife. Bringing up the rear was a hulking black man with an eye patch and a bat. It was the same guy that Jake tangled with earlier.

"We know you in here," said the Philly. "Been watching since you shot at us last time. Brought my own gun back with me. Guess we'll see how tough you are now."

The big guy with the eye patch started breaking things with his bat. Anything that was near—a small fridge that held sodas, a hat rack, a shopping basket. He smashed them all with frightening power. Up close I could see how enormous he was. Had to be 6'3" at least, and probably pushing 300 pounds. I wondered how Jake had beaten him, then remembered that Jake had softened him up with his bow and arrow first and then taken his eye out—an almost lucky move when the man had tackled him to the ground. Jake had resourcefully used the arrow in the big man's eye, and it had turned the tide. That seemed enough to stop him then, but here he was, back creating mayhem. I wondered where he got the eye patch. Regardelss, he seemed much angrier. They were getting closer to us.

Lou Orville looked at me from the floor with fear in his eyes. "They have a gun. All we have are bows. What do we do?" he whispered. I didn't know. I shrugged, shook my head, and felt a shiver up my spine when I realized we were out manned and out gunned. Then I felt the hands on my back.

"Look what we got here," yelled one of the twins. He grabbed my shirt and yanked me hard to my feet, and I dropped my bow. "Found me a Robin Hood, Bucky. Didn't you say it was a man with an arrow took out your eye?" The twin backhanded me hard across the face. The blood rushed to it and it felt like an explosion on my cheek.

"You blind my boy, bitch?" the twin shouted at me. The enormous one came walking over.

"Nah, dog. That ain't him. I ain't seen this one before. Ain't much to him," he said.

Just then Lou moved slightly from his hiding place a few feet away and banged into a rack that made a lot more noise than it looked like it should have. The man with the gun shot twice in Lou's direction, and a whine came from him that seemed completely involuntary.

"Get the fuck up," yelled the man with the gun. Lou rose immediately, hands in the air.

"Don't shoot," he yelled. "Don't shoot." His eyes were closed. He was clearly afraid. From the corner of my eye, I noticed the slightest movement across the room near the weapons area. There was no way that Jake had had time to open and load any of the guns in the back part of the store. Most were in boxes or wrapped in plastic, and the ammo had to be the same, I thought. The man with the gun walked over to us.

"Alright, where's the bitch?" he asked.

"What are you talking about?" I said.

"The bitch who works here. She shot at us. Fucked up my car. I came back to settle up."

"We're the only ones here," I answered back.

"Don't you fucking lie to me, boy," said the gunman. He walked up next to me and Lou, who was now being held by the other twin. He put his nose up to mine, stared me in the eye, and said it quieter and more dramatically, "Don't lie to me."

"I'm not lying," I said, and Lou's face looked terrified. The gunman turned to Lou, then back to me, raised his arm, pointed the gun toward the roof, fired, and then hollered in a very loud voice.

"I will fucking shoot you where you stand, assholes," he yelled, and fired another shot into the ceiling and Lou flinched as he did.

"She's here, she's here," said Lou. "Don't kill us. She's here in the back somewhere."
The gunman looked at me with a scowl, then nodded at the twin holding me and he backhanded me again. This time he drew blood, which trickled out of my nostril and onto my lips."

"That's what heroes get, motherfucker," said the twin. The gunman smiled. Then he pressed the gun to Lou's head and said, "Tell me where she is."

"I don't know. I didn't see. Somewhere in the back. She's nothing to me. Don't shoot, please," said Lou. The gun rotated slightly away, and then I heard a loud rustling in the back. Jake rose visibly, bow in hand, and fired an arrow into one of the check-out stands near us, missing the four attackers by a good five feet, but making a loud noise. The arrow knocked gum, candy and a magazine onto the floor. The gunman immediately returned fire at Jake, but Jake had already dropped to the ground and the bullet flew past harmlessly. Jake rose a second time and shot again. This time the arrow was closer, but still far from hitting the gunman, who shot once more at Jake. The shot hit a shelf right near Jake's head as he dove to the floor. I winced at how close the shot was.

"Alright. Let's try this another way. Come on out, Hawk-eye and bring the bitch with you, or I'll do your friends in front of you." He then turned the gun towards me and Lou. Lou squinted, and a squeaking noise came out of him that sounded almost feral. I swallowed hard. A long silent moment came, and I wondered if I was a dead man. Then I saw movement from the back. Jake rose to his feet, nodded at Estela, and she rose as well.

"Put the bow down, hands in the air, or these two die." It seemed like an eternity. Nothing but silence hung in the air. I wondered what Jake would do-- wondered if I was about to die in a few moments. Lou was nearly in tears. He was done —couldn't speak, drool was coming out of his mouth, and he was immobile, shaking. Then I saw Jake stand up. He walked methodically towards the rest of us with a terrified Estela next to him, hands raised.

"That your boy?" the gunman asked the large man with the bat and the eye patch.

"That's him alright," he said. "I'm gonna rip out BOTH of his fucking eyes."
As Jake got closer he squinted a bit, and I thought I saw him start to smile ever so slightly.

"Hello again," he said. "Nice patch. You look more like a pirate now," said Jake. Lou's face twisted at him in shock. I admit thinking he was being a little cocky at a bad time.

"I'm gonna end you, motherfucker. You got lucky last time. But I'm gonna show you how to hit a home run on your fucking skull," he said.

"And what makes you think I'm gonna let you do that?" said Jake.

"This is why, bitch," said the gunman, pointing his pistol at Jake now, who was only a few feet away and still approaching.

"I don't think so, dude," said Jake. "You're out of bullets."

The gunman's eyes widened, then he pointed the pistol at Jake, pulled the trigger, and only heard a clicking sound. Just then Jake sprinted right at him and clotheslined him. He hit the floor hard, and his head bounced off the concrete. One down. The twin holding me clicked a switchblade and turned towards Jake, who was moving backwards to create a single file of attackers so that he could take them on one at a time. The first twin lunged at him. Jake parried the lunge, grabbed the wrist of the knife hand, and spun backwards in a circle, flinging the twin to the ground and dislodging the knife. The twin grabbed his wrist and winced, and Jake kicked him hard in the groin and picked up his knife. He doubled over and grabbed his crotch and instantaneously vomited. The second twin was running towards him now, but Jake now had his own knife, and feinted left, then moved right and jabbed him in the neck, leaving the knife there. The second twin clutched his neck and dropped to his knees. Then Jake threw a hard left hook to his face and the second twin dropped. The gunman was still lying dazed, his eyes lolling back as he moaned.

"Looks like it's you and me in the finals again," Jake said towards the big eye patch man. Eye patch roared aloud as he smashed the nearest check out rack, sending candy everywhere.

"I'm gonna kill you now, little man," he said.

"Better be sure, big fella," said Jake. "You only have one eye left." With that the larger man roared again and swung violently at Jake's head. Jake dropped before the bat could connect, then charged into the larger man with his shoulder before he could regain his balance. The big man toppled into a clothing rack and hit the ground. He spun quickly to his feet, bat in hand, and turned again towards Jake. Now he wielded it like a samurai sword and swung straight down. Jake side-stepped the swing and punched the big man in the eye patch. He hollered in pain, cursed, then gritted his teeth, re-gripped the bat, and turned one more time on Jake.

Lou looked at me, horrified. Jake had gotten in little shots, but the big man wasn't fazed this time, and his fury was frightening. I had not noticed, but Estela had disappeared again. I scanned the room quickly but couldn't take my eyes of Jake's battle. The big man cocked the bat back as if swinging at a baseball, and Jake moved in closer when he did. The moment hung in the air. It couldn't have been more than a second, but all I could think was *Jake, why are you getting closer to him? Get away you idiot!* But the big man swung, and as he did, Jake's right hand went to his face, and his left reached out to catch the bat. He spun and blended with the swing almost perfectly, and the combined force of the huge man's giant swing and Jake's own strength pushing him in the same direction sent him sprawling violently with a thud. The big man's head bounced hard twice off the floor hard, and he slumped.

Just then Estela reappeared with a shotgun in her hands.

"Okay *pendejos*," she yelled. "On your feet. Everybody up. Time to leave."

All four slowly stirred. The twin with the knife in his neck was whimpering. His brother was trying to mop the now dripping blood on a bandana. He shot daggers with his eyes at Jake and Estela. The large man with the eye patch and the smaller man who had brought the handgun were squinting and rubbing their necks. Estela pointed at the door with the barrel, and the four started walking towards the door. As they exited the store and climbed into the car, she shot the trunk. The men reacted, aware that the next shot would be at them.

"This is the second time you tried to come in my store. You will not live if there is a third time. *Me entienden?*"

The men drove off hurriedly, spinning wheels. Estela

came back inside, exhaled, put her head on my shoulder, and started crying. I hugged her and took the shotgun from her. I let her cry for a bit, and realized that I was suddenly exhausted. Lou looked hollow. His eyes sagged, he was slumping and breathing fast and shallow. I looked around for Jake. He was sitting on a shelf, eyes closed, breathing hard, squinting hard, and looking like he was in pain.

"You okay?" I asked. He nodded back silently.

"Hurt?" He shook his head.

"Dark place?" I asked.

"Dark place," he replied.

After another five minutes or so, each of us gathered our wits and started to go about the business we had come for. Lou grabbed the cart he'd filled earlier and Jake went back for his own. Estela took back her shotgun and thanked me.

"I can't live like this," she said.

"What do you mean?" I asked.

"I can't live here, trying to defend myself and this store every day against guys like that."

"Do you have any family?" She shook her head and fought back new tears.

"Left them a few years ago to make it on my own. Here," she said.

"So what are you going to do?" I asked her.

Estela turned toward the doors, looking out the only visible incoming light streaming in the store. She took a slow, panoramic turn. She glanced at the clothing racks, scanned the baby sections, moved her gaze past the shoes, the electronics, the toys. She took a deep breath in and turned her eyes on the pet section, then the pharmacy, the groceries. Then I saw her eyes go to the back of the store. The patio leading outside to the gardening section, and next to it the paint and hardware. And finally her eyes brought her to the sporting goods area where Jake was finishing up filling his cart.

She stared at Jake a while, watching him move. Jake

moved slowly now, and with visible difficulty in some positions. His neck looked stiff, and he favored his shoulder. But his most obvious issue was his limp. He almost wobbled when he walked. It was more prominent now--after the fighting--than it was normally, I thought. Jake must have sensed us watching, for he looked up suddenly and saw us staring at him. He took a deep breath, straightened his back, puffed out his chest a little, then smiled an awkward smile back and started hobbling our way.

"Doesn't look like I have much of a choice, it seems. I guess I'll take you up on your offer. I'm going wherever *El Tejón* goes."

"*El Tejón*? It was the word for 'the badger.' I squinted. "Who's that?"

She looked at Jake, nodded, and said, "Him. I'm going wherever he goes." Jake was walking back up pushing two carts end to end. He nodded to Estela. She grabbed one of the carts and meandered towards the exit. I grabbed my cart, Lou got his, and the four of us started walking back towards the high school, heavy laden with food, weapons, and camping supplies. Jake led, and walked about ten paces ahead of us. Lou brought up the rear. We didn't speak for a while, then I turned to her.

"So, why do you call him '*El Tejón*?'"

Estela laughed a little, wiping away the last of her tears.

"Look at him," she said. "He's short, pudgy, waddles when he walks, a little grey at the temples. Seems like a nice guy. Was nice to me when I met him. But it is obviously not a good idea to fuck with him. He didn't hesitate at all to hurt those men. He would have killed them, too. I saw it in his eyes. He wouldn't have given it a second thought."

"Hell, he may have killed that one twin, depending on how deep that knife wound is."
Estela bit her lip and raised her eyebrows.

"You're right, though, you know," I said. "He is a nice guy. But I've seen him kill before. It's a little scary."

Estela shook her head slightly in disbelief.

"I saw this thing on *National Geographic* once," she said. "A badger was getting attacked by, like, three wolves in Yellowstone Park. I'm thinking the wolves are gonna eat him and fight over his corpse for dinner. He tries to just walk away, but they stay after him. I figured he was a goner, you know? But no way. Not at all. They'd go after him, he'd turn and fight. Go right after them. Bite them in the face and shit. Didn't matter how many or how big they were, the badger fucked them up. By the time it was over, the wolves were bleeding and they all left him alone. That fight back there? It looked just like that. He's *El Tejón*."

I looked at Jake. She was right. Short and a little pudgy; he walked with a limp, and in his late forties was greying at the temples too. He wasn't all that impressive to look at. I mean, he had muscles, and had obviously been an athlete at one time, but decades ago. There were bigger guys than Jake. Much bigger. More ripped. Faster. But there was something very predatory about him. Something that wasn't swayed by imposing size, or numbers, or danger. Bigger guys and multiple attackers had approached him several times over the past couple of days, thinking him to be an easier target than he appeared. And in the end, Jake had torn all of them up. Just like a badger tears up coyotes, or wolves, or whatever goes after it. It keeps to itself and tries to avoid conflicts when it can. But when conflict is unavoidable, it violently assaults anything threatening it. Mercilessly, and without hesitation.

I chuckled out loud at the comparison. Jake was a nice guy too, like she said. He was even playful, at least around me. Badgers are supposed to be playful, I think. But Jake similarly had a very dark place he would go to when he needed to in order to come out on top of a scrap. I'd seen that place a couple of times in the past twenty-four hours, and it was a trifle unnerving. It was hard to wrap my head around the fact that he was both of those people. I'd known Jake for several years. He was nice. He was playful. He was a smart-ass. He was very intelligent. He didn't have a bigoted bone in his body. I admired him for all those reasons.

In general, I put up with a lot of shit, being Hispanic in a very white part of the state. I put up with even more shit being gay in a very red-neckish part of the state. Nasty whispers of ignorant people. Side looks from countless straight white people looking down their noses at me. Folks that smile in my face and talk behind my back. Jake never did that. He joked with me a lot. To hear him you might not know that he wasn't that same kind of ignorant, but knowing him as I do, I appreciate his comfort with with me as a person. There are people at that school that think I shouldn't even exist.

I decided that Estela was right about Jake being *El Tejón*, especially about the safest place to be these days was as close to him as we could get. I also noticed that she seemed like a pretty observant girl, especially for someone who had been under siege for several days and was forced to fight for her life while befriending strangers whom she had little reason to trust. Yet trust us she did—perhaps facing no better options —and now she would join the thirty-some people waiting at Hunter's Run High School for whatever life would throw at us next. She would make a nice addition to our group. I like observant, intelligent people. I'm not much for the mindless knuckle dragging crew. I think that's why I took to Estela so quickly, and why I admired Jake as much as I did. And now that Estela was around, it was somebody else to speak Spanish with too. It's always nice to talk about somebody right in front of them and they don't know what you're saying. Not particularly polite, of course, but fun nonetheless. And being a quick study, she had learned maybe the most valuable lesson quickly. The same one I had learned after the Cataclysm. It's safer to walk closer to wherever *El Tejón* walked.

So with that in mind, we all walked with him, pushing carts back to Hunter's Run High School, where thirty six people huddled in dread of the unknown. Me, Jake, Lou, and Estela —all our heads on swivels at this point, pushed the carts up the mild slope to the school parking lot and into the building where our fellow survivors waited. Survivors with little in common, but all sharing the benefits of a group collecting together for the common goal of making it to the next day, and the next day after that.

But something told me that our cozy little group that had survived together was about to implode.

CHAPTER 7

Not Welcome

"**H**oly cow—you guys hit the jackpot," said Wes, as we rolled up with our carts. "You got everything. Including a new...person?" He was staring at Estela, who looked very uncomfortable walking up to the school.

"This is Estela," I said. "She helped us get all of this stuff."

"Where'd she get it all?" asked Wes.

"Wal-Mart," I answered back. "Where else?"

"So, she stole it," said Wes.

"She didn't steal it. She's the manager. Or was," I said.

"The manager?

"Oversimplification, but yes," I answered. Wes visibly sneered. He then turned to Mark Longaberger who matched the sneer.

"So, she *gave* you all this stuff?" Wes said with another sneer.

"Donated," said Estela.

"Donated, huh," said Wes.

"Sí. To your...cause," said Estela.

"I was afraid of that," he said.

"Afraid of what?" I asked, overdramatizing my face a bit.

"You're no better than common thieves," said Wes.

"Whoa, wait a minute," I said.

"You just took anything you wanted from that store?" said Mark. "What would you call it?"

I stared at Estela, then at Lou. She and I were both wide-eyed, yet each of us had to look guilty. I didn't have another name for it. We did steal it all. Somehow the moniker didn't feel right. We weren't common thugs, like the people we fought against. We were different. Weren't we?

"Did you use a weapon to take that from someone?" asked Wes.

"No. Well, not exactly," I stammered.

"Not exactly?" yelled Mark. "What's that supposed to mean? Did you commit armed robbery?"

"No, no. That's ridiculous. Estela here donated all of this stuff. We just had to defend ourselves from *real* thieves," I said. It didn't sound right to me even though I said it out loud.

"*Espera un momento*," Estela said. "Just wait a minute."

"Let me guess, Miss. You're Mexican?" said Wes.

"Sí. What does that have to do with anything?" she asked. Wes shot a knowing look at Mark. I wanted to take a swing at both of them. Where was Jake? Why wasn't he talking. I looked over at him and he was staring down at the floor.

"So, a pair of Mexicans robbed the Wal-Mart. And you two rode shotgun?" asked Wes.

"I'm not Mexican, you dick," I shouted.

"What's wrong with being Mexican?" asked Estela.

"Nothing. But Wes, it wasn't like that," said Lou. "We were attacked."

"By people who wanted their stuff? Or maybe didn't want you hogging it all for yourselves?"

"No, no, these guys were thugs," said Lou.

"What made them thugs, Lou? Did they take anything?" Lou winced and shook his head. He was still reeling from his experience and wasn't stable enough to handle Wes's barrage of questions.

"No? So, you held off people who tried to keep you from

robbing the store using weapons. Have I got that right, Eduardo? And then you beat feet and hustled up here to stow your stuff? Do you think you're Robin Hood or something? What makes you think we want your ill-gotten gains?"

"Ill-gotten gains?" I said.

"I'm not surprised," said Mark.

"At what?" I braced up against Longaberger chest to chest. I was infuriated.

"That you'd lower yourself to that level. That you'd stoop to that kind of thing. They say that people show their true colors in times of duress. You're no better than the people who attacked the Heffners."

"What?" I was incredulous. I looked around at the faces of the people who had walked up as we approached. Most of them matched Wes's.

"The Heffners—who you wanted to lock out, as I recall. "

"That was when we feared radioactivity. I never lacked empathy for them. They were victims. So, whom did you victimize to get all of that stuff?"

I looked around at the crowd, now gathering. They all had the same judgmental look on their faces. I gathered Wes had been working on them while we were gone, trying to gain their support against us for some reason.

I felt my blood start to boil, but couldn't think of what to say to Wes.

"We can't allow ourselves to become animals, no matter what our original cultures influence us to do," said Wes. "I've been talking to the others. They agree with me."

Lou was practically crying again. He couldn't talk. He looked on the verge of a breakdown. I looked at the others. Most of them were looking at the ground.

"Jesus, Wes," shouted Maureen. "What do you mean original cultures? What the fuck is that supposed to mean?"

"You know very well what that means," Wes said. "You just don't want to admit I'm right."

Estela looked confused. She turned to look at me, wondering perhaps if I had set her up for this, but upon seeing my face she knew I was as surprised as she was. I looked around and saw Mark Longaberger and some of the others staring me down.

"We are Christians. Maybe you aren't, Eduardo. I mean, you're gay for God's sake, so you couldn't be Christian," said Wes. "If this is the Apocalypse, we are going to make our world into a better place, not one filled with animals. God says that the righteous will be taken up when Armageddon comes."

I looked at Estela. Her face was blank. Her jaw was on the floor. I turned to Lou. He was staring at the ground. Then Jake finally looked up.

"Wes, that's enough," said Jake.

"God says," Wes started. Jake grabbed him by the collar.

"If you want to meet God right now, say one more word," said Jake. His eyes were cold and murderous. Melanie Richmond walked up to Jake and put her hand on his arm.

"Jake, take it easy. Lou, are you okay? Can you tell us what happened?"

Lou composed himself, wiped some tears and snot away from his face, and looked up at Melanie.

"We went in to take stuff from the Wal-Mart, but this gang showed up with a gun. The girl, she is Mexican, she had shot at them before we got there, and drove them off, and they were mad. They came back for revenge. But Jake fought them. He stabbed one and beat up a couple others. Then she pulled a shotgun on them and they left."

Mouths dropped, and a couple of gasps ensued. Melanie Richmond and Robin Eaves looked afraid. Even Al DeFillipo looked a little unnerved. Wes Kent looked smug and self-righteous.

"Well, Eddie. Is that the way it happened?" Wes asked.

"Yes," I said.

"Well, Jake, it seems you think all problems are solved by violence," Wes said, looking Jake in the face.

I'll give Wes credit—he wasn't backing down from

Jake. The look on Jake's face was cold rage. He was my friend, and frankly that look scared the shit out of me. I looked around at the people in the room, fixated on Jake Fisher with his fist balled up around Wes' collar. Some of the kids looked scared. I don't know how I must have looked. Inside I was enraged. Wes had spun this thing while we were gone, maybe to reestablish some kind of leadership position and erode confidence in Jake. It was working. Melanie laid her hands gently on Jake's arm.

"Jake, let him go," she said softly. "Let him go."
Jake unballed his fist. It looked cramped, and the shirt slowly unwrinkled. Wes turned to the crowd.

"You see now, don't you? It's just as I said. He's become unhinged. Jake Fisher and anyone who is around him. They are stealing, fighting gangs, committing *murder.* And that's only in the first few days. God knows what's coming next. Is this how you want to live? Is it?" said Wes.

There was a long pause. Jake just stood there. He was trying to back out of the dark place with everyone watching. Everyone looked at him, then at each other. I realized that everything we had hoped to make of this survival situation was over, and I began to fear what might happen to us.

"No," said Melanie.

"No," said Robin.

"I, I guess not," said Casey.

"Hell no," said Longaberger.

Off to the right, looking very uncomfortable and not saying a word, were Glen Billings, Al DeFillipo, Maureen Kelly, and Jada Allen. By themselves at a table in the cafeteria were the Heffners. A few others stared at the floor near them. No one in the cafeteria spoke. The group in the rotunda where we had entered had divided into two.

"You're making a mistake, Wes," said Jake. "You're dividing us when we should be together.

"You are the one dividing us, Jake Fisher," Wes said. "Your judgment is compromised. You can't be trusted to make good decisions. You have stolen, killed, assaulted people, even our own people," he paused, pointing to his rumpled shirt.

"If we are going to survive this horrible time, we need someone who is trustworthy. Someone who can make sound decisions. Who won't put us in harm's way. What we are saying, Jake, is that we don't want you or your kind around here anymore," said Wes. Lou looked up sharply, surprise on his face.

"My kind?" said Jake.

"Killers, thieves, gang-bangers. It's not what we want from our new society," said Wes.

"Killers, thieves, and gang-bangers. Me? I'm those?"

"You and your...*friends*," said Wes. He accentuated the word friends, and gestured at me and Estela.

"My friends? Wes, what are you talking about? When we left we were one group all on the same page."

"Yes, we were. Then you killed two men, maimed a third, apparently fought and assaulted four more, and stole four carts worth of items from a Wal-Mart," Wes continued.

"Wes, are you kidding me? The Heffners were attacked by armed men. No one else wanted to help them. The four men in the Wal-Mart attacked us with guns, knives and bats. One of them was one of the Heffner's attackers. I am guilty of winning two fights where I was outnumbered. And my 'friends' are a high school educator and a Wal-Mart assistant manager. Who the hell is a gang-banger? We're the only gang around," said Jake, confused.

"I'm not going to let you spin this into something it's not. I've talked to the group, and they are very concerned with your behavior. The violence, the theft. It's not what they want, Jake. It's not what *we* want. You said you wanted leadership to be determined by the group. Well, the group doesn't want you. We don't even want you here anymore," said Wes.

"I teach here, just like you," Jake said. "This is my home."

"You taught here. The world has changed. And this world doesn't want you in it anymore. It's time to find a new home."

Jake looked around. "Is that right? Does he speak for you? Do you all want me gone?"

The Heffners stared at the ground silently as if nothing were happening. Maureen Kelly and Jada Allen were starting to tear up. Al DeFillipo looked lost. Estela looked at me. I must have looked absolutely horrified. We had invited this girl back to save her life, and now she was caught in the middle of some kind of bizarre leadership struggle.

Jake took a deep breath. He turned briefly to Estela and whispered. "I'm sorry I brought you here. I had no idea—"

"You people are insane," I yelled. "He's the reason we're alive right now." I looked at the Heffners and pointed. He's the ONLY reason *you're* alive right now! These people shut you outside, and he saved your life and brought you in. How can you go along with this? How can any of you go along with this?"

"You and your new friend should go too," Wes said. "You obviously don't fit in here."

"Don't fit in?" I asked.

"We're all good Christians here. We want to do the right thing for the greater good. The decision we made with the Heffners was based on wrong information at the time. We were trying to protect the group. You and Jake wanted to endanger the group. Once we knew that the Heffners were not radioactive, we welcomed them in and apologized. They understand all that now. "

"I can't believe what I'm hearing," I said. "When did all of you suddenly come to this conclusion?"

"It wasn't sudden. It's been here all the time, and as soon as you all weren't here to bully everyone into your way of thinking, people felt safe to speak their minds. Once we did that, we realized we were all of a different mindset than you."

"You're serious. I can't believe it. All of you? You all came to the same conclusion as this asshole?" I asked.

"You all, on the other hand, have brought violence, theft, and murder onto our doorstep. You're savages. What you did to those poor boys' bodies outside," said Wes.

"The ones who tried to rob and kill us?" I asked. "Jake put them—"

"I know, he put them on display for any other would-be attackers. Very medieval of him. Everyone here was horrified by that. We gave them a Christian burial after you left. God can judge them now," said Wes. "Just like he'll judge you."

"My God, you truly don't get it," I said.

"Oh, we get it, Señor Reyes. It's you who don't get it."

I think I'm beginning to, I thought to myself. I turned to Jake, lost. I shook my head as if to say 'how did this happen?' Jake got a stern look on his face and shook me off.

"Okay Wes. Have it your way. I'll need about a half an hour to collect my things, then me, Eddie, and Estela will be out of your hair with our ill-gotten gains."

"I think you need to leave right now," said Wes. My eyes bugged out of my head and my mouth dropped. Jake's eyes glowed and he chewed on his lip for a moment. Then he walked up to Wes.

"You know Wes, considering for a moment that you have labeled me a pugilist, a thief, and a brutal killer, I'd think twice about ordering me around right now if I were you."

"You, you don't...scare me," Wes stammered.

"Well maybe I should. All those people I killed? I wasn't angry with them. But I'm pretty goddamn furious with you right now," Jake said, putting his nose up against Wes' nose.

Wes's confident look suddenly faltered and a realization of fear washed over him. He fumbled trying to come up with a response.

"Well, I think..." he stammered.

"You know Wes, there are lots of different ways to make leadership changes. Some of them only take a few seconds," Jake said. He looked around at the faces staring at him. Everyone—even the friendly ones—looked positively terrified of Jake just then.

"I'm going to get my stuff," he said. "I'll try to make it quick. Eddie, get anything you need from your classroom that you want to take with you. Estela, if anyone comes anywhere near those shopping carts of ours, blow their heads off with your shotgun."

Melanie's eyes bugged. Mark's jaw dropped. Wes looked horrified, and turned to glance at Estela. Estela smiled, and cocked her pump action almost on cue.

"Keep your distance, Señor. You know how us Mexicans are," she said.

I went up to my classroom and snagged a backpack, a jacket, and a few personal things. I didn't really have much. I'm young. My life was outside the school. I really just worked here. It took me all of about twenty seconds. I went back to Jake's room and saw him staring at his classroom. His closet door was open. It was packed full of clothes for every possible occasion. His desk had everything in it. This was Jake's bat cave, his Tardis, his castle. Jake lived here—he only slept at home. The events of the past few days had gone by so fast that it was difficult to process that it all had changed. It wasn't hard to pretend we were on a Christmas break, or a spring break, and that classes would resume next week and everything would be normal again.

Now, staring at his room, knowing he would leave it forever, Jake's façade began to waiver. He heard me coming and regulated his breathing, but I could tell he wanted to break down. The weight of his wife, Laura, being cut off when the bombs dropped, would have been enough by itself. But the anxiety about his sons, the way he was being ousted here, all on top of him literally having to fight for his life the past two days—I wasn't sure how he was holding up at all. Now he was having to say goodbye forever to a place that had been his home for decades.

"You okay?" I asked.

"Yeah. Just, just, finding it hard to say goodbye," he said. "Been here since the place opened. More than twenty years.

Hard to process."

"Yeah, it is. I'm sorry, *compadre*."

"Who am I kidding, Eddie? This whole thing's over. The world's not like it used to be. We may never have school like this again. We don't even know what's out there. Here I am getting sentimental about a room I'll likely never use again, and we've got much bigger problems to deal with now."

"Jake," I asked.

"Yeah?"

"Are we gonna be alright?" He frowned a little, then pursed his lips. He was thinking about it, but I admit I didn't want an honest answer, I wanted blind reassurance. I got it.

"Yeah, amigo. We're gonna be alright. I'm a Marine. Adapt, improvise, overcome. You're with me. We'll be okay. Better than most."

"What are we gonna do? Where will we go?"

"First, we get our shit together. Then we make sure we have shelter and food for a while. Then I'm going to find my boys and bring them back. I understand if that's not your quest."

"Where you go, I go. My parents were working in D.C. when the bombs hit. I got nothing here. Now." Jake nodded and shook my hand.

"Just my luck. On the road again. Me and a couple of señoritas." I rolled my eyes at him and we walked back to the rotunda.

When we got there, Estela was standing in the exact spot we left her. Nobody had moved.

"No, you didn't," she said.

"I did. I helped get this stuff, so some of it's mine," said Lou.

"What you did was tell those gang-bangers that we were in the back, then stood there shaking like a leaf while the rest of us fought them off. You don't get anything."

"The lady's got a point, Lou," said Jake, walking up. Lou stared at the ground. "Estelita—ready to go? Push these carts to the back of the school. My truck is parked there. We'll load up and be off."

We three awkwardly walked the four carts back to the other side of the school with everyone watching. As we turned the corner, we heard elevated voices behind us. Then we heard footsteps jogging up behind us. I turned, expecting trouble. Jake, on the other hand, was grinning.

"Wait, Jake. Wait. We, we don't agree with them. We don't want to stay here now. We'd like to come with you, if that's okay."

It was Maureen Kelly. And beside her was the gangly Al DeFillipo, and students Jada Allen, and Glen Billings. I smiled. Estela was guarded.

"Fine by me, but it's not my show—despite what Wes might have you think. You need to ask Eddie and Estela. And you need to understand that I am going to drive to southern Virginia and find my sons. If that's not a trip you want to make, fine, but I plan on leaving soon."

"Anything's better than here, now. If you'll have us," said Maureen.

"Sure thing," I said. "Estela—*son buena gente. Good people.*" Estela nodded and smiled.
We exited the building and pushed the carts toward Jake's truck. He had climbed inside and tried to start the engine. No sound came out.

"I was afraid of that," Jake said.

"Afraid of what?" I asked.

"It was the H.E.M.P.," said Al. "The high altitude electro magnetic pulse. It probably fried everyone's computers. No-body's cars are going to work."

"Maybe not nobody's, but mine is pretty new. It's reliant on a lot of computers. Not sure where everyone was gonna sit anyway."

Jake looked around the parking lot. Near the back was a short school bus. It looked like it was left in a hurry. It was parked oddly, off kilter, and its doors were open.

"Bingo," said Jake. He trotted over toward the bus, and as he neared it, he could clearly see the keys dangling from the ignition.

"Any other day this probably would not have happened, but when World War III begins and the bombs start dropping, folks tend to leave things where they are. Even school busses with keys in them. So today is our lucky day. He hopped in, turned the key, and the engine roared.

"How is it that the bus works and your truck doesn't?" I asked.

"E.M.P.'s affect different vehicles differently. This bus is more old school. Less electronics needed. And the massive amount of metal around the engine makes for a nice Faraday cage." Al smiled and gave Jake a thumbs up.

"Yes, it does," Al said, nodding with a grin.

"Faraday cage?" I asked.

"It basically is a shield that blocks electrical impulses by conducting them and grounding them. Most cars do a nice job of that—that's why people are safe from storms in them. There was an old lady who was scared to death of storms back when I was a kid. She would go sit in her car until they ended. It was a Faraday cage, of sorts. This bus did the same."

"That's science, junior," said Al to me with a smile.
We all loaded the contents of the carts into the back of the bus and hopped in. There were seven of us: me, Jake, Al, Maureen, Glen, Jada, and Estela. We had food, weapons, shelter, beds, and tools.

We also had no idea where we were going and what we would find.

CHAPTER 8

Bus ride

I had forgotten how much I hated school busses. Being gay, Hispanic, and probably fairly effeminate as a kid, the bus was the place where I took the most punishment—physically and mentally. Busses are great places to hide abuse. Too much noise for the driver to hear specific conversations. Too much activity to narrow in on trouble. Seats are too high to see a sucker punch. I was on the receiving end of a lot of all of that. Eventually I got through it; and in the end, it probably made me mentally tougher as an adult. Still, it's not anything I'd wish on anyone, and riding in one again brought back a ton of memories, most of them bad.

As we rolled on, those memories faded and were replaced by new ones. Creating those memories were the people I was with—some of whom I knew well, while others were truly strangers in all but name to me. No better time than the present to rectify that.

"Hey Al," I said. "So, where are you from?"

"Pittsburgh," he said. "Western PA, at least. North Alleghany High School, California University of Pennsylvania."

"How'd you get here to Emmitsburg?"

"Recruited. The school district does a lot of recruiting in my area. I've even done some myself."

"How long have you been a teacher?" I asked.

"Twenty years. Right out of college."

"So, you're...what? Forty-two?"

"Forty-one. Graduated early." He tapped his head and smiled.

"Science guy, huh?" I asked. He nodded back.

Though I didn't know him as well as some of my other colleagues, I knew that Al was one of those "utility teachers" who make themselves vital because they would teach anything. In our business, there are plenty of teachers who can be pretty demanding. They demand which classes to teach, focus tightly on their contracts, won't do anything they don't have to do. Al was the opposite. He was on the other extreme. He was devoted to the school, devoted to the kids, and displayed little to no visible ego. He didn't get caught up in petty power squabbles among the staff or engage in gossip. As I looked around the bus, to the best of my knowledge, we were all like that.

"Mind if I join in?" asked Maureen. She moved from the back of the bus where Jada was sitting near Glen and decided to leave the younger crew for folks more in her age range.

"Sure. More the merrier," I said.

"What are you guys talking about?" she asked.

"I was just getting some of Al's background. I just realized I don't know him as well as I should, especially now that we're gonna be traveling partners and all. Do you guys know each other?"

Both of them smiled awkwardly and their eyes darted back and forth between each other and me. I could tell immediately from looking at them that something had gone on there. Both were suppressing smiles.

"No way. How did I miss that?" I asked.

"Miss what?" Maureen asked innocently.

"You two. Are you an item?"

Eyebrows raised, eyes darted again, but silence reigned.

"You hooked up at least, didn't you?" Al began to

blush, and Maureen closed her eyes, chuckled and nodded.

"How do you do that?" she asked.

"It's like reverse gay-dar," I said. "We can see it on all you straights when you hook up. It's like putting a black light onto a hotel bed spread. Secret emissions pop up everywhere."

Maureen's face scrunched up like she just bit into something nasty. "Ugh. Nice image," she said. "You couldn't come up with a better metaphor than that?"

I just smiled and shrugged, and Al laughed. "First thing that came to my mind," I said.

Maureen took a deep breath. "We both were going through unpleasant divorces," Maureen said. "One day we were in the teacher's lounge having bad days together and started talking."

"And we all know what talking leads to," I said smiling.

"Um, yeah," said Al. He looked around to the back of the bus to find Jada and Glen riveted to our conversation. Even in a world war, teacher gossip was intesting. Jada was looking at Al as if a bit disappointed. Al looked at the ground, hunched over a bit and nodded, supressing a smile.

"We're friends, you know," said Al. "Friends help each other through rough times," he said. Maureen looked at him for a moment, then turned back towards me.

"So where's he taking us?" she asked, jerking her thumb towards the front of the bus.

"Who?" I answered.

"Your boyfriend, who else?" she said.

"Jake? He's not my boyfriend," I said. "Not my type. Too macho."

"Couldn't tell, the way you've been shadowing him lately," she said. Jake was talking to Estela in Spanish. I could hear his accent improving a little as he went on.

"Look, girl, I'm just being smart," I said. "Estela said something on the way here that I totally agree with. The safest place to be right now is near El Tejón."

"El Tejón?" she asked, smiling.

"What's that?" asked Al.

"The Badger. Estela calls Jake 'the Badger.' Says it's how he looks. And I'm inclined to agree."

"How so?" asked Maureen.

"She spelled it out. Short, pudgy, walks with a limp, graying at the temples, and though he looks harmless from a distance, it is probably best not to fuck with him."

Both Al and Maureen laughed at the description.

"She's right," said Maureen. "That's spot on."

We smiled a bit at the idea of it, then an awkward silence prevailed. Glen and Jada had moved closer behind us so that they could join in. They had been listening from a distance.

"Mr. Fisher killed somebody, didn't he?" asked Jada.

"Um," I fumbled a bit. "Well, you see, Jada," I stammered.

"He killed two people," said Glen enthusiastically. Then he beat up the other guy. Stuck an arrow in his eye. Dude is bad ass."

"Don't talk about it like that," said Jada. "It's horrible."

"Horrible? Those people attacked Tanner's family. They were gonna kill him. Coach Fisher stopped them."

"He killed other human beings. How can you defend that?" she asked. "I mean, I like Mr. Fisher and all, but he killed people." Her voice waivered slightly and a tear started to form in her eye.

"Mr. Reyes," she said. "Do you think Mr. Kent was right? Do you think Mr. Fisher is dangerous? Do you think we should be riding with him? I mean, actually killing people, that makes him dangerous, right? I don't know what to think."

The weight of the last few days' events were beginning to show on Jada. Anyone who had stayed at the school most likely had nowhere else to go, because they either knew or could guess that their loved ones probably didn't make it. Otherwise, like the majority of the people who worked or stud-

109

ied at Hunter's Run, they'd have left right after the bombs started dropping. There were over a thousand teachers and students in that building, but only a tiny amount stayed after. We never had really gotten a chance to discuss it much, but those of us stayed had done so because we really had no other place to go, no one else to lean on, and that building and those people represented something solid. Something stable.

Jada was a fifteen-year-old girl whose world had exploded. She was living with and traveling with virtual strangers. And it was starting to break her down. I moved over and put my arm around her as she started shaking.

"Now, now, *chica*," I said reassuringly. "First of all, yes, I think Mr. Fisher is dangerous."
Her eyes widened and her mouth dropped into an audible gasp.

"And yes, we absolutely should be traveling with him. He is a good man who tries to do right by people. But he is a warrior, Jada. He was a Marine and a world class athlete in a combat sport. You can't succeed in those jobs and not be dangerous. He has what it takes to get us through this, and I trust him with my very life."

I looked up at the long mirror above Jake's head in the driver's seat. He was listening in as best he could, and our eyes caught one another as I tried to soothe Jada.

"Jada, don't believe everything Sr. Reyes says. He's had a crush on me for years, and it's probably affecting his judgment right now," Jake yelled back. Jada laughed out loud. It was an honest smile, and I realized how pretty she was. Glen Billings couldn't stop looking at her.

Jake slowed up and took a left turn into a long driveway out in the country, about five miles from town. He eased in like he'd done a million times, put the bus in park and turned it off. He opened the doors and got up from the driver's seat. He had driven home to his farmette.

"What are we stopping for?" I asked.

"A few more supplies," said Jake. "Some clothes, some paperwork that might help me find the boys, and a couple of cans of diesel fuel for the bus." He said. "Does any-body want anything? There's a little food in the pantry we can snag. And I'm going to get Oklahoma."

"Oklahoma?" Maureen repeated.

"The Broadway show?" I asked. "I love that one. Just love 'Surrey with the fringe on top,' you know?" I said.

"Not the musical, you doofus," said Jake. "My cat. How gay can you get, Eddie?"

"Cat? Why are you bringing the cat?"

"Cause he might die here if I don't. I have to let him out, and let him take his chances. But it worries me a little. There are a lot of foxes and coyotes around here now. Not super sure that he'll make it. He's a smart cat, though, and pretty tough, so I like his chances. He's gonna ride with us to the barn. He likes people. Don't hit on him, though, Eddie. You hear me? He's straight."

I shook my head. As Jake disembarked and headed inside, Glen Billings went outside and around the corner in an obvious mission to urinate.

"Boys are so gross," said Maureen. Jada agreed.

"Miss Kelly," said Jada. "Where are you from? You're not from around here, are you?"

"Long Island," she said. "I'm a native New Yorker. You can probably tell a little from my accent," she said. Jada nodded.

"How'd you get to Emmitsburg, Maryland?"

"My ex-husband," said Maureen. "He's a linguistic contractor at Fort Detrick. He helps them with translations in Spanish."

"How come you got divorced?" she asked.

"Jada," I said. "That's kind of a personal question."

"No, it's alright," said Maureen. I met him when I was studying abroad in Puerto Rico. He's Dominican. He was really handsome, and a phenomenal baseball player. He got drafted and played in the minor leagues for a few years here with the Frederick Keys. We moved here and got a small apartment, and

I got a teaching job to help us make ends meet. But after about seven years here, he realized he wasn't going to get called up to the majors, so he started looking for other means of employment. He studied languages, like me. One of the coaches' wives worked at Fort Detrick and mentioned an opening, and he applied. We ended up staying right here in the area."

"So what happened? You sounded so happy," she said.

"We were for a while. But I wanted kids, and he said he didn't. He kept stalling, and we started drifting apart. He started drinking. It changed him."

Maureen hesitated for a moment and swallowed hard. I put my arm on her shoulder.

"Turns out, he already had a kid with one of the secretaries that he'd been screwing the whole time and didn't tell me," she said. Al bit his lip and looked at Maureen sympathetically.

"I'm sorry," said Jada. "I shouldn't have."

"It's no secret, *chica*," said Maureen. "Most men are shit. Some are decent. But the majority of them? Shit. I got me one of the shitty ones."

Glen Billings walked around to the side of the bus, lifted up one of the lower compartments, and put two heavy plastic fuel cans full of diesel fuel, then climbed the steps. He looked at Maureen and Jada, who both looked a little sorry they'd ventured into Maureen's marriage history, then looked at Al and me, who obviously were as uncomfortable as the girls.

"What?" said Glen. "What's up?"

After a moment, Al piped up. "It just occurred to me, Glen, that you, Jada and I may be the only people on this bus who don't speak Spanish."

"But Mr. D—I took Spanish with Ms. Kelly," he said. Maureen smiled wide and shook her head.

"As I recall Glen, what Mr. DeFillipo said is accurate," she chuckled. "That C you got was an early Christmas gift," she said smiling. "Feliz Navidad." Glen smiled back.

Just then Jake got on board with a bag strapped to his back and one more duffle in each hand. One of the duffel bags seemed to be moving. Just then, a head popped out and a small, orange, tabby cat popped its head out of one of the bags, pushing the zipper open with its neck, and meowing. Everyone laughed at what was apparently Oklahoma—our newest travel companion on the magical bus.

"Aw, nice kitty," said Jada, and she reached out and stroked Oklahoma on his forehead. The cat responded with instant purring, closed its eyes, and rubbed up against Jada's hand even more.

"Okie is an attention whore," said Jake. "He'll fit in great with you all. He's got you suckered already."

"Attention whore, huh? Wonder where he learned that from," I said. Jake cut his eyes at me.

"Probably from his Auntie Eduardo," said Jake. I gave him the finger.

"Okie isn't making the whole trip with us, though. I'm going to take him to the barn. It'll be a place where he can get shelter, be free to wander, and I can give him about a week's worth of food if the other critters don't get into it." Okie walked over to my lap and nuzzled me.

"Aw. I'd love to take you with us, Okie," I said. "But God knows where we're going or what we'll find."

"Anybody need to hit the bathroom?" Jake asked. "Get a drink? If not, it's all aboard and full steam ahead."

"Mr. Fisher," Jada said. "Glen peed outside in your yard."

"Every man's God-given right, Jada. Well done, lad," Jake said. Jada laughed and rolled her eyes.

Nobody else needed to go, so Jake clapped and sat back in the driver's seat. Estela grabbed the cat gently and placed him on her lap. She hugged him and stroked him almost desperately. It reminded me again of how each of us had lost everything, and were all struggling just to keep sane.

Jake cranked the engine, did an awkward five-point turn in his driveway, and headed off down a back dirt road to an old barn on the edge of the woods on his property. He carried Okie to the barn along with a large sack of cat food. He put the food in a bowl and Okie went after it. Jake stood up, then took a long look at the field and stream behind his house, and sighed.

The view was beautiful. Two streams crossed the property and joined at its edge. One meandered through a woods, the other ran alongside a meadow. Jake's house was on the top of a hill where he could look at all of it. A horse farm was next door, so there were fields as far as the eye could see. Wildflowers bloomed in the meadow. Birds were everywhere. Jake took a breath.

"Love this place," he said. "Hope to see her again. Okie: you're in charge while I'm gone, boy."

And off we went. We had driven about five miles in the country, and I shouted to Jake.

"So where are we going again?"

"Shenandoah Valley, Virginia. My sons, Tommy and Vinny are at college, and I'm going to find them and bring them back."

"What schools are they in?" asked Maureen.

"Virginia Military Institute and Virginia Tech. Both are on wrestling scholarships. Got a text from Tommy. It said the area had not felt any direct effects of the bombing. Hoping they're okay."

"Which Route are we taking?" she asked.

"Figured we'd better stay as far away from DC as possible. Lot of the bombs exploded directly above. Any radiation will be lingering there for a while."

"So, taking I-81 south?" she asked.

"Yeah. That was my thought. Pretty much a straight shot all the way. You travel down there a lot?"

"Used to go that way when my husband played ball. Nashville and Memphis, sometimes Jackson. It's a beautiful highway for an interstate."

"It should also keep us far enough away from DC to make me feel better," said Jake.

"You know, Jake," said Al. "I'm actually shocked that we made out as well as we did, living in Emmitsburg. Fort Detrick is only twenty miles down the road and definitely was a tactical target. It's been the home of biological and chemical weapons testing since the 1940's. They focus mostly on defense now, but it's still gotta be a main target for an enemy. I'm surprised we all made it through."

"Yeah. No question that Fort Detrick and even Camp David are prime targets, and Emmitsburg is less than a half hour from both of them. The city of Frederick is so close to D.C. that it makes me real uncomfortable about what we might run into on this journey of ours. Without any broadcasts, we don't know what areas are safe, what ones aren't. It's a bit of a crapshoot right now. Anybody have any internet?"

"Nothing new," Glen said. "And it goes in and out sometimes."

"I have been checking regularly. If anything changes, I'll let you know. Jake, have you thought of trying the C.B.?"

Jake's face responded with some recognition and surprise. Maureen's did too. I was confused.

"What's a C.B.?" I asked.

"I forget how young you are sometimes," Jake said. "Citizens' Band radio. It's what truckers use to communicate on the road. Really just a walkie-talkie with a bunch of channels that lots of people monitor, including the police. Good thinking Al! Don't know why I didn't think of that myself."

"You've been slightly distracted," said Maureen. "Think we'll give you a pass on that."

Jake reached down and grabbed the knob and twisted it on. Static was the only sound that came out. He changed channels, stopping for a few seconds on each one. Nothing. Then he went to Channel 19. That's the one where all of the chatter usually is. Static. Jake furrowed his brow.

"Nothing. That's surprising. How can nobody be on

the road and nobody be on the radio?"

The bus rode down Route 15 from Emmitsburg, Maryland—on the northernmost border between Carroll County, Frederick County, and the Pennsylvania state line—towards the small town of Thurmont, home of Mt. St. Michael's College, Catoctin Mountain State Park, and Camp David—the presidential hideaway. The rolling farmland was rife with small streams, with the blue-grey Catoctins looming in the background.

"God this place is gorgeous. I never get tired of riding through here," said Jake.

The road ran through Mt. St. Michael's University, a small Catholic college near Thurmont. The grey stone buildings loomed on both sides of the highway. Jake looked anxiously at the campus, no doubt thinking of his boys.

"There are some people over there," I said. "They look like students. Should we check in?"

I knew Jake wanted to stay on track, but we really had no idea about anything in the world outside Hunter's Run High School. Jake slowed down the bus and pulled in towards a group of twenty-somethings playing frisbee on the lawn.

"How you guys doing?" said Jake. A blonde, tan kid with some facial hair and a headband walked over.

"We're cool, dude. Who are you guys?"

"Bunch of teachers from down the road at the high school. Just checking on what things are looking like. Are you guys the only ones here?" asked Jake.

"Yeah. Most of the other folks decided to ride home. Most of us are from too far away. Flights were grounded a few days ago. I'm from California. Those guys are from the Midwest. A couple of them are exchange students."

"Is the school open?" I asked, leaning out the window and looking around for any other signs of life.

"Not officially. But the dean of students lives here on campus, and said they'd run like a skeleton crew to make sure we got fed until we could make plans to try and get home."

"How many of you are there?" asked Jake.

"About thirty or forty. Most of the guys who needed rides just found them. Hooked up with other folks riding home. The flyers are the ones mostly here."

"You guys have power?" Jake asked.

"On and off. I think they use the generator for making dinner and recharging stuff," he said.

"Just dinner, huh?"

"Yeah. They give us like cereal and stuff for breakfast. Sandwiches for lunch. Then they have a hot dinner and let us plug in our phones."

"You all got any signal? Have you had much luck with phones or internet?" Jake said.

"Some of us have no trouble talking to family. Others got nothing. We pass messages, try to get somebody else's folks to try and contact ours if we haven't had any luck. Internet's down. It's weird, some sites are fine, but nothing new is added. Most stuff just doesn't show. Sometimes we'll see something on our phones. Nothing useful though. It sucks."

"Yeah. It does indeed suck. Well, thanks for the info," said Jake. "Good luck to you guys."

"You too, man," said the student. Jake closed the bus doors, and we pulled back out onto the highway.

"That's gotta be encouraging, right?" I asked. "Colleges looking out after their students. I mean, for your sons. That's gotta be encouraging."

"Mt. St. Michael's is fairly small, more personal. Tommy should be okay at VMI. Hell, he should be thriving there, the way they roll. I'm more concerned for Vinny. He's at Virginia Tech. That place is like a city. No telling what things are like there."

I thought about that for a minute. Cities. Mass amounts of people sharing resources. In cities, order depends completely on things working. Sanitation, law enforcement, power, water. When the basics break down, things start to go awry. People start to take when they need, and later take what they want. And when those things belong to other people, folks start preying on each other. Jake had seen that first-hand overseas. I had even seen it once myself traveling abroad. Hell, all of us just saw it in tiny Emmitsburg. I hoped Jake's son would be okay at a place as big as Virginia Tech.

We rolled forward on Route 15 to the outskirts of Thurmont, heading south to Frederick. As we neared the exit for the road up to Cunningham Falls, near where Camp David was, we saw a line of military vehicles, including at least four tanks, blocking the road. Everyone in the bus went silent. There were troops there manning the vehicles. Nobody was getting up either of the roads that led up the mountain. The mountain was closed. Route 77 came in from above in Smithsburg—that would have been easily blocked off from the north. The only other road nearby was Route 550, which led to Catoctin High School, our rival. It was much older, more traditional, and completely inaccessible now thanks to the U.S. Military. The whole scene was disturbing. There was no doubt as to the fact that somebody important from the U.S. government was in Camp David. Whether it was the President, the Vice President, some generals—who knew? But somebody was there. And nobody was getting in.

"Lots of tanks. Can't say I've ever seen that many tanks side by side in one place," I thought aloud. Jake heard me.

"Yeah. That's actually pretty rare," said Jake. "Even in a forward assignment. Scattered around, maybe. But not lined up. It's unnerving. We are at war, after all."

We rode by the two roads up the mountain looking for signs of people. Nothing on the road, near the tanks, or moving around in town. Where were the people? The town wasn't huge, but big enough to support a high school, a zoo, a national park, and a decent amount of businesses. We only lived about ten miles away from this place, and we saw people the first two days in the streets of Emmitsburg after the bombings. Thurmont, however, was empty. We rode past the local zoo, which was visible from the highway. Empty. No people, no animals. Nothing. As we headed toward Frederick, which was a small city by most standards, I wondered what we would see.

Turns out we would hear it instead.

"Hello? May Day! Emergency! Hello? Is anyone there?" It was a woman's voice. Jake picked up the CB.

"Roger. Who are you? Where are you? What do you need?" said Jake, unsure of how to answer the call. He looked back at me and shrugged. The others were listening intently.

"My name is Wendy. I am at Fort Detrick. Building H. We're locked in. We've been here for three days. My supervisor is not doing well. We don't know what's out there. Can you help us?"

"We are a few minutes from Fort Detrick, but I don't know one building from the other, and there's no internet, no Google maps we can use."

"When you drive in the East Entrance off of Shookstown Road, there's a large sign there with a campus map. It will be the first right off of the entrance, then we're near the end of that street. Please hurry. I think the Colonel is dying."

Jake jammed the pedal down and zoomed down Route 15. He turned onto Shookstown Road, then pulled up to the main entrance of Fort Detrick and slammed on the breaks. The gates were closed, but something had physically torn them apart.

"What the hell did that?" asked Maureen. Jake shook his head.

"I have no idea," said Jake. "Al? Any guesses?"

Al was awestruck. It looked as if something had just ripped it open with hands. It wasn't run over by a truck, or even shoved out of the way like a bulldozer might. It looked as if someone had walked up to it and from the bottom ripped a man-sized hole in it and stormed out. Jake revved the engine and blasted the bus through the hole. Screeching noises came from the chain link fencing scraping the sides of the bus. Jada winced. Estela plugged her ears. The noise was incredibly loud and creepy. The bus rolled forward towards the map.

"It's a right. Like she said," I yelled. Building H is at the end of this street, on the left."

Jake drove another quarter mile and pulled the bus to a halt. He pulled the doors open and started to get up.

"What the hell?" he remarked. "Does that street look —I don't know—orange to you?"

"What are you talking about—holy shit!" I shouted. "It is orange. What is that?

"I don't know, but it can't be good. Everyone grab two grocery bags and tie one around each foot. We should have plenty back there. Whatever that stuff is, it's probably best if we don't get it on us if we can help it," said Jake.

"Um, should we all go?" I asked.

"Maybe not," said Jake. "We don't know what's going on here. I'll go. Glen, come with me. You're a big kid. The rest of you can stay if you want."

"No," said Estela. "*Voy contigo. Y tú*, Eddie?"

"Yeah. I'll go I guess. Al, will you stay here with Maureen and Jada?" Al looked disappointed and relieved all at the same time. Maureen grabbed his shoulder, and he put his hand on hers and nodded.

"I'll stay," he said. "But first, I have an idea." Al went to the back of the bus and fiddled around one of the boxes, pulling out some things.

"Al, we don't have time," said Jake.

"Just wait a second, will you?" said Al. He started putting something together. After another thirty seconds or so, he held up two hands with walkie-talkies.

"Ta-dah," said Al. "We can talk to you on the CB. You guys take these. The walkies only have five channels, so I'm turning the CB to channel one. Got it?"

Jake smiled and nodded, "Good thinking." Al smiled back triumphantly and the four of us were on our way. We all tied the bags around our shoes and hopped out. Everything had kind of an orange tint to it. The trees, the benches, the streets. Everything. I turned around to see how much of it there was. Except for the main entrance, flecks of orange were all over the place. There were a few spots that had somehow escaped it, but there was no pattern to it that I could tell.

Jake went up to the main door. It was open and swinging slightly. It looked bent, like the gate. Jake stepped in gingerly, looked left and right, then moved ahead.

"Wendy?" he yelled. "Where are you?" A muffled sound came from the back right portion of the building. Jake led, and everyone else followed. We went through three sets of doors made of wired glass and metal. They all seemed propped open and off track somehow. As we neared the back wall, we saw a set of double doors that was heavily dented but still closed.

"What the hell did that?" I asked. Jake's eyebrows raised. He knocked on the doors.

"Wendy? Are you in there? I'm the guy you just talked to on the radio. These are my friends." There was some shuffling, then a latching sound came from the other side, and the doors mechanically opened to reveal a disheveled but beautiful Asian-looking woman standing on the other side. She slammed into Jake and hugged him.

"Oh, thank you, thank you, thank you," she sighed. "I thought we were going to die in there."

"My name is Jake. You're gonna be alright. You're safe with us. Where's your partner?"

"Colonel Cannaveral. My supervisor. He's right over there. On the ground. Ray?" she called. "Ray, can you hear me? People are here. Tell me you have some water," she said, looking at me. "We haven't had anything for I don't know how long," said Wendy. I had brought the bottle I had been sipping on with me out of nervous habit. I handed it to her. She grabbed it and gulped half down immediately.

"Thank you," she gasped. "Ray, take some of this."

On the ground lay an older man in uniform. He looked to be in his fifties, maybe older, with a tight military haircut tinged slightly with grey. He was wearing glasses and a camouflaged top and bottom set that Jake would later tell me were his BDU's, or "battle dress uniform." Jake told me that the military had used BDU's from the 1980's to the early 2000's, then replaced them mostly with digital style camouflage. Ray took the bottle from Wendy and sipped it slowly. He was in bad shape and looked weak. The water instantly revived him. He gulped down the rest of the bottle, took a deep breath, and sat up on the floor.

"Thank you," he said. "You saved our lives. But if you don't want your efforts wasted, we need to get out of here, fast."

CHAPTER 9

Wendy, the Colonel, and the Flock

J ake and Glen helped the Colonel up to his feet. He was
wobbly. He had already downed the water and was trying
to straighten the wire rimmed glasses on his face.

"What do you mean, Colonel?" asked Jake.

"I'll explain once we're moving," said the Colonel. He
was beginning to get his legs back as we walked. Wendy led.

"How far away are you parked?" asked Wendy nervously.

"Right outside," I answered. "It's a school bus."

"Thank God," she said. They both got on the bus,
which was still running. They grabbed the first couple of seats
and plopped down. The rest of us filed in quickly and found
seats.

"Go. Now," said the Colonel.

Jake hopped into the driver's seat and zoomed out.
Wendy and the Colonel looked around nervously as we moved.
Jake didn't spare the horses. He was taking curves quickly and
headed back towards the entrance we had come in. He didn't
know what it was that the Colonel was afraid of, but he knew
fear when he heard it, and drove accordingly. He turned left
hard and we looked up at the gate we had crashed through.

There were people there. Sort of.

They were moving around strangely, almost like apes, occasionally using their hands to touch the ground. And they were orange.

"What the hell are those?" asked Al.

"Don't stop," said the Colonel. "Run through them if you have to."

Jake revved the engine and the bus started to accelerate quickly. It was one of the newer, automatic transmission busses that the school system had now. The orange colored people were starting to move towards us. Their hair was white, those that had hair at all, and their skin was a bright metallic orange. Their clothes were fairly tattered. Some had shoes, some did not. Jake turned to the Colonel.

"Through them, sir?" asked Jake.

"Through them," the Colonel answered. Jake bore down once more and winced. We could hear the sound of the bodies bouncing off the bus, like hitting a herd of deer. Bodies flew out of the way.

"*Díos mío*," shouted Estela.

"Oh my God," echoed Maureen, almost simultaneously.

"Hold on," yelled Jake. The bus slammed into what was left of the gate. The metal scraping on metal sound returned and made my spine hurt to hear it. Jake bounced the bus onto Shookstown Road and headed towards Route 15. He exhaled audibly as we pulled onto the ramp.

"Whew," exhaled Jake. "Eddie. Go into the back and grab our new guests something to eat and drink, would you?" Wendy looked up thankfully. The Colonel kept his stoic gaze forward. I found some granola bars and some bottled water.

"Thank you," said the Colonel.

"Mmm," said Wendy biting in with eyes closed, savoring every morsel. "God that's good. Thank you so much. We haven't had anything for days. This is heaven."

Both of them munched through the granola bars and downed the water in short time. Nobody spoke while they ate. Jake steered the bus along Route 15, looking for the exit to Interstate 70 West, then took it as the bus picked up speed. We were still the only vehicle on the highway. The silence started to become awkward, and never enjoying awkwardness, I piped up.

"So I'm Eduardo, this is Al, Maureen, and Estela. Those two young folks back there are Glen and Jada." Al nodded, Maureen waved, Estela smiled weakly, and the students barely looked up, as they were obviously talking about what Glen had seen on the trip inside Fort Detrick.

"It's nice to meet you all," said Wendy. "Where are you from?"

"Most of us work—er, worked, rather—or went to school at Hunter's Run High School, just outside Emmitsburg. Estela worked at the Wal-Mart next door."

"What brings you all this way?" asked Wendy. "That's a good half hour West, and you're all on a school bus?"

"Jake—that's Jake, driving, by the way—is headed south to find his sons at college. We're tagging along. We all got stuck at the school after—after the bombing began. We met Estela when we ventured out to find provisions," I said.

"I'm surprised you didn't stay at the school," said the Colonel. "That's a big, safe space. Very secure."

"We had, uh, a difference of opinion with some of the other folks we were sharing the school with. We decided to join Jake," I added.

"Hmm," said the Colonel, pursing his lips. He looked at Jake for a moment. Jake's tight hair cut and broad shoulders must have looked familiar. "You ever in the military, Jake?" he asked.

"Yes sir," said Jake. "Marine Corps. Iraq and Kuwait. Recon."

"Recon, huh? You must be fairly tough, then, son."

"Not as tough as I used to be, sir," said Jake. The Colonel smiled just barely.

"So what—or who—were those things we saw at the gate, sir?" asked Jake. It was the question everyone had on their minds, but no one wanted to ask. The Colonel stiffened up.

"I'm not sure I can tell you, son," he said. "It's classified, for one, and for two—I'm one of the few people alive who can answer that right now."

"All due respect, sir, some of those rules are out the window now," said Jake. "I'm not even sure we have a government at the moment. Nobody knows where the president is. Power's out. Internet's out. Nothing on the radio. Nobody on the roads at all. Heard nothing for several days. I'm not really sure what we're facing. I don't think anybody is. But if I have to face those things again, I'd sure as hell like to know more than I do right now."

"We have to tell them, Ray," said Wendy.

"Wendy, you're a civilian. You don't understand," said the Colonel.

"We have to tell them," she repeated. "This isn't about civilians and military anymore. It isn't even about being American anymore. This is, God, I don't know what this is. Either you tell them or I will," she said. Colonel Ray Cannaveral tightened his jaw, pushed out his bottom lip, and considered his actions.

"We are part of the U.S. Military's biological and chemical weapons defense team," said Wendy. "Fort Detrick used to make biological weapons originally, but the past few decades we have focused on defending against them. Most of the things that are scariest, we focus on them. The public doesn't even know most of them exist, because we've neutralized them before they ever get noticed. And then keep it to ourselves and don't release news of any of it to the public."

"Wendy," the Colonel interrupted.

"No, Ray. They need to know. Everything's changed," she said. "We had been hearing that several countries were working on ways to weaponize the Ebola virus. To make it into something that can be contracted through airborne means."

"I didn't think Hemorrhagic Fever could be contacted through the air," said Al.

"It can't, or at least we'd never found examples of it passing through the air in any primates. Until now," she said.

"What? Oh my God," I shouted. "Airborne Ebola?"

"Not quite. It's a synthesized strain, engineered genetically from a North Korean lab. It very nearly mimics Ebola in every way that counts."

"North Korea," whispered Maureen. "God damn."

"Airborne Ebola? Are you kidding me? It would wipe out an entire country," I said incredulously. "Fast."

"Pretty much," said Wendy. "Normally, somewhere between 85 and 90 percent of infected victims die, usually of internal bleeding or of some kind of organ failure within a few days," said Wendy. "Untreated that number is very close to 100 percent. With this stuff, though, it's quicker and more deadly."

"So, is that your area of expertise?" asked Al. "Diseases?"

"Yes," Wendy answered. "I'm from NIH. The CDC and the National Institute of Health have been working with the military at Fort Detrick to monitor and combat any attempts at using the Ebola virus as a weapon. Usually third world countries who do it use insects or animals to transmit it."

"You're kidding me," said Maureen. "Countries have been doing this? How? They just send infected animals on Federal Express and then turn them loose?"

"Not quite, but not far from it. Some of the more ruthless warlords in small African territories send trucks full of apes and monkeys and have soldiers release them into major target areas."

"Jesus," said Estela. "That's inhuman."

"It gets worse," said Wendy. "The Russians."

"Oh shit, Russians," I said. "What did they do?"

Wendy looked over at the Colonel. She cocked her head and stared at him for ten silent seconds or so.

"Wendy," he said. "I just don't feel we ought to." Wendy frowned at him. "Ray, look around. Do you see anything left of the fort? Anyone we even know? I understand your protocols. I have to adhere to lots of them myself. But without these people we're not even alive right now. Don't we owe them a little information?" she said. He took a deep breath, looked around, and spoke.

"The Russians were working on a way to use radiation sickness as a weapon. Current methods involving nuclear weapons are a bit unwieldy, and we actually agreed to reduce stockpiles of them along with the Russians near the end of the Cold War," said the Colonel.

"They actually complied with that? Did we? I thought that was all bullshit," I said.

"Both sides actually did reduce their stockpiles. Nukes themselves are an endgame. Governments prefer smaller battles to World Wars. Well, at least they did for a while," said the Colonel.
"Blowing things to smithereens also has its downside. You have to rebuild. The Russians want to win the war by maximizing human casualties while minimizing infrastructure damage. They want to move in and take over."

"Damn," I said. "Maximize human casualties."

"Makes sense," said Jake. "Instead of flipping the house, you move in turnkey style."

I looked at Wendy and the Colonel as they spoke. They were dehydrated and energy-depleted. Whatever they had been fighting or avoiding the past several days had worn on them. As they drank the water and ate the granola bars, you could see the strength coming back to them. As we spoke, I looked out the window to see where we were. Jake had passed Hagerstown, Maryland and had merged onto Interstate 81 south. We were nearing Berkley Springs, West Virginia, and headed south towards Virginia. The landscapes went from bleak to somewhat picturesque. I wondered if the people here were in anywhere near the conditions we found in Frederick.

Being a science guy, Al DeFillipo was peppering Wendy and the Colonel with questions about the particulars of what they were working on. "So how were the Russians going to use radiation on a massive scale without using nuclear bombs?" asked Al. "I mean, isn't it a side effect of the explosion? That would be the method of release, right?"

"It was until very recently. Then they developed a new element. They call it Brenerium, after the scientist who made it, Andrey Brener. It's completely unstable. It holds together for a short time, then it explodes into a more slowly decaying isotope. They were hoping to create a mega-bomb with it, but what they got instead was a delivery system for a succinct acute radiation poisoning."

"I've never heard of it. Brenerium?" said Al.

"Nobody has. It's brand new. We barely know anything as it is. But Brenerium keeps breaking down farther and farther into other elements, or isotopes of elements. As a result, it is quickly absorbed in the skin, taking other things with it. It actually affects cell permeability. I don't think the Russians knew what they had, until," the Colonel paused.

"Until they started working with North Korea. They combined it with engineered Ebola," said Wendy.

"Dear God," said Al. "Radiation that continues to break down cell membranes and brings a virus with it?"

"That's the short version, but yes. That's essentially it," said the Colonel.

"How the fuck is anyone or anything still alive with something like that in the air?" asked Maureen.

"Because it doesn't stay in the air long," said Wendy. "It's pretty unstable. It breaks down more and more. The part that is able to utilize the Ebola virus is very short-lived. After that, the virus itself just takes over and does the dirty work. Most people die within hours. But not everyone who contracts Ebola actually dies from it. A small percentage of people are naturally immune, and about twenty percent of the entire population can defeat it within a day or two just because of their DNA make-up."

"So, what were those people, things we saw at the gate?" asked Jake.

"Those people who don't die of the virus were those producing enough antibodies in their systems to hold it off. We think that those antibodies were strengthened by their contact with Livermorium," said the Colonel.

"What's Livermorium?" I asked. "Never heard of that either."

"It's one of the slightly more stable elements that Brenerium breaks down into. It first breaks into the Oganneson element, Ununoctium. Yuri Oganessian came up with that one, and for a while it was considered the heaviest element on earth. Folks believed that it was actually a metal, and shared some traits with the noble gasses."

"Okay, so most of that stuff is so way over my head it's not worth mentioning. Noble gases, though, I remember those from high school chemistry. Like neon, argon, stuff like that, right?" I answered.

"Yes," said Wendy. "But it existed for such a short time and under such strained synthetic conditions, that the scientific community waffled on it for a while. One group supposedly created it in a lab in California, but they were found to have been a fraud."

"You're losing me," said Maureen. "Not a science geek. Stick with basic English. Why is all this important again?"

"Because the radiation from Livermorium affected those people with antibodies in a strange way. It protected them from contracting the Ebola virus, but it altered them greatly," said the Colonel.

"Altered?" I asked.

"Turned them somehow into something that acted like lesser primates. Maybe even more primitive than that."

"We tried to do a brain scan on one of them, but results were inconclusive," said the Colonel.

"Inconclusive to you," said Wendy. "I'm sticking with my conclusion."

"Which was what?" asked Jake.

"Their frontal lobes essentially were rendered inactive. They followed only the limbic system."

"Limbic system? You mean, they're mentally like, lizards?" asked Al.

"No, they're not lizards," said the Colonel.

"Effectively, yes," interrupted Wendy. They will behave like reptiles and amphibians. No higher brain function. Instinctual actions only."

"And their orange skin?" asked Jake.

"A product of the isotope or the mutation from the radiation, we believe," said the Colonel.

"So, let me get this straight," Jake said. "Wherever one of these bombs goes off, the entire area is momentarily blanketed with radiation and Ebola. Most people contract and die of the Ebola, but the ones who don't revert to some kind of orange reptilian-brained creature? Have I got that right?"

Wendy and the Colonel turned to look at each other silently for a moment. "Yes," they said in unison.

"And from what we can tell, an even smaller percentage of them are affected less. Those two you saw standing upright, with good heads of hair? They seem to be the leaders. They direct the ones who walk on all fours. I'm betting if we could get a brain scan on them, we'd find something very different. Something more human, like us."

"Jesus," said Jake. "And they formed a hierarchy in a span of only a few days? Are they violent?"

"Yes," said the Colonel. "They came after us after day two. We presumed that their intentions were--less than honorable. Some of our colleagues tried to run and were captured and killed. We were able to lock ourselves back in the lab building, and they couldn't get in. But they beat on the doors nearly all day."

"Dear God," said Maureen. "And you locked yourselves in with no food or water,"

"We split a cup of coffee and some gum on the first day after the bombings. We haven't had anything since," said Wendy. "Do you have any more of these bars?"

"I gotcha," I said, and went to the back to grab two more.

"So, let me ask you this," said Jake. "Why aren't you two affected at all? Why aren't you dead or orange?"

"Lead again," said the Colonel.

"Lead?" I echoed.

"The walls of the entire portion of the building we work in are lined with lead. The most stable form of that radioactive material—Ununoctium--can't penetrate lead. I'm guessing anyone who had some kind of lead walls or even old school illegal lead-based paint might have avoided all of this," said Wendy. "Which brings me to my question: how are all of you alive? Those bombs leveled everything from Frederick to Washington. What protected you?"

"I think I can answer that, Wendy," said the Colonel. "You said you came from Emmitsburg, right?"

"That's right," I said.

"East of Camp David?"

"Yes, why?"

"Camp David, upon hearing of the dangers of Brenerium, began installing lead projecting ordnance as a counter measure."

"Lead projecting ordnance? What does that mean?" I asked.

"It means that the president set off a shit-ton of lead-spraying bombs into the air around Camp David," said Jake. "Probably some went off every time an enemy attack came close by, effectively creating a kind of temporary lead force field that the effects of the Brenerium bombs couldn't penetrate. That wall must have been enough to shield us from the radiation. That about right Colonel?"

"In a nutshell," he answered. "That would be my

guess. But the president didn't set them off."

"How do you know?" Jake asked.

"Because the president isn't at Camp David," said the Colonel. "He's airborne."

"Airborne?" I cut in. "Is he crazy? Who goes up in a plane when missiles and bombs are flying around everywhere?"

"Intelligent people," said Jake.

"What? What are you talking about, Jake?" I countered.

"Same idea as steering a ship out to sea in a storm," Jake said.

"Which is just as crazy," I countered.

"Not really," said Jake. "Boats are built to withstand waves. And boats with deep keels can even withstand very high waves. But boats or ships near the shoreline can get battered and smashed onto beaches, reefs, and rocks. Better to be out to sea in a storm."

"He's right," said the Colonel. "Same idea with being airborne during missile launches and bomb drops. Truly less of a chance of being hit with anything that high in the air."

"Well if that's the case," I said. "If the president isn't at Camp David," why bother with all of those, whaddayacallem, counter measures?"

"Somebody IS at Camp David. Not sure exactly who. Vice President. Secretary of State, or Defense, maybe. Someone important, though, to use that lead shield," said the Colonel.

"Pretty freaking lucky, and kind of amazing when you think about it," I said. "We live in the one place that can help us by being a major target."

"More like right place, right time," Jake said.

"I need to get to Washington, son" said the Colonel.

"Are you crazy, Ray? It'll be the worst there, of all places," said Wendy.

"I need to get this intel—that you just helped spread to civilians who aren't cleared for that kind of classified information—to someone who can actually use it."

"Sorry Colonel, but we're not going to Washington," said Jake. I looked out the window and saw that we were coming up on Winchester, Virginia. Wendy and the Colonel had been with us for about 40 minutes. We had covered some serious ground in that time period.

"You don't understand son, this thing is going to be of epidemic proportion," the Colonel snapped.

"It already is, Colonel," said Al. We haven't seen a person anywhere other than you two. And those things. I think most people died from the bombings."

"Well if we made it, and you all made it, I'm banking that some part of Washington made it," said the Colonel.

"I'm not sure how much Washington there is left at all," said Jake. "And if there is anything left, I'm not sure how safe it is approaching it. Assuming that communications are knocked out, just how do you plan to find anyone who might be able to utilize that information?"

The Colonel didn't answer. He pursed his lips a moment and shook his head ever so slightly.

"You're right. Wait—Colonel--how about Camp David? Someone's going to be there," I said.

"That place was locked down with tanks, Eddie. Every access road was blocked miles in every direction. You wouldn't get close," said Jake.

"They'd let me in," Colonel Cannaveral said. "Besides, Camp David is on the way to Site R. That's really where I ought to be."

"Site R?" I asked. "What's site R?"

"Raven Rock Mountain Complex," said the Colonel. "In Blue Ridge Summit, Pennsylvania. Just north of Camp David. It is essentially the underground Pentagon. Many of the big heads will be there. They could use my information there. Can you turn around, son? Take me back that way?"

"That's an hour in the wrong direction, Colonel," said Jake. "We are headed south. I am collecting my sons."

"I understand that, Marine," he said. "But I can't just sit on this information. Someone has got to be out there."

"Have you tried calling?" I asked. Everyone suddenly looked at their phones. The Colonel fumbled through his pockets to no avail.

"Oh no," he said. "No, no, no, no!"

"What's wrong, Colonel?" I asked.

"My phone," he said. "I must have left it in Fort Detrick. In the lab. In all the confusion."

"Does anyone else's phone work?" I yelled. "Mine seems to be getting some through," said Al.

"I can't. That number is classified. I don't have it memorized on the top of my head, you know," said the Colonel. "And you can't just Google it and look for the white pages. Wendy? Do you have yours?" he asked.

She shook her head. "No, me neither. But I don't have information on Site R anyway, Ray. I'm civilian." He nodded hopelessly.

"No chance you'd turn around, Marine?" asked the Colonel.

"The mission is a rescue, sir. And that's priority."

"Wish we knew more about where people sought shelter. What's going on," I said.

"Shelter. That might be the answer. Where'd you say you were going again?" the Colonel asked.

"Shenandoah Valley. Lexington, Virginia first. Then Blacksburg. Why?"

"Interstate 64 goes through Lexington, doesn't it?" asked the Colonel.

"I-64?" I said. It doesn't go anywhere. It starts in Virginia Beach, then just heads west."

"Sure does. Straight to Greenbrier, West Virginia," Jake said with a smile.

"My thoughts exactly," said the Colonel. "Can you get me there?"

"Greenbriar?" asked Estela. "What's Greenbriar?"

"Waitaminute," I interrupted. "You guys are talking about that secret emergency Congressional bunker, aren't you? It's not a secret anymore. They actually give tours through it now. I've seen the video on You Tube. They wouldn't go there. Everybody knows about it."

"That just means it's not secret," said Jake. "Doesn't mean it's not functional. There's a 15-ton blast door on that thing. It's already built. Already ready. Who cares if people know about it? Besides, if everyone is thinking like you, it makes even more sense."

"Hide in plain sight. Well, sort of," said the Colonel. "I know that some of the higher ups were directed there. Maybe someone there can help."

"That's a hell of a little detour," said Jake. "But how about after I've snagged my boys, Colonel?"

"How could we not?" said Al.

The sun was shining brightly in Emmitsburg. Hunter's Run High School was warm, bright, and the people in it were well-rested and content. The females of the group were cleaning up after brunch. Wes Kent was in the principal's office with his feet propped up on the desk. He had removed the name plate underneath the small "Principal" sign. Mark Long-aberger sat in a chair nearby.

"Any regrets, Mark?" said Wes.

"Not really," said Mark. "We're of the same mind on all of the things that went down. I agreed with you at first about the Heffners. We needed more information before letting them in. Everyone was panicking, like it was some kind of horror movie. Like if we didn't let them in immediately, some creature was just going to come up and snatch them up right in front of us. I just thought we didn't need to react too quickly. Try to find a way to see about the danger before we endangered anybody else."

"Exactly," said Wes. "And that bleeding-heart Jake Fisher wanted to put us all at risk." Longaberger pursed his lips and nodded faintly.

"And I even give him credit for what he did to those marauders. It was brutal, but he saved the Heffners' lives. But the whole, 'display the dead bodies thing' seemed a little over the top."

"Medieval," said Wes. "Unnecessary. It's not like that's going to keep people like that away. Those people that attacked the Heffners were animals. It's in their nature. Dead bodies won't scare them. Gangbangers are used to that kind of thing. It's what separates them from us. Jake Fisher is one of those modern soldiers who thinks blood and guts solves everything."

"Yeah, I guess so," said Mark. "I just thought it was an indecent thing to do, even to those thugs."

"They're not people, really," said Wes. "But we are. Our flock here can't be expected to behave like Fisher did."

"Flock?" said Mark.

"Just a term from church," said Wes. "Our group, if you prefer."

"Sure. Whatever," said Mark. "Anyway, we agree on that too."

"Good to hear," said Wes.

"Finally, his actions at the Wal Mart," said Mark. "That just seemed to seal the deal that he wasn't the right one to lead us."

"Definitely not," said Wes. "He brought that Mexican woman back with him. She threatened us with a gun! We don't want those kind of people here."

"I just don't like it that he was the *defacto* leader," said Longaberger. "He decided who would go on the hike to Wal Mart, he tried to decide all of those other things for us. I mean, who elected him king? We still believe in democracy, right? We can't just let him lead just because he was in the military.

That's not, not American."

"Not American. Exactly. And neither was that woman he brought back," said Wes. "And neither is Eduardo Reyes. We can't trust people who aren't American, Mark. It's all we have left now. Keeping the faith. Not knowing where the world is going after this catastrophe, it's up to us to keep the faith. God wants us to keep America alive."

Mark shifted uncomfortably in his chair.

"God?" said Mark.

"Of course, son," said Wes. "God. God was here when the USA was started. He sent the Pilgrims, he inspired the Declaration of Independence and the Constitution, and though we've had some rough spots over the years when we abandoned him, we were finally headed back in the right direction, then the liberals got into power."

"Hey, I'm a Republican," said Mark.

"Of course you are," said Wes. "You have some sense. You're from a proper upbringing. Those people Fisher was with. They're the reason our country went to Hell. They're the reason we got bombed."

Longaberger scrunched his face up a little. He swiveled his chair a bit. "Not sure I follow you on that, Wes."

"Gays. Immigrants. Fornicators. It's no wonder other countries find us disgusting and want to bomb us," he said.

"Um, I think it might have been other reasons," said Mark. "Political ones."

"Of course. It's political. We're the USA, so everybody wants to bring down the top dog. I'm just saying that it's not surprising that things went as south as they did, given the course we've been on. I mean, it's in the scriptures."

"Scriptures?" asked Mark.

"You believe in God, don't you son?" asked Wes.

"Well, yeah, of course. But, I mean, there's a lot of room for interpretation," said Mark.

"That's what the liberals want you to believe, Mark.

That way they can press their agendas on you. They ignore the blatant wording about sodomy and abortion, and focus on the unconditional love part. Of course they would. They pick and choose their wording of the Bible. Don't fall into their trap."

"Sodomy and abortion?" asked Mark.

"Do you know any other ways gays have sex?" asked Wes.

"I think we're digressing a little, Wes. I'm not an authority on gay sex. I don't pretend to be that big an authority on the Bible. I teach history and political science. I know a lot of history, and much of the Bible involves documented historical events, but I think there's more to it than that."

"Of course there is. Word of God. It's more than history. Glad we agree on that," said Wes.

Lou Orville entered the principal's office and nodded to Mark. Mark nodded back.

"Lou! How are you feeling, my boy? Did you get some ice on that noggin of yours? The ladies said we still had plenty of ice, and I think medical use precludes everything else," said Wes.

"Yeah, Wes. It's better. Thanks. Melanie sent me to tell you that she's got a notebook written now with everybody's name and some personal information about everyone who's still here, just like you requested," Lou said.

"Fantastic. Thanks, lad. Let me take a look at that bump," said Wes. Lou parted his hair and displayed a lump on his skull, swollen to the size of a half dollar.

"Ouch," said Wes. "Reminds me of a goose egg I got one time after I got hit by a golf ball. Either of you two play golf?" Lou nodded; Mark shrugged as if to say 'a little.'

"I play at the country club all the time," said Wes. "And before you ask me how I afford it as a teacher, the wife's family has the money. They gave us lifetime memberships as a wedding present."

"I play with some of the football coaches," said Lou. "Well, I mean, I used to." The mood went somber quickly, as each of the faces in the room deflated a little with a reminder of their current situation.

"Now don't you worry, Lou," said Wes. "We're all going to get out of this alright. Things might be tough, but America will rebound, and we'll rebuild it better than ever."

Mark smiled at Wes's enthusiasm, and nodded in agreement. "Yes, yes we will," he said. It was Wes Kent's enthusiasm that had attracted Mark to his side in the first place, along with what seemed like his own natural rivalry with Jake Fisher. Fisher had always been such a realist, seemed so cynical, so quick to assume the worst in people in a crisis. He also thought Fisher was a bit of a bully. He always did whatever he wanted, and others just seemed to gravitate towards that, and it always drove Mark crazy. Fisher was the department chair, always throwing his authority around. Why should Fisher get all of the popularity and attention? Mark felt that he was just as smart. Probably smarter. He was glad to see someone put Fisher in his place. Wes was more upbeat than Jake anyway. Some of his religious ideas seemed a little out there, but it was kind of par for this area.

Western Maryland—from Carroll County just south of Gettysburg, all the way out to Deep Creek Lake on the West Virginia border—was always very conservative. Lots of Christian right in this region of what had always been generally a very liberal blue state. Mark had been raised by old time conservatives who liked the idea of small government, fewer taxes, and people taking care of themselves. So naturally, he often voted for the same people Wes did. He could do without Wes' sermonizing, but he figured that it was because Wes was so much older than he was. Older people always like to preach. They seemed to act like they'd earned the right to be heard just because they had lived longer. At twenty-nine years of age, Mark was at the peak of his own physical health. Decently built, good-looking, intelligent. He felt that some of the old guard power brokers in the school really didn't deserve all of the influence they swung around. At least Wes Kent was giving pep talks and avoiding the rash actions of a Jake Fisher.

Fisher's actual departure, however, was a bit of a surprise. When Wes had proposed different leadership while Jake, Eddie Reyes, and Lou had gone to Wal Mart, Mark was all for it. He saw his chance to move to the forefront, even if it meant hitching his wagon to Wes Kent to get it. He and Wes agreed on a number of things, which was what he had been trying to say before Lou walked in. He had not imagined that Wes would suggest Fisher leave. That seemed extreme, considering the harsh conditions of the outside world. But before he could moderate that stance, Fisher had agreed and left on his own. Since then he'd been trying to convince himself all of it was going to happen that way anyway, and that things had worked out. Then Wes started preaching, which always made him a bit uncomfortable. But Wes's optimism was contagious, and he felt better about everything that had happened now.

"Wes, I have that list you wanted," said Melanie Richmond, walking towards the office.

"Thanks Melanie," said Wes. "Lou told me you'd finished. This will be a big help in getting to know everyone here. How on Earth did you accomplish it this fast?"

"I just spoke with everyone while we were eating brunch. Told them that we all wanted to get to know each other better and learn things about one another. Most people were eager to talk. Just having conversations again about anything besides the state of the world. I think they liked that," she said.

"Of course they did," said Wes. "That was the idea. Thanks so much," he said, taking the notebook. "I'm going to get to work on this right now," he said. "I need to study up on people. See what we're working with here."

He leaned back in the tall, black, padded office chair and propped his feet up on the desk again.

"This will give me a place to start from while talking

with these folks," he said. "Get to know our flock better."

Flock, thought Mark. There's that word again.

"You ever been on a farm, Lou?" asked Wes.

"Yeah," said Lou. "My family had some sheep when I was little. We sold the farm before I got into high school though. Why do you ask?"

"My grandfather owned several cattle ranches. Just wondering if you understand the concept of 'thinning the herd.' Sometimes you have to thin the herd to ensure their survival. Remove undesirables from the general flock, to make sure their overall health is secure."

"Yeah," said Lou. "My dad used to say that too. Why do you ask?"

"Our flock here got thinner with the departure of Jake Fisher and his undesirables. We're now stronger because of it. I just want to make sure we don't need to thin the herd a bit more," said Wes. "This notebook will help me get a much better handle on that."

Mark stirred in his seat uncomfortably again.

CHAPTER 10

Lexington

H ow much further until Lexington?" I asked. "Are we close?"

"Yes," said Jake. "About five miles now."

We had driven past large towns and one small city. I was insanely curious about who was alive, where people might be, if any of those orange things we saw were anywhere else-- but Jake was driving like a man possessed. There was absolutely no one else on the highway, which was eerie. Maureen would comment every now and then about a restaurant that she and her ex had eaten in, or a town they had visited on the way to some baseball stadium in the minor leagues. Then she would comment about wondering if he had been secretly visiting girlfriends there when she wasn't around, get morose, and shut down for a few minutes. Al was there to console her. They seemed to have moved past whatever awkwardness they had been feeling from whatever rendezvous they had previously had. Jada and Glen were holding hands a lot also—the only teenagers around. Glen was a senior, Jada a freshman— which, under ordinary circumstances might have been a little awkward—but Jada looked like an adult, and according to Glen, she was a year older than most freshman at fifteen, and Glen, while built like a Mack truck, was a youngish senior.

Estela had quieted down herself as well. We would talk in Spanish every now and then, but she seemed as if she might be regretting her decision to come along. I'm not sure how she would have fared back in Emmitsburg alone, though. Maybe being an immigrant these days is tougher than I realize. It's ironic, because everyone presumes that I'm an immigrant based on how I look. I am clearly Hispanic, and I do speak Spanish, but I was born in the U.S. to two people with advanced graduate degrees, so my experience here was nothing like Estela's. At least, that's what I was presuming. She wasn't opening up. Not yet at least. But I hoped to get her to talk a little more about herself soon.

The Colonel was coming back to life and becoming more animated. He must have really been in bad shape. He had downed four bottles of water and eaten three granola bars. Ordinarily in survival situations, that might raise some red flags, but we all agreed that these were exceptional circumstances. The Colonel was telling us a little about the workings of Fort Detrick. He was very careful, however, not to divulge anything even remotely classified. As it turned out, Col. Raymond Cannaveral was in his sixties, in very good shape for someone his age, with a tightly-cropped military haircut and wire-rimmed glasses. He was friendly, if a bit stiff, and was awkwardly dyed-in-the-wool Army all the way. For him, the answer to every possible challenge was the Army field guide.

Wendy, on the other hand, could not seem to get enough of Jake. She too, had recovered like Ray, but she had not seemed quite as affected by starvation and dehydration as her boss. She had moved to the front of the bus to talk with Jake and was spilling her entire life story to him. She was immediately pretty for a woman of her age, which seemed to be in the early forties. She had long black hair, had a thin, athletic body, beautiful skin, and expressive eyes. She was clearly Asian in background, but with softened, rounded facial features. We discovered that was because her mother was a white American woman who had met her father on a student exchange program in Japan. Dad had taken a great deal of heat at home for falling in love with and marrying a *Gaijin*—essentially a foreign white person—and they had moved to the states to make a life in Washington.

Wendy had been a hundred different things in a hundred different places and had a hundred different jobs. The conversation she was having with Jake was a punch-counter-punch between world travelers who had done unusual things. Each time Jake casually mentioned an experience he'd had, Wendy would identify with a similar one of her own. It was clear that they were mutually interested in what the other had to say. They had been chatting for almost three hours now. I had been listening in, since the others had paired off or shut down. I found Wendy fascinating, and thought anyone would have been attracted to her. She was almost too good to be true. At any rate, Jake was smiling, talking, and speeding like a madman on interstate 81, and we were approaching our destination.

"The exit to I-64 is coming up, Marine," said the Colonel.

"I know Colonel, but I'm going to get my boy first. He's only a couple of miles ahead at VMI."

The Colonel frowned slightly. "I was hoping to get this information to someone soon, son. Didn't want to dilly-dally with so much at stake," said Ray.

"All due respect sir, but this is my trip. I'm not gonna come within a couple of miles of half of my reason for coming here and then drive an hour out of my way to West Virginia," said Jake.

"Seriously, Ray. This is his son," said Wendy admonishingly. The Colonel gave a mild scowl at the rebuke.

As we exited the highway and got onto Route 11, an incredibly scenic road in Virginia akin to the famed Route 66 out West, the greenery exploded and the hills appeared. Vibrantly green fields rolled to either side, trees abounded, and houses began to look more and more like Southern mansions.

It was gorgeous down here. Not that different really from Emmitsburg, but somehow cleaner, classier, and more historic. As we got closer to Lexington, we saw something we had not seen the entire trip.

Life.

People were walking on the street, heading to the grocery store, buying gas, living life. This town did not seem to have been affected in any way. Suddenly I wondered if we had stopped in Harrisonburg or Staunton if we would have seen the same thing. Jake slowed, and everyone's mouths seemed to drop a little.

"There's people everywhere," said Glen. "It's like... normal here."

The excitement was a little contagious. Considering what the people on our bus had been through the last several days, this type of normalcy was almost shocking.

"We need fuel," said Jake. "I'm pulling in."

Jake got out, opened the bus doors, and everyone rushed out into the fresh air. People stared at us. We must have looked strange, taking in deep gulps of air and looking around with fresh eyes. Lexington was a small town, but populated enough to be a complete one. There were two colleges there: Washington & Lee University, and Virginia Military Institute. It was also a historic place in terms of the Civil War, so there was enough commerce along Route 11 for things to seem very different from the places we had just left.

"Shit," Jake said, with a gas hose in his hands. "I didn't think of this."

"What is it?" I asked.

"We need fuel, but I don't have any money. Just credit cards. And in a world with no electricity or internet..."

"Look around, Jake. These people have electricity. Hell, they might even have internet," I said. "Why don't we ask them?"

I walked inside the station where a grizzled old southern man was waiting behind a counter. Off to the side, distinct smells of bacon and gravy were wafting heavily in the air, and a couple of tables sat in front of a large grill on one side of the station.

"Howdy. May I help y'all?" asked the man.

"Yes, thanks," I answered. "We're coming from up north a little ways, and we didn't have electricity there, and you all seem to have it. Are you able to take credit cards to pay for things?"

"Kinda depends on the card. Some have, some haven't. Guessin' it has to do with what city the banks have all their computers and such as to whether they work. It's been hit or miss the past few days. We heard tell of all the trouble, bombs and all. Thank God none of that happened here. Guess the country's gonna be tryin' to climb back out over the next year or so," said the man.

"Um, so what do we do if none of our cards work?" I asked.

The man grinned a gap-toothed smile, reached down to a shelf behind the counter, and pulled out a small imprint machine and slapped it down in front of me.

"You're probably not old enough to know what this is, young feller, but this is what we used in my time. It still works. You gotta mail the slips in, but they transfer the money eventually."

"But, are you sure that's gonna happen...now?" I asked.

"That's what credit is, sonny. It's people trustin' that eventually they'll make good on what they owe. 'Round here for years, we'd buy stuff on nothin' more than a feller's word, and at the end of the month he'd pay what he could. Then credit cards and computers changed all that. Now all it takes is a good blackout for us to go right back to 'em. Your generation ain't as trustin' as mine. Maybe that's a good thing," he said. "Anyway, go get y'all's gas, and bring y'all's card back if it don't work out there and we'll take care of you."

I gave Jake the thumbs up and he started putting diesel fuel into the bus. We hadn't used as much as I thought we might, but the bus was shorter than the normal size. It was one used for transporting Life Skills and Autistic kids to the local ARC after school. The Association for Retarded Citizens was a haven for those kids, helping to find them work, helping their families adapt to their children moving on after high school, and being supportive in general to as much mainstreaming as possible. I felt a little guilty that we had taken their bus, but as Jake pointed out, whoever had been driving it had left it wide open with keys dangling, and with the current state of things, it would be a while before it was missed—if it was even missed at all.

"Here's your receipt, young man," said the attendant, leaning past the counter to give it to me.

"What are things like up north?" he said. "We don't hear much. Nobody seems to have land lines anymore except for businesses. I tried calling my sister in Fairfax at her job, but nobody's answering."

"I can't speak for Fairfax, but things up by us were pretty bad," I said. We were holed up in the high school where we work for a few days before our driver decided to come down and look for his son here at VMI, but the town had started falling apart. Power was off and on back home. There was looting, violence. Bad stuff. Those folks," I said pointing to Wendy and the Colonel, "they had it even worse. They were at Fort Detrick in Frederick. A lot of death in that city."

I decided not to mention the orange creatures at the moment. I wasn't even sure I believed my own eyes, and I certainly was having trouble processing the crazy tale told to us by our two guest riders.

"Well, you all take care. I hope your friend finds his son. VMI let their students head home, but there was a bunch of them that were staying on. I reckon your buddy's son is one of them I've been seeing when I ride by."

I thanked him, wished him well, and started to get back on the bus. I got an odd feeling of normalcy here.

I thought about the contrast of what life was like back in Maryland, and even some of the cities we saw on our way here, like Berkley Springs, West Virginia and Winchester, Virginia. Those places had not fared as well, and the streets and highways were deserted. This place seemed to be running like usual, almost oblivious to the national tragedy. It left me feeling a little unnerved. I grew up in an era where information was instant, easy to get, easy to transmit. There was so much not knowing now. Jake and the Colonel were older than the rest of us. They seemed to treat it as a nuisance, but one with which they were familiar. Everyone else on the bus just seemed a little lost.

"Okay folks, we ready?" said Jake. "VMI is just around the corner."

Jake put the bus in gear and pulled out onto the main drag and headed towards the center of town. We veered right off Route 11 onto Main Street, and almost instantly VMI rose up around us on either side. Large, stark grey-beige buildings with red and yellow signage surrounded the street. Barracks, athletic buildings, a football field, and the parade grounds were all visible from the main street. We rode under a footbridge that carried VMI's Keydets across it from the main part of campus on the right to the football fields and indoor gymnasiums on the left. We turned right and went up the hill toward the parade grounds. There were about a hundred college-aged students milling around, playing frisbee, lying on the grass. My first thought was it didn't look right. The campus looked like one great big fort, almost like a slightly newer Alamo that spread for several blocks. It did not look like a place for people to come for recreation. The kids on the field were all wearing VMI issued t-shirts, shorts, and sweatpants. The weather was nice. Jake looked at the scene and chuckled.

"They're not used to this," he said. "Huh Colonel?"

"I'd say not. I'd say they're making the most of a very rare time when there are little to no restrictions," he said.

"There's Tommy," said Jake, and he braked sharply

149

and popped out the door. Straight ahead, throwing a frisbee, was Jake's younger double. The kid looked just like his father, only much younger and taller. Dirty blonde hair, round face, squinty eyes, broad chest and shoulders and scrawny legs, Tommy Fisher even moved like his old man. When Jake got closer, though, it was obvious just how much taller Tommy was than his dad. Jake embraced him, hugging him hard, almost like a tackle. His head barely made it to Tommy's chest, which made him about 6'3" to Jake's 5'9" frame. He smiled, patted his father on the back, and the two exchanged a few sentences. Tommy then nodded, and ran towards the dorms, or barracks as they were called here, I supposed. Jake turned and limped his way back to the bus. His eyes were red.

"He's going to get a bag of stuff. He'll be right down. He's on the second floor," said Jake.

"There's not one female anywhere," said Maureen. "Is this place all male? I didn't think there were any more all male schools left."

"Not anymore," said the Colonel. "It was all male for over a hundred and fifty years, then they started taking women in the 1990's. There still aren't very many here. It's a rough life, especially for a plebe," he said.

"Rat," corrected Jake. "They call them Rats here, Colonel. The Rat line is one of the roughest places you'll ever encounter. It even rivals plebe summer at West Point." The Colonel looked dubious at that remark.

The big VMI Keydet hopped onto the bus and it shook noticeably when he entered. He cut an imposing figure, his head nearly grazing the roof. He looked around at the folks on the bus and smiled with recognition at a few faces.

"Miss Kelly, Mr. DeFillipo," he said, greeting former teachers. "*Señor Reyes, cómo está usted?*"

I shook his hand and nodded.

"What's up, Glen?" Glen smiled back and waved. He looked at Wendy and the Colonel and stiffened.

"Nice to meet you ma'am, sir. I'm Thomas Fisher."

He extended his hand to Wendy first, then the Colonel, and shook them each formally.

"In the army I see, Colonel. Hoo-ah."

"Hoo-ah, Keydet. You going in the army when you're done here, son?"

"Marines, sir. Like my dad. VMI has all four ROTC possibilities if you choose to go that Route. I'm on full ROTC scholarship here and will be commissioned a lieutenant in the Corps after I graduate."

"In that case, it's ooh-rah, son. Don't want to mess up a family tradition," the Colonel said.

"Ooh-rah, yes indeed sir. Thanks," he said. "Dad, where's Mom?"

The bus went silent immediately, and everyone from Hunter's Run High School lowered their eyes and didn't speak. Estela, Wendy, and the Colonel noticed immediately, and Tommy Fisher flushed.

"Dad," he said slowly, drawing it out, and turning to face his father. "Where's Mom?"

Jake swallowed hard. His breathed in shallowly, then looked his son in the eyes.

"I don't know, boy."

"What do you mean you don't know?" said Tommy, raising his voice.

"We were on the phone when the bombs were hitting. Then the phone just went dead."

With the word 'dead,' I winced. So did Maureen.

"I tried to call her. There's no answer. She was in Washington."

"And you didn't go after her?" said Tommy.

"Son, she was in Washington," said Jake.

"I don't give a fuck if she was in Moscow. You didn't even try?"

"Tommy don't talk to me like that. You don't know, you don't know what it's like there."

"I know that a Marine never leaves a fallen comrade

behind. But she wasn't your comrade, was she? Do you even care? Are you even worried?" Jake blanched at that. Tears were forming, and his face began to redden with anger. He got in Tommy's face and looked up.

"Now you listen, boy."

"Thomas," said the Colonel, "Washington was a hot zone, son. A hot zone. We have no way of knowing what happened there. EMP's dropped everywhere. There's no power in the entire surrounding area, as far north as Frederick. Communication is down, and no one knows anything. Your dad's first thought was getting to you, because you were in a place that wasn't affected. Your dad's a hero, son. He…"

"I know what my dad is, Sir. We hear about it all the time. What he did in Iraq. How great a wrestler he was. That's not the issue here. All due respect, I'm afraid you don't understand our family's…dynamic."

"No, son. I'm not talking about any of that. He's a hero *today.* He rescued me and my colleague there from dire circumstances at Fort Detrick. We're alive because of him. You need to cut him a break son. These are strange times right now," said the Colonel.

"Fine sir," said Tommy, and he went to the back of the bus and sat next to Glen and Jada.

I looked at Jake. He was crushed. Whatever had gone on between him and his wife, Laura, had spilled over into his relationship with Tommy, and it had affected them enough that it was the first thing that rose to the top of conversation.

"Thank you, Colonel," said Jake quietly. "I appreciate what you said."

"You okay Jake?" I asked.

"No," said Jake. "Not really."

I wasn't sure what to say to Jake. I remembered when his boys were in school with him several years ago, but I was new to the staff and hadn't really gotten that close to Jake yet. I was actually closer in age to them than I was to their father, even though both referred to me as 'Mr. Reyes.' I hadn't really gotten to know either of them past cursory greetings. They knew that their father frequently lunched with me.

I wondered sometimes if it bothered them that Jake and I had become friends. I knew that Jake was having trouble in his marriage, and evidence of that became clear with Tommy's outburst. I wondered if my being openly gay made them wonder about their father. I have seen my fair share of middle-aged men suddenly 'decide' that they've been gay all along, despite having families. In truth they were probably in denial or simply trying to conform to the world around them. I had actually slept with a couple of guys like that. Older guys, who had come out later in their lives after having wives and kids for a decade or more. I don't know if Tommy or his brother even thought like that, but after hearing him just now, I realized that things must have been worse at home than Jake let on, or worse at least than I imagined. I decided to move closer to the back to listen in on Tommy's conversation a little, and I used thirst as my excuse. I made my way back to the water bottles and rummaged around while Tommy spoke to Glen Billings. Jake, meanwhile, had shaken off the effects of his son's accusations and began talking to the impatient Colonel Cannaveral.

"Colonel, I know you want to take a stab at the Greenbriar," Jake began, "But I've got one more son to get first. Two hours south to Virginia Tech, then we'll turn around and come back through. I promise."

"Okay," he said. "Okay."

We drove through the small road that connected VMI with its liberal arts neighbor, Washington & Lee University. The stark contrast in campus styles was immediate. VMI looked like a military barracks. Like a fort with athletic fields. W&L looked like an antebellum plantation. Crisp maroon brickwork flanked by sharp white columns everywhere. Washington & Lee's colonnade was picturesque, and outlined the front lawn of the school, lying in a gentle slope that buffered it with Lee Chapel, the resting place of confederate general Robert E. Lee. Lee was big medicine in this part of the country. He was portrayed as a loyal native son who would not invade his home state for a pushy federal government. Once the South was defeated, Lee took over then Washington College and instituted a number of educational reforms and put the school on the map. He could do no wrong in a town that idolized both him and his colleague, Stonewall Jackson. Jackson's sculpture was equally honored at VMI, where he had guided young Keydets into battle against the invading Yankees in what Southerners refer to as "The War of Northern Aggression."

I knew all of this because I had been forced to read about Lee in my graduate history class while working on my Masters. Growing up in Frederick County, Maryland among numerous sites famous for Civil War Battles like Sharptown and Antietam. Living only a few miles from Gettysburg, I had always made it my favorite historical topic. It always seemed to me like my undergrad courses focused more on the battles, while my grad classes focused more on the generals. I had studied Stuart, Longstreet, Pickett—all of the biggies. But Lee had captured my heart, which I always found surprising. I'm not usually a fan of confederates.

In this day and age, admiring a confederate general usually meant keeping company with white supremacists, homophobes, xenophobes, and misogynists. The country had divided itself sharply the past few years with recent presidencies and administrations working hard to divide the country. There was little refuge anymore in America for independent thinkers. I think that's why I liked Jake.

Jake Fisher hated to be pigeon-holed or classified by anyone. I suppose you would have to call him 'moderate,' but only because the average of his extremes fell somewhere in the middle. He believed in a strong defense—a very Republican ideal generally—but he was socially very liberal, and very protective over me, his female colleagues, and anyone of color. He liked the idea of lower taxes, but also felt that the government's job was to take care of the weak, the poor, and the needy. He was a man at odds with himself. In that way, he was similar to Robert E. Lee. Lee felt strongly about his country, went to West Point, and served the U.S. proudly. But when his country decided to take arms against his state, it put a personal touch to a problem that had been overly simplified as 'slavery vs. abolition.' In the North, Lee got a bum rap as a supporter of rebels and a loser who surrendered. In the South, Lee was still a candidate for sainthood. Lee would have disliked both of those characterizations. He was more complicated than either of them. I admired complicated guys. I was studying one, and I was traveling with another.

"I'm sorry you had to see that, Colonel," said Jake. "That's personal stuff. Dirty laundry. I've taught my boys better than to do that."

"Don't give it a second thought, Marine," said the Colonel reassuringly. "These are pretty extreme times. They try men's souls, to paraphrase someone better than myself."

"My wife—Mrs. Fisher and I—we were struggling a little like most empty-nesters do. I don't know if you can relate," Jake said.

"I can," the Colonel said simply.

Jake nodded. "Well, then you know that empty nesters sometimes find it a little hard getting reacquainted with one another. After dedicating the better part of twenty years almost entirely to our boys, Mrs. Fisher and I were, well, having some trouble getting reacquainted as partners. I think the boys noticed, and maybe they misinterpret things a bit. At any rate, I'll talk to him about...everything."

"Life has some challenging milestones, Marine," said the Colonel. "They almost seem cliché once you reach a certain age. But just because you can see a milestone coming doesn't make it less of a milestone."

"Sounds like you understand where I'm coming from," Jake said. "Do you?"

"I'm divorced, and recently started dating again," said the Colonel. "I have grown kids, and we had some of our biggest clashes when they came back from college. What you're experiencing is actually fairly common. I'm not trying to diminish it in any way," he clarified, "and everyone's situation is his or her own, but there are likely a lot of people who can identify with your particular situation, Jake. A lot of people." Jake pursed his lips and nodded, slumping a little.

"Tommy, dude, you're not gonna believe the shit we saw on the way down here," said Glen Billings.

"Try me," Tommy Fisher said. "If it was college age kids acting like idiots in a crisis, I've already seen it," he said.

"No, man. It was wild. That Colonel dude up there, he and that Asian lady were at Fort Detrick. We had to go in and rescue 'em from monsters."

"Monsters? Be serious, Glen," said Tommy.

"I am serious, dude. These things looked like humans, but they were fucking orange, and had white hair, and hopped around like monkeys. It was wild," said Glen. Tommy immediately frowned and turned to me with a look that asked *Are you kidding me?* I nodded back.

"He's not exaggerating," I said. "These things were really fucked up." I winced a little. I had gotten used to guarding my tongue around students in school, and I had been a teacher when I first met Tommy, and I had to watch myself. I still wasn't used to the new reality.

"But orange?" he asked.

"Orange," I answered. "Like the inside of a blood orange, kind of dark. Really, really weird looking. The Colonel says they're a result of the weapons used on us by other countries. Have you seen anything like that here?" I asked.

"Not at all. This place seems completely untouched, except for occasional blackouts and power problems, but enough folks have solar or wind power here that they had back-up generators rolling the next day after the first loss of power. Nothing like what you're saying."

"Things back home, in Frederick and in Emmitsburg, they're kinda messed up. There was looting back home. Violence," I said.

"The Colonel says my dad was a hero. Was he exaggerating?" asked Tommy. "People often exaggerate when it comes to my dad."

"In no way," I said. "For starters, he fought three thugs who mugged the Heffners."

"Tanner's family?" Tommy asked.

"Yes. They were in their car, and three guys went up and attacked them. Your dad," I paused. Glen looked at me with a strange expression. I hesitated.

"Go on. My dad what?" Tommy asked.

"He took care of the problem," I said.

Tommy just looked at me. He frowned slightly and tilted his head as if to assure me that he could handle the details of what I was trying to gloss over.

"Go on," he said.

"Your dad killed two of them and drove off the other. Then, later on, we ran into four more thugs trying to kill us in the Wal-Mart. Your dad handled them too. He drove us here and helped rescue Wendy and the Colonel from a bad spot in Fort Detrick. Without his help they would likely be dead by now. He's been a one-man wrecking crew," I said.

"Yeah. He usually is," said Tommy. "Scorched Earth everywhere, no matter what."

I couldn't begin to put myself in Tommy's shoes. I wanted to defend Jake, but that's hard to do in front of a family member who knew him quite differently. Jake had never told me to go to bed, threatened a loss of privileges if I didn't do my homework, or rough-housed me if I got mouthy with him. My relationship with Jake was professional, equal, and friendly. Tommy's clearly was not.

"Don't be too hard on him," I said. "He's been through a lot in the past few days. He was on the phone with your mom when the bombs fell. The phone just clicked off. He doesn't know what happened to her. That by itself would be enough."

"Yeah, but how hard did he try?" interrupted Tommy.

"I'm not finished. That would be hard enough, but he has sons. Not knowing your status was extremely difficult for him. It looks fine around here, but compared to what we've seen, I can only imagine what was going through his mind. Add to that his need to literally fight for his life twice, be pushed out of Hunter's Run by a faction of conservative teachers, enter a radioactive fort surrounded by some kind of weird creature people to rescue strangers, and come down here to find you and Vinny. He's leading all of us," I said. "You need to cut him some slack. I don't know what kind of father he was or is. I can't speak to that, and I won't try. I just know that as a man, he's doing pretty damn well, and we need him sane. And I've seen what arguing with you does to him. So, give him some room, stay off his case a little, and let him finish his...quest."

Tommy stared at me, flummoxed a bit by my speech. Things got really awkward, and I wasn't sure where they'd go. I patted Tommy on the back, then moved up to the front of the bus. Maureen grabbed me on my way past.

"Where to now? Virginia Tech?" she asked.

"I guess so. Son number one is here, son number two is in Blacksburg."

"I have an idea," she said, and rose to move to the front of the bus.

"Jake," said Maureen. "We've been living on rations for days, and this town is open for business. What do you say we stop here and get a bite to eat? Just eat out, like regular people. We don't have to stay long. I know you're worried about your younger son, but it could do wonders for our spirits, you know?"

Jake pursed his lips, and frowned slightly. He took a deep breath, and shook his head.

"The mission's not over yet, Mo," he said. "I'm sorry, but there will be time to eat after."

Wendy chimed in. "Oh please, Jake," she said. "Ray

and I are famished, and this could really help us bounce back. We've all seen such terrible things. Just a little normalcy. Just for an hour or so."

Jake softened at her tone, and she gently lay her hand on his shoulder, and you could see him slump just a bit when she did. He exhaled and said, "Okay."

"Tommy, any recommendations on a place to eat?"

"I have an idea," said Maureen. "Isn't this the town where that restaurant kicked out the president's staff?"

"I remember that," I said. "The Red Hen. That's good enough for me," I shouted. And off to the Red Hen we went.

CHAPTER 11

Dinner conversation

After a very nice meal that Wendy paid for with her credit card, the entire group found itself in better spirits. The food was top notch, and the location in that quaint, historic town in central Virginia was a pleasant escape from what we'd seen the past few days. Sitting at the table all together, feasting and talking, there was a strange feeling of escape that was just what the doctor ordered. All of the death, destruction, violence—all of that was briefly forgotten, and we ate and laughed and learned each other's stories. We all took turns telling where we were from, and I had the shortest story, as most of the teacher and students already knew.

Estela's story was fascinating. She had been born in Texas, but she said her parents were illegal immigrants from the Guanajuato region of Mexico. Her parents, despite having lived in the U.S. for nearly two decades, were part of a government sweep of ICE agencies in the southwest. They had been discovered and deported back to Mexico. Estela, at age twenty, had the choice of going with them or remaining, but it had taken nearly a month in a California holding cell in Victorville in horrific conditions for the government to finally release her and admit that she was a citizen. Even then, the president had mentioned wanting to remove citizenship through birth. Estela's parents had made it back to San Miguel de Allende, where their family was from. Estela had stayed there on and off as a child, as her parents had gone back and forth to tend to sick family and to help with the family store there. Once released from Victorville, Estela decided to move as far away from Texas as she could. She had moved to Emmitsburg to be with a friend who had gone to college at Mount St. Michael's. She apparently had experienced a falling out with her friend, and was left to make her own way working at the Wal-Mart.

As the conversations went back and forth, I pressed her a little.

"What kind of friend would abandon you after your story?" I asked. "You move all the way from Texas to nowhere, Maryland. You set up shop, get a job. Your whole family is in Mexico, and she just, what, disowns you? What a bitch!" I said.

"She's not a bitch," said Estela. "She, she had her reasons."

"Reasons? You're in need. Sorry, no forgiveness for that. *No merced*."

"*Fue la merced que buscaba cuando me dejó.*" She whispered. *It was mercy she sought when she left me.* And then it hit me. How could I, of all people, be that dense. I leaned over and whispered. "Oh my God. You're gay, aren't you?"

She looked around nervously, then at the ground, then nodded. "Sí."

"Well join the club, sister," I said in my sassy voice. "I'm sorry I called your ex-friend a bitch," I said. "Was it a Catholic thing?"

"Sí. Her...professor told her it was a mortal sin, and he threatened that if she didn't leave me that he would tell the university about her, and she would be kicked out of school."

"They can't do that!" I said.

"Well, that professor made her believe that he could. I told her that she should bring it up to someone at the college, like a dean or something, and tell them that it was a friend of hers and that she was worried and see what they said. I told her that in this day and age, even the Catholic Church would not go so far. But she was too afraid. No one in her family back in Texas knows, and she's ashamed. Not everyone has the benefit of your freedom and courage, Eduardo. She made a difficult decision. It's for the best."

"I'm so sorry, Estela," I said.

"You are outwardly gay in a public school world. You will have people that hate you and disagree with your lifestyle, but you have rights. My girlfriend, she comes from a very different place. I have been hiding who I am most of my life, and she still hides. Now she denies who she is. And she denies me," she said, choking on the last words and trying not to cry. I gave her a hug, and she slumped in my arms.

"We gotta stick together, *chica*," I said. "Especially now." She nodded with her head buried in my chest.

While I began to bond with Estela, I noticed that Wendy had completely captivated Jake with her own life story. I also noticed Tommy's icy stare from the other end of the table. His father was smiling, however briefly, and paying attention to the beautiful Japanese woman whose personality was like a bright light, and everyone at the table were moths gravitating her way.

"My mom met my dad in the 1960's," said Wendy. "She was an exchange student in Tokyo in college. My father fell in love with her almost instantly, and he began to get pressure about aligning himself with an American. He decided to marry my mother and move to the United States. They landed in Washington, D.C. I was born in 1979, and grew up in Bethesda, Maryland. My parents worked for a large Japanese importer and made lots of money. I went to all the best schools, met some of the most powerful people in D.C., and they sent me away to a fancy private girl's college. After a couple of years, I rebelled. I couldn't stand all of the privileged people I was around. My parents were nothing like that. I had been raised by a humble Japanese man who simply wanted the best for his daughter, but the people I hung out with at my preppy high school and the girls I met at my college—they weren't my style at all. They were smart, and lots of them were nice, but they were spoiled. Nearly every one of them. I couldn't stand it, so I left school after my sophomore year and became a flight attendant. I traveled the world for six years before finally coming back to my roots and finishing my education at American University in Washington. One of my international fights had taken me to Nigeria, and I had seen outbreaks of diseases there and how devastating they were. I decided to come home, go back to school, and find a way to do something about it."

"So, you became a medical student at what, age twenty-six?" asked Al DeFillipo.

"Twenty-seven, and not medical school. I have a PhD, not an M.D. My focus is on diseases, but in a more theoretical sense. I don't really treat them myself. I defended my dissertation at age thirty-three and went to work at NIH the same week."

"Wow," Al said. Al was as hypnotized by Wendy as any of us were. She was truly gorgeous, and always smiled, and laughed at everyone's attempts at humor. Maureen was clearly jealous, but even she privately admitted that she couldn't hate Wendy no matter how she tried, and she couldn't blame Al for staring at her all night. It seemed everyone else was.

Especially Jake.

"So, Dad, you gonna tell your story now?" shouted Tommy across the table. "Gonna tell everyone the story of how you met mom?" There was a tinge of anger in his voice, and it was noticeable by everyone.

"My story's not that interesting, Tommy. Why don't you tell everyone what it's like going to VMI? I bet they don't know much about that," said Jake, trying to deflect a bit. Tommy frowned. After an awkward pause, Jake mumbled, "Yeah, I didn't think so," to himself. Jake frowned, and an even more awkward silence followed.

Maureen saved us from the awkwardness. She began talking about her life growing up on Long Island, her exchange program studies in the Dominican Republic, her handsome and athletic husband who played professional baseball and how exciting he was when they were young. Then, of course, she mentioned his infidelities, and went on another brief man-hating rant. She apologized to me, of course. She always did that. It was funny. She was an entertainer, and you could see how that would translate into her being a good teacher. But she was also a little sad, and that part spilled over sometimes. Al DeFillipo put his arm around her when she got to the part about the infidelities, and she smiled and hugged him back when she discussed how awful men are.

After Maureen's tales, the energy broke up and several of us went to the bathroom. As dumb as it sounds, a nice restaurant bathroom was an unexpectedly joyous change from schools, porta-potties, and the side of the road. Jake, I noticed, had gone outside onto the porch. Wendy followed him, and I decided to spy on them a little. I felt bad for Jake, but I think I felt worse for Tommy. Losing your mom and not being able to see her, to grieve, to get closure, and worst of all—believing that your father was indifferent, even if he wasn't—that was a lot to chew on. I hid around the corner of the porch in earshot as Wendy came outside.

"Jake, are you alright?" she asked.

"Yeah, yeah, I guess so," he said.

"Tommy and you seem to have some tension there. It was bound to happen," she said.

"How do you figure that? You just met me hours ago."

"It's only natural. Your kids grow up. You and your wife become empty nesters. You're not sure what your roles are anymore, you're not as fond of living with each other as you were in your twenties, and your collective goal of raising your kids is essentially over. You're living with a stranger, and you're not sure you have to continue. Stop me if I'm wrong here," she said.

"You're not wrong. How do you know all this?" asked

Jake.

"Because the same thing happened to me and my husband," she said.

"What did you do?" he asked.

"We divorced. We had kids pretty young. Twin daughters. I'm not sure we had much more in common than the girls anyway. When they moved out and went to college out West, Mike and I went our separate ways, and I took back my maiden name, Yubashiri. I really threw myself into my work and haven't really dated much. But I think that my story is the same as a lot of people's, including maybe yours."

"Minus the part about your husband getting bombed while talking to you on the phone during World War III, and your son guilting you into believing that you hadn't done enough to look for him. Her. Whatever. We were trying to make it work. But I think we both knew it was doomed, and we dreaded admitting it to ourselves or the boys, so we just walked around in denial. When the crisis came, we both still looked for each other first. But now she's gone. And I'm not sure how I feel about it. And I sure as hell can't talk to my sons about it. I appreciate you listening."

The next part was unexpected. Wendy leaned over and kissed Jake on the cheek. Jake stiffened, almost looking like he was in a panic. She laughed.

"You saved my life. You saved the lives of most of the people on that bus, it sounds like. Don't forget to save your own, Jake Fisher. Even in times like these, you deserve that much." Jake's mouth opened, slack-jawed. He couldn't seem to muster a reply. Wendy brushed his face with her hand and walked back inside. Jake put his head in his hands and gritted his teeth silently. I moved awkwardly back to try and not be seen and ended up creaking on a floorboard. Jake looked up.

"How long you been there, Eddie?" he asked.

"The whole time," I admitted.

"You rotten little spy," he said.

"She's quite a woman," I said.

"Yeah, dammit. She does in fact seem to be that."

"Don't be too hard on yourself, Jake," I said.

"Why?"

"Well, for one, you're good at it. Being hard on your-self, I mean. I've watched you this week get beaten on by several different gang members and threatened by ultra-Christian power thieves and orange mutated things and none of them came anywhere near the beatings you give yourself." Jake just frowned and shook his head. "For two, you seem to be getting plenty of help from your son, who has obviously picked up some of his father's aggressive habits." He half-smiled, half-scowled this time. I was making progress. "For three, you're about to go get another son, who's younger," I continued. His eyes rolled.

"And for four, we need you," I said.

"What?"

"We need you. All of us on that bus need you. You're the rock. You have the vision, you have the *ganas*, you have the *cojones*. We have ridden through the streets of one city and found emptiness and devastation. We've ridden through the streets of another and found normalcy. And you just keep plugging away. Every one of us is just a step from losing it."

"Eddie," he interrupted, waving his hand.

"I'm serious. Nobody knows what to expect. Like nobody in the whole world. Our world has changed completely. Most of us don't even know who's alive and who isn't, what we have and what we don't. We're sitting on a bus chatting it up like it's a road trip, but this whole fucking thing is insane. And you are the one thing that keeps us from losing it completely."

"Eddie, I don't know any more than you do," he said.

"But you do. You know how to be focused. To complete your mission. To ignore distractions and to stay on task. Even if somebody is bitching about having to go on this trip with you, what else would they have anyway? Where would they go? People follow leaders. You are a leader, and you're the one we chose. I'd take you over Wes Kent ten days out of ten."

Jake smiled, nodded and glanced at the ground.

"Well at least you didn't place any more pressure on me by hanging everyone's hopes squarely on my actions or decision-making," he said smiling. I chuckled.

"Okay, maybe that wasn't the best move. But you seem to be motivated by guilt pretty easily, so I thought I'd throw my hat in," I said.

"Nice. So my current insurmountable amount of guilt wasn't enough. You had to put your little pink icing on the top to garnish it. Thanks. Thanks a bunch." I smiled at the pink reference.

"Look, *hombre.* All of this shit is tough enough. You're gonna have to work through your issues with your family. I'll defend you as a person, but that is work you'll need to do. But you shouldn't feel guilty about finding a beautiful woman attractive. Even liking her a little."

"You're not attracted to her," he replied.

"No, but I have a decent excuse for that," I added.

"Is it any easier being a homo?" he asked. I laughed out loud. It felt good to laugh freely. I patted him on the shoulder, and we turned to walk back to the others.

"Nope. Just as tough. Maybe tougher," I said.

"Gracias, *compadre.* I appreciate the pep talk. It isn't wasted on me."

I knew that was true.

When we walked in, Maureen and Al were taking pictures with the owner. Hardcore liberals to the end, they wanted anything to do with someone who had taken a stand against our current president—who, in a way, had led us to the modern-day apocalypse we were currently experiencing. Not that the people of Lexington, Virginia would know it by their circumstances. They lacked very little here, and even the electricity seemed to be stable. Suddenly everyone's phones were working. Some of us who had friends in places far away from target areas actually were able to trade texts with loved ones. Folks in Montana, Arizona, and Utah had all touched base with someone from our group. Most had similar circumstances to Lexington. They could not find much news, nor could they contact anyone near a major city like Los Angeles, Houston, Chicago, or Denver. Most of them found portions of the country operating as normal, but out of touch with loved ones in "hot zones"—areas of large metropolitan populations, or as in the case with Denver, cities near strategic zones like the home of NORAD—the North American Aerospace Defense Command—which had bases in Colorado and El Paso, Texas.

Jake's eldest son, Tommy, was on the phone with his younger brother, Vinny, as we approached the table.

"Yeah, dude. We're leaving in just a few minutes. We should be there in about an hour and half. Can you get packed by then? Yeah. Yeah, pack heavy. No idea what we're gonna find. Yes, I'll talk to him about looking for mom. See you in an hour or so, little bro," said Tommy.

"That was Vinny," Jake asked. "Is he alright?"

"He's fine. He's packing up, waiting for us. Have we paid the bill yet?"

"Yes," Jake said. "Wendy sprung for all of it."

"Kind of her. A little expensive though, no?" asked Tommy.

"She makes a very nice government salary. Has a nice nest egg, too, it seems. I wanted to push on, but everyone wanted to do a big dinner, celebrate a little bit. It seemed like a celebratory time," said Jake.

"Then why do you look like such a sad sack?" asked Tommy.

Jake sighed and slumped a little. "I don't like fighting with you, son. And I swear to you that after we get your brother, we'll make plans to try and find your mom. Okay?"

Tommy stiffened a little. He nodded and shook his father's hand. "Don't flirt with that Asian woman, though. Alright?"

"I'm not flirting with her. I'm being polite. We're just talking. We just had a life and death survival experience. It's not like you guys have it down here. It's bad back home. People need to talk about things after occurrences like that. Don't they teach you that in military school?"

"Mostly they make us march, salute, and say 'yes sir' a lot. But I'll take your word for it."

I saw Jake's shoulders relax after Tommy said that. He breathed a little deeper and actually mustered a smile for a bit. We gathered up the troops, got on the bus with full bellies and improved spirits, and rolled out of Lexington with a full tank of gas, bound for Blacksburg and Virginia Tech.

Blacksburg lay about forty minutes south of Roanoke, which is a fairly major city in Virginia, a populous state with no really big cities. Lexington may have been a college town, but Blacksburg is a University city. Everything was decked out in Hokie orange and maroon, and the facilities at the school were massive, clean, and impressive in every respect. The buildings were all uniform in a light grey stone façade. The grass was green, the streets wide and clean. Vinny was waiting outside his dorm with two giant duffel bags and a girl next to him. The girl was sitting on a small suitcase chatting with Jake's youngest son, a sophomore at VPI.

"Does Vinny have a girlfriend?" Jake asked Tommy.

"Not that I know of," Tommy answered.

"Then who is he with?"

"I guess we'll find out," said Tommy.

The bus pulled up to the curb. Students were milling around, the streets were full, and while classes had been cancelled, the town looked like Lexington—as if nothing different were going on. Jake opened the doors, jumped out and gave Vinny a hug.

"Hey boy," he said. "Glad to find out you're okay."

Unlike Tommy, who resembled his father, Vinny had none of Jake's coloring. Like Tommy he was much taller than his dad, but Vinny had darker hair and a slenderer build than either Tommy or Jake. I could see that he looked like his mother, whom I had seen occasionally over the years.

"Dad, this is Morgan," he said. "She is from Washington, D.C."

With that announcement, Morgan's eyes started to fill. Her lip trembled a bit, and she offered her hand.

"Nice to meet you, Mr. Fisher," she said.

"Morgan would like to come with us. She has lost touch with her family back home," said Vinny.

"Of course, of course dear," Jake said, and took her hand in both of his. Jake picked up her suitcase and moved towards the bus. "Plenty of room."

The young lady walked gingerly up the steps and looked around the bus at the odd group of passengers she was joining. With her there were four other young people in their teens or twenties. Between Jake's two sons, Tommy and Vinny, Glen Billings and Jada Allen rounded out the younger folks. I wasn't much older than they were, to be honest, at twenty-five, and neither was Estela. There were a couple of thirty-somethings in Maureen and Al, a couple of forty-somethings with Jake and Wendy, and then there was the Colonel, who was in his early sixties. Morgan's eyes found Estela and locked for a moment.

"I'm Morgan," she said. "Morgan Branson. Thanks for letting me come with you."

The entire bus began to welcome her aboard, and you could see her anxiety begin to subside. She had brown, curly hair, cut fairly short and not quite reaching her shoulders. She wore round glasses and no jewelry, which gave her a kind of a bookwormy look. She was above average in height, and slender—which made her look tall. She had a friendly smile that seemed instantly engaging, though she seemed a bit reserved as she made her way back to the middle of the bus.

"I'm Eddie," I said. "Nice to meet you Morgan. What brings you aboard?"

"Vinny said his dad could maybe help me look for my family."

"Oh," I said, and caught the sight of Jake's head jerking toward us as he heard. Then he looked at Vinny.

"Dad, Morgan hasn't been able to reach her folks for several days. I told her we lived just outside DC on the Maryland side and would be riding right through Northern Virginia. She's from Vienna."

Jake just nodded and turned away. "See what we can do," was all he said, and he got back in the driver's seat and started back out onto the main road and headed towards Interstate 81 North. Vinny sat behind Morgan and in front of his brother.

"Sup, dude," he said. "I see your haircut hasn't improved much." Tommy punched him in the arm.

"I see you're still an idiot," he said. "What are you weighing these days?"

"About one eighty," Vinny said. "Down a bit from earlier. Was thinking either 174 or 165 lbs. next season. How about you?"

"About one ninety-five. I was thinking 184. The way Dad was talking on the way down here, I'm not sure there is going to be a season at all."

"You kidding?" he asked. "Mr. Reyes, is he kidding?"

"Afraid not, Vin," I answered. I had taught Vinny at Hunter's Run. He was only two years out of school. "We saw some pretty heavy scenery back home. Everybody's gone. Roads are empty. There's evidence of some really weird aftereffects of some of the bombing. Your hometown is a shambles. There's looting, even killing. It's rough."

"Jesus. There's nothing like that here," he said. "What about Lexington?" he said to Tommy.

"Nothing. Some brief blackouts, but not much."

Just then, Maureen shouted out loud with her phone in the air.

"Oh my God," she said. "I have the news on my phone! There's news on my phone! Everybody be quiet!" She turned up her volume.

The nation is reeling after massive multinational bomb attacks rocked dozens of major cities and military bases across the continent. Communication is down or sporadic across the country. Reports are still coming in, and we will be updating you as we become aware of them. For now, the following major cities are considered disaster zones. Civilians are urged not to approach these areas until further notice, and only approved military personnel are permitted to be there. These cities in the mid-Atlantic region are: New York, Philadelphia, Pennsylvania; Baltimore, Annapolis, and Frederick, Maryland; Washington, D.C.; Arlington, Quantico, Fredericksburg, Richmond, and Norfolk, Virginia; Boston, Massachusetts; Providence, Rhode Island; Stamford, Connecticut; Wilmington, Delaware; and the lower Eastern Shore of Virginia. These areas have sustained extensive damage and could present dangerous levels of radioactivity. Repeat: avoid those areas completely until further notice. Martial law has been instituted in each of those areas.

Then the message began to repeat itself and Maureen clicked off her phone.

"Dear God," she whispered. "That's like the whole East Coast. Millions of people."

"I can see why they went for major cities, but why the Eastern Shore of Virginia? There's nobody there," said Vinny.

"Chincoteague has a Coast Guard installation, and Wallops Island right next door is a major NASA and Air Force base," said Jake.

It was the first news of any kind that we had heard since the day after the bombings. Nearly all of us had been able to live in some form of denial for a few days, but this broadcast had made our nation's situation very real, and brought that reality home to us. Maureen had tears in her eyes. Wendy did too. Al was clearly affected as well. Morgan was crying softly with her face in her shirt. Vinny tried to comfort her awkwardly. No one spoke for a few minutes. Tommy got up and walked to the front of the bus and sat in the front seat behind his father.

"I'm sorry I doubted you, Dad."

"No worries, boy," said Jake in a low voice. "It was only natural."

I looked at the Colonel. His face looked perplexed. He was deep in thought, and he shook his head slightly as if talking to himself.

"Colonel? What now?" I asked him.

"If martial law has been declared in Washington, it's a decent bet that the president will be there soon."

"How do you figure?" I asked.

"It's been hit already. No need to bomb a place twice. It's a waste of resources. The military can keep the streets clear and the people away. The president can work out of his bunker, or possibly even the White House if the newer weapons were used in Washington. I'm betting they may have landed already. If you don't mind switching the plan again, Jake," the Colonel began.

"Washington, then, instead of Greenbriar?" Jake asked.

"I think so," said the Colonel. "Hard to know for sure, with the limited information coming in, but it's the best bet probably, other than Site R, and we're way too far from there now."

"Wait, Colonel—wouldn't all of those places they just mentioned be radioactive?" asked Al.

"Ordinarily, yes," said Wendy. "But if all of these places were hit with the virus-carrying Brenerium bombs, maybe not. Those new weapons go for massive mortality instantly. Then the breakdown of Brenerium isn't as strong, drastic, or as long-lasting as the standard neutron or hydrogen bombs. It might be safe to approach those areas now without danger of radioactivity. This issn't your grandfather's nuclear war. This one is different."

"'Safe' isn't exactly the word I'd use based on what we saw when we picked you up," I said.

Wendy bit her lip, and the Colonel frowned slightly. Eyes widened among the original group.

"What did you see?" asked Tommy Fisher. No one answered.

"Oh come on," he shouted. "You guys have been holding back on this ever since I got on the bus. We all have to face this, whatever it is. Glen already told me a little. Talk."

"Things, Tommy," said Wendy. "We don't know exactly what they are. They are transmutations—mutates from their original form. They're altered."

"Mutates? Is that what you're calling them?"

"Actually they're so new they don't even have a name, but I guess that's as good as any," said the Colonel.

"Just what do these mutates look like?" asked Vinny. We all looked around at each other, but nobody jumped in.

"They're orange-skinned with white hair. They're essentially the same in body, but some of them have devolved brain patterns," said Wendy.

"Devolved?" asked Vinny.

"Backwards in development. Primitive, reptile-like. At least some of them. Some seem to be only a bit reduced. But all of them are aggressive," said the Colonel.

"Aggressive. Like, why? What do they do?" asked Tommy.

Suddenly I realized that nobody from our original crew knew the answer to that one. We knew that they were dangerous. We knew that they caused damage to the base. But we didn't know their end game. I must have had a weird look on my face, because as I turned to look at the Colonel he couldn't hold my gaze.

"Aggressive...for feeding purposes," Wendy said.

"Whoa," I said. "Feeding? They eat people? Are you fucking kidding me?"

"Now we don't know that exactly," said the Colonel.

"Yes, we do, Ray. We most certainly do. We saw them feeding on dead bodies, and we watched them slam the hell out of our doors trying to get to us," she said.

"So, they're zombies?" asked Vinny.

"Zombies are dead, dumbass," said Tommy.

"Fuck you, Tommy," said Vinny.

"Both of you, be done," yelled Jake, in a voice I hadn't heard him use since the Wal-Mart. "We're trying to learn something here. Wendy?"

"They're not zombies," she said.

"Told you," said Tommy. Vinny scowled back at him.

"They do seem to be carnivorous, and they do eat... carrion. Dead flesh. They found dead bodies everywhere and devoured them."

"Dear God," I said. "That's just horrifying."

"It was very animalistic. We watched them investigate the bodies, poke around at them. Then they just, they just eventually started eating," said Wendy, wincing.

"Well, that's not great news, Colonel," said Jake.

"That's not all of the bad news, son," said the Colonel.

"What do you mean?" said Jake. "What else?"

"They don't only eat carrion," said the Colonel.

"Jesus," I said. "Jesus F-ing H, Christ. Are you saying they ate living people?"

"We had an assistant. Bill Rafferty. A lab tech. He was with us in the lead room. He panicked and tried to leave, and they hunted him down," said the Colonel.

"Hunted?" asked Jake. "How do you mean, 'hunted?'"

"They used coordinated attack patterns. Remember the ones who were standing upright? The ones with more hair? They seemed to be directing them somehow. We watched them go after Bill. I couldn't bear to watch them eat him," Wendy said.

"I observed it all," said the Colonel. "They were coordinated hunting patterns. The upright, hairier ones directed the others into position. They funneled Bill into a spot where he couldn't retreat, couldn't escape. Then they just descended on him as a group. Nasty stuff. They stripped him bare and ate him raw. Then they napped nearby like a pride of lions or something. It was difficult to watch," he said.

"Dear God," said Al. "That's a worst-case scenario. Predatory mutated humans?"

"Colonel, do you think there could be more of those things elsewhere? Besides Fort Detrick?" asked Jake.

"Impossible to say for sure," said the Colonel.

"But given what we found when we were studying all of this, there's no reason why this couldn't happen elsewhere," said Wendy. "You agree Ray?"

"For all we know, if the conditions were similar, there's no reason other people didn't react the same way in other cities, though we can't know for sure. The odd combination of weaponized viral attacks with Brenerium seems to kill eighty to ninety percent of the population and alter the other ten to twenty percent. And a few of those seem to retain a greater portion of their former humanity."

"Well, as horrific as all of this is, if they feed primarily off the dead, they can sustain themselves almost indefinitely. There will be plenty of dead left around those bombed areas," the Colonel said. "Especially the larger cities."

"Okay, but what happens when they run out of dead people?" asked Maureen.

CHAPTER 12

Church and State

"Welcome everyone. It's so good to see you," said Wes Kent. Melanie Richmond hugged the two dozen or so members of the Church of the Many Blessings as they entered Hunter's Run High School's rotunda area.

"Great to see you, Mel," said a large woman wearing a white button-down with her collar popped.

"You too, Roz," said Melanie.

"Robin, you're here too? I'm so glad you're alright," Rozlyn James said to Robin Eaves.

"It's been awesome since our phones started working again," said Robin. "We have been able to contact lots of loved ones."

"Of course, we've all lost loved ones too," said Wes. "It's a national tragedy. We're going to have to use God's strength to rebuild," he said. "And we will. We will."

"It's a little scary out there," said Roz.

"It certainly is," said Roz's husband Billy. "There has been looting, and a number of assaults in broad daylight. It's unbelievable. I thought I knew this town," he said. "So much violence."

"Don't say another word," said Wes. "We had a violent presence right here with us for a while, but that's all behind us now. Have you heard the news reports yet?"

"Yes. At least the East Coast ones. It's horrible. So many cities attacked. So many people dead. How is it that the little town of Emmitsburg survived?" asked Billy.

"God's will," said Wes.

"Amen," repeated a number of the church members.

"We are the chosen," said Wes.

"So why, Wes, are so many of you still holed up here, now that phones are working and electricity is coming back?"

"Many of us lived in Frederick," Wes said. Frederick is essentially a ghost town. You can thank Fort Detrick for that. Of course it would be a major target in Maryland. Everyone else who had somewhere to go or someone to go to has already gone. But those you still see here? We have nothing left to go to, no one waiting for us. The kids that are here can't contact their parents, but we're looking after them now. The Heffners —do you remember them? Well, they have taken it upon themselves to look after the orphans here. They're fine people. Fine people," said Wes.

"How's the church?" asked Melanie. "Did it survive?"

"Oh yes," said Roz. "We have it guarded. It's in perfect shape, and there are a lot of stored provisions there, like the Food Bank. We're making sure nobody gets in there."

"Good thinking," said Melanie.

"Father Joe rather fancies himself like Clint Eastwood in *Pale Rider*, and he has several others taking turns guarding things."

On cue, Father Joseph Clarque walked in, white collar around his neck, and hanging in front of it was a large silver cross contrasting on his black shirt. He was back-slapping Wes Kent and shaking every hand Wes could introduce him to. He smiled reassuringly, the crows' feet on his eyes deepening when he did. As he moved forward, he saw Melanie Richmond.

"Melanie, my dear," Father Joe beamed. "So glad to see you alive and well." Joe embraced her for a good ten seconds, patting her back as he pulled away.

"You too, Father," said Melanie. She smiled, and then she and Robin guided the guests into the cafeteria, where a veritable feast awaited.

The twenty-five residents of Hunter's Run High School had gone to great lengths to host the two dozen guests they had coming to visit this night. Fried chicken, tater tots, and green beans waiting in chafing dishes for the guests. It represented a good bit of the food that the survivors had originally set aside for themselves. Ordinarily, a meal might be only one of those rationed out. But Wes Kent had assured them that this was well worth the investment. Discovering the surviving church members of the Many Blessings congregation was big, he said. The Church of the Many Blessings represented some of Emmitsburg's finest citizenry. It had a daycare facility and an elementary Christian Academy there and made a habit of taking missionary trips every summer to Central America to help build houses and churches for poor communities there. Oddly, no church members were of Central American origin, and very few Hispanics attended the Christian Academy. The tuition there was considerable—comparable to some of the finest private schools in the Baltimore area that were so prevalent. Emmitsburg, being about forty-five minutes west of Baltimore, was usually too far for many of the town's finest families to send their children to "Charm City's" famous preparatory schools—and there were many in Baltimore. But there were also several private schools in Frederick, and Hunter's Run had a good reputation for a public school, so many of those parishioners' children ended up there after a stint at the Elementary Christian Academy.

"Believe me, these are people you want on your side," Wes Kent had told Mark Longaberger and the rest of the new flock. "They bring a wealth of resources and influence. It would be important to have had them here when things were, well, normal, like before. But now, with the need to rebuild society being so urgent? Now it's crucial to get a good start. To get things going in the right direction."

Mark Longaberger was forcing his warmest smile as the church members entered the cafeteria. Mark was sitting on a stool playing the guitar. Wes knew of Mark's musical background, and suggested that he provide some much needed entertainment for everyone. "What a grand entrance it will provide," Wes had said. "And what a great impression you'll be able to make on some important folks." Mark didn't mind playing in front of people. He rather liked the attention, he thought to himself. For some reason he had bristled internally, though, that it was Wes who had asked him to do it. It had made him feel a little like the hired help to serve Emmitsburg's elite. It was probably him being irrational, he thought, and he strummed away on a James Taylor song that he'd remember his dad singing when he was little.

Wes paraded the group past Mark and introduced him, and the group politely clapped as he nodded acknowledgement. Wes had told him to play throughout dinner and had offered him the chance to eat beforehand so that he could provide a soothing atmosphere for the guests.

"It just makes sense, my boy," Wes had told him. 'You eat first—you deserve it. You're providing the much-needed ambience, so you get first dibs on dinner." It all sounded very flattering when Wes had suggested it, but now he couldn't shake the feeling of being an employee. Mark played five more songs as the guests ate, then Wes had come by to tell him to play one more and call it a night so that the group could have a meeting. Dishes were cleared away by some of the orphaned students—who also had been encouraged to eat early. Wes, Melanie, Lou Orville, Robin Eaves, and several of the originally stranded teachers were sitting among the guests awaiting Wes's upcoming meeting. Wes took the time to introduce several of the others.

Jenny Custis—chair of the English Department, a graying woman in her early sixties, was the AP teacher at Hunter's Run. She had been an influential staff member who had worked on and off with the local community college as well as with the state department of education. She was the teacher that most of the students dreaded having. She taught an extremely difficult course and made sure that everyone in it worked their fingers to the bone in order to pass. Her reputation preceded her—which was just the way she liked it. Mark always felt a little inferior with Jenny in the room, and he got the impression that was premeditated on her part. Jenny's only child had grown up, gone to an Ivy League school, and moved out west to become a software engineer in Silicon Valley. Her husband had left her decades ago. Hunter's Run was her life and her domain.

Also hanging nearby was Ken Miller. Ken was one of the custodians at Hunter's Run. The one you saw everywhere doing everything. He cut grass, cleaned trash, fixed broken desks, anything he could do to serve the school, which represented home to him, much like it did to Jenny Custis. He had a little desk in a cubby of a corner in one of the storage closets, and he set up shop there daily. Ken was not the building supervisor or the building maintenance man. In fact, he was fairly low on the totem pole of importance for custodians. He was not the smartest member of the staff either, having been raised in the Catoctin Mountains nearby in a cabin that literally had an outhouse until he had reached adolescence and the county made his father put one in order to receive services for his ailing mother. However simple-minded he might have been, Ken was friendly, hard-working, and dedicated to the building and the staff. He was ready with a 'yes sir' to Wes Kent whenever he was asked to do anything, and he thought Wes was doing a wonderful job of keeping the flock together. He would often talk the ear off anyone standing still long enough to listen, and now he had wandered up to Mark, who was putting his guitar away.

"That was some fine playin' there, Mr. L. Fine playin'. I figger these folks Mr. Kent's got in here sure did appreciate that atmosphere you was bringin'. He says they're from the church across the street, didn't he?"

"Yes, from the," Mark began.

"Church of the Many Blessings, it is, I b'lieve Mr. Kent said. Yup. That sure is a fancy church. They do a lotta stuff over there. Got an elementary school, a day care facility. They even go down to Mexico and Guatemala every year on mission trips. Nice people."

"They do seem so, Ken," said Mark.

"You know, it sure bugged me when those other folks decided to leave. Mr. Fisher, Mr. Reyes, Miss Kelly and Mr. De-Fillipo? I didn't see that coming at all. They seemed like good folks too, 'specially the way Mr. Fisher took care of them hoodl-lums out front. But Mr. Kent, he says they didn't see eye to eye, and the others decided to just leave. I don't know about that. The way things look out in town, I don't know about that. I'da stayed here I think. You never know about some people I guess."

Mark just nodded and moved quietly up to the front of the cafeteria in order to hear what was going on. Wes had stood up and began to address the crowd.

"Folks, we sure are blessed to have you all here to-night and to have found each other. It seems like our town survived much better than much of the areas surrounding, according to what we've been able to hear of the news so far. Baltimore, Washington, and Frederick were all devastated, all with extremely high death tolls. God spared us here in Em-mitsburg for reasons that only He can know, but it is beholden to us to try and make a new start of things, and to do that, I felt it crucial to bring the church and the school together—some-thing we weren't really allowed to do before."

The crowd gave a collective low laugh for that. Father Joe gave him a thumbs up, and Wes smiled at their appreciation.

"But it seems to me, that if we are going to rebuild this town, we'll need not only good people and resources here, but we'll need to make contact with other areas that also sur-vived. It's hard to say just yet how extensive the damage is to the country and to the population, but in this tragedy we can also find a new beginning. Set up a new world order of things. And I hope you share my vision."

The applause, for only about forty to fifty people there, was loud. Father Joe stood and led the clapping. He was the first to begin and the last to finish. Maybe it was the acoustics, or maybe it was Mark Longaberger's imagination beginning to run away, but a chill went down his spine when he heard words like 'new world order,' and for the first time, Mark began to wonder if he hadn't picked the wrong person to back. Wes was shaking hands with the guests, and Melanie Richmond came over.

"He's very inspiring, don't you think?" she asked Mark.

"Hmm? Oh, yeah, of course," he said absent mindedly.

"It takes a real leader to do something like this. He has real courage," she said.

"Yeah. Courage," said Mark.

"When everyone was so high on that Jake Fisher, I knew that he was out of control. I'm glad Wes ran him out," she said.

"Really? I thought you were one of his fans," said Mark. "You two seemed pretty close when this thing first went down."

"I never felt comfortable around him," she said. "He's got that weird limp, and he's always hanging around with those Hispanics."

"Well, he does teach a section of Honors Spanish class, doesn't he?" asked Mark.

"He's mostly a history teacher. He just filled in for Spanish," she said.

"But wouldn't that explain why he's often with Hispanics?"

"Not necessarily. I mean, it's ridiculous--why would Hispanics be taking Spanish classes anyway? Seems like cheating to me," she said.

"Don't all English-speaking kids take four years of English classes?" asked Mark.

"That's different," said Melanie.

"Mmm. Different. Gotcha," he answered.

"You're starting to sound like one of those liberals he hung out with," Melanie said.

"I'm just asking questions, Mel," said Mark. "Don't worry, I'm still a Republican. Just using some standard Socratic method like I used in class. Teacher thing. Hard to break old habits, you know?"

"Socratic method?" she asked.

"You know, Socrates. Greek philosopher. Asked a lot of questions," said Mark.

"Socrates? Ew, gross. Isn't he the one that had sex with his mother? Why would you use his method?" Mark paused for a moment, wrinkled his brown at Melanie, then nodded.

"Beginning to wonder that myself," said Mark. Just then Wes walked up.

"Mark, my boy. Fine job tonight. Many thanks for providing a wonderful atmosphere. It helped a lot. These folks have agreed to join forces with us on some ventures. We've increased our numbers, our resources, and our allies," said Wes.

"Glad I could help," said Mark. "But you make it sound like we're going off to battle."

"Ha! Battle! Not quite, lad. Enough war for the whole world this past week, let me tell you. But we are going to revamp this town, that's for sure."

"What's the plan?" asked Mark, hesitantly.

"Well the church is going to send out some scouts in nearby areas. Quick look-sees, in vehicles. Find out the status of neighboring cities and such. They asked that we contribute someone, and I suggested you."

"Me?" asked Mark. "Why me?"

"Well, for starters, because you didn't get to go on

that Wal-Mart recon, for one. Jake Fisher screwed you. He was threatened by you, so he made you stay home. I, for one, would like to see you take a leadership role in things around here, starting with the scouting sortie," said Wes.

"Sortie?" asked Mark.

"Just a phrase, lad. Short trips for purposes of gathering information. Anything you can find out about the outside world. Take notes, pictures, whatever you can. Get back fast and stay out of danger. You up for that?" asked Wes.

"I suppose so," asked Mark. "I am curious what's going on out there. We've been cooped up in here for the better part of a week."

"Excellent. Glad I can count on you," Wes said. "You'll head out tomorrow. Let me introduce you to the fellas you're going to be traveling with. They're right over here."

Wes paraded Mark Longaberger up to the deacons of the church, Roz and Billy James. Mark shook hands with Father Joe and smiled, whose friendliness seemed to ease his anxiety a bit.

"Nice to meet all of you," said Mark.

"You were wonderful tonight, Mark," said Emery Butler. Butler was the choir director for the church. A man in his sixties, he looked older somehow. He had ash-colored, sallow cheeks, almost a grey-yellow in tone. His hair was nearly white, and his skin looked partly mummified. His words were spoken in a high pitched voice, and he nearly always had his hands on Mark somewhere. He shook hands with both hands, one on Mark's arm; he rested his hand on Mark's shoulder as they chatted; he patted Mark's arms when complimenting him on his physique. Mark's anxiety level raised again.

"Mark's going with you all when you head out tomorrow on recon," said Wes. "He'll be invaluable to you. Sharp young man, here. Sharp young man indeed."

"Great to hear," said Emery in his high-pitched voice. "Can't wait to see what we see." Mark smiled politely and nodded.

◆ ◆ ◆

The next morning, a white minivan with the church logo printed on it pulled up in front of the school. Wes and Mark went out to meet it. Wes was all smiles. Mark was feeling anxious. Emery Butler was in the shotgun seat, and a large, muscular man was driving. Mark had not seen him the night before. He presumed that the man was one of the security people that the church was using to monitor things at their compound. Billy James was in the back seated on the bench-seat. He nodded to Mark and gave a small salute, then beckoned Mark to take the swiveling chair in the middle. Mark did, and Wes Kent leaned in to speak to the group.

"Come back with as much information as you can, boys," said Wes. "Stay safe, don't linger anywhere that looks dangerous, but remember that information is power. We need you to do your jobs so that we can move forward. Best of luck."

With that he slammed the sliding door shut, patted the window, and the van pulled out of the parking lot.

The quiet, muscled driver headed onto Main Street, an alternate Route of US Route 15, that carried folks in the mid-Atlantic from Virginia to Pennsylvania and beyond. Downtown Emmitsburg looked like most small town in the northern part of Maryland and southern part of Pennsylvania. Much of the town's heyday came decades before, and the architecture of the homes and businesses there displayed it. The real contrast came with the Catholic church's properties, which included campuses and monuments to Saint Elizabeth Keough, Mount St. Michael's University, and the Grotto of Lourdes. All of those areas were spotless, manicured, and beautiful in every possible aspect. Juxtaposed with the pristine and sometimes opulent property associated with the Catholic church, there were also areas of lower income housing, and some places in the outskirts in the country that looked almost condemned.

Regardless of which socioeconomic background Emmitsburg residents came from, they were usually found bustling on the streets.

But not today. Streets were empty, cars were still and businesses were silent. Most houses had shades pulled or curtains drawn. The bombings of a few days ago had driven people inside.

"Over there," said Emery. "Look at the grocery store."

Several people scurried in and out of the building nervously, looking all around them for anyone who might be watching.

"There's some more over there, Emery," said Billy, as folks slipped into a dollar store on Main Street.

"There's some activity in that tavern, too," replied Emery. They pulled the shades, but I saw several figures.

"So, it looks like the town of Emmitsburg fared pretty well so far," said Billy. "We were lucky. My wife got word that Washington and Frederick got hit bad."

"Where'd she hear that?" asked Mark. "Our communication has been spotty at the school."

"Roz has a younger brother on the military detachment for Camp David," said Billy. He texted her. He said Frederick is like a ghost town."

"Is the president at Camp David?" asked Mark.

"Roz's brother wouldn't say."

"Mmm, I guess that's how it should be," said Mark. "I wonder how other towns fared."

"It's going to be up to individuals to come together with information when they can," said Emery. "That's why we're moving on this now. We want to be ahead of the curve."

"What curve?" asked Mark. "Our country has been attacked, and you gotta figure that at least some of it has been demolished. What possible curve could there be?"

"Life is all about curves, Mark," said Billy. "Things end, things begin. Everything is cyclical. And whether you lead or follow, the view never changes. The Catholic church has had a strangle hold on this town for centuries. We have an opportunity to add our own influence as the town rebuilds."

"Wait a second," said Mark. "World War III takes place, for all we know the Apocalypse is here, and you are worried about extending your influence over a traditionally Catholic town?"

The large driver glanced in the rearview mirror at Mark and glowered. Emery frowned a little and turned around. Billy patted Mark reassuringly on the shoulder.

"I know that sounds petty the way you're saying it, Mark, but think for a minute. We have certain ideals that we believe in as a society, and we want to advance those ideals. For whatever reason, as successful as our church is, not everyone attended it. Maybe it's due to a family tradition, maybe some folks are intimidated, who knows? But reaching out to people in their moment of need shows our good intentions and brings people into our flock and helps us spread those ideals."

"When you put it that way, it sounds much better. Sorry I reacted the way I did," said Mark.

"No problem. It's totally understandable," said Billy.

The van toured the town uneventfully for a few minutes, and the driver pulled out onto a back road that led the van to a pocket of low-income apartments behind a gas station. There were a number of signs in Spanish advertising various items, including a place where people could wire money to Mexico and Central America. A few people scurried in and out of the apartments looking distrustful of the van.

"There are some people there," said Mark. "See? Around those apartments."

"They're, uh, not really our kind of people," said Emery. The driver shot a sharp look at Emery and Billy nervously jumped in.

"Emery means that we haven't had much success getting them over in the past," Billy said.

"But your sign literally advertises services in Spanish on the marquee. I've seen it," said Mark.

"Sure, not for want of trying," said Billy. "We try all the time, but these folks are too...Catholic I suppose. They are mistrustful of white people. Probably because they're illegals. We do have Hispanics in our church, Mark. There are several families from Spain, in fact. Señor Pablo Fuentes leads our translation services with Father Joe. He helps us with our marquee messages as well."

"Spain," said Mark.

"Yup. I'm sorry you didn't meet Pablo. He didn't make it over last night because he was keeping a vigil at the church. He was on watch, so to speak. I think he may be coming over to Hunter's Run today, in fact. Wonderful man," said Emery.

"Wonderful," said Billy.

"Pablo Fuentes," said Mark. "From Spain. Well that's reassuring," he said.

"Indeed," said Emery.

The driver glowered at him in the mirror again.

CHAPTER 13

New Passengers, New Destination

"Hold on, Mo," I said. "Are you suggesting that those, those things, are going to start eating living people?"

"She said they already have eaten living people," Maureen said, pointing to Wendy.

"It was horrifying," said Wendy.

"It's why I am in such a hurry to get this intel to someone in power," said the Colonel. "I don't know how much this has spread, if it's happening in other cities where bombs hit. If we can get on the lead end of this it might curtail the devastation, save some lives," he said, looking at Jake.

"This does put quite a bit more urgency to your mission," said Jake. "I'm sorry I was the cause of slowing it up."

"You went to get your kids," I said. "Priorities, dude." Jake nodded.

"So where to, then, Colonel? The swing by the Greenbriar was a long shot. You still want to try that, or do you have something else?" Jake asked.

"There are some installations in Roanoke, but they really didn't have much to do with military intelligence there," he said.

"If there were no bombs falling now, where would you go?" asked Jake.

"The Pentagon. Without hesitation."

"DC is a mess," I said. "Radioactivity, martial law, and who knows, maybe those mutate things too. Colonel, do you think the Pentagon will be open and functioning?"

"Hard to know for sure, but they would have the highest amount of defensive strategy capabilities as anywhere else in the country. It's our nation's capital. The Pentagon isn't impregnable, but it's damn hard to hurt. They were up and running in under a week after the 9/11 bombing, and that hit them square. Yes. I think they'll be open, and I think they'll want to hear what I have to say. The only other back-up plan would be Raven Mountain. Site R that I mentioned before. But I think Washington should be the first attempt. Congress goes to the Greenbriar. They aren't the ones that need to hear what I have to say."

"Dad," said Tommy. "You said Mom was in DC during the bombings. We could look for her while we were there."

"Now hold on, Tommy," said Jake.

"Yeah, dad. We gotta look for Mom. You promised. And Morgan's family is there too. I say we head to Washington," said Vinny. Morgan smiled.

"Didn't the news say that those cities were radioactive?" asked Maureen. Wendy turned to Maureen and shook her head. "Yes, but remember, this isn't the usual radioactivity. It's Brenerium. It's run its course by now. It's not like uranium or plutonium, with a huge half-life. It breaks down quickly."

"Tactically, it makes sense," said the Colonel. "Many of the countries involved in this war aren't equipped to occupy an enemy land. None of the American or Middle Eastern countries have the means to do it. The Chinese might be able to, but ethnically speaking, Chinese are easier to identify physically than Europeans. It would be less practical for them to try, and they are farther away, so the logistics of moving any Chinese operations here would be monumental.

The Russians, on the other hand, are just across the Bering Sea. They have numbers, most of them look like most of us, and they have the wealth to pull it off. If the Russians were looking to occupy us after a defeat, they would want the country intact. That is likely why they are using the Brenerium bombs with the weaponized Ebola. They want human casualties, but not demolished cities. It's expensive to rebuild.

Remember, also, that the Russians have had to live with Chernobyl. They didn't want long-lasting problems with nuclear weapons either. The kind of radiation that went with the old A-bombs or H-bombs lasted for generations. Brenerium was used to be combined with viruses. The danger to life is greater and more immediate upon impact, but the blasts do less damage to buildings than A-bombs or H-bombs, and radioactivity shouldn't be a factor at this point, only in the first 48 hours or so, based on our experience with itd at Fort Detrick," said the Colonel.

"He's right. Washington might be a high casualty situation, but it is most likely safe after a brief period. The people we worked with would know that, and we communicated it to the highest levels before the bombing began," said Wendy. "What they don't know about yet, I'd wager, are the mutates. The information we've accumulated on them is limited but pretty crucial. If they popped up other places," Wendy paused dramatically.

Jake turned around and looked at us. The group now included teachers and students from Hunter's Run, an assistant manager from Wal-Mart, two government military defense specialists, and three college kids. Twelve of us in all, now. Jake looked over the group, cleared his throat, and spoke.

"Guys, I've done what I came to do. I have my sons. I don't have any other plan, no secondary mission. I can't make you do anything. We've found places that are regular. Lexington. Blacksburg. People are living pretty normally here in Southern Virginia. Even if the radiation is gone, Washington is a war zone. There will be thousands dead, devastation everywhere. And for all we know, those mutates are there as well. I can't decide this one for you. What do you want to do?" said Jake.

"Are you serious?" asked Al. "We have people on the front lines of this war with crucial intelligence that maybe no one else in the country has. I'm not playing it safe at this point. I have a chance to be part of something special. I'm in." Maureen kissed him on the cheek and gave him a hug.

"If you're in, I'm in," she said.

"In," said Glen Billings.

"In," said Jada Allen.

"*Estoy con ustedes*, Jake. I'm in too," said Estela.

"That makes it unanimous," I said. "I'm not staying in Podunk central."

"Really Eddie? Lotta cute guys on a college campus," said Jake, smiling.

"Podunk guys. I need sophisticated guys. You gotta go to DC for that," I said.

"I thought all you gay guys were sophisticated," he said laughing.

"Compared to you? Yes. All of us. But there are levels, and I deserve the best. Get this van moving," I said.

Jake revved up the engine and moved out full steam ahead onto Interstate 81. He decided to top off his diesel tank again in Lexington, which was another hour and a half away, so we all settled into our seats. There was an air of adventure, of lightness, and of positivity in the bus. I looked around and people were smiling. We were headed into a bombed-out nightmare that likely had little to no power, no life, and possibly some kind of cannibalistic orange zombie monsters waiting for us. But we all seemed okay with it, as if we had a renewed sense of purpose. It seemed everyone was smiling. Except for the new girl, Morgan. She was crying. So I went back and sat with her. Estela had moved closer as well to try and talk to her.

"Hey honey, what's wrong?" Estela said.

"I'm, I'm just really moved by all of this," she said. "Vinny's been my friend for a year and a half, and his dad just met me a few minutes ago, and now everyone's heading back to the area where I live to help me

find my parents. No one's ever done anything like that for me, and here you guys are doing all of that and you don't even know me," she said.

"That's how we roll," I said, smiling. She laughed.

"I know that you're going for more than just me," she said. "I'm not stupid. But it's, it's just that I contributed to it all, sort of. Like, I'm one of the reasons we're going, and that's really cool. People usually aren't that nice to me."

"Jake, Vinny's dad, is like that. He's instantly loyal and supportive. If you're tight with someone he cares about, you are automatically in the inner circle. Are you and Vinny...?" I raised my eyebrows. Morgan laughed again.

"God no. I mean, he's a great guy. I, I don't have a boyfriend. But, um, guys aren't really my thing, if you catch my meaning. I hope that's not a problem."

"Are you kidding me, girl? Most people can tell within the first five minutes that I'm gay."

"I don't like to make assumptions," said Morgan, but after hearing you talk with everyone, I kinda figured."

I looked over at Estela for a non-verbal cue that it was okay to out her. We locked eyes. She smiled and nodded back.

"Well, you and I aren't the only ones who think alike," I said, jerking my head towards Estela.

"Really? Wow. There are like, twenty people on this bus tops, and you're telling me that three of them are gay? That's unusually high. It's also pretty reassuring. I mean, if things are as bad back home as I've been hearing, it's just nice to know that, I don't know, that there are people like us who survived, you know?" said Morgan.

"Amen sister," I said.

"*Verdad*," Estela said, looking at Morgan and smiling. I caught Estela staring at her. She caught my glance for a moment and gave me a quick, stern frown as if to say, *shut up, I'll handle this*. I smiled and silently nodded back at her, and then saw Morgan turn, smile back at Estela, and give a little nod.

"So where are you from, Estela?" Morgan asked.

With that, I took my leave and moved back up to the front of the bus.

Jake's boys were sitting next to each other, catching up. I went up and sat down behind them, deciding to watch and listen to them for a bit. I had known both of them from a distance from Hunter's Run. Growing up in the community, and never really leaving, I had kept up with all things having to do with my alma mater. Those two had been very successful athletes while there. Jake was a bit of an icon as a teacher, too, so everybody knew the Fisher family. I had never had Mr. Fisher as a teacher, but he was as well-known as anyone in the building. His kids were too young to have been around me as students, but I remember them coming over to his wrestling practices as middle schoolers. They would wander into the building and go watch their dad and his team in practice and do their homework or work out themselves sometimes. They had grown enormously since then. Both towered over their dad, and he was somewhere between them in weight, but much shorter. They were broad-shouldered and muscular, and both handsome. I had had many brief, superficial chats with them over the years as they moved through high school, came back on breaks, even at occasional competitions that I went to go see when they were close by. Now, however, I was actually getting to know them.

The eldest, Thomas, or Tommy, as he was called, looked like Jake. If you smoothed out Jake's wrinkled skin, stretched him out, and got rid of his love handles and slightly protruding belly, they might have been twins. Tommy was an upperclassman at Virginia Military Institute, but he really didn't seem the military type to me. Yeah, he knew the lifestyle, the lingo, and at least gave lip service to continuing in some service after graduation, but he was not your typical dyed-in-the-wool military type. Like his dad, he was an intellectual and a deep thinker, but much of his energy went into the internet.

Tommy was a communications major at VMI, and as such, was entitled to much more time on the internet than most of his fellow Keydets. He was constantly looking at memes, videos, and daily feeds from various on-line sources, and was very up-to-date on world happenings. He was addicted to gaming as well, which was very problematic at VMI, where students have the bare minimum in terms of personal items in their barracks. When the students would get liberty on weekends, Tommy would play videogames. Most recently he had made friends with wrestlers at next door Washington & Lee University. He came over on weekends, stayed on their floor, and played videogames all weekend. His first year, he had gone to his sponsors' house for occasional visits. Sponsors are families in the surrounding area of military academies who offer up their homes to students so that they can have a touch of normal, non-military time. They are in many ways like second families, and can be crucial in the retention of plebes, rats, knobs, or any other first-year academy students across the country. Tommy had discovered that his sponsor also liked videogames, and they hit it off in his first two years. Then the sponsor had to switch jobs and move across the country. He was in the process of being assigned a new one, and in the meantime had crashed in the apartment of his W&L buddies, which was enough to satisfy his videogame cravings for the time being.

Tommy may have resembled his father physically, but Tommy's heart gravitated more towards his mother, Laura. Laura smothered him with love and spoiled him to a degree. She never let him become an entitled brat, but she always managed to lavish him with surprises, care packages, and attention. As a result, he was her absolute champion. Rarely did his mom give an opinion that Tommy didn't back, and if anyone ever vehemently disagreed with Mama Fisher, Tommy didn't hesitate to loom his massive frame over them in discouragement. That included his dad. Laura and Jake were not always happily married, especially the last decade or so. They argued over little stuff from time to time, as old couples tend to do. Jake said that he rarely started it, but he was quick to escalate. Laura would start it, push his buttons, and Jake would get loud--the kind of loud that only Marines and wrestling coaches can produce. Then, in recent years, Tommy would interject. His size made an already tense situation a whole new kind of tense. That type of awkward family dynamic had begun to rear its head more and more frequently over the past few years in the Fisher household. Jake wanted one thing, Laura wanted another, and Tommy would often shift the balance so that most decisions went Laura's way.

Vincent, or Vinny, on the other hand, looked like his mom. In fact, he looked nothing like Jake in any way. Taller and thinner than Tommy, Vinny was darker in coloring, walked completely erect, and had wiry, rippling muscles to contrast with his brother's beefier build. Whereas Tommy looked more like a night club bouncer, Vinny looked more like a tall, white version of Bruce Lee. Vinny was a bit more difficult to describe. He was fiercely individualistic--usually preferring to be left alone--yet he had a group of friends that he frequently gathered with that were his "crew," and he was no doubt their leader. Vinny often gravitated towards the underdogs of the world. His crew was usually comprised of socially marginalized individuals. They were usually a little smaller, a little more awkward, and a little more timid--and Vinny, like his brother, never hesitated to loom his impressive frame in their defense. It is supremely ironic that Vinny ended up going to Virginia Tech on a wrestling scholarship, because every time I spoke to him, he said that he hated wrestling. I asked him why he did it, and he always answered that it was a family tradition. I asked him if his dad made him wrestle, and the answer was always no. Tommy also answered that way. Jake never wanted to force his kids into something that he did, but he was always there to coach them when they chose to join him on the mat. Vinny was still doing it, though, much to everyone's surprise-- and like his older brother, he was pretty good at it.

Vinny's thoughts, being more guarded, were harder to read than Tommy's, and thus he was harder to predict. As a defender of the marginalized, Vinny was constantly on the lookout to "adopt" someone. He would often find someone who fit that awkward, geeky, outsider description, and then become their friend and defender. Now that I had discovered that Morgan was gay, I wondered if she was one of Vinny's new adoptions, and I decided to press him about it. But first, I listened.

"Dude, do you believe that crap about the orange things?" asked Vinny.

"Sounds nuts, I can't lie. But everybody here said they saw them," Tommy said. "It's just so hard for me to believe things are so bad back home, when everything here is practically normal, you know?"

"Seriously, dude. I mean, we had some internet interruptions, sure, and some brief blackouts, but those are kinda normal. This stuff about what Frederick and Washington look like, it's hard to imagine. It's like surreal, you know?" said Vinny. There was a pause, then Vinny looked at his brother solemnly.

"You think we can find mom?" he asked Tommy. Tommy looked away, and his face seemed to display anger.

"We're gonna," he said. "Because Dad sure as hell didn't."

"Dude, what was he gonna do?" Vinny said. "You heard the story right? About the school and everything?"

"I heard it. What I didn't hear was why he didn't drive straight into DC to find his wife."

"Dude he killed people in Emmitsburg. Just to survive. Just to make it through the day. First chance he got, he came for us," said Vinny.

"You always did defend him," said Tommy.

"And you always went against him with mom," said Vinny.

"Shut up. Shut the fuck up. We don't even know

what's happened with mom. Don't talk about her," said Tommy.

The two offered a couple of hard shoves each before I jumped in.

"Whoa, whoa, boys. I think you need a ref. Take it easy, alright?" I said.

They looked at me angrily, then down at their feet.

"Listen guys, it's been a tense week for us. You need to get ready for this. It's not what you've been used to. We need you at your best. You can't be at each other. We have to be a team. At the very least, we have to support each other. There were tons of people on your campuses compared to what we have back home, and some of them are about to realize what we already know. There are parts of this country that have been devastated by foreign attacks, and what remains is for us to deal with. The only thing the people of this country have heard is a radio report about what areas to avoid. We don't know if the president is alive, and if he is, what he's planning to do next. It's every man for himself right now, and you know how that goes, right?"

"Yeah. The strong survive, and the weak get crapped on," said Vinny.

"Yes. And those who stick together are stronger still. You two are formidable additions to our group. You're big, strong, smart, and athletic. We're going to need you. But we can't fight among ourselves, even if we're related."

"Okay, Mr. Reyes," said Vinny.

"Tommy?" I asked.

"Okay."

"And I need you to do me a favor. I mentioned this before to you Tommy, but now I'm flat out asking you. You need to ease off your dad a little. He needs support, not criticism right now. He is our leader, like it or not. He's not being a dick and forcing us to do anything, he's asking our opinions, then he's making decisions and acting on them. That's what a leader does. And right now, we're all counting on him. I know that to you, he's just "Dad," full of flaws and full of shit. And I know what it's like to be the coach's kid, so to speak. My parents were professors, and their students all thought they were a lot smarter than I ever did. I get that. But right now, we're entering life and death stuff, and you can't pick at him. You are his Achilles tendon. He risked life and limb to get to you. He's going to do the same for your mom, but you've got to let him work."

The boys looked at me and nodded.

"Deal?" I asked.

"Deal," they both responded in unison.

"So, Vinny," I said, changing the subject. "Tell me about Morgan. She seems like a nice girl."

"Oh, it's nothing like that, Mr. Reyes. She's, uh, not my girlfriend or anything."

"She's a cutie-pie," I said back.

"I don't think I'm her type," he answered.

"Really nice, too," I added, lifting my eyebrows suggestively.

"Mr. Reyes, she's gay," he whispered nervously. I laughed out loud.

"I know," I chuckled. "I was chatting with her in the back the past few minutes. I just wanted to hear you say it out loud. And so am I, remember? So, there's no need to whisper." He grinned back. "Alright, you got me," he said.

"She seems to be doing alright so far here as well. She's chatting with Estela right now, who is also gay."

"Really?" Vinny beamed. "That's cool." Then he thought about it a minute. "You know, that's a lotta gay folks for one bus. Higher than the national average," he smiled.

"Definitely higher," I said. "How did you meet her?" I asked him.

"She was in one of my classes, then when we got together to study for a quiz I found out she lived in my dorm, too. We got to talking some. She had been bullied in school a little and was kind of having a hard time here. Then she found a gay students' group here and felt a lot better about things. We've hung out ever since."

"That's the great thing about college. All the people you meet from all walks of life," I said.

"Yeah, that is cool," he said. "Doofus here, on the other hand," he said, punching his brother. "Not quite as much variety at VMI, huh?"

"Well, historically it was all male for like 200 years, and with so much controversy about sexual and gender preference in the military...let's just say it's probably not the best spot to encourage openness from a cultural standpoint," Tommy said. "And considering they were a staple for the South in the War Between the States, maybe not the ideal place historically to, um, blend the races," he said. "Still, there are plenty there that don't fit the mold. We all tend to find each other."

"So, you haven't drunk the Kool-Aid, Tommy?" I asked.

"Well, they don't really discuss it. There's no real Kool-Aid like that per se. Privately people voice their opinions, but the Institute doesn't really touch it. Not sure they could, to be honest. It's hard to outrun your past. I don't have a problem with it. You know what Dad always says, 'I don't care who you kiss or where you piss'," Tommy said. We all said the last part in unison aloud and chuckled afterward.

"I know he's glad to have gotten you on board," I said. "You could see the weight flying off his shoulders." Just then Jake's booming voice came from the driver's seat.

"Eddie, stop trying to convert my kids to your twisted religion," he shouted.

"It's not a religion, you Neanderthal," I shouted back.

"Well what is it, then, if not a cult?" he asked.

"The natural order," I answered back, grinning. He laughed as did the boys.

I glanced over at the Colonel, who looked fairly uncomfortable. Whenever I was chatting, or the topic of homosexuality came up, the Colonel seemed to stiffen, look away, and get a blank look on his face. I didn't want to fall victim to stereotyping or prejudice, but I had seen many, many military types have issues with my very existence. Like those folks who drove us out of Hunter's Run, most of them quoted the Bible as their reasoning. There were many people in the military who sounded the same. I imagine having to face the possibility of death on a daily basis makes one a lot closer to one's creator —whoever that creator might be. In the United States, more often than not, that was the Judeo-Christian form of God— and my experience was that people who ironically called them- selves 'Christian' these days were pretty inflexible on the mat- ter. I was an abomination to them.

That was one of the things that made Jake so special. He had been there—faced death on the daily—even caused it. He'd been through some heavy stuff in his life, and it would be understandable if his view on it was just as inflexible as I im- agined the Colonel's might be. But it wasn't. Jake gave plenty of homophobic sound bites, but he didn't have a bigoted bone in his body, really. When Jake and I got to jawing back and forth, folks who were uncomfortable with me and my perspective only got more uncomfortable. Anyone else usually enjoyed the banter and had fun with it. The Colonel very much seemed to be of the former disposition. I was only guessing, but my guess was that he didn't approve of me. I hoped that wasn't so.

Wendy, on the other hand, had a sly smile on her face watching us all, and she leaned in to talk to me.

"You and Jake are good friends, aren't you?" she asked.

"Yeah, I'd have to say yes, despite our differences," I answered.

"Differences? Was that exchange you just had for real?" she asked.

"Oh Hell, no," I said. "Not in the least. We joke like that all the time. No, our differences are age, life experience, background, that sort of thing. I mean, I'm a single gay Hispanic in my twenties. He's a married veteran and father of two and nearly fifty. We shouldn't have much in common to talk about on the surface," I said. I saw Jake's eyes in the bus mirror.

"I heard that. Stop spewing lies, Eddie," he shouted. "I'm nowhere near fifty."

"You're probably closer to seventy, you old geezer. Now get your nose out of my private conversations," I shouted. As we went tit for tat, I glanced sideways at Wendy. She couldn't take her eyes off of Jake, and she had a faraway smile the entire time. She asked me lots of questions about him. Lots of questions. And she laughed nervously whenever we talked about him or if he was shouting one of his smart-ass comments to me. There was no doubt about it.

She was smitten.

And that was going to be a big problem.

CHAPTER 14

The Church of Many Blessings

"So, Emery, what did you find?" asked Pablo Fuentes. Pablo seemed over-dressed for a regular day. That fact coupled with his Castilian accent made Mark wonder for a second if Pablo was a vampire.

"Not much, amigo," Emery said, patting Pablo on the shoulder. "Some businesses are either shut down or they've been looted and are boarded up. It's a little depressing out there."

"Tch, Tch, what a shame," said Pablo. "People in a crisis have the capacity for great good, or great evil."

"We did see some people scurrying around, but most of them seemed scared. I think the entire town is hiding. Kind of in lockdown, if you get my meaning. I think we need to reach out to them," Emery said.

"What do you suggest?" asked Father Joe.

"I think," Billy James interjected, "that we should offer food. Like have a cookout or something. People will smell it, maybe pass by and see it, and we can hand it out. It will bring people to our door, and we can get more intel from talking to them."

"I think that's an excellent idea," said Father Joe, entering the main lobby of the church, where the group had gathered.

"What about an old-fashioned barbecue?" asked Emery. "We can even do it roadside."

"I like it," said Father Joe. "In fact, it's brilliant. The smoke, the smell, it will attract people who might be hiding in their homes. And there's no doubt that they'll need food. Tell you what, gentlemen: I'll put you two on it. Mark—would you like to help with that?"

"Sure, I guess so," said Mark. "Why not? Sounds like fun. I mean, who doesn't like a cookout? But where are we getting the food?"

"Oh, don't you worry about that," Father Joe said. "We've got plenty."

"What Father Joe means is we have some food stores that we can use in these kind of special circumstances. We can pull them out for emergencies," Billy said.

"Great. That's great," said Pablo. "Mark, I don't believe we know each other. Pablo Fuentes. I am from Spain."

"Nice to meet you, Pablo," said Mark, shaking his hand firmly. "What do you do?"

"I teach Latin and Greek at the University in town," he said. "In the Classics Department."

"Wow, that's cool," said Mark. "How is the college doing?"

"It is currently closed, but maintains good communication with staff and students. Most of the students have gone home. A small percentage remain, and the staff take turns looking in on them. I myself have been there recently for my turn."

"It must be really tough for them. Who would possibly be staying during this crisis?" asked Mark. "If I were a college student I'd have gone home long ago.

"Not everyone lives close by," said Pablo. "Some of our students are from the American West, and a surprising amount are international students. Flights have been grounded and communication is not fully up and running. Those students need us right now. I invited many of them to come join our church," he added.

"That, that's great," said Mark. "I'm sure they appreciate it."

"What is a church's purpose if not to help out those in need?" asked Pablo. "It is quite wonderful."

"How long have you been here?" asked Mark.

"Here, in Emmitsburg? In the United States? Or do you mean in the church?"

"Well, all of them, I guess. I don't mean to pry, I'm just making conversation," said Mark nervously.

"Happy to answer them all," said Pablo. "I have been in the U.S. for seven years, at the college for five years, and in the church almost as long—four years."

"Your accent," Mark said. "I can't get used to it. It's not like many of our Hispanic students. It sounds different somehow."

"Understandable—a common mistake you Americans make. We Spanish are not really Hispanic. We are actually more Caucasian than most of you, coming from much closer to that European mountain chain. We speak the purest form of the language. It would be like listening to someone from England, for example, and comparing it to someone from say, Texas. The language is the same, but the vocabulary and the accent can be very different. Hispanics are a blend of Spaniard and indigenous native American Indians," Pablo explained.

"Ah. That explains it," Mark answered back uncomfortably.

"Let me guess. You think I sound like Dracula," said Pablo.

"What? No, no. That's ludicrous. No, it's...okay, yes. I admit it," Mark said, breaking into a laugh. "I do think you sound like Dracula."

Pablo laughed as well. "That, too, is understandable if you know your Romance languages."

"Transylvanian isn't a Romance language," said Mark.

"No, because there is no Transylvanian. Transylvania is the ancient name for that region. Do you know what it is called today?" asked Pablo.

"Sure, Romania," answered Mark.

"And you never considered where they got the name?" Pablo asked, smiling.

"Oh my God, I never did," said Mark. "Holy cow, it's right in the name. Roman!"

"Hence the name. Our accents are similar because the Romans left more than troops in Transylvania. They left their language and much of their culture," said Pablo.

"It sounds like you've had this conversation before," said Mark.

"Many times. Especially with my students. Today, you were my student," he said, smiling.

"I guess I was," said Mark.

The large van driver came into the lobby pushing a large cart with very large, quiet wheels. On the cart was a giant slab of meat. He pushed it down the hallway towards the kitchen.

"Wow, that's a big hunk of meat," said Mark.

"It is indeed," said Billy. "We'll be able to feed a lot of folks with that."

"*El Señor nos provee,*" said Pablo. "The Lord doth provide, no? Truly, America is the home of beef. In Spain, we have the greatest ham in the entire world. But beef is truly American."

"Billy, Emery, Mark—why don't you guys go get started packing up items for the barbecue. I'll have Oleg drive around the portable pit to the front of the church, and I'll put up the message on the marquee to welcome everyone. Pablo, why don't you come with me and help out," Father Joe directed.

"Who's Oleg?" asked Mark.

"Oleg was your driver this morning and is currently handling the beef. Fine young man, from the Ukraine, I think, who came to us last year," said Emery.

"Billy," Father Joe jumped in, "Once we get things started cooking on the pit, why don't you and Oleg drive around town with the microphone and portable speakers and announce our cookout to everyone. Better to get the word out to everyone. I'll have Pablo join you to do it in Spanish as well."

"Fine idea, Padre," said Billy.

After an hour or so, the giant slab of beef was roasting in a giant barbecue grill on wheels. The grill was about the size of a small boat and had large wheels with every conceivable accoutrement hooked to it. The marinated beef smell was wafting all over town, and the scent alone would bring people from a mile or two away. Mark and Emery oversaw it, but after a while there wasn't much to do other than let it cook. Pablo, Oleg, and Billy were driving around town announcing the event to any who could hear it. Mark looked up and began to see people walking on the streets towards the church.

"Wow, people," Mark said.

"Of course," added Emery. "What did you expect?"

"I don't know," said Mark. "This is all very different from those first couple of days after the bombings. We actually had people come to the school and attack us. There were deaths. It was all pretty crazy. This, this is totally different. I guess I didn't know what to expect after all that."

"From what I understand, from what Wes told me, much of that violence was due to one of your staff members. The man who left several days ago. What was his name? Fisher?"

"Yes. Jake Fisher. But I don't know that I'd go that far. Jake defended the family that got attacked. He did go to extremes. Actually killed two of the three attackers, but they were trying to kill him too."

"Sounds like you're defending him. I thought you were on the other team."

"Team? No, there's no teams. We were all one team. At least that's how we started. I can't say that the violence didn't scare me a little. I mean, I'm no big Jake Fisher fan, but

I don't know that we took sides. I don't know that any of us could have done any better."

"Really? Could you kill a man?" asked Emery.

Mark stared at him a moment. His forehead wrinkled in thought.

"I don't know. I just don't know. I suppose if my life depended on it," said Mark.

"But what if it didn't? Could you kill someone then?" asked Emery.

"I'm not really enjoying this conversation, Emery," said Mark.

"Because if Wes is right, that's what your Mr. Fisher did. He killed people who didn't need to be killed. Not just those thugs going after the Heffners, but those kids in the Wal-Mart as well. That makes him a murderer, Mark. You were right to send him away. To think you actually worked in the same building with that man. And him, ready to snap the whole time," said Emery.

"Yeah," said Mark. "I guess so."

"You're right, let's change the subject. Here come some guests anyway, and we can check the beef and see how it's coming along."

Emery needed both hands to lift the giant lid of the enormous grill. Smoke billowed out from underneath, blowing an enticing smell into Mark's nostrils.

"God, that smells amazing. We've been living on cafeteria food. This is going to be heavenly," he said.

"Good choice of words," said Emery. "And welcome to all of you! Come on up and take a whiff. It shouldn't be too much longer now."

Five people had ambled up timidly to the cooker. A young lady seemingly in her twenties came forward.

"Who's all this for?" she asked.

"Why, you, my dear. And everyone! This is kind of a survivor's celebration courtesy of the Church of the Many Blessings."

"How much?" she asked.

"Why, it's free, young lady. We're giving food away to whomever we can. Times have been hard, and we want to reach out to anyone who needs it. That's what we do," said Emery.

"It smells awesome," she said. "Do you have anything to drink?"

"We certainly do. Look in that cooler over there for anything you like," said Emery. With that, Mark opened up the cooler and invited everyone to pick something. He grabbed a Coke himself, opened it with relish, and downed about a third of it in one gulp. His eyes teared up a bit from the carbonation, and he pulled away and started to chuckle.

"Amazing what you miss until you don't have it," said Mark.

"Have a seat," said Emery, pointing to a number of folding tables and chairs that he and Mark had set up previously.

"Thank you," said the girl. "I haven't had real food now for a couple of days."

"Rolls, chips and dip, all over there for you as well," said Emery.

The other four stragglers sat down with their friend. Three of them were younger, like the girl. Mark noticed that one was clearly the mother of one of the others by the way they interacted.

"What's your name?" said Mark to the girl. She was small but athletic-looking, and had straight, bright blonde hair that fell about halfway down her neck.

"I'm Jen Gosling. I'm a grad student at the University. Finishing my Masters in Education. I'm not actually from Emmitsburg. I was visiting my friend, Susan here when the bombs fell. My car wouldn't start back up, and I couldn't reach my family down the road in Taneytown, so I just stayed here with them the past few days.

"Hi, I'm Susan," said a tall, slender, brunette. "This is

my mom."

Mark reached over and politely shook hands with each of the three women.

"Mark Longaberger. I teach at Hunter's Run. We've, uh, partnered up with the church to do, uh, a little outreach," he said smiling. He glanced over at Emery for approval for his choice of words, and Emery smiled and nodded back.

"I thought you looked familiar. I student-taught there for a while," said Jen. "Phys. Ed. With Mrs. Eaves. You know her?"

"Yes, I do. She's at the school right now. A few of us got stuck there also."

"I'd love to see her. Maybe we can go there after we eat?" she asked.

"Sounds good to me. Emery?"

"We'll work it all out. For now, enjoy the appetizers. I'm going to check the beef to see how it's doing."

Emery took out a large butcher knife and sliced into the beef dead center and pushed the two halves back a bit. It was still a bit red, so he moved to the outer ends and sliced off a piece there. It was pink and dripping with juice.

"The outer parts are ready. Let me slice you some and you can make some sandwiches," he said.

He cut off a large chunk and placed it onto an electric restaurant-grade meat slicer. As he pushed it through, a giant pile of roast beef began to form on the large serving tray beneath it. Mark thought his stomach was going to explode with anticipation. More and more people began coming up to the tables and chatting some with the first arrivals. Mark sat with Jen, Susan, and Susan's mother, and for a moment it was like the Cataclysm had never happened. People ate, drank, and laughed aloud. The noise and the smells attracted more and more people, and before long, there were over thirty townspeople sitting at the tables.

A few minutes later, Pablo, Billy, and Oleg pulled back in with the van, and behind them came two vehicles and nearly a dozen more pedestrians. Everyone was gravitating towards the church cookout.

Father Joe came out with a wireless microphone and went over to a panel and flicked on a few switches. The three men shut the doors of the van and came over to partake in the meal themselves. Father Joe walked out to the center of the gathering with his microphone.

"Good day, everyone. And I mean truly, good day! With the catastrophe, the Cataclysm that took place here last week, we are all lucky to be alive. By now, many of us are realizing that not everyone has been so fortunate. Many of you are still wondering about family members all over the country. Others sadly know only bad news. Today is about rejoicing in our own lives. We are here, and for whatever reason, whatever plan God has for us, he has selected us to begin his work. I say 'begin,' not 'continue,' because it is a new world that we all face. A world of uncertainty. We are uncertain if our government is up and running. We are uncertain if our previous lifestyles can be retained. We are uncertain if our lives will ever be the same."

The happy-go-lucky mood turned somber for a moment.

"But one thing we can be certain of, is we have each other. No matter what limits, faults, or let-downs your previous lives or your previous church presented you with, we here at the Church of the Many Blessings want to be the place you come when you are in need. The place you come when you need guidance, a helping hand, a boost, or even just a good meal. We want to be the true Many Blessings of the new world order that will rise from the ashes of what used to be. It doesn't matter to us where you went to church before. We want to be your present and your future. My name is Father Joseph Clark, and I want to be your pastor. Welcome to the Church of Many Blessings."

And then the applause began. It was instant and spontaneous. Mark couldn't ever remember a church clapping like that after a sermon in his recollection, but everyone at the tables stood on their feet and clapped. Mark looked around and noticed he was the only one not standing and clapping. Everyone else was staring at Father Joe and offering him an ovation worthy of political candidate at a rally. Father Joe looked out at his feast and smiled.

"Before you leave, brother Pablo is coming around with pens and information cards for you to fill out. We'd love to be able to reach out to you in any way we can. As our country moves forward, your phones and computers will come back, and when they do, we want to be the first place you call when you're in need. In the meantime, eat up, get to know our church members, and enjoy yourselves."

Pablo stopped by every table, said hello, shook hands, and handed each person there a pen with the church's phone number on it, then handed them an information card for them to fill out.

"The land line to the church survived completely, so feel free to call whenever you need us," said Pablo.

Mark's earlier feeling of uneasiness had drained away, and he felt really good about helping create a meal and a community feeling for the people who had come to the church that day. *This is very different from the first days after the bombings*, he thought to himself. He had seen vandalism, theft, brutalit, and death. It had left him scarred, and when the rift came between the Wes Kent faction and the Jake Fisher faction, he had worried the entire time that maybe they had done the wrong thing by pushing Jake out. He had been even more concerned at the religious convictions of the people he was dealing with, and some of the things he heard Wes Kent say. They were subtle, but unnerving remarks about certain kinds of people being more worthy than others. But Billy James, Pablo, Father Joe, and even Emery to a certain extent, had calmed his nerves, and he was certain that what he had helped achieve with this event was more than simply providing people with a meal. He felt part of something more important. He had helped bring people together after a mass tragedy, and that could only be a

good thing.

CHAPTER 15

Convict Compound

The bus flew up Interstate 81 as Jake and his cohorts began to settle in for the long ride. It would be several hours more. Jake had fueled up again in Lexington. He felt comfortable there, it seemed. That town had provided us with our first taste of normalcy after a crazy week, so the feeling was understandable. Now we were zooming past Harrisonburg and James Madison University as we headed for Interstate 66 East, which would take us into Washington DC.

Nobody was really talking at this point. Several folks were napping. Jada had fallen asleep with her head on Glen Billings, who was snoring. Al and Maureen were snuggling together. Even Estela and Morgan--who seemed to have hit it off pretty quickly--were asleep, with Morgan's head resting on Estela's shoulder. I was looking out the windows, trying to make a mental note of everything I saw. There were some towns where everything looked normal, and there were others that looked fairly deserted. We hadn't seen any devastation yet like we saw in Frederick, but I think both Jake and I were anticipating when the landscape would begin to change.

Before long we saw the turn for I-66 to Front Royal and got in the right lane and started to merge in with that

highway. Front Royal was a small, attractive town on the Blue
Ridge Parkway. It was near Luray Caverns and Shenandoah National Park. It was off the highway a bit and was a mix of old
Virginia hill town and newer, middle class tourist town. Today
we would pass it by, but I remember having a small pang of
yearning, wishing we could visit it as if we were tourists ourselves. I wondered how long it would be before we could do
that kind of thing again.

Suddenly I heard the brakes squeal and felt the bus
fishtail slightly. I looked up and Jake was grimacing. The sleeping couples were jarred awake, and Wendy and the Colonel
both yelled aloud, "What is it?" I looked out the window and
saw two abandoned cars turned sideways across the ramp. Behind and between them was a medium sized tree that had been
placed in the middle of the road deliberately. The two cars had
not successfully gotten around the tree and there was some
damage to each of them in the front. Jake had skidded in without running into them, in what was definitely good reaction
time on his part. We all pitched forward into the seats in front
of us. Jake looked around at what looked like a scene that was
unnatural—perhaps even staged to a certain extent. He voiced
his displeasure.

"What the Hell is this?" he shouted out loud. He
looked angry.

As soon as the bus stopped, we were surrounded by
people. They were mostly male, fairly young--teens and twen-
ties--and each of them was holding a weapon of some kind. I
saw more than twenty people and spotted several guns, including one shotgun. Some looked like they were holding Japanese
katana swords. A tall one with his face painted with camouflage approached the doors and looked at Jake.

"Open the doors," he shouted.

"Why?" answered Jake.

"Because if you don't, we'll break them down," he
said.

"If you try, I will break your neck," said Jake.

"If you don't open the doors and let us in, I will tell my people to open fire on your bus and kill your people," he said. "So, you think it over. You have ten seconds."

We all looked at Jake horrified. He had a look of fury on his face.

"Jake?" I asked.

"How many guns you see, Eddie?" he asked.

"A bunch. At least four or five, including a shotgun," I answered.

"Tommy, can you confirm that?" Jake asked.

"Yes sir. Five. And the shotgun," said Tommy.

"Shit. We have to let them in," he said.

Everyone looked around and realized that if there was any chance to fight, Jake would have taken it. His boys looked at each other incredulously.

"Dad, you're not gonna let 'em in," said Vinny.

"No choice, boy," he said. "They're armed and ready, and we're not. I'm not going to lose someone to some kind of stupid false bravado pissing contest with no intel. Let's see what they want. If we get in trouble, an opportunity usually presents itself to take some action at some point. And when it does, we can't hesitate. But now is not the time, do you hear me?"

"Do you hear me?" he yelled.

"Yes, Sir," said Tommy.

"Yes," Vinny said, resignedly.

Jake opened the door and the large camouflaged leader beckoned him out.

"Out. All of you. Now," he said. "And if you try anything, we kill whoever is in front of us."

Everyone filed out one by one from the bus. The camouflaged leader eyeballed Jake's sons challengingly. Vinny avoided eye contact, looking forward with an angry sneer on his face, but Tommy stopped and stared back to meet the challenge. The leader turned his head and glanced at a shorter man holding the shotgun and nodded. The man lifted the butt of the gun and slammed it into Tommy's ear. Tommy hit a knee, clutched his ear and yelled. Jake moved faster than I have ever seen him. He tackled the man just above the knees and drove him ten feet back onto the ground, landing on top of him with his hands on the man's throat. The man hit with a thud and the shotgun dropped to the ground. Jake started pressing his thumbs into the man's Adam's apple and the man made a gurgling noise. The sound of a click behind Jake's left ear made him freeze.

"Stand down, Marine!" the Colonel yelled. "Stand down!"

"Get off my man or I blow your fucking brains all over him. And he hates brains on his clothes," said the leader.

Jake froze, and didn't move for about ten seconds.

"Better do as he says, you fuckin' jar head. He'll blow your goddamn head off," said the man beneath him.

"This is not the first time we've done this, bud," said the leader. "You might fancy yourself a tough guy, but I got killers in my band here. I wouldn't call my bluff if I were you."

Jake took his hands off the man's throat, pushed himself off him, and stood up.

"Shoot him," said the man on the ground. "Shoot that fuckin' jar head, Lawrence!"

"Shut up, Nick," the leader said. "We don't know anything about these folks yet. We got plenty of time to kill 'em."

"Fucker tackled me," said Nick.

"He sure did," said Lawrence. "Knocked yer ass down good, too. But Mr. Grappler here isn't gonna do anything now, are you Mr. Grappler?"

Jake stared impassively back.

"When you do what we do, you gotta expect some heroics, Nick," Lawrence said. "Judging by the resemblance, I'd say you pissed him off by hitting his boy. That right, Grappler?"

Jake stared silently back. Lawrence backhanded him in the face. The slap was quick, loud, violent, and caught Jake off guard. His eyes bugged, he took a breath, scowled back for a moment as his face reddened on one side.

"Now that's just disrespectful, Grappler," said Lawrence. "I asked you a goddamn question, and you plum ignored me. So I'm gonna ask you again. That your boy there?"

Jake stared back, wordless. Without taking his gaze off of Jake, Lawrence reached his right hand out and pointed his gun and shot the mirror of the bus. It exploded into a thousand shards, some of which hit Maureen, Jada, and Estela. Morgan screamed.

"Next one's goin' into a person, Grappler. We need to establish who the Alpha male is here, and you don't seem to understand that just yet. It's a simple question. Is.That.Your. Boy?"

"Jake," whispered the Colonel. "They have the upper hand. Don't let innocent civilians get harmed on your watch."

"Well, Jake," said Lawrence. "Is it?"

Jake nodded.

"See? Not so hard after all. And just in case you were wonderin', it's me. I'm the Alpha fucking male around here. Do what I say, or you watch me do bad things to your friends. And you got a lotta nice friends here."

The Colonel stepped forward. As he did, Lawrence turned the gun on him.

"Whoa, there, soldier man. Where do you think you're goin'?" Lawrence said.

"Son, I know you have plans here, but the truth is, we don't have time for this. We have vital information that we need to get to Washington, and your agenda here is holding us up."

"What kind of information, sir?" asked Nick, the one whom Jake had tackled.

"Never mind, Nick. It don't matter. There ain't no Washington, soldier man," said Lawrence. "I know. I was there when it went down in flames. I watched them all drop to the ground and die. There's nobody there for you to take nothin' to, so shut the fuck up and get back in line."

"You don't understand. I've been working at Fort Detrick for the past five years on weapons defense" said the Colonel. "I have vital information that could help the country defend itself, and I need to warn the government about what has happened to the survivors of the bombing raids. The weapons that the Russians and Koreans used. They've started to affect people. It's possible that more conflict could take place. We don't know what our government is going to do, and no matter what local power you may have around here, you're an American, for God's sake. You've got to let us go to Washington."

Nick's face froze, slightly agape. He looked at the Colonel for a moment, then back to his leader, Lawrence.

"Boss? Maybe we ought to listen," he said. Lawrence shook his head.

"I already told you, General. There ain't no Washington. I watched it disappear."

"You were in Washington when the bombs hit?" asked the Colonel.

"Just outside. I saw them from my truck. People just dropped. Everywhere. People that were nearby took a minute or two to die. I saw people everywhere crawling around and dying. Whatever buildings were left standing didn't have any living people anywhere near. It was like spraying a can of Raid on an anthill. Everything just died all at once. I didn't stick around much after that, but I know that Washington is gone, which means the government is gone. If there ain't no government, then there ain't no laws. So, it's every man for himself, and that means the strong survive. Get me?"

The Colonel nodded, still dumbfounded by the news of Washington's destruction. Lawrence turned his head towards Jake.

"And I am strong, Grappler man. 'Case you were wondering. But your swelled up face is telling you that right about now, ain't it, Marine?"

"So, what do you want from us?" asked Jake.

"Oh, you *can* talk when you want to, huh?" said Lawrence. "Well, let's keep it simple. What was once yours is now ours."

"Take what you want and let us get on our way, then," said Jake.

"Jake, no!" said Al DeFillipo. "We worked for all that stuff."

"It's just stuff, Al. We know we can get more. We need to get out of here intact," said Jake.

"Uh, hold on there, Grappler," said Lawrence. "You ain't goin' nowhere. What was once yours is now ours. That includes your freedom."

"What?" Jake said.

"You belong to us. We have some ventures in which we could use some cheap labor. Free is the cheapest labor I know," said Lawrence.

"You're making us your slaves?" asked Glen Billings.

"Whoa, there, boy," said Lawrence. "I'm sure that word don't sit well with you, so we'll use another term. You're 'indentured servants.' Most American colonists started out that way, so don't worry. You can work off your debt."

"We don't owe you a debt," said Al. Maureen grabbed his shoulders and pulled him back.

"Oh, but you do, friend," said Lawrence. "You owe me your life."

He pointed the gun to Al's head. Al shrunk back and put his hands up.

"See? I thought you looked smart to me. Now you understand. I let you live, and you pay me the debt of life you owe me. Nick, get Troy to bring up the Jeep and the wagon. We got us some new agricultural workers."

"I'm sorry, Colonel," Nick said, and poked the gun barrel into the Colonel's back. "You have to go."

Nick and some of the others put zip tie handcuffs on all the men. Jake, Tommy, Vinny, Al, Glen, the Colonel, and me —all of us got zip tied. They left the ladies unfettered. Lawrence, the leader, noticed the confusion on the face of the ladies and smiled.

"In case you were wonderin' ladies, you all ain't zip tied for a reason. It's easier to enjoy your charms if your hands are free to take various positions," he said. "We figure you'll be smart enough not to fight back."

Wendy's mouth went agape. Jada began to cry. Maureen looked sick, and turned to look at Morgan and Estela, who were in shock.

"How can you be like this? Like animals? Our country is under attack and you are taking advantage of it like, like, a criminal!" Wendy said. "It's only been a week! How can you be like this so soon? What could have driven you to be this, this, this evil?"

"Why that's simple, ma'am. Some of us were evil long before the shit hit the fan," said Lawrence, grinning. He pulled up his sleeve and showed Wendy a tattoo.

"See this? I got this in Lorton prison six years ago. It says I was someone's bitch. I was property, and that anyone who messed with me would have to deal with my owner. It kept me alive while I was there--but the things I saw, the things I did? They weren't human. Then I got paroled, and I started driving a truck for another ex-con around here who owned the company. He wanted to give me a chance, knowing that society wouldn't. He was right. He was also the first person I killed in this town. But he weren't the last, that's for sure. Folks here wised up quick. Now this tattoo means I'm the fuckin man, at least in this neck of the woods. And every time a new car comes off that ramp, I get richer. And so do the people who stick with me. But the ones who don't? They don't live long."

Wendy made a defiant face but was unable to hold back tears as she marched along with the bus passengers.

"You're a little old, but you're a looker. Might have to keep you around here instead of selling you," said Lawrence, patting her buttocks. Wendy grimaced and shut her eyes through the tears.

About an hour later, the men had been dropped off at the high school stadium. We were sitting on the bleachers with our hands zip-tied, staring out onto the local campus. There was a lot of activity about a hundred yards away in the school greenhouse. People were bustling in and out of there non-stop, carrying packages, potted plants, and pushing carts around.

"You all are gonna become the new hired help," said the one called Nick, whom Jake had tackled and choked.

"Lawrence don't let new guys outta their cuffs for the first day or two, cuz they always try to bolt. A few days of trying to wipe your ass with two hands and you'll start to come around. You realize you gotta labor, wipe shit, eat, and try to wash with the same fucking hands, and it don't work. You'll see. This place will break you or kill you."

Nick looked at Jake.

"And don't think I forgot about you, waddles. Payback's coming. You're my bitch now," he said, and back-handed Jake hard. A bloody spot of broken skin opened up immediately, and we all looked at Nick's hand. There was an enormous ring on it.

"Like my ring, motherfucker? State champs two years straight."

Jake spat and eyeballed Nick.

"You want another one?" Nick asked.

A Gator cart came riding up, with a young man in his twenties driving. He had a tightly cropped head of hair and a cut off T-shirt that showed a muscular build.

"Hey Nick," the young man called. "Boss wants the new guys at the greenhouse. Moving a lot of shit out today, and he wants to stay on schedule."

"Alright, Troy," said Nick. "I'll march 'em over there." We walked the hundred yards to the greenhouse. Jake's face was dripping with sweat and trickling blood from the backhand from Nick. It had to sting, but his face was stone. Just as we were passing the side of the bleachers, Glen Billings stumbled and fell.

"Get the fuck up," said Nick, kicking at him.

"He's diabetic," I yelled. "His blood sugar must be off."

"I don't give a fuck if he has AIDS, he needs to get up, now," said Nick.

"He can't, you asshole. Don't you know what diabetes is? He could go into a coma and die if you don't get him either food or medicine. We have some on the bus," I yelled.

"Shut up," said Nick, who then bashed me in the face with the broadside of his shotgun.
"I'm tired of dealing with you fuckers. If he can't make it, then he dies. Leave him. Weaklings can't exist in the new world," he said.

We all kept walking and Glen lay still and flat next to the bleachers. Jake was seething, but said nothing. The Colonel grimaced, and Al made a face and looked down at the ground. Nick marched us up to the greenhouse, and as we got close, I noticed why all the activity was buzzing around it. The plants they were moving around were Cannabis. Marijuana. Weed.

"Now you know why Lawrence is such a badass," said Nick. "We been supplying the jail with weed for the past three years. Now we gonna expand our territory, now that we have more 'hired help' like yourselves. We're all gonna be rich men, cause even in the Apocalypse, people want weed. And we can supply it."

"Using the high school's greenhouse?" I asked.

"We took it over last week. Replanted our shit in there. People fucking bailed outta the school the minute the bombs dropped. Lawrence was smart enough to take it over. Local cops came to run him out the day after, and we killed 'em. All of 'em. Nice thing about small towns—ain't too many cops, and the ones that are there are just yokels."

"Using the local high school as a headquarters," I said. "Who would've thought of that?"

Jake cut his eyes at me and Al scowled a little.

"That bus you provided is gonna be a help too. We could only get our hands on one of them, but now we can move more shit faster. More shit means more money," said Nick. "Now pick up everything inside the greenhouse that ain't planted in the dirt and put it over into that flatbed.

"How are we gonna carry all of that with our hands tied up?" asked Al.

"Find a way, Stilts. And shut up," said Nick. "Colonel, you too, sir. Sorry. Job's gotta be done."

The Colonel looked quizzically at Nick for a moment, nodded, and moved forward towards the rest of us. The next hour we spent putting everything that wasn't planted and growing onto a flatbed wagon being pulled by a pick-up truck. It was exhausting, and my wrists were killing me with every movement. The plastic cut into them, leaving a mark, and I wondered how long it would be before permanent damage set in from being tied up like that. The greenhouse was now mostly empty, and the flatbed full of product for Lawrence to sell.

"Back to the stadium now," Nick said. "You can sit there till we have more shit for you to do."

I wondered why we were being put in the bleachers of the stadium, with so much space anywhere around the school. Then, as we got closer, I saw why. Up in the press box was a man with a rifle and a scope. A sniper. He could pick us off easily before we could get anywhere. Lawrence wasn't kidding. This wasn't his first rodeo. He knew what he was doing, he knew how to manage thugs and push dope, and his numbers would only grow. And he had us as his slaves. God only knows what he was doing with the girls.

I also noticed something on our walk back that Nick did not: Glen Billings was gone.

CHAPTER 16

Second Thoughts

"That was really, really good," said Mark Longaberger.

"See," said Emery. "This place does good work, like I told you."

"Well, yeah, that too," said Mark. "I was talking mostly about the barbecue."

Emery laughed. Billy James was collecting the information of the guests, which eventually totaled nearly a hundred and fifty people. Mark hadn't believed it at first, but the names on the sheet didn't lie.

"Wow. I wouldn't have believed you if you told me seventy people showed up today," said Mark. "But this did go on for about four hours."

"There are many people in need in this town," said Pablo. "I must admit, I too changed my mind about this church." Emery smiled in a very satisfied fashion, like a cat with belly full of bird.

"What do you mean, Pablo?" asked Mark.

"I was not always a Protestant, Mark," said Pablo. "In fact, I teach here at Mount Saint Michael's because it is a Catholic institution. Spain, even more than Italy, is the most Catholic country in the world.

"More so than the country that houses the Vatican?" asked Mark incredulously.

"Consider the fact that Spain became a country because of Catholicism," said Pablo.

"I thought it was because Ferdinand and Isabel married and joined their massive holdings," said Mark.

"It was, but they joined to combat a religious foe," said Pedro. "Don't you teach history?"

"I have to admit, that in spite of my being a history teacher, the particular history of Spain isn't my strong suit," said Mark. "I usually teach about either ancient Mesopotamia or the modern United States. Can you explain it to me?"

"Well, Spain was a collection of small kingdoms and dukedoms. Castle towns, surrounded by walls and protected by warlords, and run by *moros*—Muslims from North Africa. Then an arranged marriage between Fernando of Aragon and Isabela of Castilla y Leon solidified much of the land. They were the *reyes católicos*—the Catholic rulers—and they created a country in 1492 dedicated to eradicating all religions except Catholicism.

"1492—the year Columbus sailed?" asked Mark.

"Sí. They were intent upon gaining wealth and influence for Spain, and with the Pope's blessing, sent emissaries and conquistadors to the New World to do just that. But in the process, they pushed the Muslims farther and farther south. And the church offered sanctification to anyone who had fought and died against them. San Fernando—from whom my mother gets her surname—was a moor fighter. Most importantly, Santiago Matamoros—Saint James the Moor Slayer —the Muslim Killer—is his literal sainted name. He is the patron saint of all Spain. Our national hero is El Cid—a knight who fought the moros for years. Our entire country owes its existence to unifying around Catholicism."

"And apparently the destruction of Islam," said Mark.

"Well, those were different times. From the times of the Crusades, Europeans have fought to say which god is the more powerful," said Pablo. "But even now, the world divides itself between religions, no?"

"So how is it that you ended up here, at this church?"

asked Mark.

"I met Emery here at a college lecture I was giving. He talked to me about my ideas and invited me to come to the church. They showed me similarities in things I love about the Catholic church, then won me over by making me see the ways this church improved upon it. They are not so different in how they view the world—but very much so in terms of the way they run things."

"Does the college have a problem with you...converting?" asked Mark.

"I am still Catholic," said Pablo. "I have not renounced my original faith. But now I describe myself as perhaps being not so trapped beneath church hierarchical dogma. I still attend mass at the college, and still visit the Shrine of Saint Elizabeth and the Grotto of the lady of Lourdes. But I also am open to ideas here as well."

"I see," said Mark. "What ideas in particular attracted you?"
Emery and Pablo eyed each other warily, then slowly turned back at Mark.

"I mean, from an academic point of view. I mean, I'm having a positive experience here myself," Mark said nervously. "I just wonder what aspects of this place appeal to you."

"Well, Mark," said Pablo. "It's that the church and I see eye to eye about the kind of people who belong in the congregation."

"Really?" said Mark, raising an eyebrow. "What do you mean?"

"Well, Mark, it's no secret that many denominations consider themselves to be God's chosen people. Catholics, Jews, Mormons, Baptists. Each group has certain characteristics to which they adhere, and believe that God's blessing is upon theirs especially, and that those people within it demonstrate certain...behaviors, qualities if you will, that delineate them from the unwashed," said Pablo. "For years as a devout Catholic, I followed the Holy Father's instructions to the letter. I was even a member of *Opus Dei.* Have you heard of it?"

"I read *The Da Vinci Code.*"

"Dear Lord, it's nothing like that. It is simply a lay group of individuals who chose to live like members of the clergy."

"So...celibacy?"

"We deny ourselves many temporal distractions," said Pablo. "Denial strengthens faith, will, and the soul. But this most recent pope has allowed standards to relax in ways that Heaven would be much firmer with, in my opinion. This church holds firm to my standards."

"Which are?"

"There are a number of them," said Pablo. Billy James looked a little nervous.

"Now Pablo, don't scare the boy," he said.

"I think Mark has spent enough time with us to know that we have grace in our hearts," Pablo said. "But he must also know where we are less forgiving."

"In due time, Pablo," said Billy.

"Billy, the Apocalypse is upon our doorstep. World War III has begun, and millions of people are dead all over the world. God's message could not be louder. Mark, the mongrelization of what your country's earliest promises were, well it has reached levels that Heaven has moved to correct."

"Huh?" said Mark.

"The scripture is very clear about homosexuality, as well as the mixing of races. It is also clear about the roles of women in this world, and how they differ from the males' roles. First Timothy says, 'Suffer not a woman to teach, nor to usurp authority over the man, but to be in silence.' Recently the Catholic Church has allowed its firmness on these topics to lapse in their adherence. The Church of Many Blessings has always been firm on their approach to all of these, and that is why I left the Catholic Church to come here to worship."

"Are you serious? In this day and age, your beef is with gays, multi-racial people, and women? They are in the social vanguard for Pete's sake. You can't outlaw people!"

"We are not outlawing them, Mark. We are simply choosing not to socialize or be with them spiritually. We are not denying them any rights as American citizens. We are simply declaring what God has already said about them and choosing to gather among the purer souls. That is all."

Mark Longaberger suddenly looked like he was about to throw up. He glanced around at the church members on the periphery of the barbecue to see if they were listening to Pablo, and how they might react. All of them looked at Pablo with affirmation and pride. A couple of them were nodding. But when Mark caught their glances eye to eye, he read only mistrust, doubt, and concern. He was not one of them yet. He wasn't one of them ever. For a brief moment he felt that it was his responsibility to teach them, as if they were a classroom full of his students. They were ignorant, not evil, and he could convince them of his way of thinking by simply citing a few facts, some statistics, some irrefutable science. He may have felt a little in over his head, but these were educated adults. Surely they would listen.

"Pablo, Billy. You can't be serious about this. This seems more political than religious. I mean, you really think this?"

"It wasn't us that made this political," said Billy. "We contained it to our congregation. It's the crazy socialist liberals who rammed this down everyone's throat. But because we don't happen to agree, we are persecuted, chastised, even ostracized. But not anymore. It's a whole new ballgame now. We can remake America the way the founding fathers wanted it."

Mark felt a chill go down his spine.

"Mark, you must see," said Pablo. "When your country elected someone like Barack Obama-- a mixed-race Muslim, a lover of homosexuals, transsexuals, and all types of natural aberrations--it was very clear what path our country was going down. The road to Hell is paved with good intentions, and no matter how well-intended those people may have been, they were on Satan's path. The Scriptures are clear about this. And thankfully, God intervened and prevented a woman from ascending to the White House, where the murderers of innocent unborn children could be legitimized."

"Holy shit," said Mark. "I think I need to take a walk."

"Think about things Mark. The evidence is clear. God is cleansing the world, and testing us, challenging us to remake it in his image."

"And his image is that of a straight, white, male," said Mark.

"Can you think of a more accurate description of Jesus Christ?" said Pablo.

Mark stood agape, his head shaking ever so slightly in disbelief. He put his soda down and started to walk down the street. His shoulders slumped, and his feet scraped as he walked, as if all of the air had been taken out of him.

"You came on too strong too fast, Pablo," said Billy.

"I disagree. Isn't it better that we know now which side he is on?"

"We could've won that one over," said Billy.

"I'm not so certain," said Pablo. "Either way, he knows where we stand. It's up to him to decide. Chosen, or Unchosen."

"I think you can catch more flies with honey than with vinegar," Billy said.

"That may be true, but was what I was saying vinegar, or was it simply an accurate depiction of what we believe? People also respect truth and directness. He does not have to accept our way completely, but if there are parts that make sense to him, he can be won over that way as well. People do not usually align themselves completely with anything right away. That is more for fringe believers. There are, even to me, aspects of the church's doctrine that are not fully aligned with my beliefs, but overall your approach to things aligns with more of mine than it doesn't. Give him time and allow him to express his own doubts. You may find him more willing to join. Or you may simply discover more quickly that he is not going to be one of us. Either way, it is more honest."

"I suppose so," said Billy. "I know that directness is more your way. I just prefer a little more subtlety," he said. "Let things sink in more slowly. Maybe if you had tried more subtlety with your daughter, she might have come around."

"Apart from being none of your business, my daughter's issues were likely a result of laxity on the part of my former wife, and too deeply ingrained for her to accept my beliefs. It is not uncommon in a child to be rebellious of whatever her parent's ways are. My daughter is likely no more complicated than that. She knew her choices would go against mine, and she took a perverse pleasure in that somewhere in her subconscious. At any rate, I do not speak to her anymore. Her choices have brought about consequences, and I don't wish to discuss it further," said Pablo.

"I'm sorry to have upset you, my friend. I didn't mean to step on your toes and open up an old wound. You and I have different styles, that's all, but we're still doing God's work. You are an invaluable asset to this church, and the day you came to us is still one of the greatest moments of our existence. What you bring us is more than we could ever repay," said Billy, extending his hand. Pablo took it, shook it firmly, and nodded.

"I'm sorry too. It is an old wound, as you say, and I was wrong to give in to anger. We have no problems between us," Pablo said, smiling resolvedly. Father Joe entered the courtyard where the two men were.

"What's going on, gentlemen? Where did Mark Longaberger go?"

"I think I may have frightened him off, Padre," said Pablo.

"How so?" asked Father Joe.

"Pablo simply expressed a few of the church's views on...selectivity, Father," said Billy. "Nothing untoward. He was completely professional. Mark felt uncomfortable and decided to wander off."

"Wander off? Where to?" asked Father Joe.

"I don't know. Why? Is it a problem?" asked Billy.

"That depends on where he wanders and what his state of mind was when he left. If he wanders into the group of people we just began to recruit into our flock, he could cause undue damage."

"How much damage can one guy do, though, Father? I mean, given the circumstances," asked Billy.

"Consider this: He is a young, attractive, charismatic teacher of history, social studies, and current events. His career has him stand before skeptical, rebellious crowds and speak rhetorically to them every day, getting them to accept information that they themselves either don't already know or don't already believe. The very things that make Wes Kent such a resource to us are potentially magnified tenfold in this young man. Word has it that he is very intelligent and well respected. He's also young, popular, and good-looking. The kind of numbers someone like that could bring in include a demographic that is very hard to reach on behalf of the church.

Church, in and of itself, does not attract younger people these days. Wes Kent, despite his good work, doesn't appeal to teenage or twenty-something girls or young men who see themselves in him. Mark Longaberger could do that. He could also—If he decides to flat-out reject what we're selling—do untold amounts of damage to that very same demographic," said Father Joe.

"We won't make a new world with middle-aged men. We need young people as well. In droves. And young people don't usually go to church, because church usually tells them what they're doing is wrong and that they should stop doing it. They think themselves immortal, and rarely consider the afterlife. It takes a virtual act of God to shock them into considering ideas that are larger than they are, like God or Heaven, and where they'll go after this life is over. What just happened this week-- however horrible it has been to the United

States, the world, and this little town—is also a wonderous opportunity to reach young people. Because now they can walk
the streets and see the daily devastation around them. They
can see what horrible things unsaved human beings can wreck
upon one another. Thanks to this horrible Cataclysm, their
own mortality is staring them directly in the face. And we offer
something they've never considered before: a supernatural in-
surance policy. Don't you see, gentlemen? This is our moment.
This is the chance we have now to form the world we've always
wanted to see. We bring order in a time of chaos, and an afterlife in a time of daily death. This chance may never come again,
and we need to capitalize on it. Mark Longaberger is one man,
sure. But every man, especially those with gifts, is an asset.
And we must try to use every asset available to us."

Billy and Pablo stared in awe, nodding. Father Joe's
words were captivating. The men standing behind him in the
courtyard were transfixed. Some were loyal deacons of the
church, others brand new potential converts, but every one of
them was hanging on Father Joe's words. Pablo and Billy nodded in resolution.

"Very true, Padre. Your wisdom is truly an awesome
thing, and your vision is the reason I came here to begin with.
Billy and I will see if we can find Mark before he is frightened
away from us," said Pablo.

"Very well, but I would like to talk with him personally. You two do very good work—and you make a sound
combination, a fine one-two punch as it were. Billy is a little
slower and takes smaller steps, Pablo you are more direct and
forthright, and together you are formidable recruiters. Buy my
sources tell me that Mark Longaberger may require a special
touch. He is a scholar and a thinker, and not only erudite but
also one who considers himself a lifelong learner. I will try to
appeal to him on an intellectual, rational basis and see what we
can do," said Father Joe.

"Of course, Father. I'm sure you'll be able to get him
to see the light," said Pablo.

"Thank you, brother Pablo," said Father Joe. "I will do my utmost."

"And if he doesn't?" asked Billy.

"Hmm?" said Father Joe.

"If he doesn't? See the light?" asked Billy.

"We'll burn that bridge when we come to it," said Father Joe.

CHAPTER 17

Slave Labor

I was morose. Jake was fast becoming my hero, and I had seen him get through some pretty impressive shit this week. He clobbered the three thugs who had attacked the Heffners. He had bested four gang bangers attacking Estela at the Wal-Mart. He even managed to elude some kind of mutated people while rescuing Wendy and the Colonel from a war zone. But this time--this time I couldn't see what he could possibly do to get himself or any of the rest of us out of this. He was tied, beaten, and being ordered around by organized criminals. They weren't just thugs; these guys had done hard time and knew how to run an operation. We were heavily outnumbered, heavily outgunned, and were about to be either separated, sold into slavery or outright killed. Things were looking hopeless. The only smidgen of hope I could conjure up was that Glen Billings had found a way out and somehow they were so busy with us that they hadn't noticed.

Glen was diabetic, and it wasn't unlike him to have some problems. He had even fallen into a diabetic coma once during football season. I figured the same thing had happened here, and that his captors—our captors—didn't give enough of a shit to bother with him. The fact that he was gone didn't necessarily mean good news. To be honest, he could have dropped dead of low blood sugar and one of the guards found him and disposed of his body somewhere. Or even have found him in bad shape and simply finished him off. But given the comings and goings of folks as I was able to observe them while we were at the greenhouse, I didn't think so. I had not heard shouting, nor had I heard any gunshots, and it stood to reason that one of the two would have come up if any of them had found him lying there. I figured that Glen had to be faking. God, I hoped he was faking. If that was true, he had managed to sneak off, maybe even get his zip ties cut, and was just biding his time until he could help the rest of us get free.

That was our only hope as I saw it, and that still meant Glen would have to find a way to free us, get guns, somehow get those guns to us, and then we would still have to be good enough and lucky enough to beat these guys to make a getaway. That would be more classically heroic than anything Jake had pulled off this week. It honestly would be more heroic than most of the crap I saw on television. And Glen was a high school kid. Very few grown men could pull off something like that, much less a teenager with a major health problem. And even in the most desperate hope fulfilled that Glen and the rest of us managed to pull all of that off, that didn't account for the girls, either. If we had managed to do all of that and get away, it would mean leaving the girls, who had been hauled off to God-knows-where. I knew that if Jake managed to get free, there's no way he'd leave the girls. Jake was a combination of Marine Corps 'leave none behind,' bundled with a misdirected overly-protective sense of chivalry, coupled with the guilt he already felt having lost his wife. He'd die trying to free them before leaving them. And that pretty much meant we were doomed any way you spun it.

I sat there staring at our crew. The Colonel looked old and tired. So did Jake, maybe for the first time since I knew him. Jake's boys looked sullen. Tommy looked at the ground and scowled the whole time. Vinny looked on the verge of a breakdown. Al DeFillipo was almost apoplectic. He kept looking around for Maureen, asking me what I thought might happen to her. I just shook my head and told him I didn't know.

Maureen, Wendy, Jada, Estela, and our new addition,

Morgan, had been marched off in a different direction. Larry, or Lawrence, or whatever the Hell our new owner's preferred name was, had been very clear about his intentions for them: Five attractive women. Good price. Good time for his boys. I thought about Morgan and Estela particularly. Somehow their being gay and being raped by thug men just made it worse. I know that it didn't, but being gay myself, I felt an extra pang of pain for them. I just kept shaking my head. I didn't see any way out of this.

"I just don't understand how this man was able to create this compound so quickly," said the Colonel in a loud whisper while sitting on the bleachers of the football stadium.

"What do you mean?" I asked.

"The bombs went off a week ago. This man has a well-armed, well-trained crew; he has taken over the local high school; he has set up a drug distribution center; and has collected a fair amount of captives to be used as slaves for his endeavors. This kind of operation doesn't happen overnight. It doesn't even happen in a week," the Colonel said.

"I'm betting he had it running some time ago," said Jake. It was the first thing he had said out loud since his altercation with Nick when we arrived. "You heard him say he is an ex-con. It's tough for those people to get jobs. Usually it requires someone to take a chance on you for a manual labor type position. He said that he was a truck driver. My guess is that this whole set-up was already in operation in some way before the bombs hit. Once the chaos of that began to spread, they simply moved over and took the next step up."

"I think you may be right, Marine," said the Colonel. "I saw my fair share of that kind of thing happening in Iraq and Afghanistan. Local warlords, drug lords, and crime bosses already had a web set with people in it operating out of sight. Once someone in power was killed or arrested, they made their power move."

"It's like some small-town ex-con decided he wanted to be bigger than he was and recruited half of Cell Block D to help him out. Now he's some kind of apocalyptic warlord gangster trying to increase his holdings," said Jake.

"Shut up, piss-wipe," said Nick, the holder of the shotgun from before. He had come in the back entrance without our knowing.

"You fuckers don't know nothing about Larry," he said. "So just shut up."

"Why don't you tell us, Nick. It's Nick, isn't it?" Jake said.

"Shut up, grappler man, or I'll blow your fucking head off."

"No need to get violent, boss. I'm not fighting now. You were right, I was defending my son back there. It was instinct. But I'm restrained effectively now. I'm not plotting anything. I've done what you asked. I'm not a threat. So, tell us, how'd your boss—how'd Larry—get all this up and running so fast. It's an impressive operation."

Nick paused for a moment, trying to make heads or tails out of Jake's question. Then turned to Jake and scowled.

The Colonel, wiping sweat off of his forehead with his bound hands, stepped up.

"Considering how recently the world began dropping bombs on itself, this operation is moving quite efficiently. It does beg the question, son. How did you do it?" he said.

Nick breathed out, and his face softened a bit, and he nodded ever so slightly.

"You're right, sir. This operation was set up already to a point. Our boss—Mr. Dwyer—owned the trucking company. He was an ex-con himself, and he always offered a hand to ex-cons to get them work. Over half of the company was ex-cons. Some of us even knew each other in the joint. Dwyer was a bossy asshole, though. Treated us like we were his bitches in the slammer. That shit was old when we were actually inside, and it sure as shit got old fast outside.

"So, one day, Larry decides he's had enough, and offs Dwyer and takes over the company. It was the day the bombs fell. Larry had been talking about it for a while, then the day the bombing started, Larry came back from a DC run, organized a meeting, and then we took over. Larry's the fucking man. He was the man in the pen, and he's the man again now. And now we're gonna expand even more and take over a shitload of territory. People will have to pay us a toll just to drive through this area on *our* interstate."

"Impressive," said Jake. "Made his move during the chaos of the bombing. He must have been plotting it a little before, huh? I mean, to get so many moving parts in order in such a short time."

Nick scowled at Jake, not knowing what to make of his curiosity.

"It does seem like a brilliant tactical move," said the Colonel. Nick nodded, turning his head from Jake.

"He had us all ready, told us one day the time would be right for a hostile takeover, he said," Nick mentioned. "Despite what you may think, I don't mind telling you all this shit, 'cause you probably ain't gonna be here long. You bastards are either gonna get sold as labor to another of our partners, or Larry's gonna give me permission to shoot you, so I don't give a fuck what you ask me right now," he added.

"Most appreciative, Nick," said Jake. "Just one more question."

"Make it fast. I'm getting tired of listening to your ass," he said.

"What's your percentage?" asked Jake.

"Huh?"

"For joining up with Larry. What are you getting out of it now that the old boss--Mr. Dwyer, was it? Now that Mr. Dwyer is gone, and whatever operation he had set up is now Larry's, what's in it for you?"

"I'm a partner," said Nick.

"That's what I mean. Partner of what? What do you get for putting your neck on the line for him?"

"I get profit. Money. All that shit," Nick shouted.

"How much have you gotten so far?" asked Jake.

Nick went quiet. His nostrils flared and he ground his teeth at Jake.

"Has he paid you since the coup d'état?" asked the Colonel.

"The what?"

"Since the hostile takeover," the Colonel explained. "My colleague simply wants to know what have you gotten for your effort? How is your life different now than it was under the previous owner?"

"It don't work like that, Sir," said Nick.

"How does it work?" asked Jake mildly, his tone un-threatening and even a little suave.

"I don't have to talk to you about this," said Nick an-grily. "Shut the fuck up."

"Sorry, he didn't mean to upset you. He—we—are just curious," said the Colonel, eyeing Jake. I caught the subtle glance, and like the Colonel, realized that Nick was responding much more pleasantly to him than he was to Jake. The Colonel was trying to send Jake the message to back off and let him find out what he could. For some reason, the tiniest bit of hope en-tered my brain.

"I mean, you all did the heavy lifting I'd imagine. You secured this school campus, all that cannabis we moved, all these weapons. Your boss—Larry—is obviously giving the orders. He knows how much *he's* getting. I think my colleague just wondered what your take was in all of this," said the Col-onel, fluidly.

"He gets what he deserves. Larry killed Dwyer him-self. He's doing plenty. He's calling the shots. He's the brains of the outfit," Nick said.

"Oh, I don't doubt that, son. It's clear Larry has no trouble getting his hands a little bloody. And I'm sure he also gets his share of the profits. I just wondered, with an operation this large, one that's taking in drug money, slave money, and probably some gun money, what are the...*helpers* getting for all their help?"

Nick was silent again. It was all I could do to contain my smile. I realized that Jake had wanted to work a psychological angle, but obviously his earlier altercation with Nick made it impossible for him to switch gears. But the Colonel for some reason was being given some latitude. And he was sharp enough to pick up on that, and was doing the only thing he could, given our situation. He was calm, methodical, emotionless, nonthreatening. He was also breathing hard and sweating. I was worried that he couldn't keep this up much longer. But he had kept pace thus far, and his panting didn't affect his dialogue.

"We're gonna get plenty," said Nick.

"I'm sure you are. I didn't mean to imply otherwise," said the Colonel. "Tell you what. We can just drop it. I didn't mean to pry, and I surely don't want to upset somebody with a weapon held on me."

Nick looked at the ground and chewed his lip a bit.

Just then, the gunman driving the Gator drove up and stopped in front of Nick.

"Hey Troy," said Nick. "What's up?"

"Larry wants these guys at the front of the school. Says he's called a buyer who wants them, and he wants to inspect them more himself now that they've done some work," said Troy.

"Sure," said Nick, turning towards us. "You heard the man. Start walking."

We all rose and began to trek back the way we had originally come. We'd all moved about ten yards down the field when I heard Nick ask Troy if Larry had given him any money yet.

"No. Why? Did he give you some?" asked Troy.

"No. Me neither. It's been a week. We've had several truckloads go out this week, and more than a few slaves too. I just wondered. I mean, he hasn't mentioned anything about it to me."

242

"No, he ain't mentioned nothing to me neither. And we have done a lot of business in one week. I've actually seen money change hands. No, I haven't been paid, come to think of it. Been too busy chasing down new slaves all day long."

"Think we oughta ask him? Larry, I mean?"

"And piss him off? You wanna end up like Dwyer?" asked Troy.

"No, but I don't wanna work for less than I was getting when we were legit, either," he said.

"Maybe if we ask him nice. I mean, respectful and all," Troy said. "I mean, it's business, right?"

"Besides, we're about to make a buncha money on this one. We're gonna sell these people for a shit-ton. The last ones weren't very fit, and the girls were kinda ugly. This crew just loaded up all our shit in that little bit of time. Just look at 'em. There's four young ones, that tough old shit that tackled you, and a buncha hot chicks. Only one who probably won't make it is that old army dude. He's pretty old. He's limpin', sweatin', breathin' hard. Shit, he don't look like he might make it to the front of the school," Troy chuckled.

Nick watched the Colonel struggle up the hill along the path. Then looked down and started chewing on his lip again. We kept marching up the hill towards the front of the school. Al and Jake looked all around. Al was obviously looking for Maureen. I'm guessing Jake was taking in the scene, trying to make a plan of some kind. The Colonel was sweating profusely. He was in good shape for a man his age, but he was nevertheless a man in his sixties. He lifted his forearms to his face to wipe some of the sweat, then grabbed at his glasses for a moment. He squinted, then looked over at a portable classroom trailer in the back of the school. I watched the Colonel for a moment, then risked a glance over there at the trailer. I found the girls. Morgan was on the porch entrance, and another arm was visible in the doorway. Guessing either Wendy or Estela. I shot a glance over to Jake's direction. He gave a quick look at the trailer, the faintest hint of a nod, then looked back down at the ground.

After a few hundred yards we were in front of the school, on the side nearest the football field. There was a passenger van parked in front, with two men standing near it whom I had not seen when we arrived. I looked off to the right to an additional parking lot, and our bus was there with the doors open. I could see our stuff in the back seats still piled up. They apparently had not yet taken the time to remove it.

Troy had parked the Gator and hopped out and was talking with Nick again. You could see by their expressions that they were getting agitated. I hoped that the Colonel's questions had gotten to them—gotten in their heads—but for the life of me couldn't figure out how that would help us now. Even if we could sew seeds of dissent among our captors, they were about to sell us to a new owner. The girls were about to suffer indignities that I couldn't bear to think about, and the status of this gang of ex-cons was going in my 'couldn't care less' file. If things went south for them, it wouldn't matter to us. We weren't going to be here very much longer. I found my thoughts drifting back to what it must have been like being a slave on a Southern plantation, and waking up to find your family members had been sold off over a dinner meeting the night before, and knowing you could do absolutely nothing to prevent it. I felt a lump of despair in my throat as we reached the sidewalk by the bus lane.

Lawrence was out in front talking to the two men. He had a beer in his hand, a pistol holstered around his waist like an old-time cowboy, and he was talking in a loud voice with lots of gestures. Larry was a showman, after all—which is probably why he was able to charm a bunch of former prisoners to join him in killing their only means of financial support--in hopes of a new life of power and money in a post-apocalyptic Virginia hill town. The sniper in the press box had come down to walk us to our point of sale. Nick had taken point and led our group, with Troy riding along in the Gator. We were well-covered by several thugs, still tied, and exhausted from our previous work in the greenhouse. The Colonel was beginning to falter. That had to be hard for him. He had been a veteran of several tours in the Middle East, and he had been bested by American hooligans—and his own advancing age. Al's face began to twist into a sneer of disgust and desperation. He kept trying to look back a Maureen, but the reality of what was coming approached with every step. The men he had undoubtedly hoped, like I did, to be his saviors—Jake, the Colonel, maybe even Glen—were all gone. Jake walked quietly, slightly twisting his zip-tied wrists back and forth.

Finally our meager procession arrived at the front of the school, where Lawrence and his two new business partners awaited. The long sliding door of the passenger van was open, and I knew we were headed to be sold. The two men Lawrence were talking to had accents that sounded a bit like Russian. That gave me a chill. I had seen too many movies recently with vicious Russian mobsters who did unspeakable things to get their way, and I had to admit to myself that I was deathly afraid now. Ironic that someone like myself—who has always fought against racial and gender bias, stereotyping, and homophobia would succumb to some of it myself here and now that my life of freedom was over. But I guess who we are in times of strife is who we are down deep.

"*Privyet, druz'ya,*" said one of the men. He was tall and had slicked back hair and a tattoo on his neck. "Welcome. I'm sure you will like your new accommodations," he said laughing.

"They sure will, Sergei," said Lawrence, laughing as well. "This bunch does nice work. At first I thought they were gonna be a problem, but they shaped up nice. They brought some ladies with them too, if you're interested. I had my eye on one or two of 'em myself, but since you gentlemen brought so much money with you, I thought maybe we would help you fill your van up."

"*Spasibo,*" said Sergei. "I think our relationship is going to be much more profitable than the one I had with your former employer, Mr. Dwyer."

"I'll drink to that," said Lawrence, tipping his beer bottle up for a swig. "Hey Trevor," he yelled. "Go fetch the ladies from that trailer over there."

"What if they're in the middle of something, boss? I heard Clint say he was pretty horny and wanted to get right to it."

"Then you tell Clint to finish fast. These gentlemen don't want to wait any longer for their goods," said Lawrence. Trevor nodded and started walking over to the trailer where we had seen the girls.

"Now then, comrade," Sergei said with smile. "Let's see what I'm getting for my money."
Lawrence gestured with nod of his head and Nick poked us with his gun and told us to move on. We walked up to the sidewalk next to the van.

"These young ones are big and strong," said Sergei. "But these two are old," he said gesturing towards Jake and the Colonel. "And these two look like women," nodding at me and Al. Al sneered at Sergei and Lawrence back-handed him in the face.

"Don't be disrespectful to your new owner," he said. Al looked at the pavement. "Yeah, Sergei, these two are young bucks, big muscles. And I see your point about these two sissies. But don't be fooled about the old guys. One is in the army, and the other has got some fight in him. Tried to wrestle Nick here when they first arrived. Took him down pretty hard, too. They're probably a lot tougher than they look. They're worth the money, trust me. They moved a lot of your new cannabis plants into the truck today. They'll serve."

"I will trust you, my friend" said Sergei. "But you'd better be telling me the truth, or the next deal will not be so lucrative for you."

"No worries, Sergei. They'll be fine," said Lawrence. Trevor came walking up with the girls. Morgan had one of her shirt sleeves ripped. I shuddered to think what had happened and tried to shut it away.

"And here's the ladies," said Lawrence. "Nice group, like I told you."

Sergei's face lit into a big smile. He nodded while looking at each of them. In truth, I don't think I've ever been attracted physically to a girl, but if someone asked me, I would have said that all of them were pretty. Estela, Wendy, Maureen, Jada, and Morgan—who ranged in ages from teens to forties—were good-looking women. And unfortunately, I knew what happened to good-looking women in all of the Russian mobster movies I had seen.

"These are lovely ladies," said Sergei. "You were telling the truth, Lawrence. I did not trust you. Have they been—touched?"

Lawrence looked at Trevor. "Well?"

"Clint was smooching on this one here, but never got her clothes off," said Trevor, pointing at Morgan. "At least, not all of her clothes off."

"For that I will give you a bonus," said Sergei, producing a round wad of bills secured with a rubber band. "Incentive for you to continue to deal with us honestly."

Larry took the wad of bills with a smile and shoved them in his pants pocket. Nick looked at Troy and frowned. Troy's eyes narrowed and he nodded ever so slightly. Nick pursed his lips a moment, then moved forward.

"Nice bonus, boss," he said. "What you get for this bunch?"

"Don't you worry about that, Nick. You don't exactly have a head for figures," Larry said, laughing. Sergei laughed with him.

"Maybe not, but I understand buying and selling. What's the going rate for eleven people these days?" he asked.

"I said don't worry about it," Lawrence retorted, this time more sharply. "You just help get them in the fucking van."

Nick looked at Troy. "Troy, you know how much the boss is selling these folks for?"

"I sure don't," said Troy. "Boss?"

"What is this," said Lawrence. "Why are you two so fucking nosey about my business dealings?" Sergei began to shift uncomfortably and shot a questioning glance at his colleague.

"Our business dealings," Nick corrected him. "We're in this together, remember? Partners? A team."

"You do call us a team, Larry," said Troy.

"Yeah, but you're *my* fucking team. I'm the owner, general manager, and head coach. You just shut the fuck up and run the plays I tell you, got it?" said Lawrence. "This is not the time for this shit."

"Maybe not, but we haven't seen a dime since we started with you a week ago," said Nick. "And I know you've done some cash business this week. Not exactly how a team is supposed to work."

"You ain't getting three squares a day?" said Larry.

"I got that in Lorton," said Nick. "So did you. We still in prison, Larry?"

"You got booze to drink, food to eat, weed to smoke, women to fuck, and the free air to walk around in a town that I run. That sound like prison to you? I'm getting a little tired of this conversation, Nick."

Trevor looked up nervously at Troy and Nick. It was clear from his expression that he wasn't sure where all of this was coming from or where it was going. He looked at Larry, who was red in the face and furious.

"Just wondering about your finances is all," said Nick. "You sold a lotta weed this week, even more today, and now you're selling eleven people. Eleven slaves. I'm just wondering where all that money is going, cause it ain't seen my pockets yet."

"Look, let me deal with Sergei here and get this transaction taken care of, then I can explain it all to you. But right now you're making me look bad, and I've got half a mind to blow your fucking head off right now because of it," said Larry, quickly pulling his pistol and pointing it at Nick.

Nick raised his gun to Larry now as well.

"That how it's gonna be, boss? You gonna shoot me just for asking questions? Troy, maybe you were right. Maybe he is keeping it all and we're just slaves ourselves—no better than this bunch."

"Troy don't you get into this shit too," said Larry. "I'll kill both you motherfuckers right now," Larry shouted, now moving his pistol back and forth from Troy to Nick. "Trevor, put a gun on one of these two."

Trevor lifted his rifle at Nick, while Larry held his gun on Troy.

"We can all calm down and get out of this in one piece, but this disrespect is gonna cost you two," said Larry.

"Won't cost me nothing," said Nick. "I ain't been paid yet."

"There's other ways for you to pay, though," said Larry.

"Lawrence, you and I have business. Let's settle it and I'll be on my way," said Sergei.

"Gimme a second Sergei," said Larry. "Things have gotten a little tense here. Maybe it's good for you to see what happens to people that don't show me proper respect."

Just then we heard Clint trotting up the path from the trailer with his pistol drawn. He sidled up to Trevor and asked, "What the fuck is going on?"

"Nick and Troy asked the boss when they were gonna get paid, and now everybody's pointing a gun at each other," said Trevor. Clint lifted his gun up and pointed it at Troy.

"I got him, Boss. Why don't you finish up your business and then you can deal with these two," said Clint. Now Clint was holding a gun on Troy, who was holding one on Larry. Trevor had his rifle pointed at Nick, who also had a gun on Larry. Larry lowered his gun and nodded at Clint and Trevor.

"You two have crossed the line," Larry said.

"You raised your gun at me first. And you haven't answered the fucking question yet," said Nick. "Clint, Trevor. You two get paid yet?"

"Shut the fuck up, Nick," said Trevor. "We got it good here. Things are happening. Don't fuck this up."

"Don't fuck what up?" said Nick. "You're just as much a slave as these people here. Working for free. Putting up with bullshit. At least Dwyer gave me a check every two weeks. I ain't seen shit since Virginia's answer to Tony Montana here decided to take over the fucking town. It was just a simple question, Larry. All you had to do was answer. But the fact that you got all pissed and pointed a gun at my face tells me all I need to know. Doesn't it Troy? This fucker ain't paying nobody. He's keeping it all for himself. Don't sound much like a team to me. And I'm gonna help you sell these people, two of which are veterans, into white fucking slavery just so you can line your goddamn pockets thicker than they already are?"

Troy nodded, and Larry sneered and pointed his pistol back at Nick.

"You are going to die for this, motherfucker," said Larry.

I looked around at the girls. Their eyes were wide with fear. The Colonel, still sweating and breathing hard, was watching the whole seen with incredulity. Al was tense, immobilized. Even the two college boys, Jake's sons, were agape at the entire scene. Everyone seemed braced for a giant shootout, and we were standing in the crossfire with nowhere to run. Just then, a shot rang out, but no matter where anyone looked, we couldn't see who had pulled the trigger. Heads turned in desperate swivels to see who had fired, but no guns were smoking.

Then Clint slumped to the ground, a puddle of blood forming under him. Standing behind him was Glen Billings. I couldn't believe it. Just then, Jake raised his tied hands together above his head like he was praying, gritted his teeth, and brought his hands down hard with exertion and something like a growl. The plastic bit into his flesh instantly, then the zip ties exploded off of him. His hand were free. He wrenched Larry's pistol out of his hand and onto the ground. Larry clubbed him in the back of the head with the beer bottle, which didn't break, but sent Jake down to the pavement on both knees. Trevor pointed the rifle at Jake instinctively, and Glen promptly shot Trevor in the head. Trevor's skull exploded and his rifle fired suddenly before his limp body dropped to the ground. Sergei's associate was hit in the chest. He clutched at his breast before falling to the ground with a gurgling sound coming from his throat and blood bubbling out of his mouth.

"*Bozhe moy*," shouted Sergei, raising his hands.

Then Glen pointed his gun at Nick.

"Let them go. Let us all go," said Glen.

"Nick, Troy," said Larry. "We can work this out between us. Money is just money. Shoot this fucker right here, let Sergei leave with his property, and I'll give you this wad of cash right now," said Larry.

He reached in his pocket and held it out. We all stood tense, watching what Nick would do. Troy was looking solely at Nick. He held his pistol on Larry, but his hands were shaking violently now. Nick was staring at the wad of money with his pistol on Larry as well. Sergei stood completely still with his hands up, staring at his compatriot's lifeless body next to the van.

"Let us go right now or I'll blow your head off too," said Glen to Nick.

Nick just stood there for a moment, looking back and forth at Larry, Sergei, Troy, and Glen. Then he took a breath. Sergei glanced at his lifeless partner on the concrete, then slowly stepped forward.

"Excuse me, Nick, is it?" said Sergei. "I have already paid for my property, yes? And certainly this business between you and Lawrence doesn't involve me. I have already lost a valuable colleague today, for which I will not be compensated.

Why not let me take what I have paid for and leave—how you say—in one piece, and I will allow you to work this out yourselves, eh?"

Larry was motionless, his hand still out offering the wad of cash. Glen held his gun on Nick. Troy held his gun on Larry. Sergei now stood next to Larry. Nick stared at the two of them. He looked at Troy, nodded, and slowly reached out to take the cash.

My heart sunk.

Nick put the cash in his pocket. Larry smiled and exhaled. Troy looked cautiously at Nick, somewhat unsure of himself. Nick fingered his pocket a bit, feeling the wad of money in it. Then he turned ever so slightly and looked at the Colonel. Then suddenly Nick lifted his pistol and shot both Larry and Sergei in the face. Troy stood agape. Glen's eyes bulged and his mouth dropped, and he lowered his pistol in confusion. Jake was still on his knees. Larry and Sergei's blood had spattered all over his shirt.

"Troy, take that young man's gun," said Nick. Glen just handed it over without thinking.

"Jesus, Nick, what the fuck did you just do?" said Troy.

"I suppose I just put us in charge," Nick said. Troy's eyes widened.

"Do you know what those Russians are gonna do to us now?" said Troy.

"Nothing," said Nick. "They won't come after us right away, because the story they're gonna hear will be a slight variation of the truth. We just witnessed Larry double cross Sergei, take his money, and fearing the Russian mob, we killed him for it. They won't know any different, and it will take them a while to track down the transaction and where the money went. We've got two truckloads of weed, a handful of cash, and a free van to get the fuck out of here with."

"Are you kidding me?" said Troy. "Where will we go?"

"I don't give a damn. But I'm not gonna do slave labor for some junior varsity mafioso in a hick town when the whole fucking world just blew up."

The Colonel looked up at Nick and nodded.

"What about all these fucking witnesses? You don't think they won't turn on us?" Troy said.

"Gonna take care of that right now," said Nick.

I swallowed hard. This was it.

"Colonel," said Nick, "Don't mistake me. I'm not a good man. I've done bad things in my life, and I've paid for some of them in jail. But before I went bad, I was in the army for four years. Looking back now, I'd probably have to say they were the best four years of my life. I guess that's pretty sad when you think about it. They turned me into a man and made me feel like part of a team. My sergeant and my commanding officer were good to me. You kinda remind me of him a little. As good as they were to me, though, I couldn't stay in the military. I'm afraid I don't much like taking orders."

"I gathered that from your last interaction there," said the Colonel.

"I don't pretend to know what you're talking about with all the intel you say you have, but I know Fort Detrick works on some pretty heavy-duty secretive shit. If you have anything that can help save this country from the shit storm that is hitting it, then I need to let you try and do that. You all are free to go. I'm sorry for what we did to you."

Then he lowered his gun and gave a salute. The Colonel saluted him back. Then he walked off, with Troy walking behind him incredulously.

"Un-fucking believable," I said.

"Let's get back to the bus, before somebody changes their mind," said Jake. He reached up and patted the Colonel on the back. "Nice work, sir."

The Colonel smiled big for the first time since I'd met

him.

CHAPTER 18

Father Joe's Outreach

Father Joe drove up to Mark Longaberger in a golf cart as silent as a cat stalking a mouse. Mark lurched a moment, startled, once he realized the cart was there.

"Oh God, Father," said Mark. "You scared me."

"Sorry, my son. This golf cart is all electric. We were able to keep it charged with our emergency generator. Thought I'd try it out. Where are you off to?"

"Um, back to Hunter's Run," said Mark.

"You left in a bit of a hurry," said Father Joe. "Is everything okay?" Mark kept walking, forcing Father Joe to tap the accelerator and lurch forward awkwardly.

"Sure," said Mark. "No problem."

"Son," said Father Joe. "The swiftness of your pace and your inability to look at me suggests otherwise. What's troubling you?" Mark slowed his brisk walk almost entirely. He closed his eyes, lifted his head, and took a deep breath, before stopping and turning towards the pastor.

"I'm not sure I'm such a good fit for your church, Father," said Mark. Father Joe smiled an almost piteously accepting smile and nodded his head at Mark. "I thought something must have bothered you," he said. "What makes you think that?"

"I just think your philosophies don't really jibe with mine," said Mark.

"Why, whatever do you mean, son?" asked Father

Joe.

"I just had a talk with Pablo, and he discussed a few interpretations of things that I don't exactly fall in line with, that's all."

"Well now, you just described nearly everyone in the church, then," said Father Joe, smiling.

"Huh?" asked Mark.

"Why, nobody agrees with everything," he said. "And Pablo is European. They all come off a little extreme, if you don't mind my saying."

"Yeah. Yeah, he did come off extreme," said Mark.

"Give you that bit about the selected children of God, did he?" asked Father Joe.

"Yeah. Yes, he did. Isn't that what your church teaches, then?" asked Mark.

"Mark, every church feels like it's the selected one," he said. "Think about it. That's why we have so many denominations. The one church of Christianity now has so many branches that they all seem specifically different from one another. But in the end, we're really all not that different if you think about it," he continued.

"That stuff Pablo was saying sure sounded different," said Mark.

"Mark, the Jews considered themselves the chosen ones, and that was in the Old Testament. Doesn't that make them technically the oldest recorded racists? Every denomination thinks they have all the answers. The truth is, every church is competing for souls, so to speak. The more people you have, the more sustainable your church, the more universal your message, and the more good works you perform. There are always people in each church who are more zealous than some of their fellow flock. Pablo's one of ours, that's all. He comes from a pretty extreme branch of Catholicism," said Father Joe. "That's hard to shake all at once."

"But Father, that's Catholicism. Your church, I mean...the Protestant Reformation," Mark started.

"Simply changed the power structure of man's relationship to God, my son," he said. "You don't need me to talk to God. I'm just the 'guide on the side,' not the 'sage on the stage.' And apart from some of the habitual dogma, we're all on the same side. I'm sorry he spooked you. I hope that you'll reconsider. We're all just doing God's work right now."

Mark paused and furrowed his brow a little. Father Joe smiled, and silence ruled for the moment. Not an awkward kind—Father Joe just smiled patiently, obviously waiting to see the effects of his words.

"You know Father, I'm not exactly what you'd call a 'good Christian'," said Mark.

"Tell me anyone who is," said Father Joe, still smiling. "Other than Christ himself."

Mark nodded. "Okay, I'll keep an open mind. Guess I shouldn't scare so easily," he finished.

"Good man. Great news," said Father Joe.

"Look, Father, truth is, I do need to be getting back to the school—Hunter's Run. We're all taking care of each other, and I've been gone all day. I just want to check in with everyone. I'm sure we'll be back."

"Of course. Tell Wes Kent that we'll probably be having some kind of gathering tomorrow, and I'd love to have him there. I figured that by now, everyone is taking care to find out what services or utilities they have that work, which ones don't, what loved ones are in touch, and so on. It's a rebuilding time, a time for taking stock. The church wants to help the town any way it can."

Mark said "Thanks, Padre. See you soon. I appreciate your coming to talk to me." Then he kept walking towards the school.

Wes Kent was sitting in the principal's office with his

feet propped up and a smile on his face. An empty plate was sitting on the corner with barbecue sauce smeared on it. Lou Orville sat in the corner on a chair sucking on a rib bone.

"That was delicious," he said. Lou nodded emphatically in agreement, his mouth too full of bone, meat, and sauce to answer.

"Those boys sure do know how to throw together a barbecue," said Wes. "Nice of Emory to bring us by a plate. I've been too busy to leave the campus today."

Lou wiped sauce off the corner of his mouth with his forearm and made slurping noises while giving Wes his agreement with an "Mmm-hmm."

Just then the phone rang on the principal's desk. Wes cut his eyes towards it warily, then remembering that as the man in charge, any phone call to this line was, in fact, to him. He smiled again and picked it up. Lou Orville listened in.

"Hello, Wes Kent," he said with a smarmy grin. "Father Joe! Nice to hear from you. Great spread today, many thanks. I imagine we got some new blood around the church today, hmm? No, he hasn't arrived yet. Sure, sure, will do. Pablo, huh? Yes, I suppose it does. Well that's good. Yes, I'd be happy to. Sure, sure. I will report back periodically, sure thing. Thanks Padre. Goodbye."

"What's that all about?" mumbled Lou, sauce covering his hands.

"You need to find a sink, fast," said Wes. "Don't get that sauce on my furniture."

Lou gave him a saucy scowl, then ran out of the office to the next-door bathroom. Wes could hear the water run and the paper towel dispenser being batted awkwardly. Lou was wiping his mouth when he walked back in.

"It was Father Joe. Apparently, Mark Longaberger got a little spooked when Pablo talked to him."

"He does that sometimes. Pablo, I mean," said Lou.

"Yes, he does. Comes from his *Opus Dei* background. Pretty hard core, that guy. Not that I disagree with him—just some of his methods. Tends to scare off some folks. Better to ease them into things, by my thinking. Still, he's a good man who means well and does a lot for the church. Anyway, Father Joe just wants us aware of Mark's sensitive state right now and said not to push him too hard."

"Good thinking," said Lou.

"We've got lots of work to do, Lou. A town to rebuild, a new world to change, steer, and define. Great opportunities here. Guys like Mark can be real helpful. Good looking young fella like that. The kids think he's super cool, and the ladies all swoon around him," said Wes.

"Swoon?" said Lou.

"Yeah, swoon."

"What the hell is 'swoon'?"

"You know, like pass out. Collapse. Lose consciousness," said Wes.

"From what?" asked Lou.

"From, I don't know, his hotness," said Wes.

"Are you gay or something?"

"Hell no, I'm not gay. Frankly I'm glad to be rid of those weirdos that left with Jake Fisher. No, I'm saying the girls think he's hot and they pass out. They swoon."

"Pass out. Swoon. Okay," said Lou. "No girl ever swooned with me around."

"Somehow I do not find that surprising," said Wes. Lou scowled again.

"Swooning. Who'd have thought?" said Lou.

Just then, almost as if on cue, Mark entered the front courtyard and knocked on the door.

"Ah, here he is now. Lou, let him in."

Lou got up and walked to the main entrance, trailed by Wes behind him.

"Welcome back, my boy," said Wes, offering his hand.

"Hey, Wes. How are things going here?" said Longaberger.

"Swimmingly, swimmingly. The ladies have made some great advancements in the kitchen storage now that the electricity is back on. And we have started to set up more permanent quarters for those choosing to stay here. Father Joe has been helpful in coordinating some cooperation with the church. We're helping each other out. I understand you had the good fortune to meet the Padre."

"Yeah. He's a nice guy. Seems like a wise fellow," said Mark.

"Indeed, he is," said Wes. "Indeed, he is."

"We had a good chat. I've never been what you'd call a religious man," said Mark. "But there are advantages to being part of a greater community with shared values," he said.

"Couldn't have said it better myself, lad," said Wes. "A man needs to tie himself to a good church, a good congregation, a good way of life. That church can be the backbone of the entire community. In fact, we mean it to be that way here."

"Well, your influence is certain," said Mark. "But in this town—where an American saint resides next to a Catholic college—I think you're always going to play second fiddle."

Wes looked a bit perturbed by the suggestion. He pursed his lips, nodded, considered his words a moment, then put his arm around Mark and pointed down the hall. There was a great deal of bustling going on and a large amount of people were coming and going in the hallways.

"Who are all those people?" said Mark.

"Those people are the ones that are going to help ensure that we don't have to play second fiddle in our own town for much longer," said Wes.

"What do you mean?" said Mark.

"We have just announced a partnership with the Church of Many Blessings for outreach for our citizens displaced by this horrible catastrophe that has befallen our town and our country."

"Meaning?" asked Mark.

"We are offering up the school as a place for people

to stay as they get their lives back," said Wes. "The church is partnering with us in terms of supplies and services, as well as getting the word out. That barbecue you helped with was just the beginning. We've got room enough for nearly the entire town to eat here, shower here, even live here. Classrooms are being converted to family homes as we speak. It is truly God's work going on," said Wes.

"This is a public school," said Mark. "We can't really do that."

"Mark my boy, the Cataclysm changed all that. These are desperate times," said Wes. "The rules are different in times of extreme strife."

"Cataclysm, huh?" said Mark.

"It's what they've been calling it on the radio. You know it's working again. Radio, I mean. We are beginning to get back communication across the country. It's still patchy, but we are getting messages with some information about the status of things.

Anyway—yes, we can partner with the church. There's a need out there. If we don't instill some good Christian order, places will devolve into a jungle, like they did the first few days here."

"But you were one of the ones trying to keep people out those first days," said Mark.

"And it was wise then to do so. We didn't know what we were up against. Radioactivity, fallout, illness. Those first days after all the bombs, we knew very little. Now that we have a better handle on things, we can do the Lord's work and bring people in and help them," Wes countered.

"Okay," Mark said cautiously. "It just seems odd that now we're doing the very thing we pushed Jake Fisher out for."

"Now just a minute, Mark," said Wes. "You were part of that vote, remember? And Jake Fisher killed two people in front of you, possibly more at the Wal-Mart. He was violent and dangerous, Mark. I haven't killed a soul here. I think that may be your guilt talking, and I understand. But please know that I didn't like having to make that decision any more than you did. I felt then it was the best for our survival. Just like you felt about initially keeping the Heffners out, remember? But as we take in each day and what it offers, we make decisions, and it's unproductive to fret about decisions we made based on limited information. Go with your gut, I say, and do what your conscience says is right."

"Yeah, I suppose so," said Mark. "I guess you're right."

"Of course I am. None of us are perfect, Mark. We are all God's children. It doesn't mean He wants all of us living together, though. Jake Fisher was leaving anyway to get his sons. We didn't exile him. We condemned his methods. He didn't go anywhere he wasn't headed in the first place. If he returns, we can always welcome him back—but only if he abandons his life of violence and autocracy. He elected himself leader of things, Mark, and then demanded obedience of all of us. I think you saw that before any of us. When we differed from his opinion, he threatened us. When he realized his actions had consequences and that we all stood firm in denouncing his methods, he left. You can spin it all you want, Mark, but that's what happened."

Mark's face pinched a bit as he considered Wes's words. What Wes said wasn't completely inaccurate. Mark felt he had left out some things, but there was simply no debating that what Wes said was true. *Perhaps Wes is right*, he thought. *Maybe it's just my own guilt talking.* Mark nodded and walked down the hallway towards the hustle and bustle of people moving things into classrooms.

"Show me what you've got started," he said to Wes. Wes smiled big and patted him on the back and the two exited the office and turned into hallway.

They walked down the hall a bit and saw a family dragging in mattresses and bags of clothing into what used to be an English classroom. Student desks had been moved off to the side and out into the hallway and some of the mattresses had already been laid down. The entire A-Wing of the building was full of families settling in.

"Wow, this side's already full. You guys worked fast," Said Mark.

"Father Joe is a marvelous communicator," said Wes. "And he's a doer, Mark, not just a talker."

"I'd certainly say he is," said Mark. "Where did all of these people come from?"

"Emmitsburg, Thurmont, even some from just outside Frederick. Some of those poor devils barely made it out alive. They say Frederick is a ghost town. Horrible."

"My God," said Mark. "I knew that its proximity to Washington made it vulnerable, but I never imagined that much damage there."

"Consider that it's the home of Fort Detrick and is close to Camp David," said Wes.

"My God, I never thought of that," said Mark.

"Well, the Russians and the Koreans sure as hell did," said Wes. "I only hope we paid those bastards back in kind."

Mark shuddered a little. "I wonder...I wonder what it's like out there," he said.

"Don't ask, son," said Wes. "I can only wonder why Emmitsburg isn't as bad off. God's grace, I imagine. I wonder if the entire country is like this. The radio message wasn't completely informative. It listed a few off-limits areas, like Washington, D.C. and Norfolk, but not much else."

"I can only imagine how many people have died in all of this," said Mark. "Are they going to play the message again?"

"Every hour, they said, and any updates will come at that time," said Wes. "You were out when the first one came in, I guess. We all were breathless while we were listening. As little as it said, it was reassuring to hear something finally on the air. It was on every station that was still broadcasting. I believe it was the Emergency Broadcast System."

"Wow. I want to be around to hear the next one. I have a question, Wes. Do the folks who started with us here have rooms?"

"Of course my boy. I wouldn't forget the people who started all this. Most of those people had their own classrooms. Robin Eaves is a Physical Education teacher, so she was given a classroom. Melanie was a secretary, so we gave her one as well. Most of us are all in the B-wing. A few nice amenities with that. There's the handicapped shower as well as the Family and Consumer Science suite. We are closer to both of those—so that's a nice plus for us," said Wes, smiling.

"We have separated into sections by gender," said Wes. "Only proper, you know. There's always a need to keep civilized even in uncivilized times."

Mark smiled and nodded. "How about my classroom?" he asked.

"So far the only rooms we have opened up to the homeless belonged to our deserters," said Wes. "Fisher, Reyes, Kelly, Defillipo. All their rooms went first," Wes said, chuckling. Mark smiled politely back.

"Membership has its privileges, huh?"

"Indeed it does, my boy. Indeed it does."

CHAPTER 19

Back On The Road

"Thank God," Maureen yelled. "Halle-fuckin-luyah!"

Everyone was back on the bus, and Jake was flying down an empty Interstate 66 East towards Washington D.C. Al hugged Maureen hard and long. He was fighting back tears and was clearly still tense. Jada and Glen were nuzzling as well, sprinkled with the occasional kiss.

Estela was hugging Morgan, and the two of them were practically all over each other. Watching them briefly, one might assume that they were pretty advanced in their relationship, not people who had just met each other the day before. That whole thing might have seemed fast to unsuspecting onlookers, except that the catalyst on this transformation was what we had just gone through over the last four to six hours. Everyone knows that extreme situations can be powerful attractants and even aphrodisiacs. This group had gone from one life-threatening stress-filled situation to another, and our most recent event was brutal, abusive, and horrifying. If the theory about the aphrodisiac was accurate, our collective shared experience meant that we were all likely to be screwing each other's brains out before we got fifteen miles down the road.

I looked around at everyone. The Colonel seemed as if he'd come back to life. He had gotten a little to eat and drink from the back of the bus and was reflecting on his influence on the entire day's events with satisfaction and maybe even displaying a teeny bit of pride. Jake was focused on the road. He was hard to read in general, but right now his face looked someone defeated.

"You okay, Jake?" I asked. He didn't answer at first.

"Yeah, I suppose," he said. "That was nearly a day of my life I won't get back. None of us will. Because of some truly evil sons of bitches," he said haltingly.

"Maybe not," I said, trying to reassure him. "But their party is over thanks to us. Thanks mostly to the Colonel, though, right?" I gave the Colonel a thumbs up, and he smiled and saluted me back. "One way or another, we broke up their little cartel. So fuck them."

"The less we talk about that whole thing, the better," Jake said. "It's over, we're alive, the cartel is busted, and we can move on."

"Yeah, I guess all's well that ends well. Is Morgan okay?" Jake caught my eyes in the bus mirror. He had seen her ripped shirt and wondered how far her captors had gotten.

"She's fine," I said smiling. I turned to look over my head and she and Estela were locked in an embrace and were rocking slowly together. "Estela's got her."

Jake's eyebrows raised after a glance in the mirror. The two were hugging so closely that they almost seemed like one person. Every few moments they would sneak in a kiss. Jake's eyes opened and he looked at me. "Are they, um?"

"Yes. They are 'um.' Both of them. I picked up on that days ago. You're a little behind, Coach. I thought you were more observant than that," I said.

"I've had a lot on my mind lately," he said with a smile. "Without having to worry about you and your people taking over the Earth now."

I chuckled aloud at that, and it lingered long enough that it got Jake chuckling as well. Stress I guess. First big laugh since being captured and sold to a Russian. Bound to happen.

"You were great back there," said Wendy, staring at Jake in the bus mirror. I turned my head to look as well.

"Me? Are you kidding? I was completely ineffectual. It was the Colonel that got us out of that one. Props to him. Seems everything I tried back there fell flat. Including me," said Jake.

"You have been amazing since the first day I got on this bus," said Wendy. "True, the Colonel was the inspiration on this one, but you did your part. The way you got out of those cuffs."

Jake winced and held up his left wrist. There was a giant bloody cut across it from when he broke the zip ties. "Yeah, pretty stupid, huh?"

"Don't sell yourself short," said Wendy.

I looked at her face as she spoke. She was completely taken with Jake. It was clear to me now. She was wholly enamored by him. I thought back to the whirlwind set of days we all had spent together, and how she must have come to this state of mind. There was no denying that Jake's rescue of her was pretty heroic, to be truthful, and his leadership had been unquestionable since we left. There was much to be admired about Jake once you got past the limp, the scars, and his moodiness.

But the truth was that Wendy was digging on a married man who was on a quest to find his wife and mother of his children. I don't know if she had really processed that part of it yet or was still under the effects of being rescued by our leader, but this was simply not going to go well if it continued. Tommy and Vinny noticed her too. They hid their disdain for Wendy, but it was obvious they were uncomfortable with another woman admiring their dad.

As for Jake, I couldn't get a read on him in terms of what he thought or felt about Wendy. He was using his poker face. I actually never knew him to play poker, but if he did, his unreadable face would have been an asset. His face was expressionless. He was aware that his boys were close-by and listening. I think he could tell that Wendy was into him, but he couldn't let on, not with Tommy all over him about Laura.

I saw Jake's eyes cut across to Wendy when she complimented him. They hung there, just a tad too long.

He had to notice her. How could he not? By all accounts she was a truly attractive woman, and one that was close enough to his age to have to produce just the slightest inkling of a 'what if' in his mind. If I were straight, I'd have gone after her. Not only pretty, but smart, brave, and worldly. I know that we can't really know people after less than a week, but at least on the surface, Wendy was the complete package. I couldn't understand how she wasn't married or even with someone. Married to her work, I guess. Some people are.

Yeah, this had to be hard on Jake. As if losing your wife during World War III wasn't enough, but the guilt that drove him would be his pitiless master. The guilt might have driven him all by itself, but Tommy and Vinny were there to help it along. They had outright accused Jake of not caring about their mother; even hinted that his indifference might have led to her disappearance, and Tommy's tone suggested Jake's indifference might have indirectly led to her death somehow. How would Jake begin to refute it? Jake was completely devoted to his sons. That was unquestionable and evident by the way he went after them. But how devoted had he been to his wife this past year? He had chatted with me about it some. Hints here and there.

I remember one conversation we had in his classroom eating lunch a while ago. It was just the two of us, and he was clearly vexed about something:

"Things aren't great at home, Eddie," he began.
"What do you mean?" I asked.
"Laura. Sometimes I think she hates me," he said.
"Jake, she married you. She doesn't hate you."
"She didn't hate me back then. But I think things are different now," he said.
"How so?" I asked.
"Little cruelties, every day," he went on. "Passive aggres-

sive stuff. Little shots here and there. Always taking little shots."

"Like what?"

"It's gonna seem dumb to you," he said. "Besides, you're gay, so you'll side with her anyway. Snarky gay guys always side with women."

"Shut up, you turd," I said. "Give me an example."

"Okay, so sometimes she'll be telling a story, and I'll chime in with something, you know, just to join her, be part of the conversation. She'll accuse me of hijacking her topic and trying to steal her spotlight. Then another time, I'll back off and not say anything, you know, so I don't accidently hijack anything, and she'll accuse me of not listening or not caring.

"That's unfortunate. That's kind of a no-win scenario," I said.

"That's what I said," Jake replied.

"Still, that's a long way from her hating you," Eddie said.

"Okay, here's another one. I'm always the MC at school events. You know, football games, pep rallies, that kind of thing. She's been to a bunch of them with the boys over the years. She complains all the time that I'm the guy with the mic and says I'm an attention whore. So then I decide to stop doing them, you know? And I tell the school they need to get somebody else. So then we'll go to one of those events, and she complains about how bad the new guy is and says I should be doing it."

"I see what you mean about no-win-scenarios," I said.

"I'm not used to no-win scenarios. I've always been able to out-work, out-plan, out-last or out-sacrifice everybody. Even in the Marines. We had some hopeless situations, but there always seemed to be at least one scenario where we could all agree was the best possible solution, no matter how bad it seemed. We'd agree to it and move on. With Laura, it seems like she's determined to be unhappy. At least with me," he said, looking down at the floor.

"Maybe she just doesn't like you being the hero all the time," I suggested.

"What do you mean?" he asked.

"Well, you are an actual war hero. You are, in many

ways, a hero to many of your students. You are also a hero to the kids you coach. You're trying to be the hero at home. Maybe she wants to be the hero for a change. Maybe she wants you to experience that no-win scenario. You seem to win at a lot of things. Maybe she just wants you to lose now and then. Be the sacrificial lamb. Give her some spotlight."

"It's not like I seek the spotlight," he said back defensively.

"Still, you do get it a lot. Imagine what it's like for someone who never does," I said. Jake scowled at that.

"I don't want the spotlight. She can have it. I just want her to act like she likes me. She seems so angry at me all the time," he said. "Sometimes I just want to retreat, you know. Like, move away and hide. Just hide away from everyone, especially her."

"I'm sorry buddy," I said. "I guess everybody makes choices they regret sometimes," I said, trying to sound philosophical.

"That's just it," he said. "I don't regret it. She was the right choice. I'd do it again ten times out of ten. We agree on all of the important stuff. Religion, politics, how to raise kids, how to treat people. And she's a really thoughtful, selfless woman. Just not to me. I'm the exception."

"Los que queremos mas tambien nos hará daño." I said.

"I didn't quite catch all of that. Those we love, something-something?"

"Those we love most will also hurt us. It's an old proverb."

"Fits here I guess. I don't know what to do. I don't want to be single. I don't want to leave. I love our life, love our home. I don't want to be that pathetic divorcee living in a studio apartment with nothing in his life but work. Even with my boys out of the house, I just can't do that," he said.

"But you're obviously miserable," I said. "We all deserve to be happy, don't we?"

He didn't answer me then. And I felt really bad for

the guy that day. That had been a few years back, when Vinny was a junior in high school. Jake had to see him every day and keep it to himself, and I could see it was hard on him. It was his opening up to me about all of it that had made us close. He showed some rare vulnerability to me, and I never betrayed his trust. I recommended therapy, but neither of them wanted to discuss private matters with a stranger. In addition, the boys could sense the tension there. Maybe they weren't aware of how much there was, but they weren't fools.

Strange how a guy like that, who was truly fearless , put his life on the line for others, and was one of the hardest working people I knew, just couldn't find a way to make his home a happy enough. It must have been incredibly frustrating having a daily reminder of your greatest failure right in front of you like that, especially for a guy like Jake, who just always seemed to find a way to win at so many things.

I looked at Wendy again, and I felt a tiny part of me kind of rooting for her. I wanted to see Jake happy again. He had moments of humor, being a smart-ass, but real, unfettered happiness was a rare sighting these days among everyone— especially Jake. I'd just keep my mouth shut for now. His boys were omnipresent, and his situation was unthinkably complicated.

I looked around the bus for a minute. I suddenly realized I was surrounded by couples. Morgan and Estela. Al and Maureen. Jada and Glen. Maybe even Wendy and Jake. And suddenly I felt horribly lonely. As a gay Hispanic man in a red region of a blue state, I was courting danger every day just being me. I liked being single. Young people are supposed to be single. I would drive to DC and hook up with guys. I enjoyed the party atmosphere when I had time for it. I was young. But just now—now, when everyone seemed to have someone next to them—now I felt utterly alone. Now I realized why people sought out life companions. For moments like this, when your world was coming down around your ears, challenging your very existence. Sharing in something like that suddenly seemed much better than having it all to yourself. Like I did. All by myself. My self-pity party was interrupted by Morgan and Estela, who made their way to the front of the bus near my seat. Estela sat close to me.

"Hola," I greeted her.

"Hola, Eduardo," she answered, and grinned widely. She had Morgan's hand.

"You seem happy," I said.

"*Eddie, estoy tan alegre que no puedo creerlo. Es como Morgan fuera hecho especialmente para mí. La conocí solo hace dos días, pero no sé. La adoro*," she said. Morgan smiled uneasily. She had heard her name, but didn't understand what was being said.

"In English, Estela. It's bad manners," I admonished her. I turned to Morgan. "She says she can't believe it, that it seems like you were made for her, and that even though she just met you, she adores you."

Morgan beamed, and squeezed her hand tight.

"I feel the same way," she said.

"I'm happy for you," I said. And I was. The cynic in me said that relationships born out of traumatic events couldn't last. From what I could tell, they were both on the re-bound, and both were without their families, at least for now. That wasn't an ideal start, but they were young, and naïve, and no one could tell them any different. It was ironic, because I thought I was young and naïve, but here I was judging them like an old realist.

"Eddie, are we headed to find my family now?" Morgan asked.

"Yes, yes we are. We're driving to Washington. And we'll pass through Prince William County, and Fairfax County, and near where you're from. Once we get you settled, the Colonel needs to find someone in the defense department to give his report to. He and Wendy have seen things. Things that might be beneficial for our military to know. Then we all can go about our business. Wendy lives nearby; my parents are there somewhere, and so is Vinny's mom. We'll sort it all out."

"Thank you all so very much. Vinny said you'd help. He said his dad would find a way. It's odd, because Vinny picks on him a lot, and talks about him like he loathes him sometimes, but clearly he respects him enormously. He hides behind it by joking, but you can see that he'd be lost without his dad," she said.

"Jake's a good man. We could be a lot worse off," I said.

We had driven for about an hour and a half, and were closing in on Manassas, when I heard Jake start in with the profanities.

"Goddamn asshole Hell-fuck! Now what's this shit all about?" he said.

"Jake, we're both linguists. It's embarrassing. Don't force the curse words. It's beneath you," I teased.

Suddenly the brakes of the bus started to squeal and I looked up ahead on the highway. I was having flashbacks of the criminal roadblock in Front Royal. Ahead of us now, however, there were tanks. Honest-to-God tanks blocking the entire highway Eastbound on I-66.
I wondered for a moment if every town we passed was going to have convicts trying to capture slaves and drugs, but then I noticed that everyone there was wearing a military uniform. No other cars were on the road. I guess we were the only ones who made it past Front Royal. A soldier held out his hand to stop, and Jake rolled slowly until we were still. The soldier, who was armed with a pistol and a rifle, walked up to the window.

"I'm sorry sir, you cannot pass," he said. "The road to Washington is closed. The capital is in quarantine, and martial law has been declared.

"Sergeant," said Jake, looking at the stripes on the man's uniform. "We have vital information to share, and some people to take home. "After all we've been through today, we should be allowed to go through."

"I'm sorry sir. You're going to have to turn around.

There is a small access road there in the middle," he pointed to an emergency vehicle pass through off to our left. "No one is allowed in or out until further notice."

The Colonel leaned over to the window.

"Son, I have vital information to pass."

"I'm sorry sir. My orders are nobody in or out," said the soldier.

"Who's your commanding officer?" the Colonel asked.

"That's classified, sir," he said.

The Colonel's face changed. He was not in his formal uniform—only his BDU's—or Battle Dress Uniform—which essentially was camouflaged pants and an olive green t-shirt. He paused for a moment as if trying to decide if he needed anything, then motioned for Jake to let him off the bus.

"Stay on the bus, sir," said the sergeant.

"I'll be goddamned if I will, soldier. I am your superior officer. I have a clearance level higher than your goddamn I.Q., and if you live through this goddamn war it will be because of information I have provided. Now get me your goddamn C.O. right now, or so help me Jesus when this war is over I'll see to it you're scrubbing shit off of the floor in the Leavenworth latrine for the rest of your miserable life for insubordination!"

Everybody's eyes bugged and mouths dropped. Even Jake's. I didn't know the old bird had it in him. Wendy was elated. She was thoroughly enjoying seeing the Colonel shift into a whole new gear. She made a squinty smiley face and high-fived me silently.

"Go get 'em, Ray," she whispered.

The Colonel got off the bus and walked towards the tanks. An officer who was dressed more formally than the sergeant was walking briskly towards him. Then Col. Raymond Cannaveral started poking the officer in the chest, pointing to the bus, and gesticulating animatedly. The officer's face fell several times, and he began to look alarmed. Ray pointed to the bus again, and the officer shook his head. Ray became more animated, but the officer stood firm. Ray's face grimaced a moment, then he nodded resolvedly and walked back to the bus.

"What's the deal, Colonel?" Jake asked.

"They're going to let me through, Jake. But not the rest of you. Looks like this is where I leave you, Marine. I will be transported into an area where some of the surviving top brass resides. Then I'll give them my report."

Wendy looked at Jake a moment, then slowly rose.

"I'm afraid we have to part ways here too, Wendy," the Colonel said.

"What?" she answered.

"They won't budge. Despite clearances to Fort Detrick, you're a civilian, and you can't come. I'm afraid I couldn't persuade them. The situation here is critical. They have no place for you."

"But I did that research with you. I'm part of it. Hell, I'm more than part of it. It's more mine than yours," she said angrily.

"I know. I know it is. I told them that too. I'm going to try and fix things once I get into the Pentagon, but for now, these guys aren't budging.They're not going to give an inch on this. I'm so very sorry. You've been wonderful to work with. Your work could turn the tide in all of this."

"What about those things? Those mutate things? Are you going to tell them about all of that?" she said.

"Of course. Everything. In fact, any notes that we brought with us I have to take with me. I'm so very sorry. I wish I could fix this," he said. "You deserve better. Much better."

"But where will I go?" she said in a sad whine, suddenly sitting back down. "I live in Washington. I can't go back to Frederick. There's nothing there. I, I have nowhere to go." She looked like she might start to tear up, and her breaths came in shallow bursts.

"I know, dear. I'm so very sorry. I don't know what to

tell you. I wish I could help," the Colonel said.

I looked at her that moment. Strong, brilliant, dedicated—and now, suddenly lost. Just like the rest of us. We didn't know where to go or what to do. Before, she was just a rescue victim we were transporting to her next assignment. Now, she was one of us. Homeless, lost, a stray. I glanced at Vinny and Tommy for a moment, gritted my teeth, and made a decision.

"Jake?" I said. "You got this?"

Jake looked back at me. He looked nervous. I can't remember ever seeing him nervous before. Then I looked around and saw Tommy and Vinny staring at him.

"Jake! You got this?" I asked more fervently. I saw his eyes in the mirror. Then I looked at Wendy. She was on the verge of tears.

"Jake!" I yelled.

"You're with us, Wendy," he said finally. "We take strays on this bus. Of course you can stay with us. We've got you."

She laughed, teary-eyed. Tommy and Vinny were motionless.

"You're practically related already," I said. "Welcome to the family."

"Well, thank you," she said. "I'm so sorry to be a burden. It's just that work was all I had, and now." She trailed off.

"Don't give it a second thought," said Jake, his voice a little hoarse.

But obviously he had given it a second thought, or it wouldn't have taken him so long to answer. Funny—when it was him leading the troops back at Hunter's Run, he wouldn't have hesitated a second to take someone on, to embrace them as part of the group--least of all a damsel in distress as lovely and pleasant as Wendy. But with his sons there, Jake wasn't the same. He was diminished somehow. Less confident, less sure of himself. Wendy stared at him awkwardly. I was betting she noticed the change as well, even having known him less than a week.

"Dad, if Washington is closed, does this mean we can't look for mom?" said Tommy.

"Yeah, how can they do this?" said Vinny. "You're not gonna let them do this, are you?"

Jake rubbed his squinting eyes, half slouched over the steering wheel.

"Dad? Are you hearing us?" shouted Tommy.

Jake stared out bleary-eyed at the tanks and the departing Colonel. He stared at the empty highway beyond, and at the damaged mirror on the bus that had been shot out by the hoodlums in Front Royal. He closed his eyes, took a deep breath, and wheeled on his sons.

"Are you two blind? Do you not see a string of army tanks in our way? A full bird Colonel can't even get his government-cleared research assistant to be able to go with him, and we are instructed to turn around. What part of that do you think I can control?" said Jake. The boys were silent at this, their mouths slightly agape. They suddenly looked hopeless. I tried to remember that they had just lost their mother and were clinging to the slightest hope they might find her again. That hope rested in the man at the steering wheel, who suddenly was powerless to help for the second time in a day.

"The real question," said Al DeFillipo, "Is where are we going now? We can't help find Morgan's parents. We can't go look for Tommy and Vinny's mom. So...what now?"

"We go back to Emmitsburg," said Maureen, without pausing.

"Why there?" I asked.

"Because for most of us, it's home," she said. "And because now that we've made it out of the school and realize what the world is actually like out here, we are in a totally different position. Some of us can go home, try to get our lives back together. At least a little. We were trapped those first days at Hunter's Run, but now we have options. We can try to make the best of it. We go home."

Jake looked in the mirror at everyone for a moment, then nodded.

"She's right. We go home," he said.

Morgan was keening. She had expected to be able to look for her parents, and the military's blockade of the interstate was driving home the notion that she may have already seen her parents for the last time. She started rocking back and forth.

"Shhh," said Estela. "It'll be alright. Come home with me for now. It's not the end. Just a setback. We can try again, when things open up." Morgan hugged her hard, and Estela caressed her hair.

We said our final good-byes to the Colonel, who collected his things, hugged Wendy, and promised to get in touch with us as soon as he was permitted. We assured him he was doing the right thing, then we bid him adieu, and he walked past the blockade and out of our lives. At least for now.

"Home," said Jake. He shifted the transmission to reverse, then rode across the pass-through onto Interstate I-66 West. He glanced at another line of tanks on the other side of the highway, perhaps deterring last-second desperation runs by lunatics. We were not of that mindset. Soon we had the highway rolling under our wheels and within another hour had merged back onto I-81 north towards Maryland.

CHAPTER 20

Return of the Mutates

The trip was quick. We had a tank full of gas, and Jake was flying down roads he knew. This far away from Washington, things looked normal, so with nothing to see, we sped to our destination. We blew past Winchester and drove over the rapids of the Potomac and Shenandoah Rivers near Harpers Ferry, then past the rail town of Brunswick, Maryland and neared Frederick again, where Jake began to slow down.

"What's wrong, Jake?" I asked.

"Not sure what to do around Frederick," he said. "This place seems to have been hit hard, and we know that those...things are around here somewhere."

"Seems to me that if you're trying to avoid something, faster is better," said Tommy. Jake smiled and nodded.

"Point taken, boy," he said, jamming his foot onto the accelerator. We were the only car on the road moving, but we often saw some off to the side, in ditches, even on the shoulders that had been abandoned. But no people at all. It was eerie.

"I have to admit, Dad, I didn't really believe you completely. But you're right. This place is a ghost town," said Vinny.

"All of this looks spooky to me," Al said. "But we're moving fast, so at least we aren't likely to see those orange things."

Wendy shuddered at the mention of them.

Then they came at us.

A group of about ten of the orange mutates came clambering up the hill. They had been hidden behind a copse of trees and bushes on the far side of an overpass, but now, in the open, they were sprinting. It was chilling to watch them. Some ran on two feet like men. Some moved more like apes, somewhere in between. Some crawled like bears. And in the back, two stood upright, walking slowly, gesturing. They were clearly in command.

"Jesus," Al yelled.

Then a loud bang was heard as one of them literally flung itself into the side of our bus, instantly denting the side and bouncing off, seemingly unfazed by the collision.

"Holy shit," said Vinny. "Dad, what the hell are those things?"

But Jake couldn't answer his son. He was swerving to miss them, trying not to crash us or get us hung up on the hills. If the bus stopped, we were dead. A second one jumped onto the step and grabbed the big mirror hanging from the side. His snarling face stared into the window only feet from us. Wendy lurched backward to distance herself and screamed.

I looked into its eyes. The eyes were pale, almost while. Its skin was a dark orange, and its hair was thick white. The eyes were empty, and it was drooling and making some kind of horrid sound like a fox or a wounded hound.

Then it started banging on the door. Jake looked around the bus.

"Boys, are any others on the bus?" Jake asked. Tommy and Vinny instantly scanned the area.

"No," Tommy answered. "Just that one."

Jake sped up, then grabbed the handle for the door opener.

"What are you doing?" I asked. "You're not going to let that thing in, are you?"

"Not if I can help it," said Jake. He gripped the handle hard, flexed his arm muscle, then yanked on the handle with everything he had. The door flew open and smacked into the creature's face and kneecaps. It shrieked in pain, wobbled a bit, but held on. Jake pulled the door shut again.

"Dammit. I was hoping that was gonna work," said Jake.

"Try again Dad. Rapid fire," said Vinny.

Jake yanked on the handle, opening and closing it repeatedly. The creature screamed a horrible scream and rolled its head in anger. Still it held on.

"These fuckers are tenacious, aren't they?" said Jake.

"You have no idea," said Wendy. "Do you have any weapons?"

I looked up, my face brightening at the thought.

"We have a shitload. Estela, where are the guns and bows?"

Estela was up and moving to the back of the bus like lightening. Morgan sat upright, a look of terror on her face. Estela rummaged through the bins in the back seat and pulled out a handgun and a clip of bullets. The creature was clawing at the door, trying to wedge its fingers between the two folding doors. Jake was holding onto the handle to shut the door. He was struggling, and the bus was starting to swerve.

"I got it," said Vinny, and the strapping 18-year-old took over for his father. Vinny held the handle and the doors shut, while Jake steered the bus straight again. Estela was fumbling with the clip for the pistol.

"Bring it here. I got it," shouted Tommy. Estela was panicking. She dropped the gun, then picked it up and handed everything to Tommy. Within seconds he had loaded the clip and flicked the safety off.

"Ready dad. I have a .38 caliber Browning."

"Okay. Vinny, on the count of three, open the door again. Tommy, don't hit the glass. Be sharp," shouted Jake.

"Ready," said Vinny.

"Ready," said Tommy.

"Okay, boys," said Jake. "One, two, three."

Vinny slammed the door open and the creature wailed. Tommy shot it in the arm, which was flailing on the far side of the door. Flesh and blood flew out of the arm, and the creature wailed louder. But still it held on.

"You've got to shoot it in the head," shouted Wendy. "It's the only way."

"The head? What is this, fucking Zombieland?" I shouted.

"Just do it," she said.

"I can't," said Tommy. "I'd have to shoot through the door."

"Vinny, close the door half way. Tommy, can you get a shot off with one hand out the door?"

"I think so."

"Can you do it accurately?"

"I don't know," Tommy said.

"Gotta try," said Jake. Vinny started to close the door, and the creature wrapped its fingers around the edge.

"Shit," said Vinny. "It's got the door."

Tommy shot again. This time the bullet flew wide, hitting nothing.

"Damn it," Tommy said. "I can't get a good angle."

"Are there any more around us?" Jake asked.

"Not for like half a mile. This is it," yelled Al from the back.

"Tommy, if I slam on the brakes and it falls, can you nail it?" Jake asked.

"Yes," he answered back.

"Everybody hold on!" Jake yelled. "Big stop coming!" Everyone grabbed a hold of the seats and ducked down. Jake slammed on the brakes hard. We all lurched forward into the seats in front of us Vinny smashed into the dashboard, held onto the door handle and spun around as the door swung open. Tommy was wedged up against the front pole and the thin metal barrier in the front seat. He righted himself and held the gun up. The creature had fallen off and rolled forward, but not before wrenching the mirror horribly out of place. I couldn't tell if it was broken. I was looking to see how and where the creature had landed.

It had pitched forward onto the road. Wendy said later that had it hit the road on its head, the impact would have killed it. As luck would have it, the mirror had saved the creature's life. A regular person might have pulled his arm out of socket or dislocated an elbow, but the creature lay there for a moment trying to recover itself. Tommy shook his head as if in a daze, then hopped outside, aimed his pistol one more time, and fired.

The shot took off half of the creature's skull. It lurched backward, fell, and remained still on the pavement.

"Back in," yelled Jake. Tommy was frozen for a moment, then turned and looked behind the van. The other creatures were running towards the bus.

"Dad, they're coming. Jam it," he yelled, pulling himself on the bus.

"Holy shit, my arm," said Vinny. He had wrenched his own arm in the quick stop. He assessed himself and sat down, rubbing his shoulder.

We sped down the road for several miles in complete silence. Everyone was trying to process what they'd just seen. Our original crew now had gotten a much better view of the things we drove past on the way down. Jake's sons and Morgan were slack-jawed and speechless. I looked around the bus. Everyone had looks on their faces that read of terror, dread, and disbelief. Finally, someone spoke up.

"I hate those things," said Wendy.

"What are they?" asked Vinny. "You gave us the short version before. Can you explain it a little more than last time?"

"Well, as you know, we call them mutates," said Wendy. They are essentially people who responded unusually to a new configuration of Russian weapons. Most people died instantly upon exposure, but a small percentage had a bizarre reaction. Their skin color changed, their hair color changed, and the more primitive portions of their brains took over. Some reverted back almost to an ape-like state, but not all of them. An even smaller percentage seem to be less affected, retaining more brain capacity. Those were the ones you saw walking upright, directing the others. They seem to be the leaders. They somehow communicate with the more ape-like ones. Telling them what to do. We presume that it is through noises, gestures, or maybe even something pheromonal.

"So why are they coming after us?" said Tommy. "I mean, they're not zombies who eat brains, right?"

Wendy frowned.

"Right? Why are you frowning? Jesus, they eat brains?" said Tommy.

"They're not zombies in that they are not dead, and they don't eat brains. Well, not only brains."

"What are you saying? That they eat living people?" asked Morgan, shivering visibly.

"Yes. They are driven by a need to feed frequently. Their metabolisms are much higher than ours. And they seem to be carnivorous only. And they're not too discriminating about what kind of meat they eat," she said. "They are also scavengers and will eat carrion."

"Holy shit. Maybe that explains why we don't see anyone," said Tommy.

"What do you mean?" asked Vinny.

"I mean that they have eaten everyone else, dumb-ass," Tommy said.

"Screw you, Tommy. If that's true, then where are the bodies of everyone else?"

"For some reason they prefer to haul their meals into a private cache and eat together where they won't be bothered. We watched them drag colleague after colleague of ours at Fort Detrick. It was horrific," Wendy said.

"And how long have these things been around?"

asked Vinny.

"Since the bombings," said Wendy. "About a week."

"How did you learn so much about them so fast?" asked Tommy.

"We captured one right away. When there were more of us. We were able to sedate it and run a multitude of tests. Everything we could think of. Brain scans, EKG's, everything. We didn't have time to process all of the data at first. The one we captured died after a day and a half of not eating. When that happened, the Colonel and I began to dissect it."

"Gross," said Tommy. "I always hated biology lab. So, what did you find?"

"They're human. Just metamorphic humans. Something in the Russian weapons sped up a mutation process in them. Why some end up like they do—we never found that out. But we do know that in the one we found, its brain was only using the most primitive portions of the limbic system. It was effectively a reptile, at least in terms of its brain function. The outer layers were almost completely vestigial," said Wendy.

"Dad, did you know all this?" Tommy asked Jake.

"Wendy explained some of this to us on the way down to get you. You all are getting the much more detailed version. There are some parts I've never heard, however," said Jake. "Wendy, you're saying that they have to eat every day to survive? And they only eat meat?"

"From what we could discern, yes," she answered. "At least on the one we caught. We really need to test them in mass numbers to know more about them. But that doesn't seem likely."

"So you've only seen them eat human beings so far?" Tommy asked.

"We saw some snag a squirrel right out of a tree," she said. "I have to presume it's anything with flesh that they go after. The ones that give the orders, the upright ones—they sent the ape-like ones up the tree after the squirrel. There's clearly a hierarchy. The leaders look more human than the others. Almost like someone with a really deep, fake tan and white hair. The other ones almost look distorted a little. Like cavemen," Wendy said.

"This is really unbelievable," said Vinny. "I'm sorry I doubted you, Dad."

"I didn't know you doubted me," said Jake, smiling.

"I never said. I thought you were full of shit," he said. "More so than usual."

"I am at my standard bullshit level, son," said Jake. "Gauge accordingly." Vinny smiled feebly. We rode past the turnoff to Fort Detrick and headed north towards Emmitsburg. As we passed Thurmont and Catoctin State Park, the tanks were still blocking the road to Camp David.

"I wonder where that son-of-a-bitch is right now," I said.

"Not a fan of the president, Mr. Reyes?" Tommy asked. But Tommy already knew my answer. Our president was an arrogant, homophobic war hawk who entered into every pissing contest he found. He bullied, taunted and threatened other world leaders throughout his presidency, and right up until the first bombs struck, no one believed that he would bring about the world war that we were currently experiencing. Denial is the strongest drug, my parents always said.

And though the truth was that our current state was due to a plethora of factors all leading up to a perfect storm of violence, I blamed him personally for the Cataclysm and for the World War that we all, I supposed, were still in. A week had passed since the world had blown itself up. So many explosives passed each other in the air at once, that in the two days of it we found it impossible to keep track. I remember listening to the major media stations with Jake at the school. We stayed up all night into the second day, listening for updates. We had received some of the info as to who was bombing whom. The first several hours seemed like a dream. The radio and television stations were keeping score like a football game. Then as more and more countries became involved, the updates stopped coming in, and the emergency broadcast system was all that was left. Until there was nothing at all.

The status of our own country was still seriously in question, so I imagined that any news of the rest of the world was impossible to retrieve. We had not blown ourselves into the 18th century, but there wasn't enough of our country functioning yet to connect itself to parts that were. The not-knowing was maddening.

We drove past Mt. St. Michael's University. Estela looked up ominously, staring at the campus. I suppose she had a lot of baggage there. I have faced prejudice before. Anti-gay, anti-Hispanic. It's been part of my life from day one. But for her, it must have been especially difficult. Could you imagine? Moving across the country with everything you had to be with someone, then having that person—and every part of the world that surrounded her—reject you completely, leaving you alone in a strange place with no one to connect to. Such a beautiful campus in a beautiful part of Maryland. And a good school as well. But the Catholic church can be unforgiving to some things, I suppose, and homosexuality was always one of them. At least according to that professor who confronted her.

Being Hispanic, my parents had been good Catholics when they arrived in the U.S., and we had spent much of my youth in and around the college and the Grotto, and the Shrine of St. Elizabeth Keton there. They had even worked there briefly but had moved on to teach together at Hollowel when they were both offered tenure track positions at the same time. I started thinking about what must had happened to my parents again and had to fight back tears. I had successfully compartmentalized them in order to move forward and face daily survival at Hunter's Run, and the guilt of not having thought of them creeped into my mind. My throat tightened a little.

And then, as if reacting to my very thoughts, something strange happened, almost as if on cue.

My cell phone buzzed. I had a voice mail.

"Whoa—what the hell is this?" I asked. "How do I suddenly have a voice mail?"

"You have a voice mail?" Wendy asked. Jake's eyes looked up in the mirror excitedly.

"I haven't had a text or a voice mail for over a week," said Tommy. "And that was you, Dad."

"Does this mean satellites are working?" asked Al.

"Eddie, what is it?" Jake asked.

"I'm checking, I'm checking. I didn't even hear my phone go off," I said.

"Put it on speaker," said Wendy.

I pushed the speaker button and started listening.

It was my father. And he was speaking in English.

Eduardo, if you can hear this, we are alive. We managed to find our way into a government bomb shelter near the National Mall built in the 1950's that was still intact. A colleague found us as soon as the bombing in Washington began, but we are safe. There is one phone here, and it is a land line. We are waiting here with about forty other people. It is a bit cramped, but we have ample food and water, as they were using part of the room for vending machine storage. We are all taking turns using the phone, so we cannot talk long, but we are okay. I do not yet know the number of this land line, but if this call gets through your phone should identify it. It will likely be busy if you try to call back anyway, as everyone is taking turns leaving messages, and we were among the first. It was requested that we speak in English. There are some government workers that are nervous that we are South American. I believe there were some South American countries who declared themselves enemies of the United States. Peru is not one of them, of course, but people are nervous, so we are honoring the request, and speaking to you in English. We are praying that you made it through all of this. We will try again to reach you, but please don't worry. We love you, son.

I broke into tears. I couldn't help it. It was like a dam burst. I had been trying not to think about my parents at all. I had decided to presume they were dead in my own brain. That made it easier to focus on my own survival. But I wondered. We all wondered. I cried hard. Deep, uncontrollable, heaving sobs. Wendy put her arms around me. Morgan and Estela moved up and did the same. I was embarrassed that I couldn't control myself, but I just let it all go.

I looked up at the mirror in the bus. Jake was smiling. And there were tears in his eyes.

"Jake," I said, "How is it that you're crying? You are such an enormous pussy." I then started laughing uncontrollably, and so did he. It was one of those contagious laughs. Pretty soon everyone was laughing and crying together. The tension broke, and we all just let ourselves go. My voice mail must have continued listing previously saved messages throughout all of the laughter, because as our laughter finally died down, and our breath returned, and our abdominals started to relax, I heard the lady's voice on the voice mail message come back on:

-First skipped message.-

Everyone's eyes bugged again, and we all held our breath to hear another message that had come in. It could have been one that came in either before or after my parents' message, depending on whatever buttons I had hit while laughing and crying hysterically with everyone. You could have heard a pin drop.

Eddie, soy yo otra vez. Casi me olvidé. Dile a Coach Fisher que vimos a su esposa cuando el ataque empezaba. Ella es-

taba hablando por su celular, pero no nos vio. Tuvimos que entrar, y no pudimos llamarla, pero ella sí estaba viva cuando entramos. Ojalá que le ayude a Jake. Buena suerte, hijo.

Holy shit!

Eddie, it's me again. I almost forgot. Tell Coach Fisher that we saw his wife when the attack was beginning. She was talking on her cell phone, but didn't see us. We had to enter, and we weren't able to call out to her, but she was definitely alive when we entered. I hope that this news helps Jake. Good luck, son.

Estela's mouth dropped and she turned towards Jake. I wondered if Jake had understood all of it.

"Jake, did you hear that?" His face went blank.

"Dad, what did it say?" asked Vinny.

"It's about your mom," I said. "My parents saw her when the bombing began but weren't able to call out to her when they entered the bomb shelter, but she was alive when they saw her. She was on her phone.

Vinny and Tommy looked at each other.

"Mom's alive," said Vinny, and he hugged his brother.

"At least she was," said Tommy. "Keep your hope alive, little bro. We have to go look for her. Right Dad?"

Jake's face remained expressionless.

"Dad!" shouted Tommy.

"I hear you boy. We will. We're in Emmitsburg, so let's get these people settled first, make sure they're okay, then we'll grab some provisions and get on the road again," said Jake.

"But Jake, the roads to D.C. are closed," I said. "How do you plan on getting there?"

"The roads are closed, Eddie. We're in a bus. But I own a four-wheel-drive truck. We'll just go off-road," he said. Tommy and Vinny smiled at each other and nodded.

I wanted to be happy for them, but selfishly I thought perhaps I could tag along and we could look for my parents as well. Then my thoughts were interrupted when I looked up.

We were in front of the high school again.

CHAPTER 21

Return of the Pack

Mark Longaberger and Wes Kent were upstairs in the Family and Consumer Sciences wing where Wes had made his own little nest. Wes had just finished giving the tour of locations where Hunter's Run High School was now housing homeless and displaced members of the church. Wes offered Mark a cold Coca-Cola and they both sat down on the couch in the room that Wes had designated as his own. It was out of the way of the mainstream, far from the common areas of the building and diametrically opposed from the new housing areas that Wes had shown Mark. Wes leaned back with a satisfied smile on his face and took a swig from the soda.

"I did a little redecorating," said Wes. "The FACS teacher was one of the first to leave when the bombing started. She's from West Virginia originally, so I doubt she's coming back," he said. "It's homey, wouldn't you say?"

"Very much so, Wes. A nice little spot for you, and well deserved. I have to say, I'm really impressed with all that you've done for the community," said Mark. "There is certainly no end to the need, and..."

Lou Orville came jogging up, knocked quickly and loudly, then burst into the suite.

"Wes," he said. "You should come."

"What is it now?" Wes Kent answered, clearly bothered by the interruption. "You always seem to arrive at the wrong times, Lou. It's your gift." he said.

"The others. They just drove up," said Lou.

"Others? What others? What are you talking about?" asked Wes.

"Fisher and his friends. Their bus just pulled up to the front door. They're about to come in."

Mark lifted an eyebrow. "They've come back?" he asked.

"Yes. And they've got more people with them. It's like a dozen or so now."

"Well, well," said Wes. "I wonder what they think they're doing here. We will just have to go and ask them.

We all got out of the bus and stretched. Several hours in a bus, no matter how exciting, can cramp your style and your legs. The sight of the school was welcoming. I had spent my high school years here, and my first professional years here, and it was home. Al and Maureen smiled as they got out, and Jake's boys grinned at having returned to their alma mater as well. It was like an old friend who would always be there to welcome you back.

And then I remembered the circumstances under which we left. It all came back when I gave a look toward Estela, who had only terrible memories of bigotry and mistrust in the few moments she was here. Morgan sensed her uneasiness and put a light hand on her shoulder, which Estela took in her own and squeezed. "I hate this place," said Estela.

"You only know a part of it," I said. "It's not the place, it's the people you hate. Besides, we have a lot more perspective than when we left." I glanced over my shoulder up the hill towards the Wal-Mart that Estela had worked in. She looked too, and her glance that direction was no more reassuring for her than looking at the Hunter's Run entrance.

"Well, well, the prodigal son returns," said Wes Kent, making a dramatic entry into the courtyard in front of the school. "Just what do you think you're doing here, Fisher?"

"I'm coming to my place of employment, Wes," he said. "And I'm sure as shit not your son. I'm too old, and not nearly prodigal enough."

"Cute," said Wes. Mark Longaberger and Lou Orville came outside quietly and stopped behind Wes.

"You may not remember this, but this isn't your building, Wes. It's public property. And being a coach, I have keys to about half of the rooms in this place. It's as much ours as it is yours," Jake said. Maureen, Al, Wendy and I all stood shoulder to shoulder in a defiant stance. They had subtly done it, but the effect was the same, and I felt proud. Tommy and Vinny walked up and joined us. Having two, ripped six-footers join our wall was a powerful addition. To the onlooker, we were a formidable wall of eight defiant people. Wes's face reflected our show of strength.

"Then *you* may not remember that you are not welcome here anymore," said Wes. "Your former colleagues made that decision, not me. And America, and whatever is left of it, is a democracy. Even you can respect that."

"Can the bullshit, Wes. I'm not sure how you manipulated all of that, but I was leaving anyway. You didn't chase me out, as much as you'd like to think you did. And those people there behind me? They opted to join me. You didn't chase them out either. It's their school too. So, be a sweetheart and step aside, will you? Because we're going in," said Jake. Tommy and Vinny smirked. They may have battled their dad privately in a myriad ways, but they enjoyed the influence he wielded in the building. Maureen and Al had told them on the bus about Wes Kent's power play and their reactions went from annoyance to fury when they discussed it. In some ways it was clear that they were enjoying the conflict just a little.

"Always violence with you, isn't it, Jake? Tell me, do your new guests know that you're a murderer?"

Jake scowled at that. So did his sons.

"Fuck you, Wes," I yelled. "Self-defense isn't murder, and he saved the lives of most of the people who 'voted' us out."

I accentuated voted for effect. "He's no more murderer than you are."

"Tell yourself whatever you must, Reyes," said Wes. "But we all know the truth." Lou Orville had a look of assurance on his face, but I noticed Mark Longaberger's looked very, very uncomfortable. He chewed his lip, his eyes darted around, and he looked constipated as Wes spoke.

"Don't worry about what I tell myself. What I'm telling you is we're going in whether you like it or not," I said. Wes smirked at me and glanced over at Mark and Lou. Lou smirked as well, but Mark looked a little like he swallowed a frog.

"Help yourself, Eddie," Wes said. "We're not going to threaten you with violence. Like you said, it's your school too." Wes made a sweeping gesture towards the doors, like a game show host demonstrating the prizes. That made me uncomfortable. I looked at Jake confusedly.

"What's he up to?" I whispered. Jake shrugged, then started walking in. Waiting in the rotunda, near the back by the cafeteria's entrance, were all the people who had been with us at the beginning. Every single one of them looked uncomfortable. Unsure of just what to say, just what to do, they just stood there gawking at us as we walked in.

Jake looked at each of them. Some of them couldn't hold his gaze. Jennie Custis scowled at us. I always hated that bitch, and now I felt it in my bones. Melanie Richmond's look of discomfort became one of disgust as we got closer, and I realized that I never liked her either, and I wondered how I ever faked it before when she pulled her two-face routine. Robin Eaves was expressionless. She had gone along with all of the fervor that had led to our banishment, just not quite as zealously as Melanie had. The Heffners stood together and looked mildly ashamed, which I admit was a small comfort to me. They were pawns in Wes Kent's power play, but were now dependent on his charity and couldn't help it.

Jake broke the awkward silence. "Hello again. I understand how awkward this is, but if you consider that the backdrop for all of this is World War III, you also understand why I don't give a shit. We have traveled nearly a thousand miles, have seen several very different cities, been abducted into slave labor, have been barred from looking for our loved ones by army tanks, and have fought back some kind of mutated creatures who, of all things, were trying to eat us. Your awkwardness at this moment is really, really low on my give-a-shit-list. We are back, I don't know if--or how long--we are staying, and I don't care how welcome we are or aren't. Those of you who have decided to hate me, or us—there's not much I can do about that. Those of you who are still on the fence should probably have a conversation or two. For now, I am going to take a shower and probably help myself to something to eat."

Then he walked towards the athletic wing and the coaches' locker room. The others gawked wide-eyed, and I grinned like a Cheshire cat.

"I'm going to my classroom," I said. "Estela, Morgan, are you hungry? Do you need to use a bathroom?"

Morgan nodded. "Yes, to the bathroom, thanks. Vinny, can you show me around your school a little?" Vinny brightened, nodded, and gently grabbed her elbow. Estela came with me and waved almost imperceptibly to Morgan. Al and Maureen started to walk to the wing where their classrooms were, and Jada and Glen went straight into the cafeteria to talk to some of the other students who had stayed.

That left Tommy and Wendy. They glanced at each other uneasily. Tommy frowned slightly. Wendy forced a smile. "So, you went to school here?" she asked. Tommy nodded silently. A tense moment went by with no words or movement.

"I think I'll use the bathroom too. I'll catch up with Morgan," she said, and she walked hurriedly to follow Vinny and his friend. Tommy stood alone, taking in his alma mater.

"They've got some nerve," said Wes. "But they're in for a surprise when they get to their classrooms and find homeless families living there," he said smiling.

Mark looked uncomfortable still. "What do you think they're going to say?"

"I don't much care," said Wes. "What can they say? We're housing homeless people! Who would be so selfish or heartless as to have a problem with that?"

"Easy to say when it's not your room," Mark added.

"They left," said Wes. "I didn't."

"But you ran them out," said Mark. "They have a right to be upset."

"You're missing the big picture, my boy," said Wes. "We're helping an entire community."

"But it's a select community of your church's congregation," said Mark. "And their rooms were simply confiscated. They didn't volunteer them. Don't you think they're going to have some problems with this?"

"I'm not sure who's side you're on, son," said Wes. "But I don't like your tone."

"It's not a tone Wes, it's just an observation. I mean, there's two sides to every coin."

"Not necessarily," said Wes, scowling. Mark made a face of incredulity as the front doors swung open again. In walked Father Joe, Pablo Fuentes, Emery Butler, Billy James and the mysterious Oleg. Lou and Wes turned.

"Padre," said Wes. "You come at an awkward time."

"What's the matter?" said Father Joe.

"Our undesirables have returned," said Wes.

"Returned? Why? I thought they left," said Father Joe.

"So did we," said Wes. "But here they are. And they're not particularly contrite," said Wes. "They're defending their actions and just brazenly walked in here, daring me to stop them."

"How unfortunate," said Pablo. "Some people have no shame. What do you plan to do?"

"What can I do?" said Wes. "This Fisher comes and goes as he pleases. We're powerless to stop him. He's very violent."

"Violence should be a last resort," said Father Joe, looking directly at Oleg when he said it. Oleg nodded without expression. "Perhaps I can talk to them."

"I would value that greatly, Padre," said Wes. "Hopefully you can help them see reason."

But suddenly I was in a very unreasonable mood. I had taken one look at two families of homeless people living in my classroom and lost the last bit of my composure.

"What the fuck do you think you're doing?" I said, stomping back to the rotunda. Wendy and Morgan had stayed in the ladies' room, and Vinny was with me.

"What is the meaning of this? You've put squatters in my classroom to live? What right do you have to my room?" I shouted.

"What right do *you* have to it?" said Wes. "We are all just public servants here. These aren't our rooms. We occupy them as teachers. We all get moved from time to time. They don't belong to us any more than the cafeteria does, or the gym.

"Easy for you to say. I'm guessing no homeless people are living in your classroom," I shouted.

"As a matter of fact, they are," said Wes. "I moved my things to another spot to accommodate them." I didn't know what to say to that, but knowing that Wes was a snake in the grass, I supposed that just enough of it was true that he could equivocate.

"Well, I never gave you permission to do anything with mine," I yelled.

"You left. How was I supposed to know you were

coming back?" said Wes.

"You kicked us out, you asshole!" I said.

"You kicked yourselves out. You made yourselves un-welcome. Besides, these people need places to stay. We're offer-ing them Christian charity. Are you so self-absorbed that you can't even see past your own ego to notice that?" I had nothing to say to that either. Not without sounding like a giant dick.

"Look, Eddie. I didn't try to screw you intentionally. There's no question that the only thing we can agree on is that you and I agree on virtually nothing. We are worlds apart politically and religiously. But we—our church, these people you left—are trying to do something charitable here. If there is anything you need from your room, you know that you are welcome to get it."

"That's not the point, Wes," I said.

"Then what is the point?" he said. I had nothing for that either. I just made a face of disapproval and shook my head slightly.

"I, for one, would like to personally thank Mr. Reyes for the use of his classroom," said Father Joe. "I understand the awkwardness of all of this. We didn't anticipate your return, of course, so we moved ahead with our charitable projects. I'm sorry for your inconvenience, but you are truly helping us do God's work."

"And you are?" I asked.

"Apologies," he said. "I'm Father Joseph Clarque of the Church of Many Blessings. It's a pleasure," he said, offering his hand. I took it and shook uncomfortably. I knew what I thought of his church—and had heard like-minded people pri-vately call it 'The Church of Many Snobs' in my presence.

"Father," I said. "I appreciate your candor."

"Of course. Let's address the elephant in the room, shall we. I know that you all had a bit of a falling out philosoph-ically. That is none of my business, of course. But when Wes said you all had left, and I suggested we use the school to help house some of our displaced flock, Wes thought your rooms would be permanently deserted, and I accepted on behalf of the church. I'm sorry." He was good, this guy. I wanted to be really, really pissed about this, but he had assuaged my anger in just a few moments with a couple of apologies, some explanation, and apparently altruistic projects.

"Not a problem, Father," I said. Now he actually had made me feel guilty about being upset of being robbed of my room. Vinny and Tommy stood there awkwardly watching all of this. Father Joe turned to them.

"And who are these strapping young lads?" he asked.

"Thomas and Vincent Fisher," said Wes.

"Fisher, eh?" said Father Joe. "Coach Fisher's sons, then, I presume." He offered a hand to each of them. They shook dutifully and firmly.

"Yes sir," said Tommy.

"Firm grips, good handshakes, both of you," said Father Joe. "Your dad taught you well." Both boys smiled automatically. Wendy walked up alone.

"Hello," she said.

"Hello," said Wes, looking like a wolf at the attractive researcher. "And who might you be?"

"Wendy Yubashiri," she said. "I work—worked, at Fort Detrick with the National Institute of Health. These people rescued me and my supervisor from a bad situation there."

"Nice to meet you, Wendy," said Wes.

"Fort Detrick?" said Father Joe. "You have certainly faced life's trials, my dear." Father Joe offered her his hand and a warm smile. "Things there were particularly egregious," he said.

"Yes, yes they were, Father," said Wendy. "Nice meeting you."

A wet Jake Fisher came walking up with a small towel around his neck. He glistened a bit having just gotten out of the shower, and his tight haircut was even spikier than usual in its damp state.

"Coach Fisher, good to see you," said Father Joe. "I understand you're a bit of a hero, rescuing damsels in distress." Jake nodded blankly as he walked up. He took Father Joe's hand.

"Father."

"Wendy here was just telling us tales of your heroism," he said. Wendy's slightly awkward look betrayed his false embellishment.

"We arrived at the right place at the right time, Father. I'm glad we could help Wendy and the Colonel when we did."

"Saved another one, did you? A Colonel, you say? Is he not with you, then?" asked Father Joe.

"No. He had to report to people in Washington," said Wendy.

"Washington," said Father Joe. "You have been out and about. What is the status of Washington? I heard that no one can get near it. Apparently you have some clout." Jake looked at me wordlessly, and I instantly knew his thoughts. Neither of us trusted Father Joe as far as we could spit, and he was wrangling information out of us with ease. He was the kind who could use that information to his benefit. Jake always likened him to Hannibal Lecter from *The Silence of the Lambs*. I always thought that comparison was a little extreme, but there was no denying that Father Joe had the ability to worm information out of anyone with their unwilling compliance.

"No, we couldn't get in either," said Wendy. "But the Colonel could."

"You all certainly did travel some distance, didn't you?" said Father Joe. "Made it past Roanoke, I take it?" Father Joe's knowledge of our destinations irritated me and obviously concerned Jake. Wendy didn't know any better, so she simply kept up polite conversation.

"Yes, all the way to Blacksburg. It's amazing how different all of the towns are on the way," she said. "Frederick is a ghost town and fairly terrifying for a number of reasons. But Lexington and Blacksburg were virtually untouched. Communication is still not that great, though," she said. Jake tensed up with every piece of information she gave.

"I am guessing that our enemies went after our satellites first, my dear," said Father Joe. "We are an advanced country with many advantages. If I were in their shoes, that's the first place I would target," he said. Something about that answer gave me chills, even though all of us had probably thought it at one point or another in retrospect.

"So, what are your plans now?" Father Joe queried. Just then Morgan and Estela walked up. Estela had joined Morgan and Wendy in the ladies' room, but Estela had stayed a bit longer with her new love interest. They walked up to the group in the rotunda, but as they neared, Estela looked like she'd seen a ghost.

"Estela, what's wrong?" asked Morgan. "What is it?" Estela grimaced and stared at the church members.

"That man," Estela said. "Is my father."

Wait a minute, I thought. Didn't she say her parents were dead? Or deported to Mexico? I couldn't remember. But I'm certain she didn't say her father was in Emmitsburg. I decided to turn my head from Father Joe's prying questions and instead listen to Estela and Morgan to see if any of this could jog my memory.

Pablo Fuentes looked at Estela with a scowl. "I have no daughter," he said.

Wendy tip-toed over to me. "Eddie, didn't she say at that restaurant in Lexington that she came here from a detention center in California? And I thought she said her parents were in Mexico," she said.

"So did I. I thought I was remembering it wrong," I said. Pablo evidently heard us.

"Still lying to people about who and what you are?" said Pablo. "This story is a new one. Touching, I admit, and more creative than usual."

Estela's face was a mix of fear and rage.

"What is this about?" asked Morgan. "Aren't you from Texas? Weren't you held in jail?"

Pablo laughed out loud. It was a belly laugh than rang with insincerity, clearly designed to draw attention and make a point.

"The real story isn't nearly as interesting, is it?" he said.

"Estela, what is he talking about. Is this guy your father?" asked Morgan. Estela had no reply at first. She was battling to hold it together. Just seeing Pablo had set her off balance, but being pressed by so many questions seemed to push her to the brink of losing it.

"Is he your father?" Morgan said again.

"Ask him," said Estela.

"I already told you. I have no daughter," said Pablo.

"You can fool these people, Papa, but God is watching," said Estela. "And you can't fool Him." She pointed to the sky as she said it.

"It is because God is watching that I say that I have no daughter," said Pablo.

"You are a *cabrón*," she said.

"Watch your mouth, girl," said Pablo.

"If you are no longer my father, you no longer can tell me what to do," Estela answered.

"I gave up trying to tell you what to do long ago," he said. "I see that you have not abandoned your abominable choices. I'm guessing this is your new one?" Pablo asked, nodding at Morgan.

"Leave her out of this," said Estela. "This is between you and me."

"There is nothing between you and me, *mi caída*." Said Pablo. "Until you change your demonic ways, I have no place for you."

"You drove everyone I ever cared about away from me, you bastard!" Estela shouted.

"You did that yourself. The scriptures are clear, and

your little girlfriend simply wised up and decided to read them. She valued her soul, unlike you seem to do, and she made the decision to save herself from the fires of Hell. You can't blame me for that."

"You are the one who pushed her out, Papa. You made her read the scriptures that you gave her. You scared the hell out of her and chased her away from me with your dogma. Then you kicked me out of your house and your life and left me to fend for myself. If Mama was alive, she would curse you for what you did!" Pablo took a step forward and smacked Estela in the face.

"Do not speak of your mother to me," he said. "You have no idea what she would have said. You are a source of shame for me, our family, and our God." Estela shrieked as she was slapped, and clutched her face, and began to cry into her hands.

"What the hell is going on here?" I asked. Morgan and Wendy looked at me as if to agree that none of this made sense—at least according to the stories that Estela had told us. Estela composed herself for a moment and turned on the man she now claimed was her father.

"My God is love. Your god is a hateful bigot," she said, breaking into tears. Morgan didn't know what to say, but gently approached and wrapped her arms around Estela, who cried with her face buried in her shirt.

The man known as Father Joe walked up beside Pablo and silently nodded towards him in acknowledgment, then made a gesture with his hands as to seemingly offer his help. Pablo scowled at his daughter and lowered his head and turned towards Father Joe.

"Padre, I am sorry that this bit of embarrassing family business had to take place in front of you. If they are staying, perhaps I should take my leave," said Pablo. Estela remained with her face buried in Morgan's shirt. Wendy and I stood awkwardly wondering what in the hell was going on.

"Why don't you, Billy, Emery, and Oleg go wait for

me in Wes's office and we'll meet there in a few minutes," said Father Joe. The four went into the Main Office and walked back to the administrative suites.

"*Wes's office*, huh?" Jake said. "My, my, you sure have taken advantage of all of this, haven't you?"   Jake's retort snapped me back into reality, leaving for a moment the conundrum that was Estela Fuentes and her not-deported, not-Mexican father who apparently lived here in Emmitsburg and was a member of the Church of Many Blessings.

"That's not all, Jake," I said. "He has homeless families living in our classrooms. Both mine and yours!" I said.

"And ours," said Maureen, suddenly walking up with Al. "What the fuck, Wes? Who the fuck do you think you are, giving our rooms away?"   Father Joe looked uncomfortable. The situation was getting away from him. Wendy looked uncomfortable as well. Tommy and Vinny seemed to be enjoying all of this.

"Look, folks, I've already explained myself," said Wes. "So did Father Joe."

"Don't worry Wes," said Jake. "We'll get out of your hair. There's room at the Fisher house," he said. "And I have a feeling that despite the amazingly cordial welcome wagon you've put out here, that most of my people aren't too keen on staying anyway."

"Room at our house?" Tommy said. "For eleven people?"

"Nine," said Maureen. "Al and I can stay at my place in Taneytown. We've no need to trouble you anymore. We can take some food stores from the bus to get us through a few days. Things seem to be normalizing here, at least a little bit. If we get in trouble, it looks like we can call you now. Thanks for all you did for us." Maureen hugged Jake, then me. Jake smiled and nodded in acknowledgment. Al reached out his hand and shook Jake's, looking him in the eye and nodding. He looked like he was fighting back tears.

Glen and Jada looked up from their seat in the cafeteria where they were eating. The commotion in the rotunda had gotten their attention, but they had stayed and continued to tell their friends the tales of adventure they had just experienced. Jake looked over at them and waved.

"Wes, I know I'm not in a position to ask for favors, but I'd like you to let Glen and Jada stay here," said Jake. "Their friends are here, and if they have any family left, those people will try here first after looking for them at home. They don't care about the politics of adults. Keep them out of our battles. Agreed?"

"Agreed. The children can stay here. We have plenty," Wes said.

"So that makes seven now. And we do have room for seven, boy," Jake said to Tommy. Tommy nodded back.

We made an uneasy temporary truce with Wes Kent and his people. As soon as he saw that we didn't intend to stay and interfere with his plans for the school, he became cordial again. He and Lou Orville wished us luck, but no hands were shaken nor smiles offered as we walked down the long main hallway towards the teachers' parking lot.

"We are going to need vehicles," said Jake. "And ours don't start. At least they didn't a week ago. We think the EMP's knocked them out. We're probably going to need new batteries, and we will probably also have to reboot the cars' computers somehow."

"I can help with that," Al said. "I know my way around a car engine and I really know my way around computers."

"Why didn't you say that before we left?" I asked.

"Jake found a bus that could take all of us. I thought that was the plan all along, anyway," said Al.

"Fair enough," I answered back. "But where can we get car batteries in this town?"

"We have car batteries at the Wal-Mart," Estela said

shakily. "Assuming they're still there."

"Tommy, Vinny. Let's get to work putting new batteries in our truck and whatever vehicles Ms. Kelly and Mr. DeFillipo have here. Al, I'm giving you two strong boys to help you. Let me know whatever else you need. We'll all go to the Wal-Mart and see what's left, then we can divvy up the supplies and make a plan to go forward," said Jake. "Wendy, you still with us?" Wendy nodded and smiled.

Mark Longaberger was staring at Jake like he wanted to say something. It was obvious.

"Mark? You need something?" asked Jake.

"I just want to talk to you for a second before you go," he said.

"Okay. Come on out to the bus with me and we'll chat," said Jake. Wes and Father Joe exchanged glances wordlessly. The rest of us walked out towards the bus. Mark pulled Jake aside once they got past the sidewalk.

"I, I just want to say that I'm sorry things turned out the way they did," said Mark.

"I appreciate that, Mark," said Jake.

"I had some trepidation about the way you took charge at first. I don't know, maybe it was just my own ego or insecurity or something, but in hindsight, it's clear to me now that you were doing what you thought was best for all of us. You fought to let the Heffners in at first, then you fought off their attackers. You tried to protect us from going into what might await us outside, then once you realized it was safe, you were the first to do reconnaissance. I know we don't see eye to eye on everything, but I kind of feel caught in the middle of all this. I stayed, but I don't necessarily agree with a lot of things that Wes or this church are doing. I don't want you to have any hard feelings," Mark said, offering Jake his hand. Jake looked him in the eyes and shook his hand.

"You're a good man, Mark. It probably took a lot to say all that, and I will admit that I probably judged you too harshly as well. No hard feelings," said Jake, nodding. Mark smiled.

"But I do privately want to give you a little warning, and you can do with it what you want," said Jake. "I know that you are involved with this church by default now, and on the surface they seem to be doing outreach and apparent massive acts of charity. But privately, I have always had misgivings about them and their true motives. I just would suggest that you watch your step around them. If I'm wrong, you lose nothing by being careful and I end up looking stupid. I can handle looking stupid. I'm getting quite used to it. But if I'm right, then you might avoid something that could turn out to be much worse. My gut tells me that these are not good people; that they wrap themselves up in flags and Bible verses to cover up feelings that represent the very worst in us. Just be careful. It's easy to get seduced into their way of thinking. I know you were a good teacher, and I think you're probably a good man, too. I'd hate to lose you." Mark nodded, smiled, and shook again.

And then we all mounted the bus and rode over to the Wal-Mart where this whole journey began.

CHAPTER 22

Heading Home

Jada and Glen happily joined their friends back at the school. The teenagers left there like Tanner Heffner and Casey Kirby were happy to have more people their age to talk with, and that left us adults with a clear conscience for having left them. Maureen and Al were still with us, but they would eventually disembark and go off to live their new lives, presumably together. The conundrum of Estela and who she really was, and what her relationship with Morgan would become was getting more entangled. With this new revelation about Estela's past being invented, and now her father--a professor at the college--being the one who had disowned her and apparently driven away her former lover—all of that was a new revelation that only made things more convoluted. Her father's new powerful deaconship at the Church of Many Blessings, and just what that church was trying to do with Hunter's Run High School and the town of Emmitsburg were mysteries that would have to wait, but they were obviously in the back of everyone's mind.

It was clear what the remaining seven of us were going to do once we got our cars up and running and our stores re-supplied: we were headed to Washington by any means necessary. Morgan and I were headed there to find our parents, the Fishers were headed there to find Laura, and Wendy lived there. It was the one piece that tied us all together.

We entered the Wal-Mart carefully—meaning we

had armed ourselves. Estela, Jake, and I had been forced to fight our way out of the place the last time we were here, and it was mostly good luck and Jake's nerve that allowed it to happen. Now we had bigger numbers. The doors were more smashed. Someone had obviously come back to see about the store's status. It had been picked through considerably. Mostly the electronic supplies, the grocery section, and the pharmacy area had the most damage. Some clothing racks had been knocked over, and the smell of human urine was in the carpeting. I never understood how humans devolved so quickly into animals in times of crisis, the mutates notwithstanding. At least the mutates had a good excuse.

Estela was correct in her belief that the automotive section would be largely ignored. We grabbed half a dozen car batteries of varying sizes and put them in a cart, as no one seemed to know exactly what size battery their car would need. We rolled them up to the bus and put them in the compartment underneath the exterior. "Snag some tools, like wrenches and screwdrivers. Also, we're going to need baking soda and a couple of towels," said Al. "We'll need them to reset the computers."

I grabbed the baking soda and towels. Jake and the boys grabbed car batteries and tools, and Wendy, Morgan, and Estela piled whatever food was left by looters into carts and we rolled them back to Hunter's Run.

"We need to unhook the old batteries and wipe down the battery cables with the baking soda solution," Al said. He had put water and baking soda into a bucket and used his hands to stir. He had put on vinyl gloves from the box we had in the bus. We had to wait about forty minutes once we disconnected everything. Al said it was necessary for the reset. Then Jake and the boys put the new batteries in Jake's truck as well as Maureen's and Al's cars, and hooked them up.

"Now the moment of truth," Al said, turning the key to his Mazda. The engine hummed right away. We all clapped. Maureen's started right up as well. Vinny got in his dad's truck and cranked it on.

"If it was that easy all along," I started.

"We were in a bit of a hurry to leave last time," Jake said. "Get off my ass." I smiled.

Then we realized that after a week of some pretty heavy sharing of adventures, we were splitting up. The moment hung for an eternity, then Maureen walked up to me smiling. Maureen gave me another long, hard, hug. "You are a phenomenal friend, Eddie," she said. "Good luck finding your folks. Try calling or texting us when you get back. Who knows? If your voice mail made it through along with some of Jake's texts to his boys, we may have communication completely back by the end of this week or sooner."

"Where will you go?" I asked.

"We'll stay at my place for a while, see if we can get things back up and running. There are people I want to try and contact too. We'll be okay. You be careful," she said. I kissed her on the cheek and hugged Al.

"Jake, Eddie, it's been an honor," said Al. We all hugged, wished them luck, and then headed to Jake's place.

The drive didn't take long. Jake lived only a few miles from the school. The town showed a little more life than it did the week before, when we had last taken this road. It was encouraging. It meant people were trying to get their lives restarted again.

We pulled up to Jake's house, and the first one there to greet us was Oklahoma, the tabby cat we had dropped off at the barn. He looked well fed and happy to see us. "Decided to come back to the house, did you boy?" asked Jake, rubbing Okie's head. "Glad to see you made it okay all week." Okie rubbed up against nearly everyone's legs, and Estela bent down to pet him.

"Remember me, *Don Gato*?" she asked. Jake smiled and stroked him a few times before going into the house. It smelled stale, like a house that had been shut down for a week with no fresh air.

"Open some windows," Jake said, and all of us found windows and opened them up.

"We'll crash here tonight, get some good rest, get some food in us, and try to come up with a plan for how we can sneak into Washington D.C. without the military holding us up," Jake said. "Estela, Morgan, there's a guest room for you two in the basement with your own bathroom. Wendy, there's a guest room for you at the top of the stairs. Eddie, you get the couch in the living room," Jake said.

"Jake, look," I said. The clock on his microwave oven was blinking.

"Electricity!" I shouted. "It was off when we left. They must have found a way to get it back on!" Jake went over to the sink and ran the water. "Nice," he said. "Creature comforts! Eddie, try the television." I went over to the table where the remote control was sitting and pointed it at the television. I clicked it on, and the system had to reboot for a few minutes, but it looked like it was up and running. "Jake," I said. "How do you have cable out here in the sticks?"

"A rich guy in the development out back wanted it, so he paid thousands of dollars to get it run down the main road. It was cheap for us to tap into it once he'd done that, so I get country views and city cable."

"I bet with electricity and cable that we might be able to get some news," I said.

On cue, the news channels came on and there was an aerial picture of Washington, D.C. coming through. The reporter was narrating:

Welcome ladies and gentlemen, to what will be a brief and unorthodox broadcast for us tonight. We do not have full broadcast capabilities up and running at the moment, but we have been able to send this pre-recorded message through localized cable networks. The first round of bombings took place several days ago, and status reports from various cities and regions have been stalled due to the destruction of communication satellites. As of yet we have received no word about the status or the whereabouts of either the President or Congress. This is footage from a privately owned drone camera, courtesy of one of our loyal viewers. As you can see, while some parts of Washington have been demolished by conventional bombs, the majority of the city buildings have survived. Thousands are dead due to special new weaponry being used on the U.S., and it will likely be months before we have an accurate accounting on the complete death toll.

The military has established martial law in Washington and has ordered the streets cleared. It has not been disclosed yet as to the reasoning behind it, but speculation is that it has had something to do with the sightings of groups of strangely dressed people in the area who are apparently attacking and apprehending individuals on the street. We have only had drone cameras up and running for several hours now, and so usable footage is still coming into our editing room. There are alleged eyewitness accounts of gang attacks on citizens, according to one source who has spoken to us on condition of anonymity. If you look here, you can see a band of ten people, all apparently in matching masks, chasing and apprehending an individual. We should warn you that the following scene depicts graphic violence and viewer discretion is advised.

And then we saw them. The mutates. This bunch was in the nation's capital, however, not in Frederick at the Fort. Despite what the newsman said, we knew that those weren't masks they were wearing, and we also knew why they were apprehending people on the streets. The video footage was from a long distance, but for about four or five seconds, the camera had zoomed in on the face of one of the upright leaders of the mutates. It was a tall, slender woman, and she was pointing to and directing other mutates on all fours.

"Eddie, stop," Jake said. I grabbed the remote and hit the pause button.

"Back it up." I hit the ten-second reverse button.

"A little more. To the part where they zoom in on the face." I obliged again.

"Get ready to pause it. Now. Pause it now."

I hit the pause button. And the world changed.

"Oh dear God," I said. Jake's face went white. Estela and Wendy looked confused. Morgan too. But Tommy and Vinny looked sick to their stomachs. Jake's eyes bugged, and his mouth dropped.

"God almighty," Jake whispered.

It took me a second, then I realized what they were looking at. I didn't know what to say. I was horrified, and was horrified for them as well.

"Dad," said Vinny. "Do you see? That close-up. The orange thing?"

Jake nodded back at Vinny weakly.

"It's mom."

End Book 1

BOOK TWO IN THE CATACLYM SERIES: FIRST WEEKS AFTER

With the sudden realization that Laura Fisher has become a mutate, Jake and his sons are now clearly driven to find her in Washington. Wendy Yubashiri needs to find her research partner at the Pentagon, and get back to work on discovering more about the mysterious mutates. Eddie Reyes and Morgan Branson needs to find their parents. How will the crew get into the capital city that has roads blocked by tanks and martial law in effect? Will we find out the true story behind Estela Fuentes? What is the Church of Many Blessings up to with all of their recent activity and discussion of a "new world," and how will that affect the reticent Mark Longaberger, who becomes less confident in their intentions with each passing day? To answer these questions, we must join our crew in Book Two of the Cataclysm Series: *First Weeks After.*

Acknowledgements

To my Family...

--You have helped me in more ways than you will know. From exchanging ideas, to doing artwork, to wrangling computer programs, to softening my edges.

To all those who helped me Gather Accurate information & Tighten up my prose...

--Especially Renee, CC, and the Colonel. You all helped me suspend the disbelief.

To all those who inspired characters and Endured my endless discussions...

--Time and again. You are the meat, potatoes, and gravy of this series.

Thank you all so very much.

ABOUT THE AUTHOR

Jay Vielle

Jay Vielle has been writing in some form  or another since childhood. He is an award-winning educator and coach, who has worked for thirty years at both secondary and collegiate levels. He has written detective and science fiction as well as freelance non-fiction for numerous publications. He and his family live in rural northern Maryland.

BOOKS BY THIS AUTHOR

First Weeks After

Book 2 in the Cataclysm Series-- Having realized that his wife, once presumed dead, is now a mutate, Jake Fisher and his sons have to find a way to skirt past military blockades and get into Washington D.C. to rescue her. With them are fellow teacher Eddie Reyes, who is looking for his parents, and Wendy Yubashiri, the researcher trying to reunite with her colleague, Colonel Ray Cannaveral at the Pentagon. Unbeknownst to them, however, the local pastor of an extremist church has dellusions of grandeur, and is making his move to take over the town and mold it in his image. To do so, he'll have to collaborate up with some very dangerous partners, who have violent ways of dealing with investigators and malcontents--including three of Jake's friends. Meanwhile, the rest of the country is just starting to recover from the first weeks after the bombs began dropping in World War III, and formulating a plan to retaliate.

Made in the USA
Middletown, DE
21 October 2022